Full of Beans

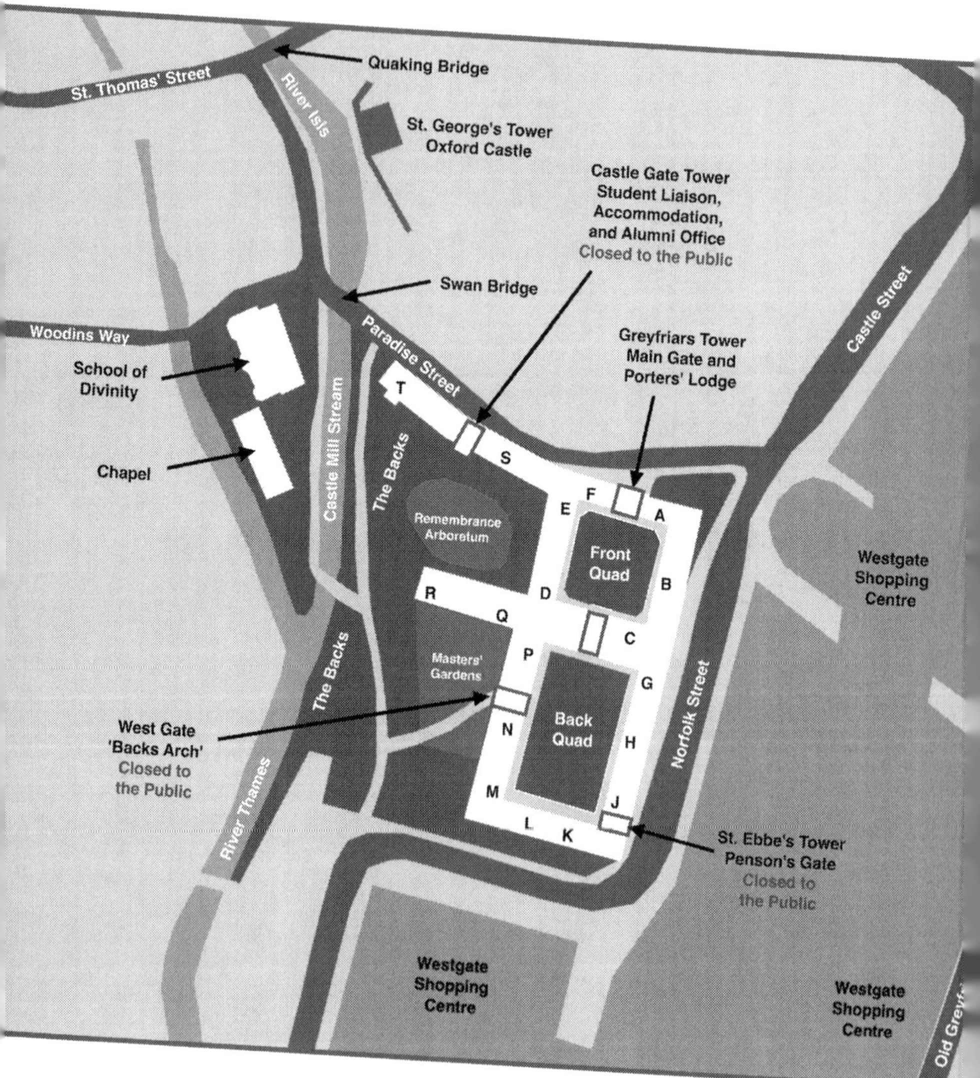

Quaking Bridge
St. Thomas' Street
River Isis
St. George's Tower
Oxford Castle
Castle Gate Tower
Student Liaison,
Accommodation,
and Alumni Office
Closed to the Public
Swan Bridge
Woodins Way
School of
Divinity
Chapel
Castle Mill Stream
Paradise Street
Castle Street
Greyfriars Tower
Main Gate and
Porters' Lodge
T
S
The Backs
Remembrance
Arboretum
F
E
A
Front
Quad
B
D
R
Q
C
P
Masters'
Gardens
G
Westgate
Shopping
Centre
The Backs
Back
Quad
N
H
Norfolk Street
West Gate
'Backs Arch'
Closed to
the Public
River Thames
M
J
L
K
St. Ebbe's Tower
Penson's Gate
Closed to
the Public
Westgate
Shopping
Centre
Westgate
Shopping
Centre

Full of Beans
A BACK-IN-TIME MYSTERY

Mark J. Wilson

Redwood Publishing

Copyright © 2025 Mark J. Wilson

All rights reserved. No part of this publication may be reproduced, distributed, or transmitted in any form or by any means, including photocopying, recording, or other electronic or mechanical methods, without the prior written permission of the author or publisher, except as permitted by U.S copyright law.

Published by:
Redwood Publishing, LLC
Orange County, California
www.redwooddigitalpublishing.com

ISBN: 978-1-966333-16-6 (hardcover)
ISBN: 978-1-966333-17-3 (paperback)
ISBN: 978-1-966333-13-5 (e-book)

Library of Congress Control Number: 2025919995

Front cover design: Mark J. Wilson
Book design: Michelle Manley, Graphique Designs, LLC

Interior graphics:
Mark J. Wilson (page 225: Oxford map and postcard)
Lauren at ScienceScribbles (page 225: Rutherford Atom pinbadge image)

Disclaimer: You'll probably notice that this book is a bit of a linguistic blend of British and American. A bit like the author. We've kept the British bits (spellings like 'colour', phrases such as 'bugger off', and the liberal use of the Oxford comma) so that the characters sound like themselves, but tidied other things up using The Chicago Manual of Style rather than the Oxford Guide to Style. Sorry Oxford. We hope to spare American readers from gasping in horror at certain quirks, like those rogue periods that dangle outside quotation marks in British writing. While CMOS preaches consistency above all, we've been consistently inconsistent—choosing which rules to keep, which to bend, and which to gleefully break. In short: we've tried to keep everyone happy—our British characters, our American readers, and our own editorial sanity.

I owe huge thanks to my wonderful wife, Carrie, whose belief in me got me started and kept me going, and whose sometimes-brutally-honest opinion made me work hard to keep improving the manuscript. The book is dedicated to Carrie and her coffee machine, which would constantly instruct us to "Fill Beans," whether the hopper was full or empty. Without either of them this book might never have been written.

CONTENTS

PART ONE: CASES ARE LIKE BUSES
1. The First Death of Corvus Durant 1
2. Chess and Pastry 7
3. All Things Brighton Beautiful 25
4. Collard Green's 35
5. Fission Chip 41
6. Fish 'n' Chips 49
7. Pedge & Co. 65
8. A Little Light Relief 77
9. Brighton Rock Star 89

PART TWO: LIFE GETS COMPLICATED
10. Arbley Scrump 99
11. Wigtwizzle 105
12. Just Popping Out 115
13. Three Goats Heads 121
14. Part-Time Ethics 137
15. Beginner's Luck 149
16. In a Manor of Speaking 159
17. Umbrella Guy 173
18. Partners in Time 181
19. Conference Conflab 187
20. Late for Their Date 197

PART THREE: BACK TO THE FUTURE
21. Em T. Trey 207
22. What the Hell Have I Done? 213
23. The Girl in the Burberry Shirt 219

PART FOUR: BACK TO THE PAST

24. Crazed Detective Mode 229
25. Let's Rewind the Tape 237
26. The Second Death of Corvus Durant 247
27. The Relationship Complication 255
28. Deeper in Trouble 267

PART FIVE: UNCOVERING THE PAST

29. A Grand Day Out 281
30. A Turn for the Worse 283
31. Birthday Blues 287
32. I Love You, Mum 289
33. What Did I Do? 293
34. Two Dozen Red Roses 299

PART SIX: CLOSING AND CLOSURE

35. Keynote Controversy 313
36. Catching the Train 317
37. Jumping-off Point 323
38. A Nice Quiet Spot 327
39. Phil in Rewind 331

PART SEVEN: JIGGETY JIG

40. Magic Tea 343
41. The Window Table 353
42. Shift Happens 357

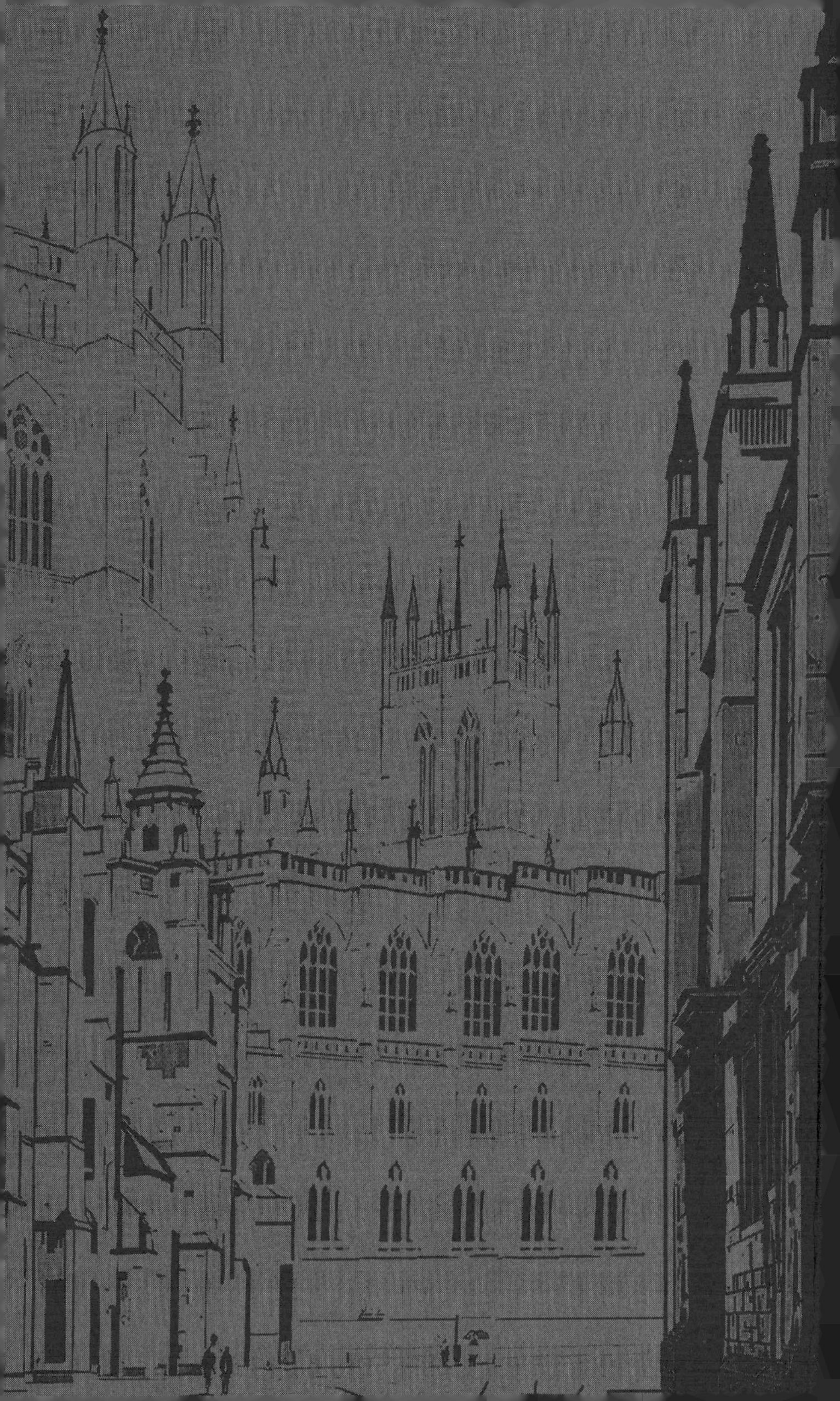

Part One
CASES ARE LIKE BUSES

1.
THE FIRST DEATH OF CORVUS DURANT

07 NOVEMBER 2022, 2.08 P.M.

Akito Takaya was pacing fretfully around the quad of Westgate College. Heavy raindrops pattered on his umbrella, but all he could hear was his internal conflict. As soon as travel restrictions had lifted in Japan, he had booked his flight to England.

Corvus Durant had been one of Akito's heroes—one of the greats in the world of theoretical physics. Admittedly, he was old now, in his fifties, and had not done anything noteworthy for twenty years. In his day, he had the potential to rival Stephen Hawking and Roger Penrose. But his day had been and gone.

Akito needed to challenge Durant, but he felt the need to contain the hurt and anger that had been frustrating him for months. Akito felt he needed answers to his questions, but also thought the professor was owed respect. He would calmly demand an explanation. Why had Durant stolen their paper? Their groundbreaking research? Akito could not bring himself to accept that Durant had done it for his own personal gain. And what had happened to Georgia? Where had she gone? Akito knew Durant had seen her that day. What exactly had happened when they met?

He pushed open the door to Staircase E. He folded his umbrella and propped it against the wall. Then, with a determined stride, he mounted the stairs. At the first landing, his heart was pounding, not so much from exertion but from dread and adrenaline. He continued up the next flight of stairs, then continued along the narrow balcony at the top of the staircase. He stood in front of a heavy oak door with a shiny brass number three.

Akito knocked. The silence surrounding Akito was a contrast to the turmoil within him. His heart pounded and his mind raced. He rapped the wood sharply and painfully with his knuckles. With his fists clenched, he banged harder, causing the sound to echo in the stairwell. As his patience ran out, Akito pounded on the door with his fists. "Open the door," he shouted. "Open the door!"

The heavy door opened wide, and an imposing figure stood before him, almost filling the doorway. "Keep it down, or you'll have the police 'round here," Durant said with a menacing undertone.

Akito looked up at his ageing, erstwhile hero. Durant was a big man with a round, red face, a salt-and-pepper beard, wild eyebrows, and a very angry glare. He had a muscular physique, with a little extra bulk around the middle from all his years of eating rich refectory comfort food. Durant towered over him, but Akito looked him in the eyes, with his arms by his side and determination on his face. Akito tried to appear as tall as he could, but his voice trembled.

"I am Akito Takaya, and I demand to know what you did! Why did you steal our paper? What happened to Georgia? Where is she?"

"What?" Durant's scowl changed to surprise, and then to indignation. "Who the hell are you?"

The First Death of Corvus Durant

"I was co-author of the paper you published," Akito stated, feeling the need to make his claim to the stolen work.

"Co-author? She never mentioned any ..." Durant protested. Akito opened his mouth to repeat his demand, but Durant spoke over him. "Never mind that. She told me it was her paper. Your colleague gave me her ideas to see if I could use them." Durant planted his hands on his hips and leant forward. "And I can prove that I was here in my rooms after she left the college."

"No! I know you stole our paper word for word. And I know you know more about what happened to Georgia." The sound of breaking glass came from somewhere inside. "Is that Georgia? Is she in there?"

Akito tried to push past Durant to get into his rooms. Durant grabbed his arms and shoved him back. Akito took a step backward and charged at Durant with all his might. Akito was small, short, and had a slim frame. All Akito succeeded in was making Durant stumble a couple of steps backward, and Akito fell forward through the door.

As Akito was getting to his feet at the threshold, the professor turned to look over his shoulder, back into the rooms behind him. Akito readied himself to charge Durant again, but before he could, Durant was running at him in a panic. As Durant's hands connected with Akito's chest, Akito stumbled backward out onto the balcony. As slight as he was, Akito was pretty nimble, and he stepped to the side and pushed Durant's hands away from him.

Durant was heading for the balustrade with considerable momentum, and as he hit the railing, he toppled and his legs flew out behind him. He grabbed at anything he could, one hand seizing a spindle, the other clutching the lapel of Akito's jacket. With nothing slowing his impetus, his legs followed his body over the railing. Gravity snatched Durant, and his grasp failed. Akito felt the hand slip from his jacket, and Durant plunged down the stairwell. There was a sickening bang as the man hit the floor below. And then silence.

Akito stood looking over the balustrade in disbelief. A panic rose inside him, and his body was spurred into action. Akito ran down the stairs as fast as he could, two steps at a time, half stumbling, half jumping. He got to the bottom of the stairs and stood, looking in horror.

Any sense of urgency evaporated. It was clear from the bizarre angle of Durant's head that his neck was broken and there was nothing to be done. He crouched by Durant's crumpled body and felt for a pulse to confirm what he already knew. The famous professor was dead. Akito would not get any answers from him now. He stared at the professor's open eyes, wondering if he should close them out of respect, like they do on TV.

Akito was in shock. Was it his fault that the professor fell? Akito relived the moment he pushed Durant's hands away. He felt an ice-cold chill run across his skin.

"Is he dead?" called a voice from above.

Akito was jolted back into reality. He looked up to the balcony from which Durant had fallen. A young woman was leaning over the railing. Her dark touseled hair fell around her face as she looked down at him. Akito felt terrible having to tell her that Durant was dead.

"Yes. I'm so sorry." Akito called up to her. "Yes, he's ... "

"Then run!" the woman blurted out, gesturing toward the quad. "Just run! Go!"

The First Death of Corvus Durant

The urgency in her voice shocked him. It was clear that she thought he was to blame for Durant's fall. Akito felt responsible. He felt guilty. He was panicked and frightened again, and he was confused. Her instruction was all he could focus on, so he obeyed it. He grabbed his umbrella and ran out into the quadrangle, out into the rain. He put up his brolly to shelter from the downpour and to hide from the world. Then he scurried out through the main gate and into the anonymity of the street beyond.

2.
CHESS AND PASTRY

18 JANUARY 2023, 10.06 A.M.

The flat was quiet. Muffled noise from the street below came up through the closed windows—the chatter of people as they walked by, the ping of an oncoming bicycle warning oblivious pedestrians, the drone of a diesel bus engine in the distance, and the clatter and swoosh of a street sweeping machine. There was the airy hum of the cooling fan of the chess machine on the dining table, and a slowly building hiss, coming through the kitchen door, from the kettle as it heated water. Apart from this background noise, the flat was quiet. No one was there. Everything was still.

A well-worn depression in a sofa cushion began to deepen. A blurred greyness hung in the air above it. The pale shape slowly took the form of a human. It developed some colour, and it became clearer and sharper. It was a man. He was sitting on the sofa, and his semi-transparent form seemed to fit the indentation in the cushion perfectly. As he became more discernible and less grey, it also became clear that he was holding a small box in one hand and a photograph in the other. Then, after a few more seconds, he appeared to be perfectly solid, and his colouring was completely opaque. He blinked and looked around.

The kettle clicked off, and the bubbling and hissing of the boiling water subsided. The man on the sofa put the box and the photograph carefully on the coffee table. He lined them up to make sure they were square with the table, then he jumped up and went into the kitchen. He poured the steaming-hot water into a mug that already contained a Tetley teabag. He mashed the teabag impatiently with a teaspoon and left the tea to brew.

Phil Beans sat down at his dining table, staring at the chessboard, waiting for the chess computer to take its turn, and contemplating his next move. He got up again to finish making his tea and then sat down on the sofa. He reached for the beige-and-pink cardboard box and opened it slowly like it was the Ark of the Covenant. He reached inside and lifted out the object of his desire.

Phil cupped the golden pastry in his hand, its exterior glistening with a thick, glossy layer of rich, velvety-smooth chocolate ganache and a flourish of drizzled caramel. He picked off the shiny garnish of gold leaf, dropped it back in the box, and then bit through the chocolate and into the delicate, airy choux pastry. The luxurious, ice-cold vanilla crème pâtissière—sweet and silky with specks of real Madagascan vanilla bean—oozed out of the side of the pastry and plopped all down the front of Phil's T-shirt.

"Bollocks!"

Phil scooped up the thick vanilla cream with his free hand and licked it off his fingers. He took a sip of tea and carried on stuffing the delightful pâtissière into his face, one big bite at a time. With his mouth full of the last bite and vanilla cream on his chin, he went to wash his hands and change his shirt.

Chess and Pastry

Phil was procrastinating. Instead of messing about eating pastries and playing chess, Phil should have been contemplating his next move in the Quinkle divorce case. Phil was a private detective. Phil didn't advertise, and nobody ever actually sought him out. He was the kind of private detective that people didn't even realize they needed. He would go and find his clients once he'd determined he was the only person who could help them. Phil would be the first to admit he wasn't a very good sleuth, nor particularly dedicated, but Phil had a talent. It was a gift that made him remarkably successful. With a little help from his Polaroid picture collection, Phil could travel back in time. Hindsight and time travel are wonderfully useful things for any detective. If hindsight is 20/20, then being able to go back in time is like X-ray vision.

Phil heard his robot briefly come to life and, with a nice clean T-shirt and a freshly laundered beard, he sat back down at the dining table. Opposite him were his childhood Radio Shack Champion 2250XL and the state-of-the-art, bright-orange robot arm that Phil had installed to move the chess pieces. The old grey plastic chess computer dated from 1996. It had been given to him for his tenth birthday, and it was one of the few good things he could remember about his father. It had been a minor miracle of electronics, engineering, and programming to make this old thing communicate with the brand-new, state-of-the-art KUKA robot arm, and for its motorized pincers to delicately pick up the right piece and place it carefully in the correct destination square without scattering the rest of the pieces across the table and onto the floor.

The 2250 had just moved its knight to h5, and it was attacking Phil's queen on g3 with nowhere to go. "Oh, bugger." A rookie error. So early in the game too. Phil regretted setting the 2250 to level 64. Not only did the machine play so much better on its highest level, but it also took so bloody long to make a move that Phil would get distracted and wander away to do something else, like get a pastry or read this month's *Cheese!* magazine. He wasn't in his usual groove; he had lost his thread, and now, surely, the game.

Phil usually took a Polaroid picture before the start of each chess game, just in case he wanted to play a mulligan. Like in golf, Phil would play a mulligan to take back a blunder and give himself a chance to win the game. The 2250 had a "take back" function, but it was slow and laborious to use, and Phil found it easier and more sporting to go back to the start of the game and give himself a clue rather than try to take back "up to 34 moves." The Polaroid he took could transport him back to that moment before the start of the game so that he could leave himself a note.

Somehow, doing a take-back on the chess computer felt like cheating. Not cheating the machine, since it didn't give a shit if it won or lost, but cheating himself of a genuine victory. He felt like it was unsportsmanlike if he just undid his mistake. Going back in time and leaving himself a clue was where Phil drew that particular line.

He would take the picture, then leave the room for a few minutes to make sure he wouldn't have to meet himself if he did come back. Not because that would cause some universe-ending temporal anomaly, but because it had made him really self-conscious when it happened the first time. He thought it a bit like hearing his own voice or seeing himself on a video, but a hundred times worse, and he was just standing there feeling really bloody awkward, like he should shake hands with himself. He'd thought it really, really weird. So at the start of a game, Phil might get out of the shower, or come in from the kitchen with a nice hot mug of tea, and find a note on the dining table that had words to the effect of *Don't get cocky in the endgame, kid. Watch for the rook on h4.*

But today, having become engrossed in his chess game for the last couple of hours, he had left it too late to go to the bakery, and they had sold out of his favourite, very probably mere minutes after they'd opened. So instead of a chess-move take-back, he had used this morning's Polaroid to play a bakery mulligan. And having used his Polaroid for the bakery trip, there was no going back again, and the chess game was damage limitation from this point. Phil was not a naturally philosophical loser; he was a sore one. Hence the Polaroid mulligan thing. The robot arm was looking quite superior, and the 2250 was humming smugly. Phil knew he wasn't concentrating properly, so he switched off the chess computer and the robot arm, which retreated to its home position and sulked. He would come back to the game when he was less distracted and see if he could recover from his blunder.

Phil grabbed the Polaroid and a Sharpie from the coffee table, and he put a big *X* on the back of the picture. "You served me well, Polaroid. Even if I lose this game, I will always remember the pastry."

Phil felt stuck. He picked up his phone and dialled

"Fergal O'Reilly speaking."

"Hi, Fergal. It's Phil Beans."

"What about ya, Phil?"

"I'm feeling stuck."

There was a sigh on the other end. Phil waited for some sage words of advice that would magically cure him of his malaise.

There was a deep breath in, and in an Irish accent that was made for reading poetry—admittedly, irritated and frustrated poetry—Fergal said, "Phil, this is the emergency number. It's for people in distress. Like standing on a ledge of a high-rise building kind of distress."

"Yes, but ..."

Fergal continued in a slightly condescending tone, "Now, you're not on a ledge, are you, Phil." After the briefest pause, he added, slightly panicked, "You're not on a ledge, are you? Please tell me you're not about to hurl yourself off the top of Magdalen Tower."

"No, no. No, I'm not."

"Then this isn't an emergency, is it?"

"No, not as such, no."

"I gave you this number in case you found yourself on a ledge or need'n to cancel at short notice. To be sure, you've never yet cancelled once, have ye?"

"No, even when I forget, I somehow manage to get there on time."

"Fair play to ye. So this number is for when you have an emergency. Ya feckin' eejit."

"It's just that I'm procrastinating. I thought you might ..."

"Boundaries, Phil. Feckin' boundaries. How many more times? Right, so how 'bout you think on what we've talked about in countless feckin' sessions, and we'll talk at your scheduled time next week. Hmmm? How 'bout that?"

Fergal hung up.

"Harsh. Harsh, but fair," Phil muttered to himself. "We did actually talk about boundaries. A couple of times."

Chess and Pastry

Phil had met Fergal after egging Professor Durant's office. He'd paid the fine and the damages, avoiding jail time in exchange for court-mandated anger management. After Fergal had determined that Phil had "every reason to be that feckin' angry," Phil decided he liked Fergal, so he carried on seeing him voluntarily, once a month, to work on the issues that Fergal had unearthed. That was several years ago, and Phil had become something of an armchair psychotherapist.

"OK, Robot, why are we stuck?" Phil began, parroting something he had heard in the course of his many sessions with Fergal. "I think it's most likely because our inner child is afraid to fail. Afraid of disapproval. It's letting my father win a battle he isn't even fighting. Well, sod that."

Phil thought of an aphorism on one of the many inspirational posters on Fergal's office wall. The one with the picture of the penguin at the gym, wearing a purple Lycra onesie, staring with trepidation at a treadmill. *If you don't try, you've already failed.*

"Would it have been so hard for Fergal just to tell me that?"

The robot just stared at Phil in disbelief.

So Phil turned his attention to the Quinkle divorce case. A lucrative divorce case suited Phil nicely. He could take whatever information he needed from today, change as little as possible in the past to win the case, and be rewarded pretty well for a day-or-two's effort.

Going back in time wasn't always straightforward, however. For one thing, Phil knew he could only use each Polaroid once to time-travel. He had tried that before to no avail. For two, he had to be sure to take a Polaroid of "now" back with him, so he could get home again to his rightful timeline. Of course, he also had to make sure it was one he hadn't already used, so he always took a fresh picture right before he left.

And for three, he knew he couldn't hang about too long in the past. Been there, done that, got the brown trousers. If he spent too long lolling about in the past, it would become harder and harder to get home the longer he was there (or rather, then?). And the further back he went into the past, the less time he could spend there/then before it became hard to return. He couldn't be certain how long before it was impossible, and he wasn't keen to test it until he found out. From the limited experimentation he had dared to do, he knew he could spend a few days or maybe a week in the recent past. But if he went back years and years, perhaps it would be just a few hours before he would be stuck there.

A relatively recent divorce case was quick and easy and, for the most part, risk-free. Plus, it made Phil feel like he was continuing his mission against philandering arseholes, like his father.

Phil's bank would occasionally get very agitated when his finances went into the red. Phil never understood why they were so upset when they were the recipient of some exorbitant charges for the privilege of lending him a few hundred quid. The overdraft charges got Phil quite stressed, however, and he would periodically have to find a good case that he could go back and fix. In exchange for vital and usually incriminating evidence, he would charge 10% of the improved settlement. Ex-wives were generally, more often than not, very grateful to pay it.

Subsequently, a period of relative calm would follow, during which time the bank would not write, and Phil wouldn't think about money much at all. He could then blithely go through life indulging his interests, at least until the bank started getting arsey with him again.

He had begun looking into the Quinkle case because the bank had written to tell him about his newly burgeoning overdraft. Phil knew Quinkle was a solid case to work on, and his current financial woes had compelled him to take his investigation seriously. A few months earlier, Mrs. Quinkle had lost the divorce settlement case against her ex-husband, a multi-millionaire property tycoon from Brighton. Perhaps tycoon was a stretch, but he had been a big shot in Brighton anyway. A big fish in a small pond. But for one reason or another, in the year before the divorce was announced, Quinkle Holdings had been all but bankrupt. A rival start-up company had poached all their big contracts, and Quinkle's money had dwindled to his last couple of million. Consequently, Mrs. Quinkle had been awarded the tiniest fraction of what she deserved of the little empire she had helped Quinkle to build over the fifteen years of their marriage.

Somehow, there had been a new investor right after the case had been settled. A mysterious new source of cash, no doubt from a bank account in Bermuda. All of a sudden, Quinkle had bought the company that had poached all his contracts, and he was a big shot once again. Phil was confident that the Bermuda bank account was where Quinkle's money had been squirrelled away.

The bigger problem was that the divorce case rested on the prenup that Mrs. Quinkle had signed fifteen years earlier. Phil knew there was no case at all unless he could challenge the prenup. If he could prove Quinkle's philandering, then Mrs. Quinkle could invoke the infidelity clause and invalidate the restrictions on her claims in their prenup. Then she could get half of whatever assets Phil could unearth in Bermuda.

Mrs. Quinkle could definitely benefit from Phil's services. Retroactively, that is. A few years ago, she could have used a proper private detective, but after losing the case, she needed someone with Phil's unique talent. Now, with his gift, Phil would have to gather some indelicate evidence, follow the money in the Bermuda account, then go back in time to before the hearing and convince Mrs. Quinkle that she needed to hire him.

The divorce had been a big thing in the news at the time. Phil had read something salacious, but lacking substantial detail, in *The Argus* online, so Phil managed to get a friend to post a copy of *The Argus* newspaper from Brighton to him in Oxford. That was where the real juicy details about the case were to be found. They were in tiny print, filling almost all of page six, aside from the adverts for an ironmonger's shop and an optician's.

Phil smelled a rat. He knew that the appearance of an Italian supermodel on the scene after the settlement was neither recent, nor particularly above board. *The Argus* had pulled no punches in telling how she had come out of nowhere only to suddenly look like a permanent fixture on Quinkle's arm.

This rat smelled just like the one from his own parents' divorce. His father suddenly had Isabella on his arm, and he'd hidden assets so that the court would award his mother a tiny fraction of what she should have had. Phil had had to sort that out, and now he would fix Quinkle. Phil would work his magic on yet another lucrative divorce case, and it would serve Quinkle right.

Phil needed proof of Quinkle's affair with the supermodel. He had searched online, but he'd drawn a blank. The supermodel was very careful about her privacy, and Phil had no idea where to look for her if he did go back in time and snoop around in Brighton.

Phil's research had hit a dead end. He had been unable to track down the Italian supermodel. He knew her name was Chianti Carbonara, and that she had moved from Milan to Brighton in early 2020 to escape from the initial outbreak of the pandemic, but the trail went cold after that. Not even paparazzi from *The Sun* had snapped her at home or with Quinkle during the lockdown. Phil had been unable to find out where she had been staying. So far, he didn't know where he would look, or even when exactly, if he did go back to do some sleuthing.

It was time to call in a favour. Well, admittedly, ask for yet another favour. Phil knew it wasn't the done thing to ask for favours all the time. But he really didn't ask *all the time*. Though he might concede that it was *often*. He picked up his phone and dialled. The phone barely had a chance to ring.

"DS Frisk." Detective Sergeant Havarti Frisk sounded bright and breezy, yet efficient and intimidating.

"Hi, Havarti, it's Phil. Hi. Hello, ummm, how are you?"

"Hey, Phil, what can I do for you?" The question was not phrased that way by accident. Havarti was one of Phil's best friends, but she had endured his need for favours, and she was a go-to when Phil needed something that he couldn't access online.

"I'll, yes, ummm … actually, I need an address."

"Address for whom? Where?"

"It's for Chianti Carbonara. In Brighton," said Phil.

"Oh, come on, Phil!" Havarti said. "Oxford, yes, easy. Thames Valley even, no problem. But West-frigging-Sussex? Really? I can't access another division without a warrant, and I hate asking favours, Phil. Especially West-frigging-Sussex."

"I think you'll find it's East Sussex. At least it's not the Met!" said Phil with a chuckle. "Pretty please?" he added, hoping that was persuasive. "It's the Quinkle case. I want that shit to pay through the nose. I wouldn't ask, but the bank … my overdraft, you know?"

Havarti let out a long, slow sigh. "Yep. That smug bastard needs his comeuppance. I saw the news a while back. It's like everyone knows, but the court case was just bollocks. A watertight prenup, and Quinkle and the judge both being Westgate alumni. It would be cool if you could make the miserable slimeball pay. And I'm sure you'll get a pretty juicy slice of the action if you do."

"I might not be catching the real bad guys like you are," Phil said, "but helping divorcées get justifiable financial restitution from their cheating ex-husbands does have its fringe monetary benefits. Enough to pay the rent on the flat and the robot arm, at least. Plus, it buys you fish 'n' chips once in a while, so don't knock it."

"Ooh, hit a nerve, did I? Bit sensitive today, Phil?"

"Oh, sod off. I just need an address. You think you can help?" asked Phil. "Chianti Carbonara. I need the address where she was staying before the divorce was announced. I think it was February 2020 when she moved from Milan to escape the Covid outbreak. She got out shortly before the borders closed. I know she quarantined at a hotel in London for a week or so because the paparazzi were all over that. Then, I reckon, Quinkle put her up in a fancy secret flat in Brighton somewhere."

"Alright, Phil. Leave it with me. I'll make a call. I was in training with Peter Fugglestone. He went on to East Sussex. I'll ask Fuggs," she said with resignation. "I hate to owe him one, though. He's a right wanker."

"Thanks."

"You'll owe me big time, Phil," Havarti said with a hint of glee in her voice. "Meet me for lunch, and I'll tell you what I need help with."

"You need help? I always said you needed help!" Phil said with a chuckle.

"Not therapy, you twit. No, from you, Phil."

"From me? Oh. OK. Well, lunch sounds good," Phil said.

"The Firkin Folly? Noon? You're paying, Phil."

"Sure," he said as Havarti hung up. "Bye, then," Phil said to his phone's lockscreen.

Phil was going to need his go-bag. Not the kind of go-bag the spies always have under the floorboards in films, stuffed full of money and guns and fake passports. No. Phil's go-bag contained a wash-bag with a toothbrush and toothpaste, little travel-sized bottles of Head and Shoulders, and hair gel. It also contained a couple of clean T-shirts and a couple of changes of undies and socks. Other essentials included some boxes of spare SX-70 film, each cartridge holding eight "instant" pictures, and a Flash Bar. He always kept his go-bag packed so he could take a little trip at short notice.

That was the funny thing with Phil. He had all the time in the world. When you can go back to a time and place, there's really no hurry. Except that Phil could be excitable and eager. When he decided what to do, it had to be done. He would go from leisurely and lackadaisical to focused and impatient in a heartbeat. Hence the go-bag. Phil knew he would need his other camera. The megapixel digital one with the expensive, high-powered zoom lens. The sort a proper detective would need for actual surveillance. Phil tucked his digital camera into his leather satchel, where it nestled softly among the T-shirts and socks.

Phil googled the date of the final Quinkle divorce hearing:

About 1,820,000 results (0.26 seconds)

The Argus for news, sport, Brighton and Hove Albion, entertainment, video, blogs

22 July 2022
www.theargus.co.uk/quinkle_case_shocker
<u>Shock Result in Quinkle Divorce Hearing</u>

Phil's mind was a sponge. A high-tech, fast, central-processing-unit kind of sponge. He soaked up ideas and information; he was always interested in new things. With an iPhone and the internet always on hand, though, he was like a golden retriever in a forest full of squirrels. Unlike a computer's central processor, Phil's output was of questionable value. In this respect, he could also be likened to a golden retriever—big and soft, loyal and loving, and quite ornamental in a pudgy, hairy sort of way, but really rather useless. He shed less hair than a retriever, though, so he had that going for him.

Phil was a geek. Or a nerd. He wasn't quite sure which. He told himself that he wasn't socially inept; he just found people awkward to be around. Phil thought the former would be a char-

Chess and Pastry

acter flaw, but the latter was a perfectly normal trait for a geek. Phil had just turned thirty-six, but as an anxiety-riddled geek, he still never knew what to say to people he didn't know. Since he avoided situations where small talk would be called for, he never really got any practice at it either. It was a kind of Catch-22.

Phil didn't care for the geeky stereotype, even though *The Big Bang Theory* had made nerds cool. Phil tried to be more of a hipster, in a late-noughties, Oxford post-grad kind of way. Now that being a hipster wasn't trendy anymore, he felt like it was OK to borrow a bit of hipster style, if you could call it style.

Phil augmented his geeky science T-shirts with skinny jeans, a light woollen sport coat (from the charity shop when he was a bit hard up), and brown full brogues (from Johnston & Murphy, when he had been feeling a bit more flush). His black hair was invariably spiked up with hair gel and styled very carefully to appear as though he'd just got out of bed, and his goatee was always neatly trimmed. His look was topped off by his signature small, round, dark sunglasses that he wore year-round, and which lived in his top jacket pocket when he was indoors. Last, but not least, Phil would be seen everywhere he went with his old Polaroid SX-70 instant camera slung around his neck, hanging from the strap of its leather Ever-Ready Case. So Phil thought he looked cool enough, and with that little bit of self-belief, he managed to just about, not quite carry it off.

But when it came to music, Phil was someone else entirely. Phil loved music. All kinds. Except opera, perhaps. It seemed to Phil that most of the awful singing spoiled some quite nice classical tunes. Best of all, Phil loved music he could dance to. And Phil could dance. He loved karaoke. And Phil could sing too. These two facts were probably the reason that Phil had ever had a girlfriend at all. He loved how dancing and karaoke meant you could be something other than an introverted, nerdy hipster without having to think of anything to say to a stranger.

Knowing the date of the hearing, Phil stood in front of the wall of shelves that housed his Polaroid photograph albums. All the albums were organized by date, each with a neat label on the spine. He pulled out the album from July 2022 and leafed through to the Polaroids from the 22nd. He picked out a nice, arty picture he had taken of a dozen punts moored on the River Cherwell in Oxford, not long after sunrise. Judging by the pictures on the previous page, it had been karaoke night the previous evening, and Phil remembered he had taken the picture of the boats on his walk home. If Phil could get to that spot on the river that early in the day, he would have no trouble getting to Brighton ahead of the hearing one way or another. By car or by train was the question. It was always a risk calculation. Traffic delays were pretty common, but the trains were nearly always running late or getting cancelled, subject to strikes or, God forbid, substituted by a Rail Replacement Bus.

His phone pinged. It was a text from Havarti:

> **Chianti Carbonara**
> **Flat 2, 42 Adelaide Crescent**
> **Hove, BN3 2JL**
> **29 Feb. 2020 – 29 Dec. 2022**

Chess and Pastry

> Brilliant! You rock

> You owe me big time! Fuggs was a complete obnoxious twat over it

> OK. Thank you!

So, Phil went back to the photo albums. He only had photos that he had taken in Oxford on Chianti's first day in the Brighton flat. He picked out a picture from Saturday, 29 February 2020. It was one of the best spots in all of Oxford to come and go, somewhere quiet where he was unlikely to be seen.

"I'll have to go back to that day in Oxford, and drive down. What do you think, Robot, about a three-hour drive to Brighton? Better make sure the car was free that day." So, he checked the calendar on his phone to see if he had ever used his car that day. Phil tried to make meticulous notes in the event that he one day had a need to use his car for the same dates and times. Phil hadn't worked out all the threads of the space-time continuum that time travel could perturb, but he knew if he turned up to use the car, and some other version of him was out and about in the Zephyr, that would definitely bugger up his plans. Since there was no note in his calendar about the car on 29 February 2020, he assumed it would be available. "Excellent. That'll be less prone to cancellation than the train. Be there on her move-in day. That's a solid plan for catching Quinkle with Chianti Carbonara."

Next, he sat on the sofa and did what he always did. He opened his SX-70 camera and took a Polaroid of the moment of departure, upon which he wrote *Queen St. Flat, 18 Jan. 2023, 10.28 a.m.* He put all but one of the Polaroids into the zippered pocket inside his satchel. Phil put on his jacket, with sunglasses in the top pocket, and picked up his satchel. He checked his jacket pocket for his wallet, his front jeans pockets for his keys and phone, and looked down at his old Polaroid camera hanging around his neck in its leather case. He was ready for his next move.

Phil took the Polaroid of 29 February 2020 in his hand. He focussed on it intently. He let the image fill his vision, and he willed the universe to help him to transform. He gradually felt the flat becoming a blur, and he could smell the outdoor air of a cold, damp February day. He felt the way he imagined a sugar cube would feel dissolving in warm, colourless water. He began to blur and fade, and he felt a greyness overtaking him.

3.

ALL THINGS BRIGHTON BEAUTIFUL

29 FEBRUARY 2020, 11.58 A.M.

Phil found himself trying to focus on something blue looming in front of him. There was a similar one beside him, also blue, towering over him. There was another one opposite, but that one was a pink blur. The air was cold, and the floor was damp where Phil was sitting, but it was peaceful and there was birdsong. He sensed colour returning to him and the greyness evaporating. He started to feel more solid, as though someone somewhere had gently coloured him in and shaded him carefully like a living, breathing trompe l'oeil. Phil was a bit discombobulated, and he had to breathe deeply to help orientate himself to his new surroundings.

As things took shape, they began to make sense. The blue thing next to him had a sign that read *Shoes,* and on the pink one, a sign read *Electrical;* the photograph in his hand had the handwritten caption, *Friars Walk Recycling, Sat. 29 Feb. 2020, 11.58 a.m.* It was a quiet, secluded spot, where people rarely recycled shoes, or electrical equipment, or anything else, for that matter.

The Polaroid in Phil's hand was spent now. He couldn't use it to time-travel again, as he'd learned from previous attempts. So, as the world around him solidified, he drew a big cross on the back with the Sharpie from his jacket pocket, as he normally did when he had used a picture.

So, what now? Phil wondered. He thought for a moment about the date written on the Polaroid in his hand. *Oh, yes,* he recalled, *this was the day Chianti Carbonara would move into her rental in Brighton, having fled Milan at the start of the pandemic.* That was the reason he had picked this particular Polaroid. The fog was clearing from Phil's mind. He needed to get to Brighton today. This Polaroid had brought him to this place and time in Oxford, but his plan was to spy on Chianti Carbonara at her new flat in Brighton.

This would mean he had a three-hour drive ahead of him, travelling to the address Havarti had texted him. He walked around the corner to Trinity Street and the home of Kelly Klunk. She was the Westgate Alumni Office administrator, and Phil had rented her garage ever since he had got his car nine years ago. Kelly and her husband, Ian, were New Age hippie artist types. They were frequenters of Collard Green's Vegan Café, and they didn't believe in cars. Not that they denied the existence of cars. They just didn't think car ownership should be allowed. So Kelly had no use for her share of the garage block near her home, and renting it out helped pay the bills that Ian's art didn't.

Phil pulled open the wonky up-and-over metal door and was mightily relieved to find that his old Ford Zephyr 4 MkIII was there. The British cars of the 1960s weren't known for their spectacular colour schemes, and Phil's sported one of the more boring colours that Ford had ever offered. Phil's car was Windsor Grey, and he loved it. He looked at its waxed, glossy paint and its gleaming old school chrome and smiled. He fished his keys out of his pocket, inserted the key into the chrome-plated door handle, and popped the lock. He grasped the handle, pushed the button in, and felt the door release with a satisfying mechanical clunk. The door opened with a creak, like an old knee joint, and Phil got into the car.

"Hello, old girl." Phil inhaled deeply, taking in the smell of vintage red leather, old rubber floormats, and unburnt petrol. He pulled the knob that controlled the choke to enrich the petrol mix, and with the strange combination of assurance and doubt that comes with classic car ownership, he turned the key in the ignition. The starter motor engaged with great enthusiasm and turned over the engine. The Zephyr's four cylinders reluctantly came to life, sputtering unevenly and throwing a big plume of dark smoke out into the garage. As Phil expertly adjusted the choke, the engine smoothed out and all 1.7 litres gently thrummed with a familiar, reassuring rhythm. "You beauty," Phil said, somewhat relieved.

Phil hated motorways. He didn't like to race the old thing over sixty. He wasn't even sure she could get up to sixty anymore. He liked the smaller roads where he could pootle behind a lorry and not get hooted at for driving slowly. So he set off on the shortest route that avoided the major roads and motorways. Just over 100 miles. About three hours. Estimated time of arrival, according to his Maps app, 3.10 p.m.

Apart from a quick pitstop at The Cricketers in Hartley Wintney, it was plain sailing. The best bit, of course, was not stopping in Reading. He arrived in Hove and drove along Kingsway. He parked in the completely empty strip of disabled parking right in front of 42 Adelaide Crescent. It was a very long stretch of parking reserved for the disabled, none of whom seemed to be using any of it, but it was the only place to park right outside Chianti's flat where he could get a good view with his telephoto lens.

There was a removal lorry, complete with three men going back and forth carrying boxes, chairs, lamps, pictures, and so on into the building. And there was Chianti Carbonara. She was undeniably beautiful with her high cheekbones and long red hair, and she was tall and elegant. But she wasn't Phil's type; she was quite lanky, and far too skinny, as you'd expect of a supermodel. And here she was, not at all the glamorous magazine cover girl in her sweatshirt, jogging bottoms, and flip-flops, with her hair tied back. Phil snapped a few pictures of Chianti directing the movers. She followed the box-carrying men inside, and, for a minute or two, there was stillness and silence.

Phil guessed that Chianti was five-eleven. In heels, she would be at least the same height as Quinkle, most likely taller in the kind of heels he was used to seeing her wear in photos on the red carpet.

There was no sign of Quinkle yet. If Phil knew his type, then Quinkle was paying for this flat, and would pretty soon be there for some kind of a "thank you." Phil just had to wait and hope for him to turn up. Phil walked across the grass to the Lawns café and got a coffee and a cake. And a sausage roll. *Who can resist a sausage roll,* he wondered, *especially those long ones with the flaky pastry that are a bit soggy on the bottom and are all warm and seasoned to perfection?*

Phil sat in his car feeling sorry for vegans who didn't know the pleasure of a fresh, warm sausage roll. Then he felt sorry for the piggies. Phil liked pigs. *Babe* was one of his favourite films! Then he separated his thoughts from his actions and tucked in. He sipped his coffee. Then he ate his cake. Then he finished his coffee and told himself he would not do that again until at least 5.00 p.m.

At 4.00 p.m., Phil got a coffee and another sausage roll. Another piece of cake, he told himself, was just being greedy.

Just before 5.00 p.m., the three men jumped into the lorry and it rumbled off down the street. Phil got his camera out, the fancy digital one with the long lens. The one he had brought for spying—or as it's officially known, "surveillance."

He trained the lens on the windows and tested the focus and exposure. Then he settled down in his car seat to watch the house.

There was a knock on his window. Phil surreptitiously put the camera on the passenger seat, behind his satchel. Peering in through the window was a middle-aged chap in a blue parka with the fur-trimmed hood up over his head, obscuring his eyes, but revealing a large, Roman nose and a smile full of crooked teeth. "Nice car, mate. What year?"

Phil wound the window down a bit so the man wouldn't feel compelled to yell quite so loudly. "It's a 1963."

"You could show her. You know, on the concourse. She's a beauty."

"Yes, yes, thank you," Phil said, as he started winding the window back up.

"What mileage do you get?"

"What? Really?" said Phil, wondering how to cut this short. "I get bugger all mileage. Petrol consumption is awful. She's a guzzler, alright. She drinks the stuff like it was margaritas on a hen night. But thanks for taking an interest," and he wound the window back up.

The old gent walked off saying something like "Please your bloody self, mate."

Phil watched the house some more, getting a little sleepy while his mind went off on its own tangent. Time passed, and he waited. A troll entered the forest. Oh, no, wait—that was the computer game from Phil's youth. The game that Mr. Pedge had given him for his eighth birthday. He thought about nice Mr. Pedge. Phil wondered about what happened to him the day he died. He thought about his miserable father and the wonderful gift of a chess computer. Phil's mind wandered like a cloud—over hill, over dale, over park, over pale.

There was a knock at the window again, and Phil was brought back to reality. "What now?" he grumbled, expecting to see that it was the old car enthusiast in the blue parka. It wasn't.

"Can't park here, mate!" shouted the traffic warden.

"Oh, no, I know." Phil reached over and wound the window down again. "I'm sorry. She, erm, broke down. You know, heap of old junk. I'm waiting for the breakdown van. I'll be gone as soon as they can get here to give me a tow."

"You'll have to get out and push it to where you can park. You can't park here. This is disabled."

"I know it is; I told you, she broke down," Phil said, feeling this was a legitimate reason to park there.

"No, I mean the parking is disabled, not the car."

Phil wasn't going to get far with this jobsworth. "Well, it's kind of fitting, then. Disabled car in a disabled space."

"Smart-arse. Alright, son, just for that, you're getting a ticket."

"So, if you give me a ticket, that means I can stay, right?" Phil said.

"If you're still here when I come back this way, I'll get you towed."

"Well, a tow is what I'm waiting for. When will you be back this way then?" asked Phil.

The traffic warden looked at his watch. "I suppose I'm knocking off in ten minutes, so that'll be Tuesday, most likely," he said, tearing off Phil's ticket and putting it under the windscreen wiper.

Phil held his hand out. "You could at least just pass it to me, couldn't you?"

"I could of," said the warden, and he walked off.

"Have!" shouted Phil. He looked back at the house. At first glance, nothing seemed to have changed, but there was now a black car parked in the row of spaces that had been vacated by the removal lorry. The lights of the car went out, and the door opened. It had gone quite dark, and Phil pointed the lens at the car door. He adjusted the exposure for the streetlights just in time to snap a picture of a man getting out.

It was hard to tell it was him. He had his head down and his collar up. But it was him, alright. That was Quinkle's profile for sure, with his angular nose and prominent chin. Six foot one and smartly dressed in a Savile Row suit. Snap, snap, snap. A sequence of pictures of Quinkle walking to the door and being buzzed in.

Then Phil watched the windows. There wasn't anything to see yet. Phil imagined the time it would take to drink a glass of wine and engage in a little sweet talk, and right on cue, the lights on the floor above turned on. That would surely be the bedroom, with its grand windows overlooking the seafront. The big overhead light was on. Then it went off again, leaving softer lighting, presumably from bedside table lamps.

Then Chianti came to the window, dressed in a silk robe and lit by the streetlight shining in through the window. She reached up to grasp the curtains on either side of her.

"Damn," muttered Phil, busily taking pictures. "No, no, no, not the curtains!"

Just then, Quinkle came up behind her and kissed her neck. He pulled at her robe and drew it down over her shoulders. Then he removed her robe, exposing her breasts. Phil was snapping shots all the while, like a paparazzo spotting Lady Di eating a hot dog.

Quinkle's face was visible, whispering in her ear and kissing her neck. Then his hands were on her bare breasts. He was groping her breasts and licking her ear. She threw back her head, and he pulled her away from the window. Then Quinkle drew the curtains, and Phil drew a breath. "Really classy guy, grabby old git!"

"Wow," said Phil, pressing buttons and scrolling through the pictures on the camera's little screen. "Unbelievable. Perfect. Just what I needed." Phil had a great mugshot of Quinkle's face as he was pulling the curtains. "Gotcha!"

Five minutes later, Quinkle emerged from the front door, and Phil had to scramble to catch him getting back in the car and driving off. He got a nice, clear shot of the yellow number plate on the back of the Jag too.

"That was a Quinkle quickie, a real come 'n' go!" Phil said to himself. "What a waste."

Quinkle's black Jaguar XF receded in Phil's rearview mirror, headed towards Brighton. Phil was feeling pleased with himself. He tucked the camera away in his satchel and put the key in the ignition.

"Come on, old girl, let's get you back to Oxford."

The Zephyr chugged to life with the first turn of the starter motor, Phil popped her into gear, and off they went. Phil focused on the small patch of road that was lit dimly by the car's old headlights. He gripped the wheel and prepared himself for a long drive in the dark.

It was late when Phil drove into Trinity Street. He was tired, and he needed some sleep before heading back to resume his own timeline. There was no point in going home in the middle of the day and going to bed. That would be a waste, since he could use this timeline to get some sleep. But here, it would be difficult to get in at his usual bed and breakfast, and awkward to ask his other, contemporaneous self to sleep on his sofa. So as soon as Phil parked the car in the garage, he grabbed the little pillow that he kept on the back seat and settled down on the spacious front bench seat for a nap.

When Phil awoke, it was almost eight in the morning, and the grey beginnings of daylight were dimly illuminating the cloudy sky out beyond the open garage door. He was cold and uncomfortable. He climbed stiffly out of the car with his satchel and his Polaroid camera. He picked up a clean cloth from the shelf on the wall and wiped some bits off the windscreen and the chrome bumper, shining it a little till he was satisfied. After tossing the cloth into a little laundry basket in the corner, he locked the car, pulled down the metal door of the garage, and then locked that too.

He walked off in search of coffee. He got to the top of the Westgate Oxford shopping centre and went into the Breakfast Club. He ate a hearty full English whilst deep in thought. He paid his bill and headed to the bathroom. First, he checked his hair and brushed his teeth. He went into a cubicle and turned the lock to show the stall was occupied without latching it. Then he leant against the door to hold it shut. He rummaged in the pocket of his satchel and got out the Polaroid picture from 18 January 2023, 10.28 a.m. He stared purposefully at the Polaroid and willed himself away.

A minute later, the door of the empty cubicle swung open all by itself.

4.

COLLARD GREEN'S

18 JANUARY 2023, 10.28 A.M.

Phil gradually saw his flat coming into focus, and he began to feel more solid, as though he was becoming part of the scene he was entering. He blinked as his eyes adjusted to seeing colour again, and he looked down. In one hand, he held the Polaroid he had taken at 10.28. In his other hand was his phone, which was busy connecting to his Wi-Fi. In spite of the fact that the lock screen was displaying the time in large numerals, Phil looked at his watch. Already 10.30. *Shit!* he thought, *how am I going to have brunch at the café and lunch at the pub with Havarti if I don't get my skates on?*

Phil got his skates on. Given that he was already wearing his tan brogues, he settled for getting a move on. He stood up and checked that he had his wallet and his keys. He put his phone in his pocket and, still wearing his jacket, camera, and satchel, he rushed out the door, down the stairs, and out onto Queen Street.

With a brisk stride, Phil set off through the busy morning throng, round the corner onto St. Aldate's, and in through the door of Collard Green's Vegan Café. Phil definitely did not want to skip brunch, and somehow it felt like today might be a good day for brunch. Any later and it would be lunchtime again, which was when he had arrived at the café over the last few days.

Phil walked in and looked around for somewhere to sit. He loitered by the door, waiting for the couple at the window table who were counting out coins and putting on their coats. So, despite there being several clean tables at which to sit, Phil sat down at the dirty one in the window. Phil liked a seat by the window with a view of the bustling Oxford street beyond. It was intriguing in a detached kind of way, and it was relaxing, like having a film on in the background with the sound off. He let out an idle sigh and, gazing out at the passers-by, he waited.

The waitress came over. Was she a waitress? Or was she a server? Phil wasn't sure what the PC, gender-neutral term was these days. *Server* was too American, though. And he knew she wasn't American. Her name tag read *Holly*, but Phil felt that calling her by her first name would be far too presumptuous before they had been formally introduced. Phil decided he was overthinking it, so he resorted to the same diffident smile he had given her over the last week.

Holly's long brown hair was pulled back into a neat ponytail, which was perfect for her Collard Green's baseball cap. Under the brim of the cap, her big brown eyes sparkled. Her glossy red lips completed Phil's idea of perfection.

"Sorry, let me just clear that for you." She smiled at Phil, which accentuated the little dimples in her cheeks. What Phil saw was that his smile had been returned in the most perfect form he had ever seen. *Just so adorable!* he thought. Her whole face lit up, and it made him feel like he was the most important person in the world.

Collard Green's

He opened his mouth to speak, but his fuddled brain had nothing for him.

Holly spoke first. "Would you like to see a menu? Or shall I just put you down for avocado toast and a latte?"

"Oh, yes, that would be lovely, please."

"Well, it's what you've ordered every day for the whole of the week I've been working here," she said with a giggle and a shrug.

Phil smiled and felt his face blush, unsure if she was judging him or finding him charming. When Phil had stared blankly at the menu a week ago, avocado toast was front and centre. It read *Collard Green's Signature Dish, "The best brunch you'll eat today!"* And once Phil found something he liked on a menu, he rarely bothered to try anything new. He had already committed to the avocado toast, and there was no point wavering now. "Ha-ha, well, at least it'll be the best brunch I'll have today."

"I guarantee it," Holly said. "Coming right up."

Service was quick, and Phil had said yes to a second organic arabica-bean almond milk latte when his avocado toast had arrived. Phil ate in silence, watching Holly and trying to manage it without looking like he was watching. She was alternating between being engaging, sweet, and smiley with the few other customers, and clearing tables without the smile. When she glanced his way, Phil quickly looked out the window at Oxford passing by. People were walking past, scurrying or strolling, mostly loaded with shopping bags or looking at their phones. A City Sightseeing bus passed. A couple stood outside the café door reading the menu. The backdrop to this view was the imposing stone tower of Christ Church college a short way down, across the street. Phil was pondering whether Holly had glanced his way just to make sure he was still eating, or didn't need another latte, or whether, just maybe, she was looking his way, hoping he'd be looking back.

Holly came over with Phil's bill and set it down on the table. "So, how long have you been vegan?"

"Oh, erm, I'm not actually …"

"Oh. Not much of a conversation starter," she said. "Vegans can usually talk for an hour about their vegan journey." Holly folded her arms across her baggy 'Collard Green's' sweatshirt, order pad in one hand and pen in the other. She gave a little shrug and a half smile. It seemed to Phil that it was his turn to speak.

"How about you? Been vegan long?" was all Phil managed to come up with.

"Yeah, no, I'm not vegan either," she replied, "but I only work here. I don't actually have to eat the food."

"Oh," Phil chuckled, "seems we're both here for the same reason, then."

Holly's brow furrowed, and her head tilted to the side, indicating she would like him to explain. "Which is?"

"You work here." Phil had started with a half-baked joke, and he wasn't sure where it was leading, but her curiosity made him bolder. He felt his heart quicken as he began to explain. "I only started eating here a week ago because I saw you through the window. I came in to order lunch and pluck up the courage to say something to you. I've been doing that all week, but you always seem so busy."

"Well, yes, this is a café, and lunchtime does that to you, I'm afraid. But you're earlier today, and there's only a few coconut lattes and chai teas."

Collard Green's

"A bit less chat and a bit more clearing of tables!" came a shout from the kitchen, in a broad Glaswegian accent. "Let's start the lunch rush with all the tables cleared, eh, love?"

"I'm on it, Collard!" she shouted back. "Arsehole," she whispered quietly.

"I've not actually seen him. Just heard him hollering from the kitchen. He sounds like a right arse. How does it make you feel having a boss like that? I'm Phil, by the way."

"I'm Holly," she said, gesturing ironically to her name tag. "How does it make me feel? You sound like someone who's had therapy. That's either worrying because you're a nutter, or reassuring because you've got your shit together."

"Ha-ha, yes. A bit of both, maybe?"

"Honestly, this is only temporary, so it's water off a duck's back. I think I'll manage Collard without too much trauma."

"We've all been there. Well, I'm pleased to meet you, Holly," Phil said. He'd waited a week to pluck up this much courage, and he had nothing to lose, so he had to speak up at that moment, before she went off to clear tables. "Do you think, perhaps, we could maybe meet up sometime and maybe, I dunno, get a coffee or something, sometime, maybe?" Phil's heart was racing, and he was convinced she would just turn him down flat.

"I finish here at two," she said, walking away to the one dirty table. "I'll be starving by then. You can take me to McDonald's."

Phil smiled a big, gentle smile at her as he got up from his table, leaving his usual £20 note that included a 39.1% tip.

"See you outside here at two, then?" he said as he opened the door to leave. She nodded as she put an empty cup on the tray she was holding.

Phil stepped out onto the street. Over three quid for a cup of OK coffee was daylight robbery, but it was a total bargain being in Holly's presence for the time it took to drink one. "Oh my goodness," he marvelled, "did she just agree to meet me at two?" Phil had spent the whole week attempting to find a moment to pluck up his courage, and at no point did he really expect anything other than a rejection of some kind. A simple "No, thanks" or a pitying "Aww, I'm sorry, I have a boyfriend." He was in a bit of a daze, amazed at how easy it had been, and his mind kept checking in with his memory to be sure she had actually said yes. Was it really only a couple of hours ago that he had been losing at chess? That already seemed like it was yesterday, and it wasn't even noon yet.

Phil stood behind a large black wheelie bin in the little alleyway next to the café. He unfolded his Polaroid camera and took a picture facing out across the street of the view of Tom Tower to commemorate the moment. A second later, the motor whirred and spat a Polaroid out the front slot of the SX-70. Phil glanced at the grey square in the white frame. He took a Sharpie out of his pocket and wrote on the bottom portion *Collard Green's Alley, 18 Jan. 2023, 11.22 a.m.*, and put the picture in his jacket pocket, in the warm, to develop.

5.
FISSION CHIP

18 JANUARY 2023, 11.23 A.M.

Phil walked back up St. Aldate's toward his flat, but this time at a more leisurely pace. The clear skies were unusual for Oxford in January, but it was cold, and the weak rays of the sun had done nothing much to take the chill out of the air. Phil felt like this was one of those moments in a movie, when the character is walking in slow motion, and the rest of the world is frantically rushing by him at double speed. He felt like the only person in this whole rat race to see the blue sky and sense that time was gently drifting by. A bus hurtled past, hitting a puddle in the lane right next to Phil and showering him with grimy, freezing-cold water. His jeans were soaked, but he was determined that nothing was going to dampen his spirits, even if it had dampened his trousers. *Had getting a date with Holly really turned him into a complete soppy twat?* he wondered. Nope, he decided, it hadn't. He realized he was already that to begin with.

Phil was heading back to his flat to use the loo. He would far rather use his own than the toilets at the pub. Any reasonable, decent, sober person would do the same, and besides, he'd have time enough to pop in at home if he got the bus to The Firkin Folly rather than walk.

Phil had to dodge a dozen people alighting from the bright-red double-decker bus that had just drenched him with rainwater. As he turned left onto Queen Street, his mind was wandering. Holly's smile, the cheery sun on a January morning, the latest news on quantum gravity, Holly's smile, whether he had any clean jeans to wear, and what to have for lunch, though he'd already eaten. And Holly's smile.

Phil crossed the street and headed for his door. It was the kind of door that was in between two shops, and one could just walk right past and never notice it, unless they actually had to find it. Phil dug his key out of the pocket of his jeans and aimed it at the lock.

"Phil Beans?" said a voice right beside him.

Phil was startled, but he kept his cool. He turned to see a stocky man in a checked suit. The man's round face was red, and his nose was redder. He was cold. He must have been waiting for a while. Trying to appear calm and collected, Phil said, "Yes, can I help you?"

"Sorry buddy, din't mean to startle ya. Cornwallis. Cornelius Cornwallis." The man sounded American. Very American. He sounded Southern. Phil took the business card being proffered:

CORNELIUS G. CORNWALLIS IV, PhD

President and CEO, Quectodyne Industries, Inc.

3920 Potomac Ave., Arlington, VA 22202

There was a +1-703-something-or-other office number, a +1-404-something-else cell phone number, and a chip@quectodyne.com email address.

Phil put the card in his pocket. "What can I do for you, Dr. Cornwallis?"

"For a start, y'all can call me Chip."

The email address started to make sense, but Phil was in a hurry and, by raising his eyebrows, hoped to invite a more direct answer to his question.

"Mr. Beans, I came to ask you to help figure out what happened to my daughter, Georgia. She disappeared last March, and the police have gotten nowhere."

The penny dropped. Cornwallis was an unusual enough name, and Phil surely would have made the connection on his own had his thoughts not been preoccupied by getting to the pub via his bathroom. Georgia Cornwallis was a student who had disappeared almost a year earlier. They found her suitcase on the train, but she'd been nowhere to be found.

"Yes, I'm so sorry. I read about that. I can't even begin to imagine how difficult … " Phil began to give Chip his full attention. The poor man looked disconsolate and hollow as well as cold. He couldn't just brush Chip off and get on with his day. As cold as Phil felt, Chip looked bloody frozen. Phil opened the large black door that nestled between the shopfronts. "Well, Chip, a missing person isn't my usual kind of case, but do come in. It's at least a bit warmer indoors. I'm upstairs, this way."

At the top of the stairs, the two men entered Phil's flat. Despite not wanting anyone to get too comfortable, he couldn't help being polite. "Please," Phil said, gesturing for Chip to sit down. But Phil was still short of time. "I don't want to be rude, but I've got about five minutes. Sorry."

"I hear ya, bud, I'm intruding." Chip remained standing. "It won't take me more 'an a minute to beg you for help. The police have no leads. Seems to me they're just giving up resourcin' the search. At the station, Detective Inspector Hunter said they're doing all they can, but I highly doubt that. On my way out, I bumped into a lady detective who said you were the man to ask for help. Gave me this address. She din't say as much, but I got the feeling she thinks more could be bein' done."

Phil put two and two together and figured that this was what Havarti had wanted to meet with him about. She had never asked for his help before, but Phil wasn't too surprised that she would recommend him to Chip. Havarti had only ever seen Phil get results. She thought he was some kind of sleuthing savant. She had no clue how he did it; she had no idea about Phil's shortcut to all the answers.

"We're desperate, Mr. Beans. My wife, Marietta, is a total basket case. She's desperate to have our little girl home again." Chip's voice was choked with emotion. He took a deep breath and sighed heavily. "I'm a little more realistic, but no less heartbroken. I just need to know what happened to her."

"I can only imagine how important it would be to get closure."

Chip raised his eyebrows as though Phil had struck a chord, and then he nodded with a shrug. "Sounds like my wife's been gettin' the same therapy as you. Jack Daniels is my therapist. On the rocks. But you're right, we need our lil' Georgie back, or we need some kinda closure. Not knowing is killing me."

Phil wasn't sure what he would be able to do to help. A missing persons case wasn't something he had done before. And he'd never tried working on a case that mattered as much as this. Besides, he was becoming something of an expert in nice, easy divorce cases. He wasn't at all reluctant to work on something bigger because he was lazy or afraid to fail, it was just that he was comfortable with the divorce cases. They paid well enough, and they didn't need him to change too much in the past. The Cornwallis disappearance seemed like a big case, and he was unsure that he was the right person to meddle with it. Perhaps he could find something that would help Havarti. That seemed fitting. What didn't seem fitting was for him to interrupt Chip to use the bathroom, while Chip was standing in his living room, appearing to be close to tears, pleading for his help. He decided he could wait the ten minutes till he got to the pub. It wasn't like he was desperate to pee yet.

"Yes, certainly, I understand. I can't promise results, but I will see what I can do. In fact, I have a meeting with DS Frisk, your lady detective, right now, and I should really be making a move. I will ask her for anything they've got so far and see where it takes me."

"I'm a wealthy man, Mr. Beans. I'm offering a million-dollar reward. Whatever it takes, I'll pay it. Find my baby girl, one way or the other. I just need to know."

Phil's usual cases were all about the money, but even Phil wouldn't own up to a reward being an incentive to help in this case. "It's not a matter of money, Dr. Cornwallis. I will be happy to help. It's a question of whether I can find a way." Time was getting on, and it was almost noon. Phil needed to be seeing Chip out and catching the bus. "Anyway, I'm afraid I should be making a move, sorry," he said while edging toward the door.

Chip was intrigued by the large orange robot and chessboard occupying much of the dining table. "This is very neat. Not somethin' you see every day. I guess you don't have folks over for dinner much."

"No," said Phil, fumbling for a business card, "but I'm getting quite good at chess with all the time I save not having friends over."

Phil opened the door and held it for Chip. He handed him the card, and they walked downstairs and out onto Queen Street.

"Oh," said Chip while looking at the card, "*Dr.* Beans, I do apologise. Doctor of what?"

"PhD in physics," Phil replied, closing the big black door behind them. "Not exactly a crucial qualification for detective work."

Phil's curiosity about Chip's mention of his wealth prompted him to ask what Quectodyne was.

"We're in nuclear energy. Started out supplying tech for good old-fashioned nuclear fission reactors. Nowadays, we're working on the new fusion stuff with a handful of universities and secret government departments. There's big money in it, Dr. Beans. When Georgia went missing, I was praying for a ransom demand, you know, for secrets or money. None came, and the months went by, and now I'm not hopeful that any amount of my money will bring her home. But I can pay you well. Please just find out what happened to my lil' Georgie."

Phil was at a loss for words that wouldn't promise what he might not deliver, and he needed to be heading off. He was trying not to rush Chip, but at the same time, he couldn't think of much to say that wouldn't drag the conversation out and make him late. Phil held out his hand. "I'll do my best."

"Please," said Chip, shaking Phil's hand. Phil could hear the pain in his voice. "I'm begging you to help us. Please, just do what you can, buddy."

"I have your card," Phil said, patting the pocket in which he had placed it.

Fission Chip

Phil turned away, feeling the cold air through his damp jeans. He trotted back to St. Aldate's and waited at the bus stop. His head was full of thoughts about what he had read concerning the disappearance of Georgia Cornwallis. She had been at the "Physics, the Universe, and Everything" conference at Westgate College back in March of last year. She'd left the college with her lime-green backpack and her hot-pink suitcase. The train cleaners found her suitcase on the train at Didcot and raised the alarm. Phil recalled that it had caused rather long delays, as the bomb squad had to X-ray the suitcase before reopening the station. But there was no sign of Georgia; she never checked in for her flight. Phil remembered being shocked when it had happened, and that it was so close to home too.

And Phil still needed the loo.

6.

FISH 'N' CHIPS

18 JANUARY 2023, 12.02 P.M.

Before he knew it, the bus had arrived at The Firkin Folly, and the doors of the bus had swung open. Phil looked up and realized where he was. He did a hurried, purposeful little hop off the bus to give the people behind him the impression that he was, in fact, not holding them up at all.

The Firkin Folly had been a popular watering hole when Phil was in college. It was a little out of town on the south side, across Folly Bridge by the river, but not too far from Westgate College for a pleasant stagger home at the end of an evening. It was also a very short walk from the Thames Valley Police offices where DS Frisk worked.

During Phil's first couple of years in college, the evening shafts of summer sunlight would stream in through a thick pall of freshly-blown smoke, and the air carried the smell of cigarette ash, stale beer, and damp floorboards. The smell filled every nook and cranny of the pub, wherever beer had been spilt or a cigarette had been smoked. In his third year, the law changed, and the smoke had been banished from the pub like a Dementor would be by a Patronus

Charm. Once the cold weather came, Phil had relinquished his roll-ups rather than have to go outside for a nicotine fix. He hadn't smoked anything much since that late autumn of 2007.

Now, The Firkin Folly smelled only of dank, musty floorboards and stale beer. It had somehow resisted the modern trend to become a brightly lit wine bar with polished chrome and a hundred flavoured gins lining the wall behind the bar. Instead, it stood as a bastion of warm, draft beer, a basic selection of spirits, and a couple of standard cocktails.

Phil stepped through the double doors, but the pale, wintery sunlight refused to follow him. It was resolute in remaining outside, barely even filtering in through the windows. The gloomy interior was lit by weak, low-wattage, old-fashioned light bulbs. There were no garish spotlights or harsh, fluorescent strip lights. Just dimly lit corner tables and booths that would have been romantic in a less grubby setting.

DS Frisk made a loud, two-fingered whistle, the kind that Phil had always envied, since he'd never been able to master it. She was close enough that she could have just said his name in her normal speaking voice, but she knew it would irk him if she whistled at him.

Phil turned. "I'm not a bloody dog."

"Here, Phil. Here, boy. Sit!"

"Just got to pop to the loo."

Phil walked to the back of the pub and found a sign on the door telling him the gents was out of order. "Bollocks," he muttered and pushed the door open anyway. He closed it quickly when he saw the mess the plumber was standing in, while the plumber shouted, "Out! Can't you read the soddin' sign? Is it not big enough or red enough?"

Phil came back grumbling. "Plumber's in there. There's a sign on the door."

Havarti laughed. "Just use the ladies!"

"Can't do that!" exclaimed Phil in an outraged whisper. Though he was tempted.

"It's just cubicles, Phil. I'm not suggesting you pee up the wall, like you do in the gents."

"No, I can't. What if somebody sees me in there? I'll end up on some government watch list for perverts. No, I'll just hold it." He sat on the wooden bench opposite Havarti and put his camera on the slightly sticky table between them.

"Good boy!"

Phil glared at her.

Havarti tossed the menu onto the table so Phil could have a look. "You're buying, remember. Pint of Guinness and the fish 'n' chips," she said.

"Dunno how you stay skinny." Phil picked up the menu and stared at it. "Talking of healthy eating, have you tried Betty's Buns yet?"

"Whose what now?"

"The fancy new bakery on Alfred Street," Phil said enthusiastically.

"Oh, yes. No, I have not tried Betty's Buns. Not likely to either, to be honest. It may have escaped your attention, but I work for the Oxfordshire Constabulary. I don't have the money to drop ten quid on an iced bun garnished with gold sodding leaf. I'm more likely to stretch to £1.85 for a four-pack of Tesco chocolate eclairs."

"I'll treat you sometime. You'll never go back to those eclairs."

"You Betty's pastry pusher now?"

Phil laughed and he did the awkward, bum-first slide out of the booth, for which neither bench nor table would budge to help make his exit more elegant. He took the three steps to the bar and returned the menu to the top of the pile. He was not feeling like eating much, partly because of the pastry and the avocado toast, and partly because of the unappetizing peek in at the gents. Phil resigned himself to ordering something light and healthy.

"Pint of Guinness, a London Pride, fish 'n' chips, and a Caesar salad, please, Ruby."

"And for the lady?"

Phil chuckled and raised his eyebrow at her. Ruby's one-liners had been tried and tested over several decades. Ruby's small, wiry frame was drowning in a baggy sweater and an apron. Her short white hair was as untidy as the myriad wrinkles on her face, and her eyes reminded Phil of his gran, as they had a kindness to them, but you knew they would turn fierce if you stepped out of line.

"Thirty-eight fifty, please, love." Ruby gave Phil the brief, forced smile that people often display when they are taking your money, and she held out the contactless terminal. Phil tapped his card. The pub had kept up with the times in some respects, at least. Contactless payment was a godsend when it came to getting drunk patrons to settle up.

Phil sat back down and whispered, "You know, I've seen that little old lady throw strapping, six-foot rugby players out of here. She once told me running a rowdy pub is like lion taming. I wouldn't want to piss her off."

Havarti glanced over at Ruby, who was pulling Phil's pint and humming to herself. "I don't think you would ever piss off a sweet old lady. All the old ladies love you." She looked back at Phil and took a deep breath. "OK, first off, I should warn you, this morning I gave your details to Cornelius Cornwallis. He's the father …."

"I already had the pleasure of a house call from Dr. Cornwallis today. Poor man. I told him I'd do what I can. So, what d'you have on Georgia's disappearance? You really think I can help?"

Havarti's long black hair fell forward over her face as she nodded. Her hair was so straight and shiny that it belonged in an advert for conditioner. Her olive skin and Persian beauty would have been at home in Persepolis. Havarti swept her hair back behind her ears and looked up at Phil with her incongruously pale, grey-blue eyes. She leant toward Phil, her elbows on the table and her hands clasped. "Well, Hunter has really got nowhere in months. CCTV of her at Oxford Station is pretty much all they came up with. We know she got on the train. She'd just missed the 13.32 direct to Paddington while she was buying her ticket. The next train was the 13.37 stopping service, and she would have had to change at Didcot. She had to wait a while at Oxford, though, as it was running late and didn't leave Oxford till 13.56."

Havarti leant back in her seat. "The train got in at Didcot, and her suitcase was there, but she wasn't." She shook her head with a little shrug and said, "No sign of Georgia anywhere." She paused and sighed. "Hunter's investigation focused on Didcot, based on the idea that she wouldn't have gone further without her suitcase. But that's it. That's your lot."

"Not much more than I already knew from the news. S'not much to go on," said Phil, wondering how he was supposed to do anything with that, when the police had got nowhere.

"I know, right? Their door-to-door enquiries turned up nothing. They never even found her bright-green backpack! Poor old Cornwallis got so steamed up this morning. Asked Hunter what the feck he was doing and called him *Short Bus*. He said, 'Listen, Short Bus, I don't care what else you need your precious freakin' resources for.'" Havarti tried to mimic his Southern accent, making *care* a two-syllable word, and she succeeded well enough that Phil was able to picture it happening. "We had to look it up later. Made me laugh. Not very PC, but it works for Hunter; he really is a complete imbecile."

Havarti sighed, then continued, "I wish I had been working on the case. The poor girl deserves better. Hillman Hunter is bloody useless. The twat couldn't organize a piss-up in a brewery." Havarti was agitated, and her hair fell loose again, framing the frustration on her face. "He made DI by playing golf with the chief, not solving bloody cases. Hunter is treating it like it's a cold case already. Makes my frigging blood boil!"

"I see that," muttered Phil in conciliatory fashion, picturing Hunter playing golf with the chief and using the chief's bald head as the ball. "You need to channel that anger into something constructive."

"Is that what you covered in therapy this month? In actual fact, channelling that anger is what I am doing. That's why you're here. We're going to do something about it." Havarti ran her fingers through her hair and gave an exasperated sigh. "That poor man is desperate just to know what happened to his daughter. It must be tearing him apart just imagining."

"Well, I can see that's worth exchanging a favour for."

"Ah, well, not exactly. That's just a freebie for you. Not actually what I wanted to ask the favour for. You see, I just got handed a new case, and I wanted to ask your help to try to solve it quickly."

Fish 'n' Chips

"You want two favours?" Phil asked, feeling hard done by. "You know I only needed that address from you, right?"

"It's called returning favours, you cheeky shit. I need to look good, you know, and solve this one quickly." The anger had gone, and Havarti was subdued. "Feather in my cap and whatnot. I really could use a break; a bit of a boost career-wise, you know?" Havarti leant forward again, looking very conspiratorial. Phil leant in too, and noticed her aromatic perfume, which carried the scent of oud along with hints of saffron and vanilla. She tapped a bright-red acrylic nail on the table. "I'm telling you this strictly off the record. You're helping me in the background. *Deep* background. You tell no one. Besides, you'll enjoy this one."

Phil was intrigued. "I get it. OK, I can do discrete." How could Phil ever say *no* to Havarti? She was his best friend, and she had always helped him. "I'd love to help." He sat up and rubbed his hands like he was about to open a surprise. "Especially if the case is a juicy one. What do you need?"

"It's the Durant case. Your dear old prof's death is being treated as suspicious, did you know? There was enough for the coroner to let us treat it as a murder enquiry."

Phil's mouth fell open. "No. Really? Right. Wow." He slumped back in his seat and stared off into the distance over Havarti's shoulder, remembering how much he had despised Durant, and how much he hadn't been sorry the old bastard had died. He sat forward again. "I heard about it a couple of months ago, you know, when it happened, but nothing much since. They said he fell down the stairs. Made it sound like it was an accident. I'm not sure the coroner's report actually made the *Nine O'Clock News*, though."

Havarti brightened, and her eyes sparkled. She spoke in a low, muted tone, saying, "No, they just said misadventure and weren't releasing details, but he definitely didn't just fall down a flight of stairs." She was getting animated; she took a deep breath. "Durant fell headlong over the balcony from the top floor with someone's pin badge stuck in his right hand." She leant closer. "Seems there was possibly a struggle, and Durant might have been pushed."

Havarti pulled a slim Manila folder out of her bag and pushed it furtively across the table. Phil picked it up just as two beer mats landed on the table and two pints were delivered.

"Thanks, Ruby."

"Cheers, Phil."

Havarti took a swig of her beer as Ruby walked away. "That folder is strictly on the down-low, OK? You. Tell. No one. I'd get fired for sharing that. I'm trusting you on this one. When you've read it, shred it!"

"Yep, I hear you. Cheers," said Phil without looking up from the file. He sipped his beer. He leafed through a few pages of police reports and crime scene photos. "Pfff. You'd have to be a big bloke to toss Durant overboard like that. He wasn't exactly easily pick-up-able, was he?"

There was a picture taken from the balcony, with Durant's body crumpled at the foot of the stairwell. Phil stared at the photo; his old PhD advisor lying twisted on the floor. "Couldn't happen to a nicer guy," he muttered. It should have been more shocking to see the body of the man he had worked with for five years like that, and it was likely quite improper to be thinking that the miserable old git probably had it coming. Best not to share that thought with Havarti, though.

The next photo was a close-up of Durant's right hand with a pin badge between his cold, dead fingers, the pin sticking into his flesh. Phil winced. It looked painful, but Durant had probably died without even feeling it.

Seeing the photo that Phil was studying, Havarti said, "The pin badge is supposed to be an atom. You know, nucleus in the middle and little electrons whizzing round it. Well, you'll know. That physics shit's right up your alley."

"Yes, I see that. It's a Rutherford Atom," Phil said absently, studying the file.

"It's off Etsy. Guess who was a customer at that same Etsy shop a year or so before? Georgia Cornwallis! We're running down who else was a customer, but that one stands out. Right?"

Phil nodded and muttered, "Big time," then read on. The report said time of death was between 2.00 p.m. and 3.00 p.m. on 7 November 2022. The body was discovered at 3.55 p.m. by a student, Fabian Harbinger, on his way to a tutorial in Professor Sheepshuffle's rooms, number two, up the stairs on the first floor.

The food arrived, and Havarti sprinkled her meal with salt and vinegar, squirted ketchup on the side of the plate, and got stuck in. Phil started picking at his salad, pleasantly surprised to find little bits of anchovy among the generous parmesan shavings.

"Turns out Sheepshuffle wasn't in his rooms and turned up at five past, late for the tutorial, just after the police arrived. He'd forgotten about it and had been in the Masters' Common Room drinking and playing cribbage all afternoon. A decent alibi anyway. He was sozzled, apparently, and laughed when he heard Durant was dead. Harbinger was ruled out too. He had been in a lecture at Wolfson College, from two till three, and made his way from that concrete hellhole in time for his four p.m. tutorial."

Havarti watched Phil studying the contents of the folder. She picked up a large chip, dipped it in the ketchup, sat forward, and wagged the chip at Phil. "All but one person from CCTV has been eliminated," she said, then stuffed the chip in her mouth.

Uh, oh, Phil thought, wondering if he was about to be told he was a suspect. He had motive. A bloody good one. He didn't actually wish the old shit dead anymore, but he certainly hadn't exactly been disconsolate when he heard of Durant's demise. Phil's mind flashed quickly to the day and time to double-check. No, Phil was in the clear. He had been ninety miles away, in Wednesbury, getting trained on his KUKA robot.

A faint look of relief washed over Phil's face. *He* knew he wasn't guilty, but he couldn't be sure the police would believe him, Havarti included. Phil was sure she loved him to bits, in a platonic sort of way, but he was also sure she wouldn't let friendship stand in the way of doing her job. If she was desperate enough to ask for Phil's help in closing the case, he was quite sure she'd bang him up if she thought he might have done it.

"Who is that then?" asked Phil.

"If we knew that, I'd be busy arresting them, not sitting here wasting time answering your inane questions, you dozy twat."

"Oh, yes, of course. A mystery man. What about the CCTV?"

"Or woman. Plenty of CCTV. He, *or she*, was wandering around the front quad of Westgate with a massive bloody umbrella. All we see on the CCTV from the college is a pair of grey trousers and light-coloured trainers. Of course, crappy college CCTV is in black and white on VHS tape, so we have no clues what colour they actually are. The trainers are those trendy sort of Skechers, not the sort you actually train in. But that's it. He, *or she*, leaves through the main gate and turns left. No CCTV up that way."

Phil flicked to the grainy, black-and-white CCTV still image of Umbrella Guy, as he'd decided to call him, *or her*, and it had a timestamp of 14:06:29. This gave him a description of the suspect, as well as a date and time. Now all he needed was to do a quick search through his Polaroids. "Well, I've got plenty to go on here," he said.

"Okey dokey, then. Sorted," Havarti said with her mouth full of battered cod.

Phil felt the jibe. She had probably been studying the evidence for a while before coming to a dead end and the decision to ask for help. Maybe Phil was coming across as a bit of a cocky bastard. "I just mean you've given me a lot to look into here."

Havarti nodded. "No, seriously, anything you can work out would be good. I could really use a break. I'm not saying I'm discriminated against, but you definitely get on if you fit in, you know, wear the right school tie and play sodding golf! I just don't fit in. I've got to do it the hard way by solving cases. Though I suspect having a pair of bollocks would help too."

"You've got bigger balls than most of that lot at St. Aldate's nick," said Phil.

"Why, thank you, kind sir, so lovely of you to say."

"The DCI has no balls at all," Phil continued.

Havarti laughed. "Except he has his golf balls, right?"

There was a pause as their smiles subsided. Phil felt for Havarti. She had left Oxford University after her undergrad to join the force. She'd had such enthusiasm and great intentions.

"Right, so I'm supposed to work out what happened to Georgia Cornwallis *and* who killed Corvus Durant?" Phil said, rolling his eyes.

"Yep. 'Bout the size of it." Havarti sat back in her seat. "Look, you have the knack for coming up with evidence, pictures, and theories and whatnot long after the fact. You tell me it's just luck because you take a lot of photos. You're like Oswald frigging Bates out of *Shooting the Past*. So, let's just see if you get lucky again." She chuckled and added, "You got lucky once before in college, right?"

Phil forced a laugh. "Ha-bloody-ha. Twice, actually." He was used to Havarti teasing him like this. Of all the banter they shared, though, this one always stung, and each time he had to look like it didn't. She'd had a lot more girlfriends than he'd had, and she enjoyed winding him up about it. But Havarti's encounters always seemed to be one-night stands. Phil got the impression she was married to the job. At least Phil's two girlfriends had been bona fide attempts at a relationship. He just smiled and let it go.

"Have a rummage through your photo albums, or whatever it is you do, and see what you can come up with," Havarti said.

"Will do. Rummage, yep, I'll have a rummage." Rummage? Cheeky tart. Did she not remember how meticulously his Polaroids were organized? The talk of Durant had taken his mind off needing the loo, and Phil had begun to worry about how much he had to do now, and the fact that he did not know where to start.

"I would love to watch you figuring this shit out. How do you do it, Phil?"

"Luck, mostly. Another pint?" he said, changing the subject.

"No thanks. Some of us have jobs to get back to this afternoon, remember?"

Phil thought that was a bit rich. "Well, it looks like I've got my work cut out for me on three cases, so you're not the only one with stuff to do."

"What are you up to next, then?"

"I'm planning to get Quinkle's finances from Rusty. With a bit of help from Hasty, we'll be able to hack into Quinkle's accounts and get details of payments for the rental. If I can link that address you gave me to the rental agents, I'm sure I can prove Quinkle paid for it."

Havarti slumped back in her seat, shaking her head. "Hacking his accounts? Bloody hell. It's no wonder you private dicks have an easy time getting results. You don't play by the rules. S'not fair. It's like I'm doing my job with one hand tied behind my back." She shrugged and laughed. "Well, good for you if you can get away with it. I'd bloody do it if it was admissible. You still in cahoots with Rusty and Hasty, then?"

"Cahoots? Ha-ha. Yes. Still in cahoots," Phil chuckled. "The good old Detective Collective. With your help, the forensic accountant, the hacker, and the private detective are invincible!"

Havarti finished the last couple of chips and washed them down with a final swig of Guinness.

"You done, love?" Ruby asked Phil, indicating his half-eaten salad. "Didn't like it, my lovely? I told chef nobody wants bloody anchovy."

"Surprisingly good salad, actually, Ruby."

"Why surprising? Everything on our menu is good," she said defensively with her hands on her hips, her eyes flashing with an intensity that made Phil feel the need to placate her.

"Yes, yes, for sure it is. But for me to actually enjoy a salad, though, is surprising. I actually really liked the anchovy."

"Glad you enjoyed it, sunshine. Chef will be absolutely bloody delighted." Ruby turned away with the plates and Havarti's empty glass and muttered loud enough to be heard, "Saucy little tosspot."

"I think you pissed her off," Havarti said with a grin. "I hope you get Quinkle. Hope that address helps, coz Fuggs is an arse and I hate owing him. You'll need to come through on the Durant case for me!"

"Roger that, Havarti. Ten-four, good buddy," said Phil, trying out some lingo.

"Roger who? You great knob-end. You've been watching too much old American telly, Phil."

"Probably have. Well, thanks for that address, anyway. I'll buy you a pint. Oh, wait, I just did! You sure you don't want another one?"

"Another time, matey," said Havarti, standing and putting on her camel hair coat. "I've got work, even if you haven't. I've got bad guys to catch, remember? Seriously, though, good luck. Let me know how you get on."

"You'll be the first to know," he replied.

Havarti put one hand on the table and leant in. "I'll be the *only* one to know. Yes?" When Phil nodded, she added, "Cornwallis was talking about putting up a million-dollar reward to find out what happened to his daughter, one way or the other. Whatever that is in pounds, it should beat 10% of some crappy divorce settlement, right?"

"It certainly would. He did mention that," Phil replied.

"DI Hunter advised him against going public with a reward because it'll bring out all the cranks and con artists and make the truth harder to sniff out. I told Cornwallis you're his best bet. But I think the reward might be a serious offer." Havarti picked up her red ostrich-leather shoulder bag and said, "Alright, you saucy little tosspot, I'll see you soon."

She pulled open the door, and Phil called out, "May the *force* be with you!"

Without looking back, Havarti gave him the finger and walked out.

Phil was due to meet Holly in a bit over half an hour. But first, he wanted to go to see Rusty and Hasty to get details on the Quinkle case financials and find a functioning toilet.

Phil drained his pint glass and went to where it was quiet, toward the back of the pub, where the toilets were. He heard the plumber swearing through the door of the gents, and the ladies was occupied. He popped open his old Polaroid camera and pointed it toward the bar. *Click. Whirrr.* The picture came out, and Phil took his Sharpie, glanced at his watch, and wrote *Firkin Folly, 18 Jan. 2023, 1.24 p.m. Meet Holly at 2.00 p.m.* He didn't want to risk being late for Holly, and this should give him plenty of time.

Right now, Phil's head was full of the cases he had to work on, and he really wanted to get going. He was already champing at the bit to go and find out what the hell had happened to Durant, and maybe even congratulate Umbrella Guy, if it was him, *or her*, who had tossed Durant over the balcony. Phil wasn't in a hurry, really, because he knew he had all the time in the world, and preparation was key. He had to take his time and make sure he had everything he needed before setting off.

Either way, Phil wasn't feeling stuck anymore, and it was time to get going. Phil put his empty pint glass on the bar. "Cheers, love!" Ruby called to him. He waved a thank you to Ruby and left. He crossed the street and took the quick bus ride back toward town.

7.
PEDGE & CO.

18 JANUARY 2023, 1.37 P.M.

Phil got off the bus, walked a few yards, and stood in front of Pedge & Co. The shopfront was a narrow, single-storey wooden structure sandwiched between two elegant Georgian stone edifices. Phil noticed that its paint was cracked and peeling, and was a faded navy-blue, though he realized it had probably been originally painted navy-blue and left to fade. Of course, he couldn't discount the possibility that "faded navy" might well be a real paint colour. Nevertheless, this was definitely not a fresh coat of faded navy-blue. On the large, single-pane window, the words *Pedge & Co.* were written in worn gold lettering, and to the right of the window was a scuffed, wooden door. Its dilapidated state gave the distinct impression that the rent would be cheap and the landlord even cheaper.

Phil pushed hard to open the door and stepped into the reception area, where he stood in front of a little desk on which a plastic sign bore the name of the room. The young lady seated behind the desk looked distinctly surprised, largely because of the arched, black eyebrow-pencil lines where her eyebrows used to be. She put her hand over the receiver of the telephone and simply said, "Yes?"

"Can I possibly just quickly use your loo?"

"Hold on, Mum," Laira said into the receiver. "This is an accountancy firm, not a bloody public convenience," she said to Phil.

"Oh, no. I'm here to see Mr. Pedge, if he's available. I could just do with a pee first."

"We ain't got a loo, anyhow."

"Oh, bollocks," he muttered. Phil looked down at a little handmade sign, which was a piece of white card folded over and upon it, written in purple felt-tip pen, starting out in nice big bold letters and getting a bit squished against the right-hand edge, was the name *Laira Woolfardisworthy*. Phil was reminded of the old joke sign that read *Plan Ahea$_d$* and he smiled to himself. Underneath that, in pencil, the words *Executive Assistant* had been added over the spot where *Receptionist* had been mostly, but not altogether successfully, erased. Laira was a recent addition to the staff, which now totalled two.

"OK, perhaps you would let Mr. Pedge know I'm here?"

Laira pushed a button on the intercom and said in a high-pitched tone, as though she were announcing an alien invasion, "There's a bloke here, in reception, wants to see you."

"Who is it?" said the intercom.

"Who is it?" she relayed.

"I'm ... " Phil began, then stopped himself and reached over to push the intercom button. "It's Phil."

"It's Phil," she repeated into the intercom, as if to make it official.

"Send him through, Laira, thank you," the intercom replied.

"Please go through," Laira said in her best formal voice, pointing to the door on which a plastic sign was Blu-Tacked, reading *Chris Pedge, Forensic Accountant*. Laira continued her conversation on the phone, saying, "Well, that's Dad for you, innit. What was he thinkin'? The dozy old sod."

Wondering what Dad had done wrong, Phil knocked and went into Pedge's office. He was met by the strong smell of a nice malt whisky, and a gloom that was not merely because the office was windowless and poorly lit.

"Hey Rusty, how are you?"

Rusty remained seated and swivelled to face Phil. His slight frame seemed too small for the large, ergonomic office chair, and his pasty white complexion contrasted with the black leather. "Phil, have a seat, mate. Care to join me?"

"Bloody hell, it's a bit early even for you, isn't it?"

"Don't worry, I'm not actually working," Rusty said, turning back to lean his elbows on the desk and put his head in his hands. "I was going to take the day off, but it just felt a bit shitty sitting at home on my own. In hindsight, it probably would have been preferable to sit at home getting pissed than sitting here listening to the less interesting half of 'Tales from Rural Devon' through the door," he said gesturing toward reception and running his hand across his balding head and ginger stubble.

"Bad day?" asked Phil.

Just as Rusty replied, "It's twenty years today," and held up the bottle of Scotch, Phil mentally kicked himself for being a crappy mate and a tactless git.

"Oh, yeah, your dad. I'm sorry, mate. Shitty day, indeed. Yes, go on then, I'll join you."

Rusty slopped more whisky into his own mug that read *Amortized but Still in Use*, put another mug on the desk that read

Accountants Work Their Assets Off, poured a couple of fingers, most of which actually made it into the mug, and pushed it in Phil's direction. He put the bottle down in the middle of the puddle of expensive whisky that had formed on his desk in the last hour or so.

"I guess every anniversary is tough, but yeah, twenty years," Phil said, trying to be conciliatory. "Suppose you never get over it."

"Yes," Rusty replied, "they said in grief counselling that I shouldn't really expect to get over it, but they did say I'd get used to it. Hasn't happened yet."

Phil was stuck for words. He never knew quite what to say when Rusty's melancholy was talking through the alcohol.

Phil had never realized, probably because he'd never needed it, that Rusty's office didn't have a loo. He tried to think about his burgeoning workload to take his mind off it. Rusty continued as Phil tuned out.

Havarti had made the Quinkle case suddenly seem a small task and one that could wait. But it was the easy case, and it was the kind of case he was used to. Murdered professors and missing American students were something new. Those seemed like the kind of urgent and important cases he should be wanting to get his teeth into. He was very curious about Durant's plunge down the stairwell, and he really ought to try to help poor Dr. Cornwallis. So he wondered if he should have bothered coming. Other than to support his mate on a tough day, obviously. Maybe the Quinkle case wasn't so urgent.

Phil was brought out of his rumination as Rusty's monologue went quiet, and the room fell into a heavy, desolate silence. Phil got the sense he had missed something.

Rusty was staring off into the distance. Then he looked at Phil and said, "Do you? Know what I mean?"

"Oh, yeah. Yes. Sure do, mate," replied Phil, nodding, without a clue what he was agreeing with. "Sure do." It was time to quickly change the subject.

Phil had been thinking twice about asking, as today might not be a good day for favours. But then maybe it was as good a day as any. He really didn't want to put off getting the help he needed with at least one of his investigations, and he really needed to change the subject.

"Any chance we could talk business? You know, before you get any further down that bottle? Maybe you could get Hasty over here too? I think we're going to need the Detective Collective in full force."

Rusty looked at him, and Phil could clearly see he was hurt that, of course, Phil hadn't come to see how he was doing. Phil felt bad. It was obvious he had turned up wanting a bloody favour. Rusty raised a disapproving eyebrow, then shook his head and shrugged.

"Sure, why not. Wallowing won't do any bloody good anyway, and I can always get pissed some more later. Go on. Keep my mind off it for a bit."

"I'll pay if it pans out. Hopefully it'll be worth your time."

"Bloody hell. OK. Let's do it. It must be big if you're actually paying."

Rusty looked up the number of Hasty's newest "business" burner phone and texted. After a couple of brief exchanges, Rusty announced, "He's on his way. 'Be chill,' he says."

"Okey dokey," said Phil, doing his best impression of someone chilling and drinking whisky.

Rusty continued. "All my dad left was a suicide note and an accountancy business. What were we supposed to do with that? Apart from end up as a bloody accountant."

Phil felt awkward. All this grief was a reminder of losing his mum. But that was a whole different life, and Phil didn't want to think about it. He didn't have an answer for Rusty today any more than he ever had, so he shrugged and took another sip of whisky. *Ooh, that's good stuff,* he thought. "When you get down like this, you might try thinking about the good things in life. Did they suggest that in your grief counselling?"

"Therapy much, Phil? Actually, they did. Told me to count my blessings. Mum couldn't claim the life insurance, so she had to work at the bank to get me through school. I love my mum. She's a bloody rock star. Westgate College gave me a scholarship. I love Westgate. I love cheese. I love whisky."

"Don't tell me you love me next."

"You're an arsehole, Phil, but I love you. A little bit, anyway."

"I love you too, you cheeky twat."

At that moment, Hasty and his joie de vivre breezed into the office without any involvement of the intercom, leaving a giggling Laira out in reception. Hasty didn't actually need to duck in through the doorway, but the top of his beanie brushed the woodwork. Hasty had a slim, muscular build that Phil thought would be perfect for a basketball player. With his handsome face, perfect smile, and charisma oozing from every pore of his smooth, brown skin, Hasty was very popular with the ladies. Phil envied him for all of that.

"Rusty, ma man." Hasty took off his black leather jacket, revealing his biceps and his Jimi Hendrix T-shirt. He sat down and reached under his office-wheelie-chair and pulled out the knob with a clunk. The chair immediately reclined to its maximum extent, and Hasty's immaculately braided dreadlocks spilt over the back of the chair. Nodding along to whatever was playing in his earbuds, Hasty added "Sorry today's a shitty day, mate." Then he turned to Phil. "Hey Phil, how's it going?"

"Good, you?"

"Yep. All good. Shove up a bit, Phil," Hasty said, waving his hands in the direction he wanted Phil to move. The office was small, so there wasn't a lot of room for two people between the desk and the door. Phil moved over to give Hasty more room. "Cheers," Hasty said, then pulled his enormous laptop out of his large leather messenger bag and opened it. "Right, wassup?"

"OK chaps, here's the deal," Phil began. "I need information on Quinkle's finances. Where his money went before the divorce, for starters. Where the recent shady investment money came from for a main course, and who paid Chianti Carbonara's rent for dessert."

Phil was ready to continue, but Hasty started tapping on the keys. As Phil drew a breath to resume, Hasty held up a long, slender finger, as though he expected everyone to hold their breath, and said, "Rusty, I'm gonna need …" He then looked up over his laptop screen to see Rusty holding out one end of a blue cable. "Ethernet! Thank you. Gimme three." He turned to Phil and added, "About three minutes, mate."

That didn't sound like much time at all to Phil. "Does he even know what I need?" Phil said quietly in Rusty's direction.

"Seemed pretty clear to me."

"To you, maybe," Phil said, pointing to his own ears to indicate he doubted Hasty was listening with the earbuds in his ears.

"Yeah, yeah. I think they're probably in transparent mode, so I'm pretty sure he can hear us. Besides, it's not exactly rocket science, what you're asking for. He probably heard the name Quinkle and figured out what you need. And deduced the existence of income tax and rice pudding while he was at it," Rusty said, his *Hitchhiker's Guide* reference making both himself and Hasty chuckle.

"So, I was today years old when I learned that you don't actually have a loo here," Phil whispered.

Rusty laughed. "No, mate. This spot was used to park a car till the eighties, when my dad rented it. He never had one fitted."

"What do you do, you know, when you need to ... "

"Starbucks in the morning. The Wig and Pen round the corner in the afternoon. With the amount I spend in there, nobody cares if I pop in just to use the bog."

Hasty carried on tapping on the keyboard, clicking the trackpad, and nodding along to his earbuds. Then, without looking up from the screen, he made a beckoning gesture and held out his hand. Rusty put a whisky-mug, captioned *It's Accrual World,* into his grasp.

Without missing a beat, Hasty drank the whisky in one gulp while still tapping with his left hand, then put the mug on the desk, and tapped on the trackpad some more. Hasty sang quietly along with whatever he was listening to on his earbuds.

Phil and Rusty exchanged an anticipatory glance. Phil looked at his watch, wondering how much of the three minutes had passed so far. Rusty leant his elbows on the desk expectantly. Phil folded his arms and sat back in his chair as though it would be a long wait while his mind began to drift.

Phil was jealous of Hasty's relaxed Jamaican vibe. Hipsters seemed so lame by comparison. Hasty had adopted his super-cool attitude partly from his grandma and grandpa, who had come to live in England from Jamaica in 1954, and partly from Bob Marley, who hadn't.

Christopher Chilton Taylor had started at private school the same day as Chris Pedge. Two kids called Chris in the same class. The teacher told them they would have to be known as Chris P. and Chris T. The other kids in school gave Chris P. nicknames like Rice Krispie and Findus Crispy Pancake, but he was also ginger-haired, so he suffered many other nicknames as well. His favourite was Ginja Ninja, his least favourite was Sunscreen, and in the end, Rusty was the one that stuck. The kids nicknamed Chris T. Agatha, after the crime novelist, but that one didn't stick. Chris T. had decided to adopt Slo Hasty as a DJ name, with every intention of one day becoming a DJ. And, because it was cool, it stuck. The boys had been known as Rusty and Hasty ever since.

Hasty had qualified in computer science and information technology, and then got a job with a prestigious, high tech cyber-security firm and became a White Hat. On the side, he did a bit of Grey Hat hacking, which is doing hacking stuff that is technically borderline illegal, but for good reasons, which he usually did as a favour for Phil. And he was a DJ in Brighton on the weekends.

As a child, Phil had known Chris Pedge Sr. because he had been Phil's father's accountant, and he had been a frequent visitor at Lydington Manor, near Oxford.

Phil subsequently met Rusty and Hasty when they all arrived at Westgate College. Phil had attended the mandatory Westgate Welcome Cheese and Wine event on the first day of Freshers' Week, and there were Rusty and Hasty. That day, they had become a threesome.

"Bingo!" Hasty announced proudly, with a clenched fist held up in triumph.

Phil was brought out of his reflections to see Hasty grinning at him.

"Aced it!" said Hasty. "Two minutes, fifty seconds." He leant forward like being more than horizontal was too much effort, but Phil knew the abs on this guy would put him to shame. As Hasty sat upright, the chair snapped back to vertical. He leant on the desk and scribbled a long string of hexadecimal code on a Post-it and handed it to Rusty.

Hasty folded his laptop and returned it to his leather bag, leaving the blue Ethernet cable dangling. "You know I work remotely, right? This could've all been done on SMS, mate," he said. "Save me coming all the way down here."

"You came from two doors away! Besides, I thought it'd be best not to put it in writing." Phil said, getting defensive.

"That's fair. But it's why I got the burner." Hasty got up and said quietly to Rusty, "That's the password. I'm texting you the URL to Quinkle Holdings' accounts computer." He pressed send on his phone, then put his hand on Rusty's shoulder and patted him gently. "Chin up," he said, then walked out, saying, "Likkle more" to the room and flashing a peace sign behind him.

"See ya, mate," said Rusty without looking up from his computer monitor. As the door swung shut, a guffaw of girly hilarity came from reception.

It was Rusty's turn to tap on a keyboard. Glancing from screen to keyboard to Post-it, he typed in the password slowly and deliberately.

"Sorry about your shitty day, though. Sorry about your dad," Phil said. "You remember me telling you I saw your dad a couple of weeks before it happened? It was on my sixteenth birthday, and I saw your dad with my father and Professor Durant in the library at Lydington Manor."

"I think about that sometimes," Rusty said as he carried on clicking his mouse. "You telling me how kind my dad was. You were with your mum in Headington by then, though, right?"

"Oh, erm, yes. Yes, I was." Phil needed to be careful. He had to remember how his and Rusty's timelines differed. Phil had changed things in the past and ended up in Headington with his mum. But Rusty had no idea how that had happened. "I was just at my father's for a little bit that day. But I was there long enough to overhear them in a meeting when they were talking about scuba gear and insurance. I had supposed that they were talking about going diving. Seemed a bit odd though, because my father never did anything like that."

"No, nor mine. Really weird," said Rusty, looking up from the screen, "My dad couldn't even swim." He shrugged. "But you didn't hear anything else?"

"Not really, it was hard to hear anything clearly, and Isabella, the wicked young step-mother, came along and caught me snooping. My father was angry with me and told me to leave. Your dad was sort of protective. He put his arm round me and saw me out, made sure I was OK, and then he put me in the car with the chauffeur. I didn't see your dad again after that. My father was such a miserable bastard. Your dad was always kind to me. I used to wish he was my dad."

Rusty smiled. "Yeah, he was kind. And yet he just abandoned us and threw himself off that bridge." He turned back to the screen and clicked a few times. Then the ageing LaserJet printer started slowly churning out pages, and Rusty finished the whisky in his mug.

Phil picked up the printout and smiled back at Rusty. "Cheers for this," he said, flicking through the pages. So, Pedge Sr. couldn't swim, let alone scuba dive? Phil was getting a niggling feeling about that day and the bits of bizarre conversation he'd overheard. At the time, even after Pedge Sr. died, that day at Lydington Manor had all been drowned out by the fact that Phil's mum was alive.

8.

A LITTLE LIGHT RELIEF

18 JANUARY 2023, 2.42 P.M.

Phil waved a goodbye to Laira as he passed through reception. She looked at him but didn't respond. She had the phone receiver clamped to her ear with her shoulder, she was chewing gum, and she was filing her long acrylic nails. Phil wondered if Rusty had actually advertised for a caricature when he hired her, because he'd hit the stereotype jackpot. He walked out of Pedge & Co. onto the street, holding the information he needed to blow the cover on Quinkle's hidden assets. The Quinkle case rested on the infidelity clause, and Phil already had the photos to prove Quinkle and the supermodel were involved long before the separation.

Phil set off on the walk back to his flat. By this point, and it was made worse by his suddenly being back in the cold air, he *really* needed the loo. He scurried quickly past colleges and shop fronts, dodging students, shoppers, and tourists. Winter wasn't devoid of tourists, and they were the dawdlers, never looking where they were going, consulting their phones or guidebooks, and staring up at buildings. Phil was in a hurry and had to weave in and out, occasionally hopping off the kerb and using the bus lane to go around people. Buses were easy to spot, but he had to have his wits about him because the kamikaze cyclists used the bus lane too.

Soon, Phil was on Queen Street. It was pedestrianised, and the few people here were spread out across the whole width of the street. Phil made a beeline for his door. He fumbled with his keys the way that only ever seems to happen while busting for a pee. He ran upstairs, into his flat, and immediately went and found relief.

He sat at the dining table, opposite the robot arm, and his mind was now able to concentrate on something other than his bladder. He glanced at his watch and thought about his date with Holly, which should have been three-quarters of an hour ago. He had a moment's panic until he located the Polaroid from the pub in his jacket pocket. He breathed a sigh of relief. This picture was now the most precious thing he owned.

Phil had a pretty long to-do list. What was he going to do first? Georgia's certain death was too grim a prospect. He would build up to that one. He felt much better prepared for Umbrella Guy, but he was nervous about dropping himself right into the middle of Durant's murder. Not with as good a motive as he had. Perhaps he should think that through a bit more first.

"So, what's next, Robot?" Phil wondered out loud. He was aware that he spent too much time on his own, and that anthropomorphizing a robot did not constitute a healthy relationship. "Let's get a few things done before we meet Holly, shall we? Let's start with Rusty and Chris Pedge Sr. I can't believe it's been twenty years. So, if Mr. Pedge couldn't swim, why would he be discussing scuba gear with Durant and my father?" He hadn't anything concrete to go on aside from an uneasy feeling about that day at

A Little Light Relief

Lydington Manor. It occurred to him that he should try to find out what was going on, and why it was now bothering him so much that Mr. Pedge drowned in the Thames only two weeks later.

Phil walked over to the bookshelves that covered one whole wall, perusing the Polaroid photo albums that filled the shelves. "Right, let's start getting organized, Robot. There's a lot to do, and I'm going to need a lot of pictures to get where I'm going."

He found the album from his sixteenth birthday and took out a photograph of roses in a hallway. Those roses had been the proof that his father had been cheating on his mum, which still made him angry. He would need that picture to find out more about Mr. Pedge and the library meeting. He put it on the coffee table with the one he'd found earlier for the Quinkle divorce hearing.

"What about poor Chip Cornwallis?" Phil asked the robot arm, thinking of Chip's woeful appeal for help, which had been made right here in the living room, and Chip's words still lay heavy like a melancholy lead weight. "Havarti's just powerless, and Hunter is useless." Phil knew he was Chip's only hope. But as for finding out what happened? Phil was confident he knew the ending "Sure as eggs is eggs, Robot, that poor girl is dead."

"So, where do I start looking for Georgia Cornwallis?" Phil asked, turning to look at the robot "Find out the conference dates. Good idea." Phil flicked through his pile of papers in the kitchen by the bin; stuff that he didn't know whether to keep or recycle. Old bills, his mum's recipe for baked Alaska, letters from the bank, a brochure for holidays in Greece, the warranty for the washing machine he'd recently had to replace, and, near the bottom of the pile under the passport he thought he'd lost, the brochure for the conference dated 21–25 March 2022. He found the album that encompassed those dates and started flicking through the pages. On the last day of the conference, a Friday, he had taken an arty photo early in the day in a quiet spot on Broad Walk, looking east towards the Christ Church Meadow, with the low orange sun catching the clouds. He took it out of the album and carried on looking.

Later that same day, he'd taken two more pictures in the afternoon, around the time he'd met up with former colleagues attending the conference from far-flung universities. The colleagues were physicists he hadn't seen for a while, and a few of them had planned to go out for a drink or three after the lectures were over, before they all jetted off on the Saturday. Those photos were of far too busy a scene for him to gradually appear in, so they were of no use. And besides, Phil really rather suspected the girl would have already been dead by then.

Thinking of death caused Phil's mind, like a golden retriever spotting a squirrel, to suddenly become preoccupied with Durant's death. "Maybe doing the favour for Havarti is next? Maybe paying her back for all the favours she's done me over the years should be my first priority? What do you think?" He glanced up at the robot, which stared, unhelpfully, back at him. "Or maybe it's just the deliciousness of Durant's downfall, pardon the pun, that's just too much to resist. I *really* want to know what happened and who had it in for him."

Phil woke up his Mac and began looking into Durant's death. He googled "Professor Durant death." The screen displayed a plethora of results, and he scanned them quickly. His eye was drawn to the second link, which he double-clicked.

A Little Light Relief

About 8,350,000 results (0.47 seconds)

New York Times
www.newyorktimes.com/tragic_fall
Professor "Chronos" dies in tragic fall

Oxford Mail
www.oxfordmail.co.uk/oxford_prof_horror_tumble
Oxford professor, 58, in horror tumble

The Sun
www.thesun.co.uk/death_plunge_suicide
Famous prof in death plunge — was it suicide?

Phil's understanding, which was confirmed by the story in the *Oxford Mail*, was that Durant had been ridiculed in recent years for his outlandish and unsupported scientific claims, and that he had found glory a few months ago with his now-famous paper solving the quantum gravity conundrum.

This was a man who had been at the top of world physics twenty-odd years ago. He had been a popular figure on TV and in publications such as *Scientific American* and *Reader's Digest*, explaining the complexities of modern physics in ways that everyone could understand. "Durant could have been up there with Hawking, Penrose, Feynman, or even Magnus Pyke," Phil explained to the uninterested robot.

But then, Durant drifted into obscurity, with nothing new of his own. His students had gone on to do great things, but his own work had foundered. He was superseded by a younger generation of sound-bite scientists who could make science exciting and relevant, and they could capitalize on social media.

Even just a few months ago, Durant had been washed up and marooned on the shores of obscurity. Phil found a Reddit thread about how Durant had been humiliated at the conference held the previous March at Westgate College. Durant had given the keynote speech on the last day, and the questions he'd gotten had resulted in hilarity and ridicule.

"Hey, Robot, it says here that Durant stormed off the stage, red-faced and angry, and went straight back to his rooms. We would have loved to see that! Apparently, he didn't even emerge from his rooms for two days."

He clicked on the article in *The Sun* that speculated about his death being suicide. Phil could see that a normal person might well want to end it all as a result of the ridicule. And he might have thought that might apply to Durant if he'd thought for a picosecond that Durant was normal, or that Durant cared one iota whether anyone else thought badly of him. Durant was an unprincipled, arrogant, narcissistic arsehole. Not the personality type to give in and hurl himself over the balustrade because of a few Reddit threads.

The robot, in its usual equivocal fashion, sat quietly, unsure what to make of it all. "You might be right," said Phil, "that's what I need to find out. Did he fall or was he pushed?"

Phil's mind wandered back to 2011, when he'd wanted to kill Durant himself. Durant had stolen Phil's theory on antimatter and had published an article claiming that there was a parallel universe made entirely of antimatter that was going backwards in time. He

A Little Light Relief

had completely ripped off Phil's theory that both matter and antimatter universes would expand, then contract, and ultimately collapse into a singularity, causing an immense annihilation that would trigger a new Big Bang. Durant had stated that this had already happened many times. Each new iteration of the universe was like a gigantic fractal, and uniquely different from any that had gone before. An infinite loop of existence through an infinity of time.

Not only had Durant stolen Phil's work, but he'd also gotten Phil expelled for plagiarism a year into his postdoc. Durant took an early draft of Phil's paper, changed it a bit, then put his own name and an old date on it, and entered it into the university's database. As soon as Phil submitted his final version for review, the university's search engine came up with an 82% plagiarism score, and Phil was up in front of the Westgate disciplinary panel. He denied it, of course, and naturally, the panel believed the computer and Professor Durant. Consequently, Phil was sent down. No matter where he looked for a new position, Corvus Durant was one of his references, official or unofficial, and Durant made sure no one would hire Phil.

Phil had been really, really angry about Durant stealing his work and getting him thrown out of college. Angry enough to cave his head in with a Nobel Prize, assuming a Nobel Prize came in the form of a heavy blunt object, and wasn't just an Ikea gift card. Yes, Phil could have happily thrown the old git off a balcony. Back then, at least. But all he had managed to do was to egg Durant's office. It had been an impressive effort; he had constructed a Ghostbusters-style backpack that fired a hundred eggs in under two minutes, and he had slimed the entirety of Durant's ego-sized office from his desk to his oversized chalkboard.

After Phil had been expelled from college, he had set himself up as a private detective. He enjoyed it. It was a nice, easy life on the whole, and he was happy watching the world of superstring theory from the outside. He could dip in and out to satisfy his curiosity, rather than becoming embroiled in impossible mathematics that would have had Einstein baffled. Life was good, and he didn't have to contend with any of the professional competition or petty jealousy. In the end, he didn't really care enough anymore to actually do Durant any harm. For certain, Phil wouldn't have pissed on him if he was on fire. Phil wouldn't have called out his name if a bus was heading in Durant's direction. He'd felt a seething indifference, but he didn't actually feel murderous any more.

"I was bloody angry for months and months after that, Robot. I could have cheerfully throttled the old bastard. I admit the egging thing was bad form, but it was jolly good fun, and I felt a lot better after. Then I met Fergal and realized my path lay in a different direction. I hate to admit it, but Durant might have done me a favour. Still not going to forgive him, though."

Phil focused on the search results on his computer again and found an article Durant had published in *Modern Physics Magazine*, titled "Schrödinger's Cat *Is* the Observer!" In it, Durant discussed various theories of quantum probability and how a particle can be in two places at once, like electrons in the double slit experiment. He concluded that quantum collapse is a continuum of probability. Matter should be less likely to be in two places at once, with an exponential improbability, as more and more superstrings are bound together in larger and larger molecular structures.

A Little Light Relief

"Remember that, Robot? He said that, in theory, it is possible for the *Titanic* to exist in two places at once, but that it is just vastly improbable. I mean, that might be true, but fancy turning a good theory into a stupid soundbite just for the publicity. What a twat!"

Durant had been ridiculed for the *Titanic* reference in both the scientific and the popular press. His career was sunk, like the ship. It had been a humiliation, and Durant went on to become something of a miserable and angry recluse after that.

Phil pondered, "If you ignore the bit about the *Titanic*, that might actually be a really solid theory. One thing I'm damn sure of is that it wasn't Durant's idea. No way, Robot."

What if Durant had stolen the quantum collapse paper from someone else? Phil wondered. He could imagine they might have wanted him dead too.

"But why wait three years for revenge? Opportunity? Lockdown? Seems unlikely though, eh? What about the new quantum gravity paper? Do we think he stole that too? I think we do. It seems to be what the old scumbag was good at."

A few months ago, in September of 2022, Durant had published his paper on the resolution of the quantum gravity conundrum that had confounded the world for a century. He had proposed that gravity doesn't really exist, and that it is time that warps the space-time continuum, not matter.

"Gravity is just a side effect of time's interaction with matter. Seems nuts, but there you go, Robot, that's the quantum realm for you."

This might have been ridiculed too, except that Durant had given the most elegant and complete mathematical description in the paper. Pure, perfect, and beautiful. No one could refute it. It was an absolute masterpiece.

"Just breathtaking," Phil said, looking at a screen full of equations, of which he barely had any grasp. It made Einstein's derivation of $E = mc^2$ look like child's play. Phil was utterly certain that quantum gravity, with its mind-boggling mathematics, was not Durant's own work. "Not a snowball's chance in a supernova," muttered Phil.

Phil's impression was that Durant had been known worldwide as a full-time, professional, expert charlatan and a dickhead, and so eliminating anyone who wouldn't have wanted to finish him off would probably be a lot quicker than sifting through the people who would have. He figured there must be a list of people a mile long who would have cheerfully thrown the miserable shitweasel off the balcony.

There was no doubt that Durant had been unpopular in the scientific community, and with at least a handful of individuals whose work he had stolen in particular. Durant had stolen Phil's work, and it seemed to Phil that he had been at it again. Had Durant stolen both of those recent papers, and from whom?

The quantum gravity paper was a major breakthrough. Surely, that latest intellectual theft really would be a motive for murdering Durant. Phil knew first-hand how that felt, and his mind went to the picture from Havarti's folder; the CCTV image of Umbrella Guy.

"Whomever Durant stole that paper from would totally want revenge. That's our prime suspect, Robot. What do you think? Umbrella Guy, right?"

Phil looked again at the CCTV still image of the Umbrella Guy that he had studied at lunch with Havarti. It was black and white, grainy, and from a bad angle, high on the wall of the Westgate College main entrance passageway. A black umbrella, mid-grey trousers, and light-grey tennis shoes that were possibly Skechers. Phil had a hunch, and his hunches were good. "You know what, Robot? I reckon he's also wearing a Rutherford Atom pin badge on his lapel. Purchased from Etsy."

Phil would need to have a little sniff around at Westgate College on the day of Durant's demise, just to see what he could see, and maybe he'd get a good look at Umbrella Guy. If Umbrella Guy really was wearing the pin badge, Phil would know for certain, and it would surely be a big help to Havarti. Beyond that, Phil would need to find clues to the identity of Umbrella Guy, but he would have to play that by ear.

"I just need to spot clues for Havarti, right, Robot? Change nothing. Come back with evidence, an identity, and Polaroids. Get Havarti a quick result. Should be easy enough. Pretty harmless if we don't change anything. Don't disrupt the timeline. I think we can start there, don't you?"

Phil went back to the wall of Polaroid albums. "So, what about the day the prof died?" He reached up and selected the album from early November, in which he found several pictures from the day, all taken in Wednesbury. All of the photos featured impressive orange robot engaged in all manner of delicate tasks like breaking eggs, playing violin, and arranging flowers.

"Lots of pictures of your cousins, Robot. None of them any bloody good for this, though. I don't want to be in Wednesbury again."

He flipped to the previous page. "Lots of pictures from Bonfire Night," he noted, but the scenes were all far too crowded for him to use. "Nothing on the sixth? Nothing? Bugger! Not one picture between Bonfire Night and the prof's plunge."

There was one picture taken on Friday, 4 November, out on the Westgate College backs, along the peaceful Castle Mill Stream in the shade of the trees in the peace and quiet behind the college buildings. "Oh well, this'll have to do." It was another arty shot, as so many of them were, featuring sunrises, sunsets, rivers, or the "dreaming spires" of Oxford. He slid it carefully out of the album and put it with his little collection of Polaroids on the table. "I'll just have to spend the weekend in November, waiting for Monday to roll around. That's not too long to spend three months ago. Four days. Should be easy enough to get back. Maybe I should think that over first."

Phil had too much on his mind. He was used to a nice, easy life with nothing but chess and intermittent money worries. He felt like he needed to tackle something he was comfortable with just to get the ball rolling. "First things first, the Quinkle case. Get to Brighton, sort the Quinkle court hearing. Paying Havarti back can wait till after her help actually pays off."

Phil gathered all his stuff together for another day out in Brighton. Then he took the Polaroid he'd taken on 22 July 2022. He stared purposefully at the misty picture of the little flat-bottomed boats tied together on the river in the early morning mist. In his mind, he let go of now and willed himself into the scene, at that time and place.

9.

BRIGHTON ROCK STAR

22 JULY 2022, 6.02 A.M.

Phil was standing on the riverbank below a bridge that arched over the River Cherwell. In front of him were a dozen punts tied together in the still water. The backdrop to the scene was a meadow shrouded in mist, with the golden glow of dawn diffusing through it like a watercolour painting. He was looking at the scene in the photograph he held in his hand. The usual disorientation was aided by reading the caption on the Polaroid. It was significantly warmer at six in the morning in July than it was in the January he had just left behind. On his walk back across town to Trinity Street, he got more than warm. He unlocked the garage and got in the car.

He set off on his usual route to Brighton again. It was a couple of years later than the trip he had taken yesterday to spy on Chianti Carbonara. This time, he stopped in Reading to get some pictures printed from his SD card. He was heading to court in Brighton to take Quinkle down. He couldn't do it alone, so he got out his phone and called Singh & Anse, the law firm to which Mrs. Quinkle had entrusted her claim against her philandering husband. Phil had been able to help Mrs. Quinkle's lawyer a couple of times before.

"Singh and Anse, how can we legally help you?"

"Could I speak to Danesh Singh, please?"

"Please hold."

Phil negotiated a roundabout and spotted a police car in the lay-by ahead. He dropped his phone on the passenger seat and cruised past the speed trap, staring ahead and looking like a man who was not on the phone.

"Hello."

Phil reached over and put the phone on speaker.

"Could I speak to Danesh Singh?"

"Yes, I'm Dan Singh."

"Good morning, Dan, this is Phil Beans. Private investigator. Remember me? I have some information pertaining to the Quinkle divorce case. I wonder if we could meet prior to the hearing today?"

"Oh, yes. Hello, Phil. It's been a while. Tell me what you've got for me this time."

"I think you'll enjoy what I have to offer. I have some rather incriminating pictures. Very revealing, let's say. I also have proof that Quinkle paid for Chianti Carbonara's flat, and I've got the offshore account details of where all his money has been hidden."

There was a long pause with palpable disbelief at the other end of the phone. For a moment, Phil thought Singh had hung up, but as Phil pulled up at a red light, he heard him clear his throat.

"Sounds intriguing. Too good to be true, if truth be told. Just where, I mean, how? How have you got all this?" Singh asked.

"Let's not get too hung up on how. Why don't I just come and show you. You can make your mind up when you've had a chance to see for yourself. I'm heading to Brighton now. My ETA is, let me see … " Phil picked up the phone as the light turned green and switched to the Maps app. "It will be 10.36, according to my phone."

"You can't really be any later than that, Phil."

The car behind honked. "Oh, sod off, you impatient twat." Phil raised his hand to apologise for holding everyone up, put the car in gear, and set off as quickly as the sixty-four horsepower engine would allow. Phil heard Dan say, "You what?" and quickly replied, "Oh, no, not you, Dan. Sorry. So, can we meet?"

"Very well, Phil, I will be arriving at the court building with Mrs. Quinkle around 10.30. Get there as soon as you can, and I'll have a room ready where we can meet. Come to the court reception and ask for me. If it's a scam, I'll have them arrest you for contempt."

"Contempt for Mr. Quinkle, perhaps?"

"Ha-ha, indeed. We're all guilty of that! See you at 10.30," Singh said.

"See you then. Bye-bye." Phil hung up and put Maps back on the phone screen.

Phil drove straight there, parked on the double yellow lines outside the court, and arrived in the atrium at twenty to eleven. He was pointed toward a room just off the lobby, and he knocked on the door, which was already open. The small room had been painted a magnolia colour, and it had harsh fluorescent lighting, a Formica table, and chairs with cheap plastic seats. Danesh Singh and his client, Mrs. Quinkle, were already seated and waiting. Danesh was a handsome, well-dressed young man. His dark-grey suit and shiny black shoes gave an impression of someone one should take seriously, and his bright-red tie punctuated his air of confidence. His black hair was combed into a neat quiff, and his overpowering cologne smelled expensive. Phil shook his outstretched hand, and Dan's yellow-gold bracelet gave a heavy, deliberate clink.

"Hello, Phil. Please come in, take a seat. Phil, this is Harriette Quinkle. Harriette, this is Phil Beans."

Phil shook the elegant, tanned hand of the woman seated at the table. She had short hair that was coloured auburn, with grey at the roots. Her high-necked black dress and pearl necklace created a conservative, stand-offish vibe. Her lined face was knitted with concern, and Phil felt for her and the months of pain she must have endured in getting to this divorce hearing. There was a feeling of defeat that hung heavily around her.

"Pleased to meet you, Mrs. Quinkle."

"Mmm-hmm," she replied.

Dan leant in close to Harriette and said something very quietly. He sat back. "It's worth a shot," he whispered.

"Bloody better be," she whispered back. "OK, Mr. Beans, I'm all ears."

Phil sat down opposite the others with his satchel on his lap. He passed them the printout from Rusty. Dan and Harriette leafed through the pages in open-mouthed silence.

Dan broke the silence. "This is a lot of money, Phil, and these are very detailed accounts, but I'm not sure whether this document is admissible without some kind of provenance. Legal provenance, like a warrant. But the case hinges on the infidelity clause. You mentioned photographs?"

Brighton Rock Star

Phil passed a glossy cardboard Boots envelope across the table. "I'm so sorry, this is going to be a bit, erm ..."

Harriette tore open the envelope, pulled out the prints from Adelaide Crescent, and quickly dealt the photos—face up, one by one—on the table. Then she paused, holding the last one. "Bastard. I knew it. I bloody well knew it!" She placed the picture of Quinkle, with his hands on Chianti's breasts, on the table in front of Dan.

Phil took out a single sheet of paper. He slid it across the table, next to the 8" x 6" photograph of a handsy Quinkle. It was a pro forma document which simply outlined that if, as a result of the information provided, there was an increase in the offer or settlement from the defendant, then ten per cent of the difference would be paid into a certain bank account, the details of which followed, along with spaces for signatures of the plaintiff, legal counsel, and *Phil Beans, Private Investigator.*

"Ten per cent?" noted Dan, turning to Harriette.

Mrs. Quinkle looked at Phil. "I'd give you all of it just to see his face," said an astonished Harriette, grabbing the pen from Dan and signing Phil's little contract with a dry, hollow grin.

"Well, that would be generous indeed, Mrs. Quinkle," said Phil. "Thank you, but I like to think my terms are perfectly reasonable. I will also gain satisfaction from knowing you get the outcome you deserve."

Dan countersigned, smirking, and Phil handed over the SD card with the photos on it, and the rest of the printout with all of Quinkle's Bermuda bank account details. "The metadata on the SD card has date, time, and location."

"You're a bloody rock star, mate," said Dan, flicking through the financials again, and letting his professionalism drop for a moment. "This is priceless." He turned to Harriette and added, "I'll call for a brief adjournment with their council, and if I present this right, imply that we have some legal provenance for the financials, then present the photographs, that bombshell will have them on the back foot. I'm confident they'll ask for a longer adjournment and come back with a new offer to settle out of court. It'll be conditional on not making the photographs public, but we can live with that, right? We've got nothing to lose."

"Thank you, Mr. Beans, this is so utterly unexpected," said Harriette in an upbeat tone. "It's not the money, though. It really isn't," she added cheerily.

"No, no, of course not. I understand."

"I highly doubt you do," she replied in an altogether darker tone of voice. "The pecuniary retribution will be nothing compared to the unmitigated joy of sticking it right up the cheating little shit so far that he can clean his teeth with it. This is spectacular, Mr. Beans. You're like a little miracle. Thank you so very much, from the bottom of what's left of my twisted, bitter heart."

"You're very welcome," Phil said, hiding his discomfort and wondering if any amount of therapy could help her. "Ten per cent is all the thanks I need."

"Well, court will be convening in a couple of minutes, we need to get in there," said Dan.

Phil bid them all the best and left them to the hearing.

On the drive back, Phil thought about what was next, and his mind was now full of the murder of Professor Durant. The stolen research papers, the professional ridicule, Umbrella Guy, and the pin badge. He also knew that he needed to pay Havarti back for the lead on Chianti Carbonara. The meeting in Brighton had gone much better than he could have hoped for, and his ten per cent would surely be a pretty decent chunk of change. He knew the next thing on his list had to be finding clues about Durant's death for Havarti. He needed to go back to Westgate before the prof's plunge and wait to see who Umbrella Guy was.

Once back in Oxford, Phil returned the car to its rightful place. He made notes in his phone to reserve the use of the car. He locked up the garage and stood enjoying the warm summer air.

He rummaged among the stash of Polaroids in his bag and found the one he needed. It was a picture he had taken on the college backs, by the canal, on the Friday before Durant's death. It was the Polaroid closest to the date that he had been able to find.

Phil snuck behind the garage and out of sight. He perched on a low wall, took a deep breath, and held the photograph of *Westgate College Backs, 04 Nov. 2022, 4.22 p.m.* in front of his face and willed the world to change around him. The picture stayed in sharp focus, and his world became a grey blur once again.

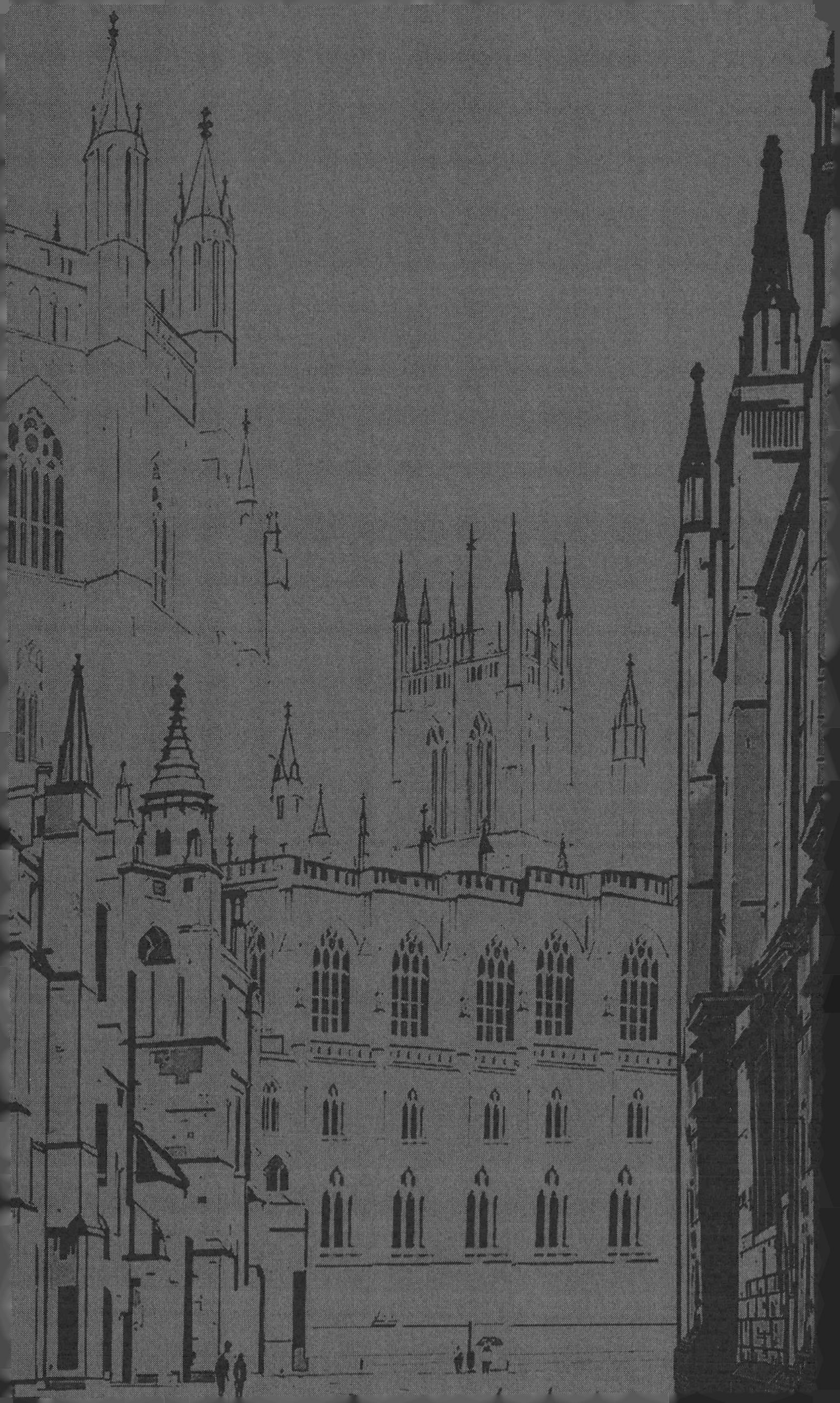

Part Two
LIFE GETS COMPLICATED

10.

ARBLEY SCRUMP

04 NOVEMBER 2022, 4.22 P.M.

The first thing Phil felt was the cool November air. Then the low afternoon sun began to take shape through the vague darkness of silhouetted trees. He sensed the autumnal dampness of the grassy lawn, still wet from the previous sombre, drizzly day, as the green hue gradually turned into dark and light stripes, and then into individual blades of grass.

As he began to focus, footsteps were receding a little way off to his right. A dark-haired guy in a jacket and skinny jeans was walking away from him and back through the archway into back quad. He recognized himself, the past version of himself that had just taken the photo, right where he was now sitting. Phil recalled that he had waited around long enough for the photograph to develop to be sure he would be alone on the backs if he ever needed to use the picture. And sure enough, there he was, alone.

Westgate College was one of the smaller, lesser-known Oxford colleges. It dated from 1445 AD and was built for the education of Greyfriars from the Westgate Abbey in Chester. It was established with an endowment from the wealth generated by the Abbey's stranglehold on the cheese market of much of Northern England and the Midlands. These theological scholars were known as the Profound Greyfriars, which in the French of their time was *Frères-Gris Profonde*. They sat around debating philosophy and theology at the School of Divinity, laughing and eating a lot of cheese, so they became affectionately known as the *Frères-Gras Profonde*, or the Deep Fat Friars. They kept the tradition alive, enjoying cheese and having fun, and it persisted into modern times. It is reflected, in Latin, in the college motto: *Integritas, Risus, Caseus* (Integrity, Laughter, Cheese).

Westgate College was designed as two square quads, referred to as front quad and back quad. Surrounding each quad were ancient yellow Cotswold stone buildings housing the classrooms and living quarters. The square in the middle of each quad was laid to lawn and tended immaculately. The rich hue of the stone and the neat lawns gave the college a peaceful ambiance, nestling gently on the air of formality. The college was a serene oasis, surviving against a tide of hideous modernization outside its walls, the worst of which was the Westgate Oxford shopping centre. The shopping centre was an enormous monstrosity that dominated the locality, lurking directly across Norfolk Street.

Beyond the west side of the main buildings, among the ancient oak trees, were the quiet lawns of the backs alongside the bank of Castle Mill Stream. It was in this tranquil haven on the backs, upon lawns that were steeped in history, that Phil had just materialized. He sat on a damp wooden bench, looking at the sun, which had sunk low in the sky and could be seen through the trees. This was possibly his favourite spot in all of Oxford. The last of the leaves were falling from the huge oaks that lined the river's edge, and many had collected on the lawn since it had last been raked. Phil loved autumn, especially the russet-coloured leaves and the cool air.

The Polaroid photograph in his hand had transported Phil three months or so forward in time, from the Quinkle hearing to the weekend before Durant's death, but even now he was still about three months behind his own real timeline, and it took Phil a little time to orientate himself.

A few quiet moments later, there were footsteps coming from the archway, accompanied by some tuneless whistling. "Afternoon, again, Mr. Phil," came the familiar voice of Arbley Scrump, who paused near the bench on which Phil was seated. Scrump was a short, rotund chap in scruffy clothes, an old Barbour wax jacket, and a wide-brimmed canvas hat. Scrump was holding broken pieces of what appeared to be the remains of a pine wood box across his arms, gripping it for all he was worth with stubby fingers that protruded from his fingerless gloves. Scrump looked at Phil a little bemused, raising his eyebrows and glancing backwards in the direction of the archway. He looked back at Phil sitting on the bench. Poor Scrump had just passed Phil walking the other way, and now here he was sitting on a bench, wearing a different T-shirt than he had been wearing less than a minute earlier.

"Good afternoon to you, Mr. Scrump," Phil replied. "That looks heavy. Need a hand?"

"Yes, it is, and no, I still don't need a hand, but thank ya kindly. Again."

"Ah, yes. I did just offer, didn't I?" said Phil, remembering back to this day. "Lovely autumnal weather. Not too cold yet."

"Autumn, ah." Arbley Scrump thought for a moment, shuffling uncomfortably under the weight of the firewood in his arms. "Nice enough day. I reckon I wouldn't mind autumn so much, but for them friggin' leaves. Seein' as I'm the poor bugger who has to rake 'em up."

"Indeed, Mr. Scrump. And a fine job of it you do too."

Scrump walked across the grass to the woodpile and dumped the load he was carrying on the ground. "Remember, remember, the fifth of November. I trust you'll be attendin' tomorrow night. It ought to be a good show. If this pile of soddin' damp wood lights up, it might. Petrol," Scrump began to mutter, "I should get more petrol. That oughta do the trick." He began stacking the wood at the top of the stack of wood that would soon become a bonfire. "I hope them students has the Guy ready for the top of this fire. It won't be the same without burning Guy Fawkes."

"Oh, yes, I'll be here," Phil said confidently, recalling his presence at what was doubtless the best fireworks display ever put on at Westgate College. He got up off the bench and took a few steps toward Scrump. The grass was soft underfoot, and he thought back to the event that would happen this evening. "I'm looking forward to the treacle toffee, and the parkin too!"

"Oh, ahh, s'nothin' better 'an the treacle toffee, in my 'umble opinyun."

"Indeed not, Mr. Scrump."

"Anyway, I can't stand 'ere gassin' . . ." said Scrump, turning back to building the wood pile. "This bonfire in't gunna build itself, now is it?"

Phil turned and headed off toward the Hare's Wharf footbridge. "A good evening to you, Mr. Scrump," said Phil, and he strode off in the direction of the B & B.

"A good evening, eh? We can 'ope so, Mr. Phil. We can only 'ope," said Scrump, tossing the last piece of packing crate onto the would-be bonfire and turning toward the back quad.

Phil strolled past the School of Divinity building, out onto Paradise Street, and turned left. He thought for the umpteenth time how far that street was from anything he would call paradise. Funny how the street name still bore a reference to where the monks would have sat in silent contemplation hundreds of years ago, long before the college was even built.

Bumping into old Scrump wasn't going to change anything in this timeline; he didn't need to worry about that. He pulled up the collar of his jacket and put his head down. Phil just needed to lie low for a couple of days, and Mrs. Thistle's B & B was just the spot. He crossed Castle Mill Stream, and in next to no time, he was outside his former digs. He rang the doorbell and waited.

11.

WIGTWIZZLE

04 NOVEMBER 2022, 5.00 P.M.

Holly transformed into her alter ego, Honey, when she changed into her outfit for work, as though her change of clothes altered her persona, and she left Holly behind her. It felt as though it wasn't really Holly who was going to work. Honey was the one with the part-time job.

Today was Honey's day with Professor Wigtwizzle. She wore the outfit she knew Limehouse Wigtwizzle liked the best. Tiny little skirt, tight spaghetti-strap top, and bright red high-heeled pumps. She knew how good she looked, and she quite liked feeling how powerful it was to dress in a way that was so unashamedly sexy.

Wigtwizzle always pretended not to look, and Honey always pretended not to notice him looking. But she was happy to give the old boy his thrill. It was a big part of what he was paying for, after all. It was always a pleasant and relaxed couple of hours or so with the old prof, and she'd earn a fair bit more than she would waiting tables till midnight.

At the foot of Staircase D, she stood on the ground floor in front of the heavy oak door with the ancient brass number one on it. She knocked gently, and it opened immediately. Wigtwizzle always reminded her of the way a puppy acts when its owner gets home. He clasped his hands together and grinned from ear to ear, stepping to the side to welcome her inside. He was always this thrilled to see her.

"Honey, my dear, it's lovely to see you. Do, please, come in. Come. Let me take your coat."

"Good evening, Limehouse," she said, leaning in and kissing his cheek as she entered.

He closed the door behind her and asked if she would like wine. As she walked across the large, oak-panelled living room heading to the sideboard, Wigtwizzle followed, taking in the view.

"Yes, please. Shall I do it?" she asked, knowing full well what the answer was as she reached for the bottle of cabernet that Wigtwizzle always had there, at the ready.

"Oh yes, my dear, if you wouldn't mind awfully doing that. How are you?"

"Oh, I'm just fine. You know, same as ever. How are you?" Honey replied from the sideboard without looking back. She opened the bottom drawer, knowing that Wigtwizzle was watching, and bent down unnecessarily far to tease him as she retrieved the corkscrew, then stood up straight to begin opening the wine.

"Tickety-boo, my dear. Always am on a Friday. Delighted to see you. I had some interesting cheeses delivered from Waitrose."

The cork popped, and Honey carried the bottle and two glasses over to the sofa. "Back in a jiffy, then," she said with a sweet smile. She went through to the kitchen and prepared the cheese and crackers. She carried the small tray with cheese, plates, and knives back to the lounge where Wigtwizzle stood watching her. She placed the tray on the coffee table and sat down on the sofa. Wigtwizzle shuffled as quickly as his arthritic knees would carry him to join her and sat close.

"Chess?" she asked, seeing the board and pieces set out on the coffee table.

"Not altogether up to such demanding intellectual gymnastics this evening if you don't mind, my dear."

"Want to watch a film?"

"That would be lovely. But something fun, a bit light. A Shakespearean romcom, perhaps?"

"*Othello? King Lear? Coriolanus?*" she said.

"Oh, beauty and wit," he replied wistfully.

"*A Midsummer Night's Dream* it is, then."

"Oh! My favourite," he grinned.

She knew that already. He'd said it each and every time they'd watched it.

She stood and leant over the coffee table to slowly pour the wine. She was sure to let her little skirt ride up at the top of her soft, smooth thighs as she bent down. Honey felt like an actress, innocently playing the role of a temptress on stage. She moved the chessboard to one side and the cheese tray to the front. As she turned to sit back down, Wigtwizzle quickly looked away, quite flushed. Honey thought it was so old-fashioned that, after all this time, he still pretended so unconvincingly that he hadn't been staring.

"Umm, new shoes?" he asked, glancing down at the bright-red four-inch-heeled pumps.

"Yes, do you like them?" she asked, holding his wine glass out for him to take.

"Oh yes, dear. The colour suits your ... I mean suits you, you know the, umm, heels do marvels for your ... I do so love the colour."

Honey reached for her bag and sat back down.

Limehouse took a breath and sighed. "You are more beautiful every time I see you. *Velut caseus aevo*, as we might say at Westgate, you are as cheese with the passage of time."

"Oh, aren't you just the sweetest." She pulled her little iPad mini from her handbag. She quickly had the film playing on the large-screen TV through screen mirroring.

"Like a little miracle," she said as the overture began to play over the opening credits.

"Yes, you are. Heavenly."

"I meant the iPad business," Honey said.

"I know," he grinned.

Honey rolled her eyes at him and gently shook her head, in spite of her fondness for his cheesy nonsense.

The film began, and they watched intently as the drama of the play's opening scene unfolded.

As more classical music began to play, Wigtwizzle seemed a little distracted. "Honey, my dear. Can I just ask? I suppose you wouldn't visit if I weren't paying you."

"Was that a question?" Payments were all taken care of by bank transfer without needing to exchange cash in person. She didn't like to talk about money, and she felt as though it broke the spell and cast a shadow on the fantasy that was at the heart of her visits.

"Well, yes. I think it came out as more of a rhetorical statement, but I meant to couch it in the interrogative," he explained.

"Then, I suppose you're right, I probably wouldn't." She wasn't about to lie to him, but she wasn't sure where he was going with his question, so she tried to soften the truth a little. "That's the nature of my job, really. But that doesn't mean I don't like being here. It just means that if you weren't paying me, I should really rather have to be somewhere where they did."

She took a sip of wine, leaving a bright-red lipstick mark where her lip had touched the glass. She looked at his kind face. His gentle eyes were fixated on her beauty. She smiled and shrugged.

"Quite so. Yes, indeed, of course. So, in a roundabout way, that makes me wonder whether you now have an opening after Westgate Wednesday Worship?" he asked.

"I don't follow. I don't actually go to chapel."

"No, quite so, but Chieveley Spatchcock did, followed by cheese and wine for lunch with the provost. I didn't blame him for being so eager to scuttle home as promptly as he did every week. I was merely wondering if his death has created an open slot in your calendar."

"Chieveley died?" Honey asked in a whisper. Wigtwizzle nodded. "Oh, I'm sorry to hear that," Honey added. Chieveley Spatchcock had been a client for the last year or so. It was Limehouse who had introduced them. He was a cheerful old soak, and so full of life. Honey was shocked to hear that he was gone.

"Oh, you hadn't heard? I'm sorry, my dear. He keeled over in the Common Room yesterday, mid-sentence and halfway through a G and T. Nothing suspicious by all accounts," Limehouse explained.

"Oh God, that's awful. I was with him on Wednesday. Poor old Chieveley."

A short, respectful silence allowed the film to fill the room. Honey thought of Chieveley's silly antics. He had been a practical joker, and he had often roped her into doing some of his dirty work, variously involving a tube of superglue, a fake tarantula, some cling film, or a plastic dog poo, all for the sake of a good laugh at some other prof's expense.

"So perhaps that has created an opportunity, an opening *per se*? In your calendar."

"Hmmm? Yes, I suppose it has. Wednesdays, two till five. Are you wanting to fill it?"

"As much as I would dearly love to fill your open slot, so to speak," he said, barely containing his mirth, "but this old emeritus professor's stipend will only stretch so far when it comes to such luxuries of life. No, I thought perhaps I might make a discreet enquiry with a colleague, like I did with old Chieveley, to see if there was any interest."

"Oh? Who might that be?"

"Chap here at Westgate, Professor Durant. Not a friend as such, he's a good twenty years younger than me. Part of the next generation of physicists that left me behind. Someone I've known for years, though. He made an enquiry a few weeks ago about the lovely-looking young lady he has seen around Staircase D these last couple of years. He was hinting strongly at getting an introduction. Seemed very keen."

"That would be very kind of you to put me in touch. I would, of course, need to iron out all the details with him directly. Terms and conditions, you know."

"He's some years younger than your usual clientele, though. Could I enquire, rather forthrightly if I may, if you were to fill that slot with such a new client, would they be allowed to, ummm, you know, as it were?"

Honey wondered where this was going. She wasn't keen to discuss her other clients, but she wanted to put his mind at rest. "Well, I have three clients at any one time. With Professor Spatchcock, it was mostly getting tipsy and playing games or practical jokes. We were just silly. Gin and tonic, and gin rummy. Twister was his favourite, he used to call out the colours and just watch me play."

"That sounds like a lot of fun," said Limehouse dreamily.

"As for my other client, even if it isn't any more sober, it is a far more serious and professional engagement. I dress up in a nice little cocktail dress, and he takes me to dinner at his country club. You know, dry champagne and foie gras canapés followed by sole meunière or boeuf en croûte. It's all fancy paired wines and lots of cutlery. Then he has his chauffeur drop me back at home. It's all for show for his golf-club cronies."

"Yes, Wolfram Belchin is always bragging about you."

"So, none of my current clients gets to 'you know,' as you so elegantly put it, during their allotted time, so let's say it would be best to set that expectation during any discrete enquiry you might make. It would save wasting their time if they were indeed hoping to fill my slot, so to speak."

Wigtwizzle was smiling from ear to ear. "Oh, my dear, I am so very glad to be reassured about that. I have always hoped that you would be saving yourself for someone worthy, someone with whom you are, perhaps, in love. That is something I would feel happy about. I'm very old-fashioned that way. Because, you see, I don't like to think of your perfect beauty being sullied for anything less than true love."

Honey reached down and took Wigtwizzle's hand, and he gave her hand a gentle squeeze. Honey rather imagined that she would miss him if he stopped being a client, and thought perhaps she would visit him sometimes as Holly. She was sad about Chieveley. Poor old Chieveley, with his Dickie Bows, his monocle, and his lisp. He was a really fun drunk.

Wigtwizzle's old arthritic hand was soft and frail, and she felt a pang of sadness for the day he would be gone too. She was sure she would miss him. Then she made herself remember that she was probably the only person, and the only thing apart from whisky, that brought him any real happiness, and the sadness melted into warm fondness. She gently squeezed his hand in return and turned to the TV screen.

As red wine poured down on Kevin Kline's head, Wigtwizzle giggled. That seemed to prompt him to remember his empty decanter. "Ah, yes, erm, would you mind terribly, you know, decanting me a fresh bottle of whisky?"

Honey smiled, knowing it was both a genuine need and a feeble ruse. "Sure," she said, and walked over to the sideboard. She bent down to get the bottle of Ardbeg whisky out of the cupboard, knowing full well that the old boy was no longer staring at the movie. Honey had long since worked out that all he wanted to do was admire her. That was his thing, and it was what he was paying for. That was the superficial layer. Honey really quite liked being admired. It was all kind of innocent, and yet a little perverse. It was all very complicated beneath the surface, especially considering how much they enjoyed each other's company and the fondness they felt for each other.

She straightened up, took off the foil cap, pulled the stopper from the bottle, and slowly, gently poured the contents into the beautiful Waterford crystal decanter. She loosely replaced the large, arthritis-friendly, crystal stopper and walked back to the sofa. As she sat down close to Wigtwizzle, he whispered, "Thank you for that."

"What for? Decanting your whisky, or the leg show?" she asked with a cheeky grin.

"Both, of course, my dear, both."

Honey took his hand again, and they turned to the screen to watch the film as Stanley Tucci made his appearance on the screen. Wigtwizzle's lips began to move along with Puck's dialogue.

"I once played Robin Goodfellow at the Playhouse, you know," he said.

"I do know. And I bet you were bloody brilliant."

Wigtwizzle smiled, and Honey snuggled up to him with genuine affection.

12.

JUST POPPING OUT

04 NOVEMBER 2022, 5.12 P.M.

The door opened reluctantly, as though it were too tired for new and unexpected guests. Phil grinned. Suddenly, the old lady who had made the door open in such an unwelcoming fashion brightened up considerably.

"Phil, my lovely! What a nice surprise! Oh, come in, come in!" Mrs. Thistle stood aside in the narrow hallway to allow Phil room to squeeze by. She was a short, round, absolute treasure of a woman, and she was like a grandma to Phil. She wore a smock dress and sheepskin slippers. Her grey hair was arranged in carefully prepared ringlets that were protected under a hairnet. Her chubby face was quite unlined despite her seventy-something age. Her ruddy cheeks and beaming smile made Phil feel like he was home.

Phil stepped in and was immediately met by the distinctive smell of old house—a homely mixture of musty carpet, ancient wood, recently applied furniture polish, and long-since-fried bacon, as well as the curious, faint whiff of lead-based trim paint. This was what home smelled like to Phil. It was the same smell as he grew up with in Lydington Manor, and the smell of his digs through college.

It didn't seem to matter which end of the social spectrum you were on. Old, old houses tended to smell this same way. New builds, like his mum's house, smelled of fresh pine trim and latex paint, and they had no soul. It took decades for a home to get its fusty, old soul, and Phil felt right at home with his first inhale.

"Cuppa tea, luv?"

"Ooh, yes please, Mrs. T.," said Phil, his independent streak having evaporated, regressing to the younger man who loved to be fussed over.

"Is it time you started calling me Marion?"

"Could be, Mrs. T., but old habits and all that."

They walked through into the kitchen, and Phil was met with the strange but familiar smell of burnt gas that always lingered after the ancient gas cooker had been put to use. Phil had never worked out the chemistry of that smell, which he never detected with a new cooker. It was distinctly the B & B's kitchen smell. There was also the delicious aroma of freshly-baked rock cakes, which were sitting on a plate in the middle of the little kitchen table, still warm.

Phil sat, careful not to pull the oversized gingham tablecloth with his knees. He knew from experience that the tablecloth moved freely on the shiny, frictionless, little table. Anything in the middle of the table seemed to be subject to gravitational attraction that reached up to the tabletop, beyond the laws of physics. Consequently, the tablecloth would cheerfully glide, dumping a cream tea in an unsuspecting individual's lap on a regular basis. Phil had eaten cucumber sandwiches and rock cakes that had been on the kitchen floor a few times before. There were many delicacies in the world, but Mrs. Thistle's rock cakes were one of the best and most irresistible. Phil bit into the crisp, lightly-browned, sugar-coated crust and into the sweet, doughy middle with juicy sultanas spread evenly throughout.

"Help yourself," said Mrs. T., sarcastically, after Phil had already taken a second bite.

The big ceramic teapot was on the stovetop, with a low light under it and what looked like a non-flammable asbestos tea-cosy over it, keeping the already-brewed tea piping hot. There was nothing worse than cold, stewed tea in Mrs. T.'s opinion. She always served hot stewed tea. Holding the teapot handle with a tea towel, she poured the dark-brown English breakfast tea into two cups, added two sugars to each, and stirred. Then, she added a splash of milk.

She put the tea on the table and sat down. Phil lifted his cup by the saucer, picked up the cup with his pinky out, and took a big sip. He tasted the sugary, tannin-laden tea and was transported. He hadn't had the heart to tell Mrs. Thistle that he gave up sugar in his tea over a decade earlier for the sake of a long-since-recovered-from girlfriend. He felt there was something comforting about drinking a good, old-fashioned cup of a past life; the soothing ambrosia of stewed, sweet tea felt a little decadent and very reassuring. Phil sat back in his chair and let out a contented sigh.

"Great tea, Mrs. T., umm, Marion," he said with a wink, trying her name out to see how it sounded. It felt nice, informal, grown-up. Like he was now in her inner circle.

"They doing work on your flat again?" she asked.

"Oh, umm, no," said Phil, thinking fast. "They're fumigating the opticians' next door."

Who knew whether an opticians' shop ever needed fumigating, but it was a fresh reason for needing an out-of-the-way bed and breakfast for a few nights at short notice, and Phil's brain hadn't come up with anything better before his mouth had spat the words out. He shrugged as if to say, *what can you do?* and followed up quickly to avoid further interrogation on the subject. "And Mum's just so busy these days, I don't want to be a burden. Her jewellery is doing really well on Etsy, and she'll only stop and fuss over me if I turn up there. You know what mums are like."

"What a considerate young man you are, Phil. Well, you're welcome here any time. I'm not too busy for you. Your attic room is available. Freshly made-up. Twenty-five quid a night, as usual. How's that?"

"Perfect, Mrs. T., sorry, Marion," he said. "Thank you."

"So, how's your mum, apart from busy?"

"Oh, she's doing well. Happy and healthy," Phil said, taking a last sip of tea and being sure to leave the tea leaves that had always somehow made it through the strainer. "But she's even busier these days with her theatre group. You know, the Old Headington Players. She's doing this year's pantomime. She's Cinderella's mother, so it's not a big part, but she's also getting ready for the opening of *Othello* after panto season is over, sometime in January. She's playing Desdemona, and every time I go, she has me reading parts while she goes through the script. I do that once a week as it is, and once is enough."

"She gets up to all sorts, your mum does," Marion said with genuine admiration. "I might go and see Cinderella, but I'll give Shakespeare a miss, if that's alright. I never know what they're talking about. How she can remember the lines is beyond me. So, you're still going for Sunday dinner every week?"

Just Popping Out

"Yes, indeed," said Phil.

"Oh, you are a good lad," Marion said. "Tell her hello from me when you go this weekend, then. Tell her we'll catch up soon."

"Will do," said Phil. There was always a chance that Marion and his mum might actually get round to catching up, so Phil just had to hope that the two dotty old women would put their confusion about his comings and goings down to their age.

Phil took his lead from Marion, putting his cup down and following her through to the hallway. She pulled a Yale key from the rack on the wall behind the little reception stand that had the guestbook perched on it. She held it out, and Phil took hold of it by the small plank of wood from which the key dangled. On the piece of wood was burnt a scruffy number 5 in Plumbus Thistle's ham-fisted writing.

"How is Mr. Thistle?" enquired Phil.

"Oh, he's alright. He's still the curmudgeonly old sod I married. He's out at darts night, so he's happy tonight at least, and I get some peace and quiet."

Phil thought the latter comment was comical, given how hard it was to get Plumbus to utter a single syllable. "You want gravy on your chips?" "Ahhr," was a typical interlocution in the Thistles' kitchen. Otherwise, Plumbus did the odd jobs around the place. The odder the better, because he quite liked being busy away from Mrs. T.'s almost incessant nattering.

Phil thanked Marion with a nod and a half smile and headed up the stairs with his bag. "Don't touch the banister on the landing," she called after him as he mounted the stairs. "There's been a bit of touch-up done. Some clumsy bugger with a huge suitcase.

And the bathroom on the top floor'll be chilly coz Plumbus has the window open to air the smell of the paint."

"Right-oh, Mrs. T.," he called down from the landing and continued up the narrow stairs to the attic room.

Phil set his bag down on the single bed that was pushed up against the wall on the right. On the left was an old oak wardrobe. It was one of the wooden articles, with peeling varnish, that lent some of its history to the smell of the house. There was just enough room in the middle for the door to open against the wardrobe, and to walk from the door to the little window in the gable end. This had been Phil's view for the four years he pursued his PhD. The small stretch, four paces long from the door to the window, was the only part of the room unencumbered by the slope of the roof. Phil sat on the bed. He was sure this was still the same threadbare burgundy bedspread that had been his for those few years, as well as countless guests before him and since.

Phil checked the time. Almost six already. He jogged down the stairs and called to Mrs. T., "Just popping out for a bite to eat. I won't be late," and went out onto Hollybush Row. The door, on its big spring, banged shut behind him, and the shiny brass door knocker clanged.

13.

THREE GOATS HEADS

04 NOVEMBER 2022, 5.54 P.M.

Phil set off up the street through Castle Quarter. He'd settled on the Three Goats Heads pub. It had been a regular haunt a decade ago, but now, Phil thought it a fairly safe bet that no one would recognize him. The burly guy behind the bar was in his fifties and carried himself with a gravitas that said he was the management. His tight, black T-shirt suggested that he worked out and had no need for a bouncer on the door, and his hand made the pint glass he was holding look small.

"Two ticks, mate," he said, glancing in Phil's direction.

It had been quite a while since he had eaten much. The rock cake at the B & B had filled a small hole, but now he was craving some proper food, and this was the spot for that. Phil put his camera and jacket on the counter seat with its back to the bar. He stood at the bar, having already decided what he wanted off the chalkboard listing the specials of the day, but he had a glance at the menu anyway.

The barman wiped his hands on a small towel and took payment from a customer at the other end of the bar. "Cheers, Jim,"

Phil heard, as the customer raised his glass and sipped his Guinness. Jim came over to Phil. "Yes, sir?"

"Pint of imperial stout and the steak and ale pie, please."

"Chips and peas alright?"

"More than alright, thanks, yes."

"Coming right up," said Jim, as Phil tapped his card on the contactless terminal. "I'll bring it over."

The pie was good, Phil thought. *Really good.* As he scraped up the last bit of pie gravy with his dessert spoon, he heard a young woman's voice behind him ordering a double Baileys. She sounded familiar. He turned around to see a young woman with long dark hair facing the bar. She was wearing a jean jacket, a short skirt, and red, high-heeled shoes. *Wow,* thought Phil, trying very hard and completely failing not to notice the backs of her perfect legs.

"There you go, Honey," said Jim, taking the £10 note she held out.

Phil wondered if Honey was the girl's name, or just a familiar term of endearment.

As she took a sip of her Baileys, she turned to decide where to sit. Phil saw her beautiful brown eyes and knew right away who she was. And then she saw Phil looking at her. She lowered the glass slowly and smiled. "Hello," she said. "I'm Honey."

Phil's mouth fell open. It was Holly. The girl from the vegan café. The same girl he had arranged to meet at 2.00 p.m. for lunch at McDonald's next January. But of course, this Holly had never met Phil before. Phil smiled back. Phil had just changed his past, and Holly's. The first time he had seen Holly was through the window of the vegan café. But then he had come here, bumped into her, and now they had met over two months earlier. In an instant, Phil's mind began racing through the potential implications. Then he looked at Holly's big brown eyes and stopped thinking.

"Hi, I'm Phil. Are you meeting friends for a night out?"

"No, I just finished work."

"Waitressing?" asked Phil, wondering which place in town would have their servers in such an outfit.

She glanced down at herself. "You're funny."

"What do you do?" asked Phil.

"I'm in my third year of a Master's in Philosophy and Practical Ethics."

Not the answer Phil was expecting given the outfit she was wearing, but intriguing all the same. "Third year. You're coming to the end then. I guess you must be finishing your thesis."

"Yep, I've got a bit of editing to do before I submit," she said.

"What do you plan to do when you're finished?" Phil asked, struggling with small talk, and worried that his conversation wasn't exactly scintillating so far.

"Well, then, I will either be philosophical or practically ethical. I haven't decided which, yet." She laughed and finished her drink. "What can I get you?"

"Oh, umm, whisky please. Lagavulin."

Honey turned back to the bar. "Jim! Another one of these and a Lager Voolin." She turned to Phil to check if she'd said it right. Phil nodded and smiled.

Phil didn't catch what Jim said, but Honey turned to him and asked, "Single or double?"

"Oh, single, please," Phil said, trying to be polite.

"Single," Honey called out. "Ice?" she relayed back to Phil.

"No, just neat, thanks."

"Neat and tidy, please, Jim," Honey called back.

Jim set two glasses down on the bar. Honey handed him a £20 note and picked up the glasses. Jim smiled and turned away to carry on putting pint glasses in the little dishwasher.

Phil wondered if the double Baileys she had just finished was her first drink of the day. Phil thought she seemed a bit more tipsy than that.

"Have you eaten?" asked Phil.

"No, not exactly," she said. "Some cheese and crackers earlier."

"You want to get some food?" said Phil, thinking it might help to soak up some of the Baileys at least.

"McDonald's," said Honey enthusiastically, gulping her Baileys straight down. "I bloody love Baileys. Liquid ice cream. And now I want a Big Mac."

Phil, likewise, finished his whisky and put the two glasses on the bar as Honey headed toward the door.

"Oi," said Jim, and Phil turned back. "You take care of her, alright?" Jim placed his huge hands flat on the bar and leant forward. It wasn't a direct threat, but it felt menacing when Jim said, "Don't forget, I've got your details in my credit card system. You remember that. You treat her nice."

"I'll see she's alright, don't worry." Phil gave Jim a smile that he hoped said less "serial killer" and more "thank you for caring."

Phil and Honey walked round onto Cornmarket Street and into McDonald's. Honey managed to walk in her heels in spite of, or perhaps because of, her relative state of intoxication. They both stood studying the menu that most of the whole world knows off by heart.

Three Goats Heads

"Can I help the next guest, please?"

"Yep, Big Mac, large fries, and a vanilla milkshake, please," Honey said.

"Just a small fries for me," said Phil.

Once they'd got their food, they sat down at the cleanest table available. Phil unfolded his camera and asked, "May I?"

"S'pose," she said with a doubtful, curious shrug, reaching for the red Big Mac box on the tray between them.

Phil attached a Flash Bar and clicked the camera's red button just as Honey was stuffing the Big Mac into her mouth and taking her first big bite.

"I bloody love the first bite of a Big Mac," she said with her mouth stuffed full.

"I usually eat around the edge and save the middle bit as the last bite. That's the best bit of a Big Mac for me," countered Phil. "But to be honest, the chips are my favourite."

"Fries," corrected Honey.

"What?"

"They're fries, not chips," Honey told him. "Chips are what you get at the chip shop—chunky, crisp and golden outside, soft and fluffy in the middle. She took another big bite of Big Mac, picked up an example fry, waved it at Phil, and continued. "These are fries. Altogether higher surface-area-to-potato ratio."

"Bloody hell, a first date and a first-rate education in deep-fried potato."

"Is this a date?" she said. "Cool. You stick with me, kid, there's a lot more where that came from. I'll teach you a thing or two."

The flirty innuendo wasn't lost on Phil, and he blushed. Phil was enraptured. Honey was like Holly's alter ego. She was the same cute, smiley, down-to-earth, sarcastic young woman, but her appearance and the way she talked were very sexy compared to the sassy waitress he had met in a Collard Green's sweatshirt and baseball cap.

Honey finished her fries and said, "D'you dance?" Without even waiting to see Phil's shrug and slight nod, she said, "Come on, let's go dancing. Varsity Club?"

Phil had always loved to dance, and he was keen to impress Honey with his moves and his very best enthusiasm. In the back of his mind, he was still trying to calculate the consequences of the changes to their timelines, but he had already changed things, so it seemed that he might as well just go with it for now. He looked at Honey's smiling, excited face and blurted out, "Sure, let's go!"

This could turn out to be a late one, thought Phil. *Oh, crap, I hope Mrs. T. will think to not double-lock the front door.*

It was a short walk and a lot of stairs to the rooftop at the Varsity Club. Phil was a bit out of shape and took a couple of deep breaths. They stood looking out over the rooftops and the dreaming spires of the skyline. There were some early fireworks flashing and popping in the distance. "This view doesn't get old, does it?" asked Phil.

"Come on, you," Honey said with a wink, and she went out into the middle to dance. Phil put his camera and jacket on a chair nearby and joined her. The propane heaters were taking the chill off, and the canvas covers overhead were keeping the warmth in and the worry of more drizzle out. The fresh air was invigorating, and Honey took off her little denim jacket, revealing a tight little sun top with spaghetti straps. She tossed the jacket to Phil to put on their chair. Phil felt flush with something more than the whisky. She was stunning. Her hair flowed with the sway of her body, and she moved effortlessly in time with the beat, with her arms above her head and her hips moving to the music.

"White wine spritzer, if you're buying," she shouted.

Phil went over to the bar and was served pretty quickly. It was early yet, and the place wasn't full. But it would be in a couple of hours. Phil hated crowds. He handed Honey the spritzer, and she drank it all and handed back the glass. He obediently put the glass on a nearby table and started dancing with his beer bottle in his hand. Honey came closer and danced right in front of him, and he tried to turn on his moves to match hers.

They danced through several tracks, and it was nice and easy not having to think of things to say. One minute she was doing cheesy dance moves from the 1960s, the next minute she was bodypopping. Phil was entranced, and he just had to go with it, trying to keep up with her boundless vivacity and infectious sparkle.

They took it in turns to go to the bar, and each time Honey was served a lot quicker than Phil was. Eventually she shouted, "My feet are killing me; if we stay much longer, you'll have to carry me home." And Phil thought if she drank any more that would be inevitable, feet or not.

Honey put up a finger to indicate that Phil should stay where he was, then she walked away. Phil stayed, like a good boy, wondering, *Why does everyone treat me like I'm a dog?* Honey came back from the DJ's sound desk, and when the next track started to mix in, she put her hands in the air and shouted a "Wooooh" to acknowledge the DJ. Phil thought the alcohol might be a good excuse for the wooooh-ing, and he decided it was cute. *So long as she doesn't do it again*, he thought, *it's cute*.

Honey shouted, "I love this one!" as the vocals began.

Phil recognized the song straight away and shouted, "Me too!" As they danced, they looked into each other's eyes and sang along."

When the song hit the chorus and got really boppy, they moved as though choreographed, like they had rehearsed for weeks.

The dance floor was becoming more and more packed as their song mixed into the next track, so Honey said, "Come on, walk me home."

They grabbed their stuff, then walked downstairs and out onto High Street. They walked and talked, and it was so much easier than Phil ever thought it would be.

Phil wondered if this was what love at first sight felt like. He had admired women from afar before, and he had been friends with women, and a couple of times things had turned into a relationship, and love had kind of quietly snuck up on him. Those times, it had seemed more like making the best with someone who liked him in spite of his being nerdy. But here he was, knowing almost nothing about this girl, and he was totally smitten already. He had gone from wondering what problems he might create to thinking how he could make this work across their timelines, until 18 January, when she would catch up with his timeline.

"You've done a lot of work on your dance moves," said Phil.

"Yes, suppose so. I used to study dance. Even did ballet. But I was queen of the dance floor in college. I was a bit of a diva, I think."

Was? thought Phil, thinking of the "white wine spritzer, if you're buying" thing.

"You're not so bad on the dance floor yourself," she said.

Phil smiled to himself. Glad that he'd made a good impression.

"So tell me, what do you do, Phil?"

"For a living, you mean? I kind of do legal work. I specialize in divorces," said Phil.

"What, you mean like a solicitor or a paralegal?"

"No, not exactly. I'm a sort of private investigator. Let's just say I have some unique skills and a bit of a knack for it," he added.

"Oh, a private detective, eh? Divorces? Not so much catching the bad guys as catching the bad guys *at it?* A *privates* detective!" she giggled.

Phil knew it was just a joke, but it was a bit close to the bone. "S'bout the size of it, yeah. It sounds so noble when you put it like that," he said. But men like his father *were* bad guys, and he knew that what he did was good work. "I like to think of it as getting cheating shits the comeuppance they deserve."

"Oh, well, yeah. It does sound quite noble when you put it like that," she said.

Worried the divorce thing might have sounded a bit unimpressive to Honey, he added, "I'm also doing some work to help out Oxford CID. Murders, missing persons, cold cases, stuff like that," thinking that sounded more admirable, provided she didn't press for too many details.

"Oh, very cool," she said. "That's neat. That sounds exciting and dangerous. Very James Bond. Very sexy."

They walked on quietly, heading up the canal side footpath between Castle Mill Stream and the Oxford Canal. It was dark and dimly lit, and there were narrowboats lining the water's edge on the right. Light and music were streaming out of some, while peace and quiet emanated from others. It was not the done thing to disturb the occupants with chatter.

The cold air swirled around them. Phil was tipsy. Honey stumbled a little and laughed. Phil felt her put her hand on his arm to steady herself. It was very peaceful and pleasant, but it didn't really feel romantic exactly, until Honey took Phil's hand. His heart soared. He wouldn't have dreamt of being that forward with her, and he was so excited that she wasn't being at all shy. They walked in comfortable silence for a while, just enjoying the relative peace and the cool night air.

They crossed over the canal on the footbridge that led to Jericho and wound up in Combe Road.

"Is this the street from the first Inspector Morse episode?" he asked.

"Yep, the house just over there," she said, gesturing with a nod. "You know your TV detectives, then?"

"I love Morse," he said.

"This is me," she said, standing by her front door and turning to face Phil. She took both of his hands in hers, leant forward, and kissed him gently, softly, on the lips. She didn't need to be too much on tippy-toes in the one-inch platforms. The kiss started soft and sweet, and it lingered, so as to make clear it was not just a friendly peck. Very clear. Then a passion ignited. This was a proper kiss from a black-and-white film. This was a Celia Johnson and Trevor Howard kind of a kiss, with Rachmaninoff playing on the soundtrack. This was a kiss Phil would remember forever.

Three Goats Heads

With his hands in hers, there wasn't the awkward question of how to embrace or where to put his hands, and he could focus on her sensuous lips. Her lips pressed harder, more passionately, and then Phil felt the pressure ease. The kiss ended slowly, she pulled away, and they opened their eyes and looked at each other. Phil was breathless; his heart was pounding.

"Call me," she whispered as she backed away. Key in hand, she turned toward the door and answered the question forming on his lips, "Top jacket pocket." She closed the door behind her without looking back to see Phil triumphantly holding the piece of paper with her phone number on it.

Phil wandered back down the canal path to the B & B. The time just drifted by in a haze as Phil thought about Holly dancing, Holly eating a Big Mac, and her kiss! Phil knew he was in trouble. Big trouble. Partly because he was falling in love, head over heels, and what if Holly didn't feel the same? The freight train of heartbreak might be heading in Phil's direction. But his problems didn't stop with the possibility of rejection. In one way, that would be the easiest problem to manage. What if Holly *did* end up feeling the same? Phil had messed up their timelines now, and he would be dating someone three months in his past. He'd never before spent more than a few days at a time in the past. He would have to come and go across the timeline, but this could be very tricky. He was a smart guy. Surely Phil could work it out.

The B & B was not double-locked, so he let himself in with the key hanging from the clumsy chunk of wood.

"Cuppa tea, my lovely?" came the immediate greeting from the kitchen.

"Oh, yes, please," Phil called back, closing the front door.

Phil walked through to the kitchen and sat down as Marion poured the deep-brown liquid from the stovetop teapot into his cup with the sugar already in it. A quick stir and a splash of milk, and the teacup was placed before him just seconds later. He took a sip of the familiar hot, sweet nectar.

Phil's dainty little cup and saucer were patterned with red and gold, and the cup had a picture of the Queen on it. He held the tiny handle between his thumb and forefinger with his pinky out. As he took another sip, he noticed his pinky and thought how posh that looked, so he tried tucking it in. But when he put the cup down, his little finger caught the saucer and he sloshed his tea. With such a tiny cup and saucer, he thought, isn't it just natural to hold your pinky out of the way? But the simpler explanation was the more likely, and if he was honest with himself, he had to concede that maybe, just maybe, he really was a little bit posh. And a bit of a clumsy twat.

"Did you get waylaid? You was only poppin' out for a bite to eat," Marion said, nodding at the clock, which read 11.05, indicating that she thought this was the "late" that Phil had said he wouldn't be. "That door normally gets double-locked at 10.30. You're lucky it was off the latch for Plumbus tonight. Did you have a good evening?" Marion enquired, throwing Phil a cheap kitchen roll, and standing attentively with her arms folded.

"Yes, a very good evening, Mrs. T. I bumped into someone I sort of know," said Phil, mopping at the spilt tea with a few sheets of kitchen roll.

"Was this someone a lady, by any chance?" Marion ventured.

Three Goats Heads

"Indeed, yes," Phil said, recalling Holly on the dance floor, holding a handful of soggy, tea-soaked paper towel (Phil was holding the soggy paper towel, not Holly on the dance floor).

"The most wonderful girl. So beautiful. Funny too … dry, you know, sarcastic. Amazing on the dance floor."

"Oh, you've been clubbing, then?" Marion said. She seemed to be giving Phil a bit of a grilling.

"Yep," Phil replied, with a big smile.

"Walking on the towpath too?" Marion continued in an accusatory tone.

"Yes, we were actually … "

"That'll explain the goose shit on your shoes then, will it? Traipsing it through my hallway and into my nice clean kitchen!"

"Oh, bollocks. Sorry, Mrs. T.," said Phil, looking down at his muddy shoes and the brown-and-white footprints leading from the front door. "That's most probably swan shit, actually."

"Makes no odds, really, does it? I'm no ornithologist, and shit is shit, love. Take 'em off before you go anywhere else."

Phil tore off more paper towel and started glancing round for cleaning supplies.

"S'alright. Don't fuss. I'll mop when you've had your tea. You're cleaning your own shoes, though. There's Dettol wipes by the sink for that."

After Phil had wiped his shoes, he washed his hands in the little hand-wash sink. It had a sign over it that read *Employees Must Wash Their Hands*, after which Plumbus had added *Weekly*.

Phil trod carefully back to the table to pick up his tea and then stood by the door. "How did Plumbus do at darts?"

"He's not back yet. I've got the best part of an hour, less the time for mopping bloody floors, before he'll come in wanting a cup of tea and a fish finger sarnie."

"Ooh, that sounds good," said Phil, sipping the last of his tea and carefully leaving the dregs.

"This is a bed and breakfast, not a bed and breakfast and midnight bloody feast, she said, taking his empty cup. "If you're that keen, you can have a fish finger sarnie for breakfast, but late-night snack provision is exclusively Mr. Thistle's preserve."

"Naturally, Marion, I was merely expressing my enthusiasm for the culinary delicacy, I wasn't actually cadging one. Not at all sure I could eat another thing today. But no, I'll stick to the full English in the morning if it's all the same. Good night, Mrs. T., I'll leave you with what's left of your peace and quiet to mop the floor. Sorry."

"Good night, Philip. Sweet dreams."

Phil trudged up the stairs carrying his clean shoes, shut his door, and sat on the bed. He was as elated, as elated as anyone could be, in spite of having been scolded for bringing wildfowl shit in on his shoes.

Phil thought he might need the car for dates with Holly this weekend. Taking the bus wouldn't be particularly romantic, so he pulled out his phone and checked his calendar for the coming few days. Finding no notes or entries about using the car, he smiled and started planning.

He tried to think through the trouble he was in now, related to the potential of dating Holly in this past timeline. It could mean trips back and forth frequently for dates. Phil knew he wouldn't be able to stay in this timeline for three months until he caught up with his own real time. His mind started to boggle, so he decided to play it by ear and see if Holly was interested in more than one date. He had all of the next day to think it through.

He got in bed, not wanting to sleep because he knew that no dream, not even a sweet one, could possibly rival the evening he'd had.

14.

PART-TIME ETHICS

05 NOVEMBER 2022, 10.57 A.M.

Phil walked out under the bright-red awning of the Jericho Café with a latte in each hand and sugar and coffee stirrers in his jacket pocket. He strolled as nonchalantly as he possibly could, considering that he was too excited and nervous for words. He knocked on the door, then stepped back and waited.

He knocked again, a bit louder, and waited some more.

He was just thinking about knocking again when the door opened slowly, and Honey stood peering out into the bright daylight, her eyes squinting and her hair all tousled and wild.

"Hi, Honey, how's your head?" said Phil, holding out a coffee.

"Aww, thanks. Just what I need," she said gratefully. "Don't call me that, though. Holly. My real name's Holly."

"Hi, Holly, how's your head? Sugar?" he said, holding a hand out with little packets of sugar.

"Don't call me 'Sugar.' 'Holly' will do," she said.

Phil opened his mouth to explain, and then worked out that the look on her face was a wry smile.

"Oh, funny! You do funny with a hangover? Impressive. You take sugar? I hope I'm not intruding. Am I intruding? Are you busy?"

"Oh, so many questions for this early in the day! What time is it, by the way?"

"Just gone 11 … a.m."

"I suppose you'd better come in before the coffees get cold."

Phil followed her down the narrow hallway past the stairs and into the little kitchen at the back of the house. Holly was wearing a slightly baggy T-shirt that was just tight enough to reveal the curve of her breasts. It was just short enough to show all of her legs, but just long enough that Phil had to assume that she was wearing panties to go with the bra she definitely was not wearing. Phil hadn't thought there could be an outfit sexier than the one she'd had on last night, but here he was being proven completely wrong.

Phil smelled potpourri—sandalwood and cinnamon, if he wasn't mistaken. The kitchen was neat and tidy, and everything was clean and white except for the shiny silver appliances, a bright pink SMEG toaster, and a carnation-pink SMEG kettle. Phil tried hard not to find the word *SMEG* funny, and failed. He could imagine Lister from Red Dwarf telling Kryten, in his Scouse accent, to *"Put the smeggin' kettle on."*

Holly sat at the kitchen table, and Phil sat opposite, placing the sugar on the table between them. He was trying not to glance at her breasts, nor to be tempted to try to read what was embroidered on her T-shirt, in case that looked like he was trying to look at her breasts. Instead, he settled for trying to gaze into her brown eyes, which was not all that easy when they were half shut and behind a curtain of hair.

Part-Time Ethics

Holly was busy tearing open little sugar packets, and she tipped the contents of three sugars into her coffee and stirred in silence. She took a big drink of latte and said, "I'll be busy working on my thesis today, but I'm free this evening."

"Sorry?" said Phil.

"You asked if I was busy. And no, you're not intruding."

"Oh, yes, I did ask," he said, laughing at the absurdly long gap since he had tried to be polite with the questions that were more or less redundant now that he had been invited in.

Holly took another sip of coffee and sighed, saying, "Ahhh, that's good."

"You want to get breakfast?" he asked, thinking back to the bacon, eggs, and black pudding he had eaten not much more than an hour earlier, and thinking that he could eat again.

"No, thanks. I couldn't eat a thing just yet. Coffee's great, though, thank you. You're sweet," she said, smiling, looking up at him through the fringe of ruffled hair.

Phil just smiled back at her, his heart floating like an untethered helium balloon.

Holly drew a deep breath and said, "OK, so … " and Phil's heart sank like a brick. It was the kind of *OK, so,* that prefaced the *You're a really nice guy, Phil, but …* chat.

"I told you I'm a master's student. Well, I also have a part-time job that pays the mortgage on this place, and I think if we're going to start doing coffee in the mornings, you should probably know about it."

Phil sipped his coffee, trying not to show the concern that had flitted across his mind. Maybe this wasn't that talk, but it was clear that it was serious and that she wanted to get it over with. <listeningmode>

Holly took a sip of her coffee. "I've had this chat a couple of times before, and it hasn't gone well, so I think it's only fair."

She looked down, seeming almost as apprehensive as Phil was feeling. Phil didn't breathe. He felt like his heart had stopped too, while waiting for what was coming.

"Well, I get paid by older gentlemen to spend time with them. Technically, I'm an escort," she began.

Phil's eyebrows raised involuntarily, and it took him a moment to get them under control. He nodded and hoped that his face looked interested rather than worried.

Holly continued. "My clients are three lonely old profs at Westgate. I entertain them and look sexy for them. They pay me for my time. It's only a few hours a week and leaves me plenty of time for my studies, and it more than pays the mortgage."

Phil was feeling flushed, and he could feel jealousy starting to rise. He could easily imagine an overpaid don parting with a couple of hundred quid a week for this beautiful girl's undivided attention. *Oh, sorry, not girl,* he apologized in his head for thinking something so un-PC, *woman, sorry.* But what kind of attention, exactly? What does *entertain* mean? Phil was pretty sure she wasn't doing card tricks or making balloon animals. He was desperate to ask for details, but he stopped himself. He needed to be patient and just listen. "That is quite an unusual part-time job."

Holly looked him in the eyes. "I mean, what are my other options? Wait on tables? Work at McDonald's? Sales assistant in Ann Summers? It'd be a lot of hours to make the £200 an hour I get from being an escort. It's not actually illegal, being paid for my time to entertain old men."

Holly looked down at her coffee cup. Phil felt the little bit of doubt she had, and it seemed as though she had paused, waiting for his judgement. With the information she had imparted percolating in his head, jealousy and judgement bubbled up as he made a desperate effort not to be a jealous, judgemental prick. But what *did* "entertain" mean, exactly? His mind was racing. What, precisely, was she prepared to do for these old men?

Neither of them spoke for a minute while Phil tried to be patient, picking at his thumbnail, trying not to fidget, and giving her time to think. His jealous curiosity got the better of him. "I'm kind of surprised your older gents are up to, ummm, you know, ummm … much."

"Well, actually, I don't know if they are. Maybe they would be, if they had a bit of help from a little blue friend. Never asked them. I suppose I should have been more explicit; it's nothing actually physically intimate. I wouldn't be the right girl for the job if they did want to get up to 'ummm, much,' as you so delicately put it. No, I dress nicely, or I dress sexy, depending on what they want. Well, you saw my outfit last night. But that's really as far as it goes. That's how come it's not illegal. I just keep them company and give them some eye candy. A bit of a thrill, you know? So …"

Phil could imagine the thrill; he had experienced it last night and again this morning. He was relieved that there was nothing physical to it, but after listening anxiously, he still felt possessive, like he wanted her all to himself. He wished he could be cool about it all, and he tried hard to conclude that it was OK. He waited in silence, expecting Holly to say something else. Phil had heard of GFE—the girlfriend experience—where a woman might be paid for sex, but also to act all sweet and loving like a girlfriend might. He thought maybe this was more like an old-married-couple experience—just sitting watching telly without the sex. He tried not to smile and failed. Phil had thought she was going say something else, but the longer the silence, the more Holly's "so" didn't seem to have been indicative of anything to follow, so ... with a faint smile already on his lips, he said, "You make it sound practically ethical," somewhat consoled by the fact that it all sounded innocent enough. Only *just* enough, but enough all the same.

She looked up at him, a little surprised. "I just thought you should know, so you can decide whether that's OK with you before anything gets serious."

As the haze of jealousy subsided, he realized that if she was sharing this with him, it meant she was thinking about properly dating, and considering the possibility of them maybe getting serious. Phil's mind was full with all of this new information, and he felt a swirl of emotion. He needed a minute for it to settle. In the meantime, however, he decided there should be no more awkward silence. "Have you been? Tomorrowland?" he asked, subtly indicating the word written on her T-shirt.

She looked surprised, apparently taken aback by the change of subject. "Umm, yes. I was there last year. Went with a friend."

"That's one of the biggest festivals. Belgium, right?" Phil thought this was a pretty cool topic to pursue.

"Yes," she said.

"How was it? I bet it was good."

"Oh, yes, so good. A whole weekend of the best dance music. Oh, God, we were so stoned. But it was better than drugs. You're just on a high for weeks after. The euphoria stays with you, you know?"

Phil didn't know. He'd always wished he wasn't too uptight to go to a festival, but they just weren't something he'd ever felt he could manage after reading about Glastonbury—the tents, the mud, the overflowing portable toilets. *Hell, no.*

"Very cool," he said, feeling encouraged by the thought that she might be serious about dating him, but trying not to let it show. He wanted to see if they were really going to be an item before he would worry about the future. If things were still going well on Monday, he would have to work out the timeline problem. "So," he said nonchalantly, "would you like to go out again tonight, maybe? It's Bonfire Night. We could go and see some fireworks, if you'd like." He opened Google on his phone.

The surprise on Holly's face had turned to relief. She sat back with her head up. She swept the hair from her eyes, looked at Phil, and smiled. "Yeah, that would be nice. Westgate is supposed to be putting on quite a show tonight," she added enthusiastically.

Phil had remembered that his other self would be at the Westgate fireworks tonight. And his mum. And most other people he knew in Oxford. He had to avoid that, not because of any bizarre time travel anomaly, but because bumping into himself in public would expose his secret. He glanced at his search results. "Erm, you know, I'm not sure about Westgate this year. I was thinking about the ones at South Park. They should be even better. It's a display put on by the national firework champions, apparently, and there'll be a funfair too."

"Oh, cool," she said. "I love a funfair. I've always gone to the Westgate ones before. Something bigger sounds great."

"Great! I'll pick you up at what? 6.45?" Phil asked.

"Sure. Right, it's a date."

"Will it be our first proper date?" Phil asked.

"No, second, I think. I'm going to count last night even if you thought I was Honey. I think it still counts. But not this morning, if that's OK. This didn't feel much like a date." Holly said.

"Cool." Phil stood to leave. He kissed her sweetly, not full on the lips, but not on the cheek either. It was the kind of in-between that was full of promise. The edges of their lips touched sensually, softly, lingering as though there could be more. Then he pulled away and smiled. "I'll leave you to get on. See you later."

Holly smiled back. "Thanks again for the coffee," she said, raising her paper cup with a half-hearted "Cheers."

Phil let himself out, leaving Holly to recover in peace.

Phil pulled up outside the house at 6.40 p.m., prepared to wait till 6.45 on the dot before knocking. He had planned to open the car door for her and be all chivalrous, but Holly emerged from her front door at 6.41, got in the car, and said, "Good evening, kind sir."

"Good evening, milady."

"Blimey," she said, putting on her seatbelt, "I could hear you coming a mile off. Does this thing not have a silencer?"

"It does. One that doesn't work very well, I suppose."

"Well, it comes in handy. Next time, I won't need to stand by the window looking out for you." She leant over and they kissed hello.

PART-TIME ETHICS

Phil blushed a little.

"South Park, sir, and don't spare the horses," Holly demanded. She glanced around. "Nice old car," she said. "How old is it?"

"It's a 1963, so it'll be sixty this year," Phil replied as he started the car. The old engine sputtered unevenly back to life. "It's the original four-cylinder, 1.7-litre engine, and all of about sixty horses, which I probably *will* spare for fear of losing a big end or the head gasket. But what she lacks in power, she makes up for in personality."

"Bit like me, then," Holly quipped.

They drove east, out of the city, toward Headington. Phil was distracted. He was a bit worried they might be spotted at the fireworks. Doc Brown, Phil's movie hero from *Back to the Future*, might have been right about not changing anything in the past, but Phil had already gone and started dating Holly. Their first date was supposed to be next January. How would this new timeline affect that?

Phil would need to think hard about how to handle the new timeline he was creating with Holly. It needed some careful planning. Of course, the relationship was kind of based on a lie. A lie by omission, but a pretty big omission. But how could he possibly come clean and explain the time travel thing? Phil had kind of fucked up.

The fireworks were fabulous and the funfair was fun. It was really busy, but they didn't bump into anyone Phil knew, who were probably all at Westgate. They had remained silent, apart from the *oohs* and *aahs*, during the actual fireworks display. Then they had laughed and giggled all the way round the funfair, eating candy floss and toffee apples, and trying in vain to win one of the big teddy bears or the huge gonk at the hook-a-duck stall and the air-rifle range. In the end, Holly won a large stuffed flamingo at the hoopla stall, which she put in the back seat of the car and buckled up its seat belt. It felt nice that they were being so silly and fun together with almost no alcohol at all. They'd only had one mulled wine each, and Phil was OK to drive.

"You want to come in for coffee or a cup of tea?" she asked as Phil switched off the engine.

"I'd love to. Tea, please."

"You can't park here, though. Double yellows," Holly said, pointing to the edge of the road.

"It'll be fine for a few minutes, surely, how often does a traffic warden come by on a Friday evening?" Phil said with a shrug.

They got into the house, giggling because the flamingo kept giving Phil kisses. They didn't drink tea. They sat on the sofa in the lounge, and in the time it took for the kettle to boil, they were kissing, as in properly kissing. Passionately. Intensely.

"Shall we go upstairs?" Holly asked gently. Phil nodded.

Holly led Phil by the hand up the stairs and into the bedroom. Holly turned to Phil and took off her jeans, peeled off her sweater, and stood before him in nothing but a pair of little white cotton panties. Phil followed suit, undressing while Holly leapt into bed and got under the covers.

"It's bloody freezing up here," she said, "Quick, come and warm me up!" Phil climbed in beside her and they embraced, kissing passionately again. Underwear was tossed onto the floor, and they began kissing, touching, and eagerly exploring each other.

PART-TIME ETHICS

Holly collapsed into a breathless, tender embrace with Phil. It had been little more than an hour, but it felt like almost no time had passed. They remained still, melded together in fading ecstasy. She was lying beside him, snuggled up to him in a soft and sensual embrace. No words were needed. They had had their very own fireworks. The best fireworks Phil had ever known. He was now absolutely certain he was in love. They drifted in the afterglow, drowsy, and sticky, and euphoric.

15.

BEGINNER'S LUCK

06 NOVEMBER 2022, 8.32 A.M.

Phil woke to the smell of coffee, and as he sat up in bed, Holly handed him a hot mug. "Good morning, sunshine," she said.

"Thank you," Phil said. Holly was wearing her T-shirt and panties outfit again, and Phil was getting hopeful that they might get to do a matinee rerun with bonus scenes. "Tell me I didn't dream it."

"If you did, I dreamt it too," she replied. She smiled at him apologetically. "I don't want to be rude, but I really do need to get to work on my thesis again today. Maybe we could have breakfast before you go?"

"Oh, sure, of course. I don't want to hold you up," he said as his hopeful bubble of lust popped.

"I had a wonderful time last night. The funfair, I mean. I love my flamingo!" she exclaimed, then she giggled.

"Me too. The funfair, obviously," he replied.

Holly threw the flamingo at him.

"Oh, no! Now I slopped coffee on the sheets!" Phil cried out.

"Don't worry, I think they need a good wash anyway," she said with a smile. Then she winked and said, "I really did have a wonderful time last night."

Phil grinned. "Satisfaction guaranteed!"

"Ha-ha," Holly said as she rolled her eyes at him. "Yeah, I was a light breeze away from that happening without you having to do anything! I'm sorry, but I'm going to need you to prove it wasn't just beginner's luck," she teased. "Tell you what, I'll go and put some toast on while you get dressed," she said. "You want strawberry jam or Marmite?"

"Oh, erm, Marmite, please," said Phil.

"Oh, thank God! I don't think I could be with someone who didn't love Marmite!"

When Phil came downstairs, Holly was sitting at the kitchen table with coffee in one hand and her phone in the other. "Looks like the nurses are going on strike," she said. "I bet someone could write a practical ethics paper on that."

"Yes, I'm sure they will strike. Doctors too, I reckon," Phil added, with the benefit of hindsight.

They ate Marmite on toast and drank a second coffee in relative quiet while Holly scrolled on her phone, and Phil played chess on his. Holly locked her phone and asked, "Did you get enough toast? You want more coffee?"

"Yes and no. I'm good, thanks," he said, feeling like that was a hint for him to bugger off. "I should be making a move and letting you get on with your work." Phil got up and put his jacket on. As he walked through to the front door, she reached up on tippy-toes, kissed him gently, and whispered, "Call me," as he turned away.

"I will," he said as she closed the door.

Phil stood by the driver's door of his car, peeled the parking ticket off his windscreen, got out his phone, and dialled. "Hi, it's Phil."

The door opened again. Holly had her phone to her ear. "Yes, can I help you?"

"You said to call you, and I'm calling!" he exclaimed.

"You dozy great knob-end," Holly said with a giggle.

"If you're free this evening, I think there's something I'd quite like to show you."

"A mystery outing? OK. I've got nothing on."

"Oh, God, don't make me imagine you with nothing on! I'm trying to leave!" he replied.

"Ha-ha, you randy little git."

"I'll see you right here," he said, pointing to the spot he was standing on, "at 5.00 sharp. Don't get in the wrong old grey Ford, or who knows where you'll end up."

"No danger of getting in the wrong car; I'll listen for your exhaust!" she said, hanging up and closing the door.

Phil parked the car in the garage on Trinity Street and walked to the B & B, arriving after breakfast had finished. After an impassioned appeal to the normally implacable Marion, he enjoyed a brunch time pitstop that involved a shower, a cup of tea, a bacon sandwich, and a good grilling over where he'd been the previous night.

Then he thanked Marion with a hug, and set off walking to his own flat, knowing it would be empty until about 5.30 p.m. because today was Sunday and this would be his contemporaneous self's day in Headington with his mum.

He let himself in and sat at the dining table. There was no robot to talk to. Not yet. It wouldn't be delivered until next week, after he'd got back from his training day in Wednesbury. The room felt oddly empty without the robot's passive presence, like a sullen metal emo, so he had to talk to himself. Today was a good day to take stock of where he was and what he was doing. But the robot was a better listener than he was, and Phil realized he was actually missing his bright-orange companion.

His mission in this previous November was to look into Durant's death, so he put Holly out of his mind as best he could. He pulled the Manila folder from his satchel and looked at the picture of Durant's cold grey hand with the Rutherford Atom pin badge stuck in his palm. Phil had agreed with Havarti that it was a pretty sure sign of a struggle. The pin badge couldn't have been Durant's. It wasn't his style to wear any kind of adornment. *The miserable shit never even wore a poppy for Remembrance Sunday,* thought Phil. Then he remembered the current date and made a mental note to buy a poppy for Remembrance Sunday.

He went over to the desk and woke up his Mac. Then he searched and found the Etsy store that was selling the exact same Rutherford Atom pin badge. According to Havarti, Georgia Cornwallis had been a customer, and yet Phil suspected it was more than likely she had died months ago, so she wasn't a very likely suspect. But it didn't seem as though it could be a coincidence. If she had purchased the pin badge that had ended up in Durant's hand, there had to be a link. But how would it have ended up in Durant's dead hand tomorrow? Phil had already imagined Umbrella Guy wearing the pin badge. That was his big hunch. Did Georgia Cornwallis know Umbrella Guy? Who *was* this Umbrella Guy?

After he'd made himself a mug of tea, he settled back down at the computer to look into Durant's life. Durant was a sad, lonely old piece of shit, and Phil came up with nothing new on him. Durant lived alone in his rooms at Westgate College. He had no social media presence, which came as no surprise to Phil, since Durant wasn't social. But he had a lot of media coverage on TV and in the news. Some of it could be found on YouTube, mostly posted by his rivals, and with a lot of scathing remarks in the comments section beneath. Many commenters questioned how Durant had mastered the SU(7) mathematics. Phil had wondered about that too.

Phil looked into Georgia Cornwallis. Beyond the news of her disappearance, there wasn't a whole huge lot to find. There were several scientific papers, and Phil skimmed the abstracts. She had an impressive publication record over the previous few years. Phil found her LinkedIn profile and began scrolling through her connections. Perhaps that list of 1,682 people would yield some leads, but based on the few he'd scrolled through, he was not hopeful. She had an Instagram account, but since high school ten years earlier, it was sparse and not very informative. According to her Instagram picture, she was pretty and had striking blue eyes. But there was no sign in any of her posts of a scorned ex who might wish her harm. Phil knew the stats: exes are most often the culprit when it comes to doing harm to women. He could see that she had travelled across the globe to conferences in places like England and Japan. Apart from having been in track and field at Princeton and writing some interesting papers on theoretical physics, she was quite unforthcoming on social media.

The internet was revealing nothing new or useful. He felt frustrated, and his mind turned back to the problem of dating Holly across the timelines.

He began trying to work out how he could sustain a relationship over the next couple of months until their relationship caught up with his own actual timeline. That would involve coming back in time to date Holly, perhaps once or twice a week. They could have dinner and a bottle of wine, see a film, take walks by the river, and maybe, ummm, more. He would have to concoct a story for why they couldn't text or talk in between dates. He could manage all that. *How hard could it be?*

Oh, wait, he thought, *his Mum!* Suddenly, it dawned on Phil that his mum would be the problem. Holly would have to be a secret from his mum for two months or more, otherwise his mum would ask questions of the wrong Phil, the other Phil, the one from this timeline. He knew that ordinarily, he would tell his mum about Holly straight away. Keeping Holly a secret would upset his mum when she found out. And maybe Holly would think it was odd not to be introduced to his mum for so long when he and his mum were so close.

So, he would have to keep Holly a secret and eventually upset his mum.

Oh, bollocks! he thought. *What if Holly bumps into the other Phil?* The Phil from Holly's timeline who had not met Holly yet. He would be clueless as to why she was so friendly, and worse still, she would be upset that he would act like he didn't know her. That scenario didn't seem all that likely, but not impossible, and far too problematic to leave to chance. That would be a problem too.

He considered the possibility that he might tell his mum about Holly, and enlist the Phil from this timeline to help. That would solve two problems, and he would only be deceiving Holly by neglecting to tell her about his time travel and the timeline problem. But he didn't feel that that was a particularly brilliant idea, and he didn't want to start their relationship on a lie. Well, any more of a lie than it already was.

How could he even consider involving his other self in the deception, anyway, in case that Phil ended up texting with Holly. Maybe they would meet up. What if the other Phil from this timeline started sleeping with Holly too? She would be impossible to resist, and why would he? It wouldn't exactly be cheating. He wondered if it was possible to be jealous of himself. It took Phil a split second to realize that the answer was yes. He decided that would surely be too complicated, and thought he should think that through better before trying to involve other Phil in deceiving Holly.

Phil hadn't come here, to November, to date Holly. And yet he had. Holly had been honest about being an escort. He wondered if he should reciprocate by telling her about how he had messed up their timelines. But he realized that if he just came clean with Holly about the time travel, she would think he was a nutter. She surely wouldn't believe him, and he would have to prove it. He would need to do something ingenious, and it would have to be something personal. He would need to do something really clever to prove that he could, but he had no idea what yet.

Phil realized, for sure, that it was actually going to be really hard. This was all too much, even for Phil's intellect, to fathom. He was going round in ever-decreasing circles in his mind, like drowning in a whirlpool of all the possible problems, those of his own making. He was baffled, and he was frustrated, and the feeling of impending panic made thinking feel like wading through treacle. It dawned on Phil that he had not been thinking with his head when he got involved with Holly in this timeline. He realized that he should have just smiled and left the pub when he first saw her. He concluded that there was no logical solution to the situation, and that he was basically buggered.

He needed to keep things simple and focus on the facts. He was waiting for Durant's death-day, which was tomorrow. He had bumped into Holly when he'd arrived on Friday, and he'd spent last night with all the fireworks. He would see Holly again tonight, and then tomorrow he would go to Westgate College in search of clues for Havarti.

He didn't have long to come up with a plan for dating Holly.

It all seemed like too much for him, and his head hurt. He put the kettle on. He went to the bathroom and took some ibuprofen. He hadn't had a lot of sleep lately, so when he sat on the sofa with a nice hot mug of fresh tea and took a few sips, trying to relax and calm his mind, his eyes began to get heavy.

Phil woke with a start as cold tea poured into his lap. "Crap!" he exclaimed as he jumped up with an empty mug in his hand. He put the mug in the kitchen and took off his jeans and underpants. He threw the wet clothes into the washer-dryer and checked his watch. It was 3.30 p.m. He had an hour before he needed to leave. He set the machine on the quickest wash and dry cycle.

He found a clean pair of undies to put on and had a rummage at the bottom of his chest of drawers for a couple more T-shirts that his other self wouldn't notice missing. He found an old Foo Fighters T-shirt and a nerdy pink one. He had already worn the T-shirts he had brought in his go-bag, and he definitely didn't want Holly to see the same one twice.

Phil deleted his search history from the Mac. No point leaving traces behind for his earlier self to be curious about. He got his clothes out of the dryer and dressed again. He washed the mug and tidied up any evidence that he'd been at his own flat.

Phil decided it was time to leave to get to Holly's on time, and so that he didn't risk meeting himself. Not because meeting himself would create some kind of universe-ending paradox, or anything like that; he just couldn't face answering his own inane questions, like *What are you doing here?* and risk ending up being late for Holly. He put the last few things in his bag, put on his shoes and jacket, walked out the door and locked it behind him, and then set off to Jericho to pick up Holly.

He hadn't decided yet whether he could tell Holly about the timeline problem he had created. He wanted to come clean, but he didn't want Holly to think he was a raving bloody lunatic.

16.
IN A MANOR OF SPEAKING

06 NOVEMBER 2022, 4.59 P.M.

Phil pulled up in the car with a full tank of petrol. He quickly jumped out of the car with a bunch of petrol station flowers in his hand. He trotted round to the passenger side as Holly came out of the house. She was wearing a very cute short summer dress with ankle socks and white trainers. She wore the little denim jacket that Phil had seen a couple of days earlier. He thought she looked very girl-next-door, and so sweet and innocent, which was a real contrast to Honey, or the sexy woman she had been last night. *Different clothes, different person,* he thought. *It's like this is who she wants to be today.*

Phil opened the car door for her. "Thank you kindly, sir," she said, accepting the flowers.

He got back in the car. He was mesmerized by his confusion about which version was the real Holly. Phil looked down at her legs momentarily and took in the flawless pale skin of her soft thighs. He thought that she really was very beautiful. He started the car.

"You look nice," he said.

"Nice, eh? Such fulsome flattery could go to a girl's head!"

"Well, I guess you'll do," he said as he put the car in reverse with a gentle crunch and let the clutch out.

"You don't look too bad yourself, matey," Holly said, making a show of taking a long, deep smell of the flowers. "Mmmm, end-of-the-day, BP-garage chrysanthemums. Lovely! My favourite. But how did you know?" She snapped off the flower that was dangling by a broken stem and slid it into her hair.

They headed out of town and onto the A44 signposted toward Much Fussing, Dimley Swithering, and Chipping-on-the-Green. Phil put his foot down and really opened the old girl up, and eventually, they hit 45 mph, with traffic streaming by in the outside lane.

"I should tell you," Holly said, "Freesias are actually my favourite flowers. For next time, you know. In case you thought the petrol station offerings really were my fave."

Phil laughed. "Freesias. OK. Noted."

"Where are we off to?" Holly asked.

"A bit of a trip down memory lane," Phil replied.

"Okaaay. Very mysterious," she said.

"It's nothing too fascinating. Don't get too excited. It's just where I grew up."

"Oh, OK," she said, "Well, that should be interesting, at least."

Phil drove on, up the dual carriageway, thinking that at least her expectations wouldn't be too high, and that she wouldn't expect a magical mystery tour of anything hugely entertaining.

"I was never much of a one for the sciences in school," Holly said, breaking the comfortable silence. "Physics went over my head a bit. I got a B, but I don't remember any of it now."

"It's not everyone's cup of tea," Phil said.

In a Manor of Speaking

"But in my philosophy undergrad, we did talk about Aristotle in a seminar one time, and how he said that the past is gone so it no longer exists, and the future hasn't happened yet so it doesn't exist yet either. He said that the present is the unity between being and non-being."

"Oh, yes, I think he's credited with laying the foundation for modern thinking about time." Phil was really excited that there seemed to be an overlap between their disparate fields of study. "Yesterday is history, tomorrow is a mystery. Now is a gift, and that's why they call it the present," Phil said, trying to quote the line from *Kung Fu Panda*.

"Are you a fan of kids' cartoons and aphorisms? Maybe you should get a job writing greetings cards," Holly said, chuckling. "Well, I think Aristotle was saying that existence is the very, very small instant of time that exists between the past and the future," she said, getting animated. "I thought that was a fascinating seminar, and we really got into a whole lot of existential metaphysics."

"I hadn't thought about it like that. That's amazing. I guess Aristotle was postulating Planck time," Phil said.

"What's plank time?" she asked, genuinely curious.

"It's a measure of a quantum of time. It's the smallest sliver of time that makes any sense. It's the time it takes light to travel the smallest distance we can accurately theorize."

"Well, that does sound like the tiny slice of time that makes up the reality that Aristotle was talking about," she said.

"I think you might be right. It's a very, very small bit of time." Phil thought of a fact that he figured would be sure to impress. "There are more Planck times in a single second than there are stars in the entire universe."

"What? Really? Pfff," said Holly. "Fancy that, an Ancient Greek philosopher predicting all that. How cool would it be to go back in time and explain to Aristotle that he was right. That would be something."

"Wouldn't it? Speaking of philosophy … " Phil said, "how did your day go, editing your thesis?"

Holly said she had been working on her conclusion. She said it had gone OK, and she was getting there with it. And then she carried on talking as Phil stared at the road ahead, soaking in every word she was saying. <listeningmode>

She talked about the difficulties of drawing a conclusion about whether it was possible to have a moral society when people didn't believe in God anymore. She said she has a chapter on the human psyche, integrity, and Freud's superego, and how the development of integrity and the superego was not something that just happened. It had to be taught, she explained, and it had to be instilled. Phil nodded in agreement. Phil was a big fan of people having integrity and a superego, and he shared her concern that it was not something that happened by itself.

"Yes, it's hard to see what incentive there is to be good if you don't believe in God looking over your shoulder," Phil said, and he wondered what made him try to be good, and then he wondered if he really was good. Phil didn't believe in God. Not an omniscient one, anyway. So why did he think it was important to be good? Phil thought about his mum.

Then Phil listened in again as Holly talked at length about how human beings are inherently greedy and selfish as a species, though not necessarily as individuals, and that for everyone to be a good person, we require something more than trust and more than laws. "You see, laws don't help if you don't get caught. It requires a collective sense of doing right. If people think they will get away with something unethical, they most likely will do it if they believe they won't get caught."

Phil thought of Durant and his plagiarism, which cheated people of their renown or even their livelihood. "You're not wrong there. People can be pretty crappy."

Holly continued, "And it's a vicious cycle with each passing generation, as more people don't do the right thing, more people refuse to be at a disadvantage. It becomes more normalized to do the wrong thing, and the cycle spirals."

Phil thought of Georgia Cornwallis, and the likelihood that she was in a shallow grave somewhere. "There's a lot of evil in the world." He thought of the word *dystopian,* and then *nightmare.* But he wasn't sure what else to contribute, so he switched back to <listeningmode>.

"What will instil integrity or a superego? What will cause people to do the right thing when nobody is looking, if they don't believe in a God who sees everything they do and will judge them for it one day? It's one thing to argue for theological pluralism with a moral unity, but it doesn't matter which version of God you don't believe in, and none of that helps when nobody believes anymore."

She was thoughtful for a moment, and then her tone changed. "For me, it's my dad. If I think about what he would say, or what he would do, or if he would be disappointed in me, then I know what the right thing is."

Phil wondered if her dad knew she was an escort, but decided not to ask.

Phil responded, "For me, it's my mum. She's the voice I hear when I think about what's right. Mum is just so level-headed, and she always does what's right. Never known my mum to even have to think about it. She'd hand over a twenty-pound note if she found one."

"Not sure my dad would do that!" Holly exclaimed. "Bloody sure I'd keep it too. I'd be too sure whoever I'd handed it over to would just keep it, and it would never find its rightful owner again. But I think that's my point. You do a small thing, like pocket a twenty-pound note, and it's just the thin end of the same wedge. But in the end, ethics have to be practical."

Phil thought of the time he and a friend had superglued a two-pound coin to the flagstone floor outside Westgate College and laughed at all the passers-by trying to pick it up.

Holly continued with her thesis and explained that she was coming to the conclusion that people wouldn't naturally have high moral standards, or choose the right thing, unless it was powerfully instilled in them.

"Without a God to believe in, people—most people—will choose selfish acts, fuelled by their greed or entitlement. Maybe just laziness because the right thing is harder. Or perhaps it is driven by necessity, by their needs. I could find an excuse for necessity, but if you make an excuse for that, surely then you have to draw a line somewhere between a degree of wrongness, and the magnitude of the need that drove it. And that is too complicated, like our judicial system, which shifts and changes with public opinion. And, like I said, the law relies on people getting caught, you know? The idea that God would catch you every time makes it kind of foolproof. How do we replace that?"

In a Manor of Speaking

Phil blushed at her unwitting judgement of his current situation. His heart, along with another part of his anatomy, had ruled his head. He was acutely aware that he had not chosen well. He had been selfish and not thought about what was really the right thing to do. He turned right onto a smaller road in the direction of Bunbury and Lymp-in-Baddeley.

"I'm an atheist," Phil said. "I don't want to derail your point, but it has to be possible to be good without believing in God. I like to think I would usually do the right thing."

"Well, it is. Weren't you listening to the bit about instilling a superego?" she retorted.

"Yeah, just saying, it doesn't have to be done through the fear of God," said Phil. "The idea that you can only have morals if you're religious pisses me off a bit; just as much as people that claim that science proves God doesn't exist."

"Well, yes, but that's not what I'm actually saying," Holly said, getting agitated. "So, what do you think science proves, then?"

"Sometimes, when you learn mind-boggling stuff about how life works and what makes the universe tick, it's hard to not believe in some sort of intelligent design," Phil said. "I think that if there is a God, all science does is show us how He did it."

"Or She," Holly muttered.

"Sorry, just conforming to the biblical pronoun. Bloody patriarchy, eh?" Phil said, with a little smile. "I'd probably go with 'It' if God had non-biblical pronouns."

Phil wondered what had made him never want to let himself down. Sure, he thought, he wouldn't want to disappoint his mum, but more than that, he wanted to live knowing that he would do, or had done, the right thing. Maybe that was his mum's doing too.

"Anyway," Holly continued, "when social media makes everyone jealous, and everyone has FOMO, and greed is too powerful a driver, how is this horribly polarized world ever going to right itself? Where is anyone's incentive to have a high moral standard and to instil that in their children if they feel that everyone else is doing it differently? Moral standards put you at a disadvantage, so why bother? It's not right, Phil. It's not going to work. Humanity's moral crisis is a way bigger fucking predicament than global warming. Who gives a shit how warm the oceans are if it's going to be a world not worth saving?"

Holly was passionate and emotional, and Phil just loved how much she seemed to care. Holly sighed heavily.

They slowed down from 40 mph as they passed the 30 mph sign and the *Welcome to Wychwood Norton, Please Drive Carefully* sign. They drove slowly through the village, and Phil was thanked for driving carefully by another sign as they left the village. The sign thanked everyone for driving carefully, whether they had or had not.

Phil sensed that Holly was a little despondent. "Well, I definitely hadn't thought of it like that. I wish it was different too. You've convinced me it's a crisis. I'm still going to recycle, though."

"I really wanted to conclude, you know, in some idealistic, hopeful, and humanitarian way, and say that people are inherently capable of being nice to each other. I think deep down I always knew that my ideals weren't going to be exactly supported by my research, but I did want my conclusion to have leant that way. Or at least not rule it out altogether."

In a Manor of Speaking

"I'm sorry about that. It sounds like a lot of work went into it."

"Fifty thousand words, just to conclude that people are, on the whole, a complete bunch of shits."

"Damn, that's bleak, girl!" was what Phil came up with, delivered in a sort of American accent, trying to lighten the air of despondency that hung in the car.

She laughed, realizing that she had been on a bit of a rant.

"Lordy Lord of the Flies! We're all going to crash and burn in a dystopian nightmare," he added, encouraged by her laughter.

"Yes, we are. And you'll be first if you keep up that kind of insolence, you cheeky bugger."

"You really care, though," he added, glancing over. Their eyes met, and he smiled quickly before looking back at the road and indicating to turn left. "You're really impressive. And very sexy when you're passionate."

"Sexy when I'm passionate? You patronizing pillock. I know you meant it as a compliment, but still, come on. And let me tell you something, I'm just as sexy when I'm completely apathetic."

Phil laughed, conceding the point.

Holly looked out of her side window. They were driving up a long, narrow driveway that wound gently through spotlit trees, with lawns laid to each side. "Where are we?" Holly asked.

"Nearly there," said Phil. "Though, now we're here, I'm starting to think this is a bit stupid. It seemed like a good idea this morning."

"Oh, no, Phil, it's not stupid. I'm quite interested to see where you grew up." Then a golden dome came into view through the trees ahead of them. It was lit by spotlights that shone brightly in the gloom, and the last of the pale, indigo daylight was fading in the sky beyond. A stately mansion came into view. "Is this it? Holy crap!"

They turned onto the courtyard outside the mansion. A large, ostentatious sign read *Welcome to Lydington Manor. Golf Resort and Spa.*

"Are we getting mani-pedis or something?" asked Holly.

"No, sorry. We're not actually going in. I just thought I would show you the house. It's not really much of a secret, so I thought you might as well come and see it with me. It's not something I ever really talk about. For some reason, I just wanted to show you. This was home till I was twelve or so, and Mum moved us to Headington when my parents separated."

They got out of the car and stared up at Lydington Manor. Phil's head was full of memories, some happy and some that made him angry. It brought back a welter of emotions from delight to fear.

"Oh, wow, Phil, this is amazing. So beautiful. And *big*. How many rooms are there?"

"A lot. All very grand. It was built in 1724, and the gardens were designed by Capability Brown in 1748," Phil said, like a tour guide gesturing to the spotlit avenue of trees that stretched for half a mile across the field behind them.

"Wow. Just wow."

"So, yeah, this is where my father lives. When my parents divorced, my father was already seeing Isabella," Phil explained. "She moved in the day after me and Mum moved out. After the divorce, my father was forced to convert the ancient family home into this golf resort and spa. He had to renovate the whole place, and according to the pictures on their website, it is fabulous. Much nicer than when I was a kid. Big investment, I think. They live in the east wing, and the west wing is a very exclusive boutique hotel. On the website, they call them guest suites, but that's where the rich and famous stay. My old bedroom is what some Saudi prince probably uses as a dressing room now. Probably cleaned out my father's bank account to make this place what it is now, but he would have had to sell it if it didn't start earning its keep."

"So, will you inherit this place, then?" asked Holly.

"God, no!" Phil said with an ironic laugh, "I'm completely estranged from my father. No chance he'd leave me a penny. Though I suppose when the old man croaks, I ought to become the new Lord Lydington, but that's not really worth anything."

"But still, Lord Lydington. Very grand," Holly said.

"Mum got money in the divorce. That's all we'll ever get from the miserable old skinflint. It took some doing to get him to pay Mum what she was really due. That's a big part of why I wanted you to see this; it's one of the biggest reasons why I do what I do. You know, divorce cases."

Phil looked at Holly. She looked at Phil and said, "Yeah, it makes sense now. I get it. The divorce case thing sounds a lot more worthwhile when you put it like that."

Phil smiled, happy that he had brought Holly. "No, I'm not welcome here. That's why we're not going in. I haven't been back since my sixteenth birthday."

"Oh, Phil, I'm so sorry. That's sad."

"Sad that I won't inherit it, or sad that I'm not welcome, or sad that my father is a total dick and doesn't deserve me as a son?"

"Well, when you put it like that, I suppose the latter. I'm sorry your dad's a dick."

They stood looking at the elegant, spotlit facade of the Cotswold stone manor house, with its grandiose portico and gold-domed hallway. Phil just let Holly take in the spectacle for a few moments more.

Behind her was the elegant fountain with its marble-walled pool and underwater floodlights shining up to the central sculpture of winged angels. "Wow, that's beautiful," she said.

"I used to get a right bollocking for jumping in there on a hot day."

"I can't even comprehend what it might be like to be a kid in such a palatial and majestic setting, with a dick for a dad."

"You've seen enough?" asked Phil.

"I guess so. I'd love to see inside sometime."

"Maybe I'll book you a spa weekend."

They got back in the car, and Phil felt relieved to be driving away. "I helped Mum in the divorce by uncovering my father's assets. He had hidden his money in Bermuda and pretended to be bankrupt. It happens a lot in high-end divorces. That's how come I'm a bit of an expert at it."

"Oh, that makes a lot of sense. Clever of you to find his stash in Bermuda," Holly said. "Wait. What? You found where your dad hid his money when you were thirteen? Smart kid."

"There's a bit more to it than that. It wasn't actually when I was a kid. It's complicated and really hard to explain, so I think that can be a story for another time. And I had help. I'll tell you about the Detective Collective sometime too."

"I'm intrigued," Holly said. "So your mum didn't get her share for a while after the divorce? What did you do?"

"When they separated, me and Mum went to live in Headington. She got a house there, and enough money that we could survive, but she worked to keep me at my private school. That Christmas was the best Christmas I can remember as a kid. The freedom was the most glorious relief for us both. We stayed at home and watched films on the telly and ate whatever we wanted. *The Wizard of Oz* and cold turkey sarnies for tea, and I was in heaven. For my birthday the next January, Mum bought me my Polaroid camera. She got it second-hand. It was twenty-five years old, but it was in perfect condition, still in the box." Phil indicated the folded camera in its slim case on the back seat behind him.

"It doesn't look like a Polaroid to me. I thought they were kind of boxy and plastic."

"This one is older than those ones from the 1980s. This one is a bit special, I think. I really will have to tell you about it sometime. So, what about your parents?" Phil asked, changing the subject.

"My mum and dad are still together. They still live in the same semi where I grew up in Sevenoaks. I'm a bit of a daddy's girl. My dad's a real softy, which is sort of surprising for a Scot. You kind of expect Scots to be a bit gruff. Perhaps it's just the accent. He's from Edinburgh. It's too sad to think about not having my dad in my life."

"That's nice. Are they happy, your mum and dad?" Phil asked.

"I really think they are," she said. "They had a second honeymoon after I went off to college. My mum's lovely too. They make such a sweet couple. I guess that's what I want someday." She paused and then added, "You know, when I grow up."

Phil chuckled and focussed on the road ahead. The journey back to Oxford was spent in a comfortable silence. Holly watched the countryside passing through her passenger window. Phil was filled with hope that he might be the guy who would make a sweet couple with Holly.

When they parked in Trinity Street, Phil said, "Come on, let's go and get a drink."

They had a drink at the Three Goats Heads, and, seeing him with Holly again, Jim was much more kindly disposed to Phil. Then Phil drove to Holly's house and parked outside her door.

"I don't want you getting sick of me, but I'm not going to be around much over the next couple of weeks. So I wondered if there's any chance I can see you tomorrow? I'm going to be busy in the afternoon, but maybe I could call for you later and see if you fancy doing something?" Phil asked.

"I'm busy too, tomorrow. But, yes, I'm free in the evening. Come over at 6.00 and maybe I'll make dinner or we can order pizza, and maybe you can tell me more about your detective thing?"

"OK, that sounds perfect," said Phil.

They kissed, slowly, softly, gently. A goodbye kiss that wasn't leading anywhere, and not getting either of them worked up. Just a lovely, sweet, memorable way to part. "Good night, handsome. And thanks for the flowers," she whispered.

Holly winked at him, then she got out of the car. Phil watched as she let herself into the house, and he sighed.

Phil's mind was already churning with how he could explain the whole time travel thing to Holly. Should he do that tomorrow? Explain how he had fixed his mum's divorce, and how he was dating her three months early in the wrong timeline?

Phil decided to focus first on going to Westgate tomorrow to investigate Durant's death. He put the car in reverse and backed out of the narrow street.

17.

UMBRELLA GUY

07 NOVEMBER 2022, 8.28 A.M.

Phil had some time to kill. He had hoped to sleep in and at least get through the morning unconscious, but he had woken early with a knot in his stomach. He thought about the day ahead. He knew Umbrella Guy would be on the college grounds shortly after two this afternoon, and that Durant would be dead by 3.00. The autopsy concluded that he had sustained injuries from the fall that caused his death, including a crushed skull, a broken neck, and a broken rib that had punctured his aorta. Any one of those would have killed him.

Phil realized how long he had to wait and how slowly the time was passing. When something good happens, time goes by in a flash. And time goes by so slowly while waiting for something. This morning, time was dragging its heels, and it was being particularly stroppy. Phil was on edge.

He got up, had a leisurely breakfast at the B & B, and watched the clock. He remembered to make notes in the calendar on his phone for when he had used the car the previous day. He rarely used the car because he walked or travelled by bus around town. He often caught the train to go places, like when he visited Wednesbury, which was exactly what his other self was doing today. But he knew there might come a day when he'd need to know if the car would be unavailable, so he kept meticulous notes, or at least he tried to.

Phil went for a walk around a drizzly, cold Oxford. He took one of Mrs. T.'s brollies with him; she kept them in a stand by the door for the guests. Phil got a takeaway coffee and wandered down past the castle.

He saw the British Legion lady out in the rain with her plastic mac and her tray of poppies. He put a £2 coin in her plastic *Please Give Generously* receptacle, and because he had his hands full with coffee and a brolly, the British Legion lady pinned a poppy on his lapel for him. Phil thanked her kindly and set off wandering aimlessly and checking his watch periodically. Eventually, the time for fretting came to an end. He set off, heading for Westgate College.

The frontage and main entrance of the college faced north onto Paradise Street. Greyfriars Tower housed the main gates and the Porters' Lodge. This was the bustling heart of the college. The passageway through the tower into the front quad was observed by CCTV cameras and patrolled keenly by the porters. The porters were tasked with serving the needs of the students, stopping them from picnicking on the quad lawn, and to keep the tourists out.

As he approached the main entrance to the college, Phil had to push his way past a gaggle of indecisive tourists. He walked in through the main gate at a couple of minutes past the hour and stood under the CCTV cameras opposite the Porters' Lodge. From his vantage point in the passageway through Greyfriars Tower, he could see, as could the cameras, from the archway onto front quad on his left to the big wooden gate out onto Paradise Street on his right.

UMBRELLA GUY

He headed into front quad. He turned left and walked around to the far side of the quad and stood in the shelter of the doorway to Staircase C and folded his brolly. There was no sign of Umbrella Guy in the college yet. The CCTV image must be of him entering the college via the main entrance. Phil felt instinctively that this was a moment he might need again, so he popped open his Polaroid camera and took a picture across the quad back towards the Greyfriars Tower. He wrote *Staircase C. 07 Nov 2022. 2.05 p.m.* across the bottom of the photo.

He opened the umbrella again and headed back towards the main gate, ready to get a first glimpse of Umbrella Guy. Phil's purpose was to find clues to Durant's death. With camera at the ready, he could snap a photo like a tourist, and give Havarti something for facial recognition to work on. He wanted to know what had happened to Durant, but he didn't want to be in Staircase E when it happened. He thought being at the main gate in full view of the CCTV was a good bet for not ending up being implicated. He wanted to spot Umbrella Guy and find clues for Havarti. That was all. Simple.

Phil turned to walk around the corner from the quad back into the passageway, and … *Bam!* Umbrellas clashed, and he collided with a young man hurrying quickly around the corner. Phil's brolly flew out of his hand and fell to the floor as he put out his hands to stop the guy from falling. Or maybe it was to steady himself, he couldn't really tell which. The young man dropped his brolly too, and sheets of paper flew from his hand and scattered across the flagstones.

"Sorry," said Phil. "Oh, shit!" he exclaimed, not actually meaning to, as he realized this was Umbrella Guy.

"No, it is I who should apologise. I was not looking. I was very far from here in my mind. I was in a hurry. I am sorry."

Phil looked at the guy properly and saw a young Japanese man. His dark hair was straight and neat. He wore a brown jacket, a white shirt, camel-coloured jeans, and white Skechers. His big, black umbrella was upside down on the floor next to Phil's red one. And pinned to his lapel was a Rutherford Atom pin badge.

"Let me help you," Phil said, starting to gather the dozen or so sheets of paper that had spilt out of the Manila folder and had spread themselves across the wet courtyard pathway.

The two of them were crouching, reaching out for sheets of manuscript before they became too wet on the soaking flagstones. But the black inkjet ink was already spreading across the pages, turning them purple, and they were getting quickly soggy and buckled.

"Thank you. I am Akito. Akito Takaya." As they stood, Akito reached out his hand and Phil shook it. "I am pleased to meet you," Akito said. Phil felt Akito's cold, wet hand trembling. Akito was clearly agitated and looking around for something other than the fallen papers.

"I'm Phil," he said. "Likewise, pleased to meet you, I think."

Akito held out his hand for the pages that Phil had collected. Phil looked down at one sheet of paper in his hand and noticed it was the cover page to the document. It didn't have much writing on it, and his eye was immediately drawn to the names: "S. G. Cornwallis, PhD, and A. Takaya, PhD."

Cornwallis, Phil thought, *Georgia Cornwallis! Joint author on a paper with Umbrella Guy, the pin badge from Etsy, Georgia's purchase, on Akito's lapel.* The clues all fitted. Phil's hunch was right! But what was Durant's connection to Akito and Georgia? What was the link to her disappearance? And why was Akito Takaya about to murder Durant?

Phil stood, just staring at the piece of paper. *Let There Be Time!* was written in bigger type with the subheading *Chronons and How Gravity Can Be Explained by Quantum Time*. Phil recognized the subtitle straight away. This was the exact title of Durant's last big paper!

Georgia Cornwallis went missing after seeing Durant in his rooms, and this was the paper that Durant had published in his own name. Things were adding up fast. Phil was making connections, and he was convinced there were more links that he needed to understand. This young man would have at least some of the answers.

"What's this?" Phil said, knowing full well it was a stupid bloody question, but one that would stall things long enough to allow his brain to formulate a better one.

"It is a scientific paper by me and my colleague and friend, Georgia Cornwallis. Please," Akito said, quickly grabbing the pages from Phil's hand. "I must go, sorry."

Akito grabbed his umbrella and headed out into the quad, looking for Staircase F.

Phil wanted to know why Akito was here and what he had to do with Durant and his death. There were many questions crystallizing in Phil's mind, but asking any one of them might affect what was supposed to be happening in the next few minutes. Phil was full of doubt about changing the past any more than he already had. If he changed nothing, would that be ethical? But if he prevented Durant's death, the risks were incalculable. Phil was in turmoil. He realized that this was why he shouldn't meddle in things that matter more than a divorce settlement. Life and death! He couldn't do it. He couldn't let Akito become Durant's killer. Now that he was here, the right thing seemed all too clear.

"Wait!" Phil heard himself say. Akito turned to face him, his face filled with angst. "What are you doing here?" Phil added, resigning himself to the impulse to try to mend what he knew would soon be terribly broken.

Akito turned, staring back at Phil, then looking toward Durant's staircase entrance. He took a couple of steps toward Phil. "I am here to see Professor Durant." Akito half-turned back towards the quad and took a step away from Phil.

Phil couldn't let him go. He couldn't let him do it. "You want to ask Durant about Georgia Cornwallis. About her disappearance, right?"

"What? Yes, how do you know that?" Akito was rooted to the spot. His shoulders dropped, and he stared at Phil.

"I saw her name on your paper. Isn't that the same article that Durant published last September? I want to ask him about Georgia Cornwallis too." Phil said, hoping to keep him from walking away. "Do you think challenging Durant all angry like this is a good idea?"

"I cannot find any peace until I do. I need answers. I want recognition for my friend, Georgia-san. She is gone, and this is her legacy. He stole our work, and I can prove it."

"That all sounds very familiar. It's not the first time he's stolen other people's work," Phil said, taking a step toward the young man. "Akito, I want answers about Georgia too. I'm actually a detective investigating her disappearance. Will you help me first by telling me what you know? Will you help me build a case against Durant?"

"A detective? Very well," Akito said, stepping forward. He spoke quietly. "I have waited some months to be able to come here. I can wait a short while longer to speak to Professor Durant. I am willing to help the police to find the truth about Georgia-san, if I can." Akito hung his head. He looked up at Phil with sorrow in his eyes. "It is my fault. I was the one who persuaded Georgia-san to ask Durant to be third author on the paper."

Phil couldn't help but hear Akito's pain. "And she agreed to that?" Phil asked.

"Georgia-san was going to see him at the end of the conference in March to ask him to publish with us. With his fame, our theory would surely have been published by a leading journal and propelled to the forefront, rather than languish for a decade in an obscure journal. It's my fault he stole our paper."

"Would you tell me what you know about that conference and the visit Georgia paid to Durant on the day she went missing?"

"I will tell you what I can."

"Let's go somewhere dry and get something to drink. I could use one."

Phil and Akito walked out of the college and over to the Slug and Lettuce by the castle. Surely, now, Phil had changed what was going to happen today. He knew it was the right thing to do. He knew it would have consequences, and he would have to find out what they were. The responsibility sat heavy on his shoulders.

Durant's time of death was between 2.00 and 3.00 p.m. Phil checked his watch. It was quarter past two. Forty-five more minutes, and Phil would be sure to have saved this young man from doing something he would always regret, or at least never be able to forget. Phil felt some relief on Akito's behalf. He was trying very hard to justify changing this event. He thought it was for the best—for Akito and Durant, at least.

They walked into the warmth of the pub, and Phil got a chill, like someone had walked over his grave; he felt that something was different somehow. Phil checked his watch. Just gone twenty past.

"What would you like to drink?" Phil asked Akito.

"I like the sound of Fentiman's Dandelion and Burdock. I have no idea what it is, but I like the sound of the words." Phil assured Akito that it was a very British drink. Phil got a large Lagavulin and paid. They sat on armchairs, out of the way, where it was quiet.

"Your pin badge. I like it; it's very cool," said Phil.

"I wear it always. It was a gift from Georgia-san. She sent it for my birthday during Covid. We were working together, but we could not visit anymore."

"OK, so tell me. How come Georgia knew Durant?"

"She didn't know him. She knew *of* him. We both did. His papers on quantum probability and antimatter helped Georgia come up with the idea for quantum time. She saw through the public opinion and the ridicule of his work. She saw the grains of truth hidden there, and she had an idea, and I helped her with the difficult equations." Akito took a deep breath. "It is a long story."

"I have all day. Please, carry on."

"In 2019, I went to a conference at Stanford. Georgia's university … "

18.
PARTNERS IN TIME

24 OCTOBER 2019

Akito Takaya arrived at Stanford by taxi from San Francisco International Airport. He was met by his appointed buddy. The postdocs had a tradition of welcoming students from abroad, showing them around, and shepherding them to their room and to the conference venue. Akito's buddy was a young woman with a blonde ponytail, a pale complexion, and azure blue eyes. She was so startlingly different to all the women Akito knew in Kyoto that he thought she was what an angel might look like. She was vivacious and chatty. She was very sweet and took Akito under her wing. Her name was Georgia.

Akito and Georgia spent a lot of time together during the conference. She really liked him. He was quiet and polite. He was a good listener, and she liked to talk.

She told him that she was born and raised in Atlanta, but her father had moved the family to Washington, DC, and she went to Thomas Jefferson High School for Science and Technology just down the road from their home on the waterfront in Alexandria. She did her undergrad at Princeton, and then she went to Stanford for her PhD and stayed on as a postdoc.

Akito said he had lived and worked in Kyoto all his life.

The conference was coming to an end. The pair had been inseparable all week, and they were both excited by the science in their own way. They walked back to Georgia's "Premium Studio" room in the Escondido housing complex. The little studio had a bathroom, a kitchenette, a bed, and a sofa. Georgia was still talking as they entered and simply pointed to the sofa for Akito to make himself at home while she got two cans of Coke Zero from the fridge. Akito sat down and looked around, thinking that the space reminded him a little of his parents' home in Kyoto.

Georgia was loquacious and babbled on at Akito about the lectures they had attended. "Oh, and that's the bathroom, right there," she said. Akito nodded. Georgia continued, "I loved the presentation on M-theory, didn't you? You know, they said there are eleven or thirteen dimensions, depending on how you apply supersymmetry? I don't think that's right. God wouldn't pick such a crazy number of dimensions. I don't think he'd do something ugly like that! I think it has to be simpler, so I've been workin' on a theory of hypersymmetry that might just bring that number down to seven dimensions, and I can live with the idea that God would do that. Seven seems right, don't ya think?"

Akito didn't believe in a God as such. He was fond of the notions of Buddhism as a way of life, and like Jonathan Livingston Seagull perfecting flight, he considered that learning about the way the universe works was his own path to enlightenment. He contemplated Japanese art, and his hobby of bonsai, and concluded that seven was indeed a beautiful and natural number. He thought that she might be right that the universe should have such a harmonious beauty to it.

"Yes, it is a nice number," he said. "I have studied SU(7) mathematics. That can help to determine what happens in the higher dimensions, though it is very hard to do. Please explain, what does your hypersymmetry mean for superstrings?"

"Well, I reckon it might mean there are three dimensions of space, and three dimensions of time," Georgia explained. She was animated and excited to have a new audience for her theory. "I have a feeling these are mirrored in Durant's antimatter universe, like they're the flip sides of the same dimension, like heads 'n' tails of a coin. And then there's one further, seventh *hyperdimension,* where the D-branes exist that link together all the superstrings in all the universe."

"I like that," Akito replied.

"Yeah, I reckon there's a lot you can explain," Georgia went on, clearly wanting to convince Akito that her theory explained all the mysteries of the universe. "For a start, there's how quantum events can happen independently, but always obey the same rules. Like if a lump of radioactive uranium decays. The atoms collectively decay at a certain rate, right? But how do all the atoms know how long it's been since the last one decayed? What governs an atom's weak force that causes it to decay, and when that is allowed to happen? Which atom decays next is random, but the time element is not really random at all, right?"

"Correct," said Akito, feeling the need to respond to her rhetorical question.

"That's the D-branes linking all the superstrings together in the higher dimension. The D-branes all know what's going on. They're linked across time—past, present, and future—so they can obey the laws of physics that rely on time."

"Yes, like the *branes* in M-theory. That's very clever to use it to explain how time works," said Akito, starting to make connections with everything he already knew.

"I think it's bigger than that. Time is governed by tiny particles, right?" Georgia said.

"The proposed chronons, yes, they are another kind of superstring," agreed Akito.

"Exactly! Each one vibrating at a certain frequency. Now, I think they interact with matter via the Higgs field. Matter then causes the chronons' frequency to change. Time slows down when there's matter around. We know that—we can measure it with an atomic clock. Astronauts on the International Space Station experience time different from us on earth because they're farther from the earth's mass." Georgia was unstoppable at this point.

"Yes," said Akito, following her logic, but struggling a little with her accent as she rattled off her thoughts.

"And when a particle travels fast, like, close to the speed of light, it gets heavier with all that extra kinetic energy, just like Einstein said it would, right? Well, the interaction with chronons means that as it gets heavier, time slows down, just like Einstein said it would. As time slows down, and down, until it can't slow down any more, that means the particle can't get any faster. So in the end, it cannot go faster than the speed of light! Right?"

When Akito didn't respond, she realized she was going too fast for him. She was getting too excited, so she took a breath and slowed down because she was coming to the complicated bit.

"What if chronons, in the presence of matter, cause a time gradient—slower where the Earth is and faster out in space. Mass doesn't make gravity happen. Mass creates a time gradient, and that's what warps space-time, warped just like Einstein said it was. It ain't *matter* that warps space, it's *time!* And gravity doesn't cause the warping, time does."

Akito was silent, his mouth slightly open in amazement.

"Think about it," Georgia continued, "if light has no mass, how come gravity can bend it? It can't! It's the time gradient that is slower in the direction of the mass, so light curves toward the slower time. The time gradient bends light, not gravity! Makes sense, doesn't it?"

Akito just stared at Georgia, nodding slowly. She had just explained something so fundamentally different than anything he had heard or thought before that he was speechless, and his mind was whirling with the possibilities in what she was saying. She looked a bit like Penny from his favourite American TV show, *The Big Bang Theory*, and yet her mind was sharper than a scalpel. She was even smarter than Sheldon. Akito was in awe.

Georgia became calm and turned toward him just a little. Akito saw her lay a hand gently on the sofa between them, as though she was passing the conversation to Akito. It was like a silent gesture indicating *This is where you come in.* Then she said, "Now, I had the idea, but I sure don't have the math for it in my toolbox. Not now, not yet, and maybe never will. I can't do SU(7) math, so I need your help. I have to confess that me being your buddy wasn't an accident. I've seen your bio; I've read your papers. I reckon you are one of the most brilliant mathematicians of our generation. You're a real, bona fide genius. Heck, you're a *Mathemagician!* So tell me, do you want a real good project to work on? Are ya in?"

Georgia's piercing blue eyes flashed with brilliance and excitement. She stared at Akito, enthusiastic and exhilarated, and eagerly awaiting his affirmative response. How could he possibly say no?

Akito sipped his Coke. He looked at Georgia. He broke into a huge grin. "I am in. I will be your Mathemagician!" She had got him with that *The Phantom Tollbooth* reference.

Akito delayed his return to Japan and spent two weeks working with Georgia on her theory. He struggled with the mathematics, and they spent hours talking things through, and they learned a lot from each other. Georgia travelled to Kyoto for a month at Christmas and New Year's Day to visit with Akito, and she stayed with his family on the shores of Lake Biwa. They did a great deal more work and were able to consult with Akito's supervisor, who had taught him the $SU(7)$ mathematics. They made great strides together.

Then, before they were going to meet up again in March of 2020, the pandemic hit, and travel was restricted. Their work was made difficult by their having to do everything remotely. It had been so much easier sitting in the room together, and Zoom just wasn't up to snuff. Working remotely did not cut the proverbial mustard.

Work was slow, and while Georgia wrote the text for the paper, Akito developed the bizarre and complicated formulae that would demonstrate it and form the basis of a real, solid theory. Theoretical physics is a strange beast. An idea is not a theory without the mathematics to show how it works. An equation means nothing without the ability to explain it. These two enthusiastic young physicists had the two pieces meshing together like well-oiled cogs. But due to their working remotely, it took them until early in 2022 to put everything in place.

The two ambitious scientists were very keen to get published in a prestigious journal and to have their shot at a Nobel Prize.

19.
CONFERENCE CONFLAB

25 MARCH 2022

As soon as travel restrictions were lifted, Westgate College hastily arranged to host a conference. It was the first conference to be scheduled since the pandemic, and the physics world was ready for it. Georgia booked her accommodations and her flights. Akito did not, as Japan had not lifted travel restrictions. He was trapped at home and unable to join Georgia in Oxford.

Akito had emailed Georgia to suggest that she should ask Professor Corvus Durant to be third author on their miraculous paper. Akito admired Durant for his work many years earlier on superstrings, and he knew that Durant would read their paper and agree in an instant. Professor Corvus Durant's name on the manuscript would mean they would get accepted for publication much more quickly and in a far more prestigious journal.

But Georgia was reluctant to share the paper with anyone. She conceded that Durant's recent papers had been somewhat inspirational for her. She admired the quantum probability paper because it led to her idea for how atoms decay, and how probability is really a mechanism in the quantum world, as opposed to God just rolling dice. And she respected his antimatter theory because it helped her to simplify the dimensions, and to see how time was actually a force, and not just something that flies when you're having fun—it was the power behind probability and the influence behind the force of gravity.

The lecture hall was in the Westgate School of Divinity. It was a cramped space for the hundred or so delegates, and the ornate stone walls echoed with chatter and the scraping of chairs on the flagstone floor as delegates squeezed in to sit at the tables that were far too close together for comfort. Each small round table seated eight, and it reminded Georgia of Thanksgiving dinners with cousins and uncles all too close together to use a knife and fork properly. In the middle of each small table was a stack of paper cups, a bottle of warm still water, and a small bowl of individually wrapped mints.

On the last day of the 2022 conference at Westgate College, the lectures were scheduled to end at noon to allow people to get to the airport and begin their long journeys across the globe. Georgia watched the keynote address, which Durant delivered from the temporary raised podium at the front of the hall. Durant dwarfed the little podium.

Georgia knew that Durant was famous for some of his more outlandish opinions and theories, and she had been reluctant to involve him in their work because of his notoriety. But she also knew that to Akito, Durant was a hero.

Notoriety or not, Georgia was shocked at the impertinence of the audience when their questions were derisive and churlish. It

CONFERENCE CONFLAB

was like watching bullies in the playground. It seemed as though people who were normally hidden behind a keyboard, and had got into the habit of being mean on Twitter and in YouTube comments, had suddenly been unleashed on a post-pandemic world and were attacking Durant in real life.

Durant stormed off.

Georgia could not miss the rest of the morning's lectures, so she waited until noon to make her way to the Porters' Lodge. She trudged from front quad into the passageway, bent forward by the weight of a backpack loaded with papers, books, and laptops, and she was dragging a large suitcase. She stood at the counter in the Porters' Lodge to ask if she could speak with Durant. The man in uniform seemed unsure that it was allowed, so Georgia fibbed, telling him that Durant was expecting her. She showed her conference badge, and the duty porter directed her to number three at the top of Staircase E.

Georgia left her suitcase inside the door in the hallway and climbed the stairs with her backpack. She knocked and waited, shuffling nervously and impatiently. Durant opened the door and curtly asked what she wanted.

She held out her conference badge, a bit like the FBI agents do on an American TV show, hoping it would seem like an official visit. "I'm Georgia Cornwallis. Conference delegate. First off, I'm ashamed of the behaviour I saw this morning from my fellow delegates. Grown men oughta know better than that. They've got no respect. Real jerks, in my opinion."

Durant laughed. "Indeed, young lady, arseholes, all of them," he said, slowly looking her up and down. "Well now, miss. What can I do for you?"

Georgia took a deep breath, and in her sweetest, chirpiest Southern lilt, just as she had rehearsed it, she said, "I have a new theory, and being as you're a real expert, and quite the celebrity, I'd really like to ask you a real big favour. I want you to take a look at my paper an' see if you'd like to be a co-author with me and my—"

"Why don't you come in, my dear," said Durant, giving her his very best smile. His mouth broadened slowly to a grin that showed all his teeth. It was a creepy smile, but it was his best one. Georgia was hopeful that the smile was a good sign and that the reference to his celebrity had landed well. She was enthusiastic about her paper, and she wanted to do her best for Akito.

"Take a seat. May I take your coat?"

Georgia sat. "Oh, no, s'alright," she said, plonking her backpack down in front of her. "I really just came to ask if you'll take a look at this paper, and see if I can tempt you to help publication along by lending your gravitas and reputation to a truly wonderful new idea."

Georgia reached into her backpack. The printout that she had brought with her had a cover sheet that bore the title *Let There Be Time!* Durant was notorious for his TV interviews in which he made clear that he was an atheist. Georgia thought better of the idea of leading with a biblical reference to Genesis. So, thinking they might discuss the title later, she left the cover sheet with the title and the names of the authors in her bag. She handed Durant the rest of the pages.

"Yes, yes, we'll get to this in good time," he said, taking the pages. "Cup of tea? Coffee, I suppose; you Americans don't do tea, eh? Something a little stronger, perhaps? Glass of wine?"

Conference Conflab

"Oh, no, thank you, sir, I'm good. I'm not thinkin' of stayin' too long. I'd hate to be disturbin' you, and besides, I've got a train to catch. Thank you kindly, though."

"Let's see what we have here, then," he said as he sat down and began to read. He glanced at the abstract. His brow furrowed. He held the pages closer. His sleazy demeanour evaporated. He stopped trying to be charming, and he sat forward with his elbows on his knees.

"I'm thinking the title could be *Chronons and How Gravity Can Be Explained by Quantum Time,*" she said, providing the subtitle that she knew would meet his approval.

Durant looked at Georgia, one eyebrow raised in surprise. He grew serious, and his attention deepened. He scanned the introduction. He glanced up again at an apprehensive Georgia. Then he began studying the main body of the text, flicking pages, and looking at the equations. He was pensive and intense.

"This mathematics is all your own work?" Durant asked.

"Yes, it is all original work. It took me more than two years to put together."

Durant scrutinized the equations and then skimmed the conclusion. "How did you come by this theory?" he said.

"It was partly inspired by your recent papers on the antimatter universe and quantum probability. That's really why you would be the perfect co-author."

"This is remarkable," he said. "It is a whole new paradigm for the world of physics. It's unifying relativity and quantum mechanics. It's the answer to life, the universe, and everything!"

Georgia was beaming. She knew he would be impressed. "You know, I love what Arthur Eddington said when he was talking about

Einstein's relativity, and in the beautiful complexity of our new equations, I sure can hear God thinking. Ya see, when I was thinking of a title, I thought of how in Genesis it says, 'Let there be light.' I believe that for light to exist, the chronons had to come first. Time had to start first for light to propagate, right? So I was thinking our title would be *Let There Be Time!*" She went to reach for the title page she had left in the backpack.

"I don't hear God thinking," Durant said dismissively. "I liked the title you told me a minute ago, and besides, I think we have plenty of time for working on a title for our new equations."

"Oh, OK," she said, feeling a little deflated, and left the title page where it was. In her sweet Southern way, she perked up instantly and said, "But you said 'our.' That means you'll do it? You'll be co-author?"

"First or second? We'll need to agree on that, but let's not get ahead of ourselves, my dear. Why don't you leave it with me, and I'll let you know my final decision."

"I'll be first author," she said, thinking of her conversation with Akito. "That's already been decided. Here's my email for if you decide you're interested," she said, handing him a piece of paper.

The paper read *savannah@georgiacornwallis.com*. "What's 'Savannah'?" asked Durant, getting to his feet and walking over to the door.

"Savannah's my first name. I go by my middle name."

"Oh, Savannah is such a pretty name, though. Anyway, what are your travel plans?" he added, casually, like he wasn't really interested in the answer.

"I'm getting a train to London now," she replied. "I'm gonna stay overnight at the airport, and then fly back home about lunchtime."

Conference Conflab

He stood with his hand on the door handle. He just wanted her out the door. "Yes, well, safe travels. Interesting reading, I think," he said, clutching the paper in his other hand. "I will be in touch this afternoon. Catch you later, as you Americans might say." He chuckled in a cold, self-satisfied way that Georgia found disturbing.

Georgia stepped out through the door and onto the balcony. She turned briefly to thank Durant and say goodbye. She walked down the stairs feeling like she had tried her best, and she was quite confident that Durant would not turn them down. As long as she was first author, she would let Akito and Durant duke it out for second and third. But the three of them could share the Nobel. She was OK with that.

She grabbed her suitcase handle and began dragging it behind her. She took out her phone and texted Akito one-handed as she walked:

> I met Durant
>
> He seemed real positive
>
> I sure am hopeful
>
> Said he'll let me know

> That's great!
>
> When will you hear?

> Dunno for sure

> Later today I think

> Didn't expect you to be awake!

< I set my alarm

< I wanted to hear you

< *from you

She smiled and said goodbye to the nice porter, walked out of the main gate, then turned left and headed toward the train station. She had been told about thetrainline.com, and how easy electronic tickets were, but she hadn't got round to it, and now she wasn't sure she had the time or the signal strength to start downloading apps.

At the station, she attempted to fathom the ticket machine. She heard the announcement for the arrival of the 13.32 to Paddington, and wished she'd bought a round-trip ticket the previous weekend. She dug the money out of her purse that was left over from the £100 she'd got out of the cashpoint at Paddington a week earlier, and inserted the cash into the ticket machine. It eventually spat out her ticket. She grabbed it and ran with her suitcase trailing behind her, leaving the change in the tray.

Just as she got to the platform, the doors closed, the engines began revving, and the train started pulling away.

"Oh, man! Goddam lollygaggin' ticket machine!" she exclaimed.

A man standing next to her glanced at her with a raised eyebrow.

Conference Conflab

The destination display board showed that the next train should arrive in only five minutes, but that she would have to change trains at somewhere called Didcot.

"Where the heck is freakin' Didcot? Why's it so darn hard to get to London?" she complained as she pulled up the rail map on her phone.

The man moved away, farther up the platform. An old lady arrived to stand next to Georgia, looking up at the *Next Train* indicator board. Then they announced a delay, "The delayed 13.37 is now expected at 13.56."

"Oh, come on!" Georgia grumbled. "I can't catch a break. Goddam trains. I knew I should've rented a car." The old lady stared at her suspiciously, tutted, and decided to stand farther away, next to the nice quiet gentleman.

Georgia checked her email. Nothing from Durant yet. Georgia waited impatiently for the train, staring into the distance in the direction the train would come from.

20.

LATE FOR THEIR DATE

07 NOVEMBER 2022, 2.57 P.M.

Akito took a sip of his Dandelion & Burdock. Phil presumed that he liked it, as this was his second. Akito concluded by telling Phil that Georgia's text was the last he had heard from her. "She left Durant and got the train. The police saw her on CCTV at the station getting on the train. I texted; I wrote emails. I never heard back from my friend."

"So, what did you plan to do when you challenged Durant? What were you expecting to achieve, exactly?"

"He cheated her out of publishing her work. He stole it. He took her legacy. He ought to give us credit for our work, and not be the sole author of a paper in the journal, the greatest paper of the last century." Akito ran his hand through his straight black hair. Looking down, he added, "But I also want to find out from him what happened, because he was the last person to talk with Georgia before she went missing."

"So, why not go public and prove he stole your paper?"

"That would cause him disgrace," Akito replied in a disapproving tone. "It would be dishonourable not to allow him to rectify his wrongdoing. I would not wish to be the person who brought shame on one of the great physicists of our time."

"OK," Phil conceded. "Well, the way I see it, the best thing we can do is to approach the publisher in confidence. I have a good friend at Oxford University Press. Pretty high up. She could handle this discreetly, and she would be very keen to avoid getting sued, I'm sure. So, will you let me handle that part of it through the publisher? What do you say?"

"I came a long way for this. I waited for travel restrictions to lift in Japan before I could make the trip. I waited so long to challenge him. Can you understand if I am reluctant to agree?"

"I do understand, but surely you also see that there is little to be achieved challenging him face to face? You can see that he would just deny everything, and you'd be no nearer your goal."

"I do see that, yes. But I want him to explain," Akito said.

According to Phil's watch, it was 3.00. Durant's time of death had been and gone, and Phil felt optimistic about the change in Akito's fortunes. "Let me see what I can do. I promise, I won't let you down. I will investigate Georgia's disappearance, and I promise to tell you what I find out. I'll keep in touch if you give me your email."

"I will trust a police detective to help me, thank you," Akito said, handing Phil his business card, holding it with both hands. Phil accepted it likewise and smiled reassuringly, deciding not to correct Akito's assumption that Phil was a police officer.

"OK, so," Phil said enthusiastically, "tell me about quantum gravity. I'm dying to hear all about it."

Phil settled back in his chair as Akito sat up and became animated.

LATE FOR THEIR DATE

Phil and Akito talked for a good couple of hours. They explored Georgia's theory in the manuscript and exchanged stories and opinions on the great minds of physics. It had completely absorbed Phil into a world that he had not realized he was so hungry for. Akito was delightfully engaging and impressively knowledgeable. Phil glanced at his watch, and though it seemed only a few minutes since it had been 3.00, it was now well after 5.00. Phil had been lost in the forest of physics, as though he were a puppy surrounded by squirrels, chasing after every one of them.

"I will much appreciate your help to find out about Georgia-san," Akito said, "but I think I have time to go to see Professor Durant. I came a long way to ask him questions. Perhaps you would accompany me?"

"I would hold off on doing that. Really, I would. I know Durant. He isn't going to take kindly to being challenged." Phil thought he'd persuaded Akito from seeing Durant face to face. "I'm really curious about Kyoto, though. I've always wanted to visit Japan. What did Georgia make of it?"

While Akito told Phil about Georgia's trip to Kyoto and proudly explained how much Georgia had liked his home city, Phil texted Holly:

> Hi Holly. Running late

> Will text when I'm heading your way

After another hour of trying to delay and dissuade Akito, Phil said, "I'm late, and I should be making a move. Can I help you get somewhere?"

"No, thank you," Akito said. He seemed crestfallen and defeated. "I will return to London now, but I leave England with a heavy heart. I now put my destiny in your hands, Dr. Phil, and I trust that you will do your best for Georgia-san."

"I will, I promise," said Phil. "Let me walk you to the station."

Phil sighed with relief as Akito's train pulled out of Oxford Station. He checked his watch. It was 6.35. "Shit, half an hour late already. Bollocks."

He texted Holly:

> On my way now. Sorry

He kicked himself for not taking a convenient Polaroid to go back an hour, but they were only going to be spending the evening at Holly's. *There's no big hurry,* he thought.

He rushed to Holly's house on Combe Road as fast as he could—half walking, half jogging. *She'll be OK when I explain that I was on a case,* he reasoned.

It was 6.50 when he arrived outside Holly's door, sweaty and out of puff, fifty minutes late.

He knocked on the door. He waited. *Damn.*

He knocked again. He waited some more. *Damn.*

He knocked again. He peered through the front window. The only light on was a table lamp in the lounge. No sign of Holly. *Damn. Damn.*

LATE FOR THEIR DATE

He texted.

> Hi Holly. So sorry

> Won't lie. Was in the pub

> Talking about physics and investigating a case

> If you're still free I'd love to see you

Nothing came back. No three dots. Not even a *Delivered* underneath his text.

He called. Her phone was off.

Maybe she was so pissed off with him that she'd gone out and turned her phone off. There was still nothing by text. He wasn't sure what to do.

Phil had originally set out to change nothing, just get clues to repay Havarti. He hadn't exactly done what he'd set out to do. He had identified Umbrella Guy, which had been his plan. But then he had altered the timeline for Akito, so now Havarti would have no Durant at the Bottom of the Stairwell case at all. Akito would be in the clear, just waiting for Phil to tackle the stolen publication problem and investigate Georgia's disappearance. Phil was starting to think that had worked out quite well.

Phil couldn't have just walked away from Akito and let him kill Durant, could he? He had to do the right thing. He was convinced that helping Akito had been a good thing. Saving Durant, though? That was kind of *meh*. Phil didn't want him dead as such, and he certainly didn't care much to save him. But Phil really didn't want Akito to have been responsible for Durant's death.

But, by changing that, what else might he have changed?

Phil had also started dating Holly. And now he was in love. Everything had started so well between them, but now it seemed that Holly was ghosting him. Phil didn't really know much about Holly, though. If she wasn't at home or at the Three Goats Heads pub, he had no idea where to start looking for her in this timeline.

Phil wanted to be at home in his flat, but he couldn't be there in this timeline in November. His other self would be living his life there, right now. His other self would be back from Wednesbury, full of the excitement of looking forward to getting his brand-new robot arm. No, Phil would have to return to his own time to be able to be at home. With the benefit of skipping forward in time, perhaps he could find out more about what saving Durant had done to change his timeline. There, he could make some tea, talk to his robot, and think straight. And then he could sort out a Polaroid that would get him back here early enough to be at Holly's on time.

But if he did come back here, he would still have to date Holly across two timelines for three months. Phil began to mull over all the complications, including his being deceitful with Holly, the bizarre and complicated double life, and the risks of his mum or his own self uncovering his secret. He had never resolved that problem.

He wondered if this was an opportunity for him to go back to his own timeline and to try to pick up with Holly in January. He was bright enough to think of a reason he had been missing for nearly three months. Something she would forgive him for, or maybe even something a little bit noble or heroic. It could be one small white lie, a not-too-tall tale, that would explain his absence in the interim. That would correct his timeline problem and save him from having so much difficulty. And, in the end, if it didn't work out, he could resort to Plan B, and use another Polaroid from November to come back and not be late for dinner at Holly's. *Brilliant!* he thought.

On second thought, he realized it was a stupid idea. He decided he couldn't possibly pull it off. Holly was too smart to not catch him in a stupid lie. And Phil didn't want to lie. Not more than he sort of already had.

Phil was getting desperate to figure out where he could find Holly. Flicking through his Polaroids, it occurred to him that he knew where Holly would be. In his own timeline, on the day they would have had their original first date in January, Holly would be ending her shift at Collard Green's at 2.00 p.m. That was what he needed to do next. Find Holly, and arrange to meet so he could explain where he'd been for nearly twelve weeks. Then go home, get a cup of tea, and think what exactly to say to Holly.

Feeling excited and optimistic, he gathered everything into his bag and fished out the photo from The Firkin Folly at 1.24 p.m. on 18 January 2023 that read *Meet Holly at 2.00 p.m.* He stared into it and willed himself back to a moment in which he knew he would be in time to see Holly.

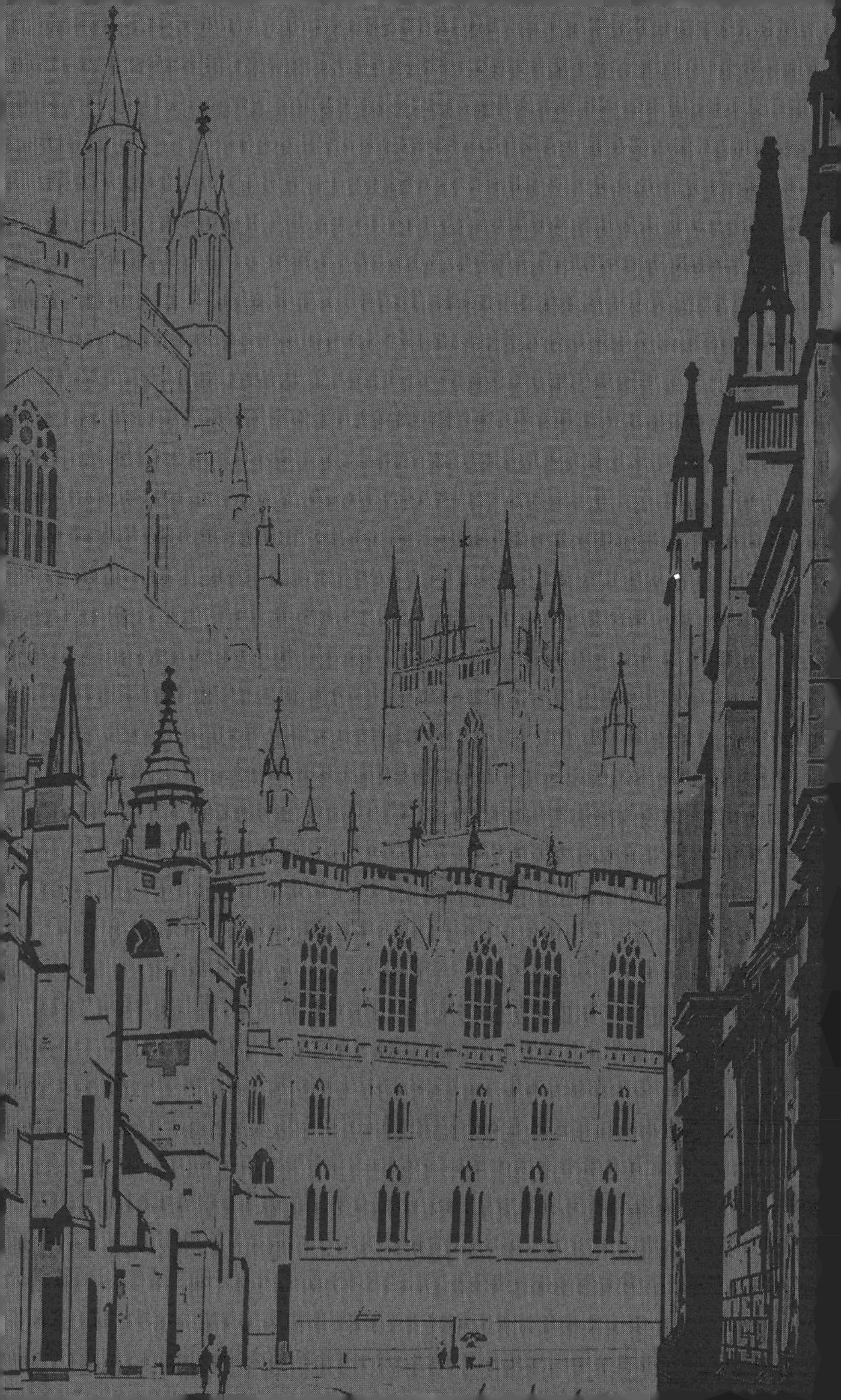

Part Three
BACK TO THE FUTURE

21.

EM T. TREY

18 JANUARY 2023, 1.24 P.M.

Phil found the inside of The Firkin Folly slowly coming into focus, and colour began to fill the scene. He hated the times when he arrived standing up. It was much nicer to get to a new time sitting down. Reality swirled, and Phil was dizzy. He was just starting to feel his feet getting steadier and sturdier when a man almost bumped into him coming out of the ladies' toilets. "Sorry, mate, didn't see you there. I was just … The gents is kaput, and I was busting. You know how it is."

"My fault," said Phil weakly, willing himself to solidify faster.

He walked up to the bar and leant on it for a minute. He got out his Sharpie and wrote a big X on the back of the Polaroid he had just used. He had planned to use this particular Polaroid of the bar so that he could get to Collard Green's Vegan Café by 2.00 to meet Holly, but now that he had been dating her, and things were messed up, Phil thought this was where he needed to be.

He called out, "Thank you," to Ruby, who looked at him quizzically and asked, "Did you forget something?"

"Got it, thanks!" Phil said, holding his Polaroid up for Ruby to see, and he headed out of the door onto the street. His pace was quick, and he was desperate to get to Collard Green's. He wasn't looking as he quickly crossed the street right in front of a bus, causing it to stop abruptly with a hiss and squeal of the air brakes. Phil gestured at the bus driver, who opened the door reluctantly. Phil jumped on.

"There's an actual bus stop right there, mate. No need to throw yourself in the road!"

"Sorry, I'm in a hurry. Thanks for stopping. I'm going to be late."

"Well, good job I did stop, coz if I hadn't stopped, you'd be late already. Late in this world, early in the next," said the driver, shaking his head, and suddenly Phil felt the rest of the passengers on the bus glaring at him because of the emergency stop.

Phil helped a woman whose shopping bag had fallen over and spilt its contents on the floor of the bus during the sudden braking. He picked up a loose apple that had rolled down the aisle and held it out to her.

"You can keep that one, it's been on that floor," she said, shaking her head.

"Sorry, sorry," Phil said to the woman and the bus in general, apologizing for the minor mishap.

Phil stood for the rest of the short journey, eating the apple after giving it a cursory wipe on his T-shirt, and ignoring the disgusted looks from the woman seated next to him. He dinged the bell and jumped off with a cheery "Thank you" to the driver, and headed the few doors up to Collard Green's.

It was 1.45 p.m. He waited for a few minutes, pacing up and down nearby, starting to worry about what kind of reception he would get after nearly three months. He reassured himself that his backup plan was to find a Polaroid, then go back a few weeks, so as to not be late and spend the evening with Holly last November. All he needed to do now was apologize for his absence, convince Holly he had a great tale to tell, and arrange to meet up this evening.

He was going to wait outside, rather than interrupt the end of her shift. Holly would be out any minute. He checked his watch. He looked in through the window. No sign of her. He paced some more. Time passed, and he fretted.

He looked at his watch again. Just gone 2.00. He looked in through the window. Still no sign. He went in.

"Hi, is Holly around?"

"Who?" asked the waitress, who Phil assumed was the late-shift girl and would be relieving Holly at 2.00.

"Holly. The other waitress. Does the lunchtime shift. She finishes at 2.00. I'm meeting her here. I might be; I think. Or, at least I was going to meet her here." Phil looked at the girl's name badge. It simply said *Em*.

Em looked at Phil blankly.

"Em, please, could you let her know Phil is here?"

"Nope, sorry. Don't know her. I do the lunchtime shift," she said in a flat monotone. "Collard!" she shrieked.

"What now?" came a gruff voice from the kitchen.

"Bloke here asking after Holly," Em called out.

"Who?" asked Collard from the kitchen, sounding annoyed with the question.

"Holly!" Em turned to Phil to double-check. "Right?"

"Yes, Holly!" Phil called out in the direction of the kitchen, becoming impatient.

Collard emerged from the kitchen. "I don't know the names of all the feckin' customers! Do I look like a bloody phone book?"

"No, he says she's a waitress here," Em explained.

"No' here," said Collard. He was a short, wiry, middle-aged man with tattoos on his bare arms, and he was wearing a black T-shirt and a blue-and-white-striped apron that was covered in flour. He looked at Phil and gave a nod as a greeting. Phil looked at Collard's apron, which reminded him of the deckchairs on Brighton Beach. The blue-and-white stripes did, not the flour. Phil nodded back. "She's nae here. No waitress called Holly. No' here, anyhow. You've the wrong café, mate."

Phil just looked at him, helpless; impatience giving way to concern. *No Holly. Where was she?* He knew in that moment that he had saved Akito from a horrible fate, but now Holly's timeline had changed too. What could he possibly have changed for Holly that meant she didn't work at Collard Green's Vegan Café? Phil started to realize something was wrong, and it was more than simply being ghosted.

Collard looked around at all the empty, dirty tables, each one strewn with the lunchtime jetsam.

"Come on, Teatray, can we get some of these friggin' tables cleared?" and he turned to go back into the kitchen.

"Teatray?" Phil said, more or less to himself.

"He calls me Teatray," Em explained. "My last name is Trey, T-R-*E*-Y. My middle initial is T, for Tracy. 'T. Trey.' Get it? He thinks he's funny," she explained. "But he's really just an arsehole," she added, whispering.

"And her first name is Em. Look at what she's got in her hand!" came Collard's shout from the kitchen. "Em T. Trey. Friggin' hilarious! And why, oh, why, is it still friggin' empty?"

EM T. TREY

Phil looked down at the empty tray by Em's side and just shook his head. He wondered briefly if he would have found it funny on a normal day. Collard really was a dick, and Em didn't seem suited to the job. She wasn't with-it enough, and she was certainly not equipped to deal with a highly strung twat like Collard for a boss. He briefly felt sorry for Em and recalled how easily Holly had been able to deal with him. Where was Holly now? Phil grew more impatient, and his concern was giving way to panic.

"Holly? I need to find Holly. Can you help?" Phil asked Em as he began to feel hopeless, like a little boy lost in a supermarket, desperate for someone to help him find his mum.

Collard emerged from the kitchen again. "Come on. It'd be nice to start the afternoon tea rush with somewhere for people to sit, eh? Why am I payin' Carl to just stand next to a sink full of hot, soapy water and stare out the friggin' window?"

"Well, he can clear the *blimmin'* tables, can't he?" said Em.

Phil's mind was in a whirl. The world seemed to be separating from him, happening at a distance and in slow motion. Where was Holly? What had he changed?

"That's your job, Teatray. I don't want Clumsy Carl out here looking like a Death Metal Quasimodo and dropping plates in the customers' laps. That's why I chain the fucker to the sink," said Collard.

"I can hear you," came a slow, sullen voice from the kitchen.

Phil's knotted stomach and rising panic were getting too much for him

"Shape up, Teatray, come on," growled Collard.

"Yes, chef," she muttered.

Collard turned to Phil briefly. "Sorry, mate, no Holly, no' here," he said, disappearing back into the kitchen.

"Sorry, I've got to get on," Em said to Phil, turning away to clear a nearby table.

Phil didn't want to leave the one place he knew Holly should be, but he now knew in this timeline that she was never actually there. He walked out onto St. Aldate's, disconsolate and panicky, and breathing fast.

He slipped into the alleyway next to the café and ducked behind the wheelie bin. He did what he had done earlier that day and snapped a Polaroid. He needed the picture in case he had to get back here, to this moment, while investigating Holly's whereabouts.

He pulled out the Polaroid and wrote *Collard Green's Alley, 18 Jan. 2023, 2.09 p.m.* He walked toward the street and turned toward home, his mind racing. *What was going on? Where was Holly?* Something had changed.

"What the hell have I done?" he said under his breath. "I've got a bad feeling about this."

22.

WHAT THE HELL HAVE I DONE?

18 JANUARY 2023, 2.12 P.M.

Phil let himself into his flat. First, he checked his phone again. He had been back in this timeline plenty long enough for his phone to connect and update. Holly had never replied to his texts in the intervening couple of months. What could he do? He called her number just to see if she would pick up. The automated voice told Phil that the number he had called was not in service. The best interpretation Phil could come up with was that she had just written him off and changed her number.

He could go back in time and rectify that. He could get to Holly's on time, and it would all be OK. He told himself to stay calm. Deep down, under the veneer of denial, Phil knew it was worse than that. Why would she overreact like that? That didn't seem very likely. She seemed quite rational and perfectly capable of just giving him shit for it.

Why wasn't she at Collard Green's? The knot in the pit of Phil's stomach was due to his worries about making up with her and wondering where she was, but making it worse was that he was worried something bad had happened. He surely must have changed things for Akito and Durant. And now it seemed he had changed things for Holly too.

But had he really changed things for Akito and Durant? Was Durant alive? That had been his hope, at least, to distract Akito and save him from being the cause of Durant's death. He decided to check that. That could be accomplished quickly. Phil fired up his Mac. A quick Google search, and *boom!*

About 2,120,000 results (0.32 seconds)

New Scientist
www.newscientist.com/time_rules_gravity_redundant
Time Rules the Universe as Gravity is Made Redundant

Oxford Mail
www.oxfordmail.co.uk/oxford_professor_on_top_of_the_world
Professor Durant to be Nominated for Nobel

The Financial Times
www.FT.com/corvus_durant_lifetime_achievement_award
Corvus Durant (58) to Receive Knighthood

The internet was full of the sensational paper he had published a few months ago, news of many recent interviews and TV appearances, and how he would likely be nominated for a Nobel Prize. Durant was currently touring the world and lecturing on the subject, and he was on evening TV chat shows everywhere the conference circuit took him: "Professor 'Chronos' Durant, The Man Who Made Time."

WHAT THE HELL HAVE I DONE?

Phil thought about Durant stealing Georgia and Akito's paper. He had some of the feelings of anger toward Durant that Akito must be feeling a million times over. "Fame and fortune for Durant? I should have let Akito throw him off the balcony!" Phil said out loud to his robot.

It seemed to Phil that Georgia's disappearance had been very fortuitous for Durant. With her gone, he must have had nothing holding him back from publishing.

But what about Holly? Phil took a deep breath.

Phil looked at his phone again, and the lack of replies from Holly. He looked on Instagram. Holly hadn't posted in months. He looked at her website. He found nothing new—no blog entries and no new excerpts from her thesis. He had a worsening sinking feeling; he knew this was bad. He decided to google *Holly Farthing*.

About 22,870,000 results (0.68 seconds)

The Guardian
www.theguardian.com/missing_student_holly_farthing
No Leads in Search for Missing Student (29)

Oxford Mail
www.oxfordmail.co.uk/oxford_masters_student_missing
Oxford Master's Student Missing

The Sun
www.thesun.co.uk/holly_escort_scandal
Missing Girl Holly (29) In Oxford Escort Scandal

Phil felt just how fast adrenaline spreads through the body. His stomach churned, he was flushed, and all the hair on his body prickled. He tried to focus on the screen, but he was starting to feel light-headed. *Oh, shit. What have I done this time? Durant is alive, and Holly is missing. Presumed dead? Holly, oh my God, what did I do?*

"Calm down, Phil, you're not helping. Come on, you idiot, get a grip," he said to himself.

He tried to think things through. There was no need to panic, because he could go back and fix this. Surely. Right? He just had to figure out exactly what he had changed and how to go back and undo it.

"Stay calm. Work the problem, as Gene Kranz would say," he muttered.

He clicked on the Oxford Mail link and read that Holly Farthing, a Master's student at Oxford University, went missing on 7 November. She was last seen at The Alchemist at 1.50 p.m. in the Westgate Shopping Centre, wearing blue jeans and a distinctive pink-checked Burberry shirt. She had on a matching Burberry scarf and pink ballet flats, and she was carrying a burgundy canvas tote bag. The article stated, *Police have no clues to her whereabouts and are appealing for anyone who might have seen her to come forward.* There was a reference to a forthcoming Crimewatch reconstruction of her journey from Jericho, which had aired in late November. The Uber driver had, apparently, been traced and eliminated from police enquiries.

"Police!" Phil exclaimed. "That's it! Havarti will know!" He picked up his phone.

WHAT THE HELL HAVE I DONE?

"DS Frisk."

"Hi, Havarti; it's Phil. So, tell me about the missing girl."

"Hey Phil, I'm fine, thanks for asking. How about yourself? Doing well? Great. Lovely. What can I do for you?" The question was not phrased that way by accident. Havarti Frisk was one of Phil's best friends, and she had endured his need for favours, and the fact that she was a go-to when Phil needed help with something he'd seen online. "I just had déjà vu. I'd say it was odd, but I get them a lot when I'm talking to you. Since you're calling for another favour, maybe that's not actually so bloody surprising."

"Hi, yes, ummm, maybe getting déjà vu with me isn't as weird as you might think. Anyway, this missing student, Holly Farthing. I'm looking for some information on her disappearance."

"Well, now, that is a coincidence, because I have been thinking about asking if you might help me out a bit. I really could use your input on both the missing girl cases. I've got two disappearances, and I'm desperately trying to stave off speculation about a serial killer. But there's no link I can find between the two."

"You're in charge of both cases now?"

"Yep. I was given the Farthing girl when she disappeared. And then Hunter got shipped off to Reading and left me with the Cornwallis case too."

"So, no leads on either?"

"No, but that's all the cases have in common. No suggestion of any link. No reason to suppose it's a serial killer."

"Except that they were both young, beautiful, and in Oxford."

"Well, yes, there is that. No other link that I can find. But, anyway, we drew a blank on both cases, and I could really use some help. I know Hunter is a complete lazy, useless bastard, but I'm starting to understand the challenges a lot better. The trail just goes cold. We don't see Holly Farthing on CCTV after she goes into The Alchemist to get a drink. Why don't you come to HQ so we can talk while I don't show you the footage we have?"

"OK, I'll come right over."

"Bring lunch, I'm bloody starving."

23.
THE GIRL IN THE BURBERRY SHIRT

18 JANUARY 2023, 2.42 P.M.

Phil sat next to Havarti on an office swivel chair, staring at Havarti's computer screen, and resisting the urge to swivel.

Havarti was sitting back in her chair, devouring a tuna and mayonnaise sandwich and gulping Coke Zero. She'd seen this movie a million times. *The Girl in the Burberry Shirt*, starring Holly Farthing. A silent, arty film that ends with some sort of bloody infuriating vanishing trick.

"Dare say we're not breaking any laws with you sitting in the room while I review CCTV footage. What d'ya think, Phil? All legal and above board?"

"What? Yes, sure. All good," said Phil, transfixed by the screen. "Mum's the word."

Phil was intently watching four different camera angles on one screen, all of them from the CCTV of Westgate Oxford shopping centre. The camera out on Old Greyfriars Street clearly showed a young woman in a checked shirt and scarf getting out of a dark-grey Honda Accord and going in via the side entrance.

The next view was from inside, and it showed the same woman walking in and going up the escalator. There she was again on the next level up, getting on another escalator. And finally, the fourth camera showed her walking into The Alchemist.

Havarti pointed at the screen, wagging her finger as if to say *hold on,* then finished her mouthful, and told Phil, "That's the barman right there, and that's Holly ordering a drink. The barman said she ordered a white wine spritzer, and stood at the bar and sipped it while they made small talk. He turned away to serve two other people who were ordering lunch. Said it was busy for a Monday lunch, and he was on his own behind the bar. He said when he looked back, she was gone, and he didn't see her again. He didn't see her leave, but said she must have left while he was serving the couple farther up the bar."

Phil watched CCTV for a while, and Havarti was right. The girl in the Burberry shirt was definitely Holly, and after she left frame in the shot of The Alchemist on the CCTV, she was not seen again on any of the camera views. Phil asked Havarti to rewind.

"There's Holly," he said, "in the distinctive Burberry. She chugs the second half of her drink. Then she walks toward the camera, toward the door. She goes out of shot, we presume she leaves, but she's not on the CCTV outside the bar. You're right, Havarti, she just bloody vanishes." Then Phil went quiet.

The tape continued playing, and a minute later, several people could be seen entering the bar. There were, perhaps, eight of them milling around, each one in and out of shot and hard to keep track of. Then Phil noticed that one of the small throng had long dark hair, and she seemed to be pushing between the others. On a different video feed, she could be seen walking to the escalator.

The Girl in the Burberry Shirt

Phil looked closer, squinting at the screen. He recognized her and thought, *It's a young woman wearing a short skirt, high heels, and a jean jacket. It's Honey!*

"Rewind again."

It dawned on Phil that Holly was busy that day because "Honey" had a client!

Holly goes out of shot, he thought. *She isn't leaving, she must be heading to the loo to change! Change her outfit, and change into Honey!* Phil continued watching. *The group enters,* he thought, *they loiter for a minute or two waiting to be seated, and … it's hard to see. There! Honey has to push through the crowd to get to the door and leave the bar.*

Phil watched the other quadrants of the video feed from the other cameras. He saw Honey among the many shoppers going down the escalators and walking off in the direction of Norfolk Street and Westgate College.

Havarti finished a mouthful and wiped her mouth on the back of her hand. "We eliminated the Uber driver who dropped her off. He had a fare to Bunbury, and then one to Chipping-on-the-Green before he was back in Oxford on traffic cameras around 3.00, and his wife swears he was home by 3.30. He even had a receipt from a kebab place in Bunbury. And the barman is seen on CCTV here and there until the bar closed, gone midnight. Long day because someone called in sick. Said he needed the cash. Gonna bet he earns more than I do."

"If it was so busy, why'd the barman remember Holly?"

"He said she was very pretty, so he got a bit chatty with her, but if that wasn't enough, he said she didn't have a coat and it was bloody cold and wet that day. He knows his designer brands and recognized the Burberry. Not the couture of your average student, so he was surprised when she said she was one. He said she clearly wasn't interested in him, so he went off to serve other people."

"Hmmm. Fair enough. Do you have footage from Westgate College?"

"No, why? What are you thinking, Phil?" Havarti asked. "What have you seen? Don't be a sneaky shit, talk to me."

Phil wasn't ready to give up what he knew about Honey just yet. He was sure it was Honey on the CCTV, and it looked as though she was headed in the direction of Westgate. He didn't want to own up to knowing Holly's secret, even if *The Sun* had already exposed it. He was thinking he could get further on his own than with Havarti. She couldn't help him if Honey was dead already. Only he could help her if she was.

"Oh, nothing, really. Just thinking that the shopping centre CCTV puts Holly close to Westgate College, and she was a student there. Maybe she fancied a drink before meeting her tutor or something?"

"We'd need a warrant for their CCTV. They're not exactly free and easy with their private footage," said Havarti. "They'll say it's an 'infringement of liberty for the students to be spied on while going about their lawful business.' Don't want us catching the buggers buying their cocaine, more like. We have to have a very specific purpose for a warrant, and they will only ever give us the footage for the particular times requested. Not exactly forthcoming. We haven't had any leads in that direction, anyway, so we haven't had due cause for a warrant."

"It just seems like a good line of enquiry, though," said Phil.

"Oh, well, sure, we made enquiries, of course," Havarti replied. "Nobody at the college saw her there that day. Sheepshuffle, her tutor, wasn't due to see her till the Thursday. The porters didn't see her, and they see everyone coming and going. The groundsman didn't see her, and he was out and about that day putting new signs out in the quads," she concluded as she stuffed the last bit of crust of her sandwich into her mouth.

Phil wasn't so sure that Honey hadn't gone to Westgate. All Phil could think was that Durant was alive and Honey was gone.

"What about Durant? Did anyone see him?" asked Phil, certain that Durant was involved in all of this somewhere.

"No, why? He was in his rooms all day, after he got back from breakfast in the Masters' Common Room, from about 9.45 a.m. on. Or so he told us. Nobody in or out," said Havarti. "Not much to go on there, I'm afraid. Come on, Phil, are you going to tell me what you're thinking? Don't be such a dick."

"Hmmm. I don't know what to think yet. Just something seems off, so close to Westgate. Oh, well. Tell you what. I'll make some enquiries. Contacts and so forth. I'll see what I can uncover and let you know."

"Doubtless you'll spend plenty time in the Alchemist," she joked.

"Ha-ha! No reason not to." Other than sorting out whatever happened to the woman he was in love with, of course.

Havarti finished her Coke, crushed the can, and tossed it into the blue recycling bin by the door. "OK, Phil. You do your thing. Work your miracle. Dunno how you do it, but I'll be grateful forever if you come up with anything on either girl. One case could crack the other."

"Yeah, thought you said there was no link? I thought it wasn't a serial killer," Phil said, quite sure that the cases *were* linked.

"Oh, sod off, Phil. That's the official line. Who knows. I'm scared shitless in case it's a serial killer. That means it'll happen more frequently now he's getting confident. I need your help, Phil, not your smart-aleck bullshit."

Havarti was stressed. Phil thought she was definitely looking older, much older, and seemed more disillusioned, and he wondered if he was seeing grey hairs. The strain and lack of sleep were taking their toll. Phil had always thought she was such a young-looking thirty-something. She used to say looking young held her back. But at that moment, her face appeared to be lined with the stress of doing her best for the two missing women.

"Sorry," Phil said, then gave her a hug and added, "I'll do what I can," and walked out.

He thought he might want to come back here, so he found the fire exit and took a Polaroid at 3.29 p.m. *You never know when you'll need it, you just know you will,* Phil thought. He needed to follow Honey's trail to Westgate on the day she disappeared. Havarti might bend a few rules to share information or CCTV footage with Phil, but she had a rulebook that Phil didn't. When it came to accessing Westgate's CCTV, Phil didn't have the same constraints. He had other ways and means.

Then he rummaged in the pocket of his satchel and pulled out a picture of front quad at Westgate College. The one he had taken in Staircase C on the afternoon just before he bumped into Akito, on the day that Holly went missing.

225

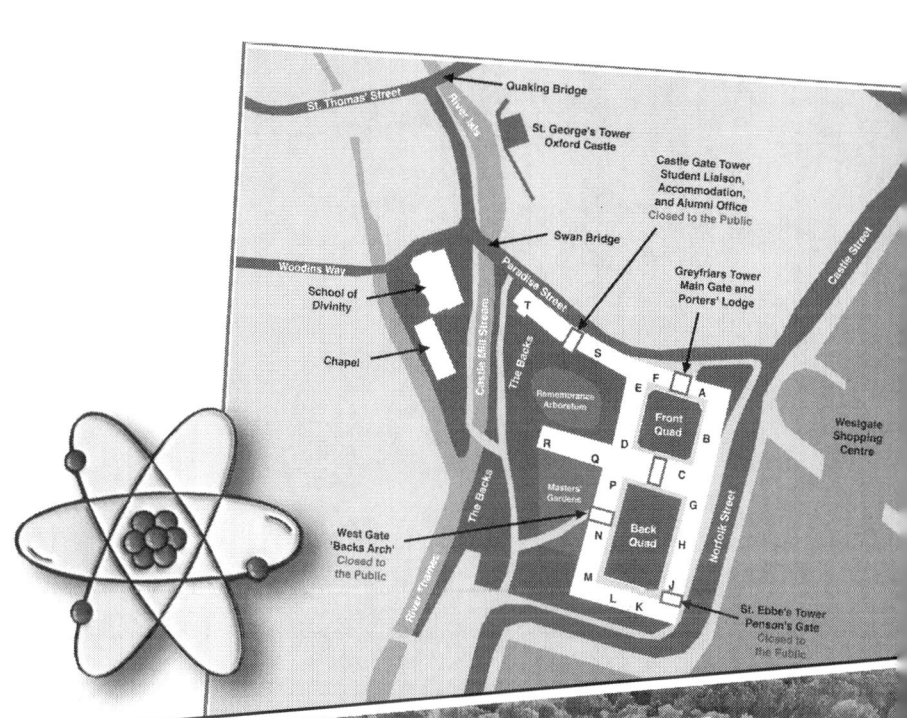

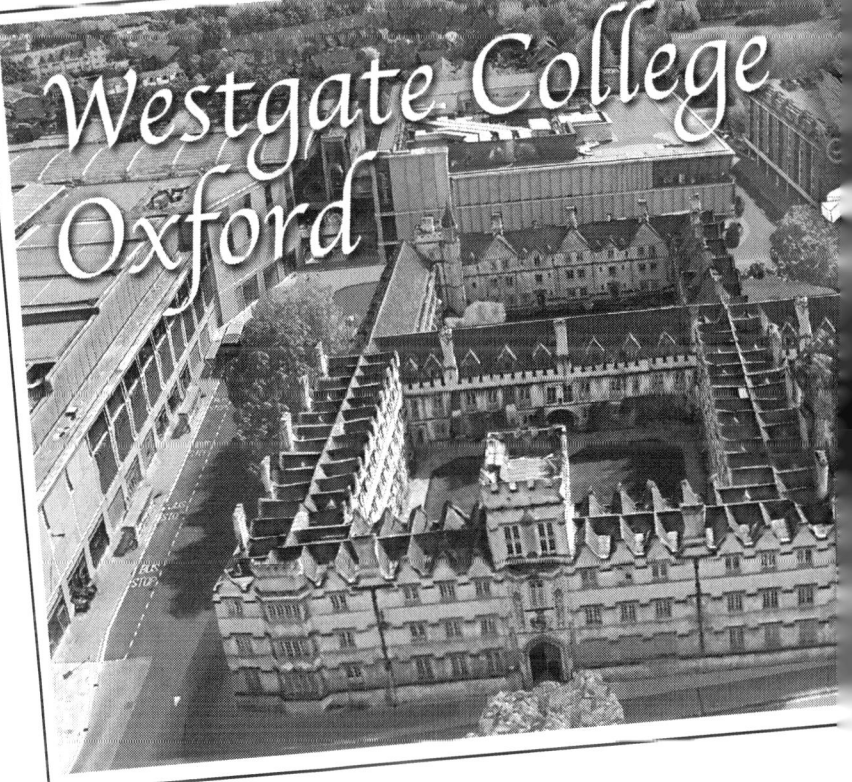

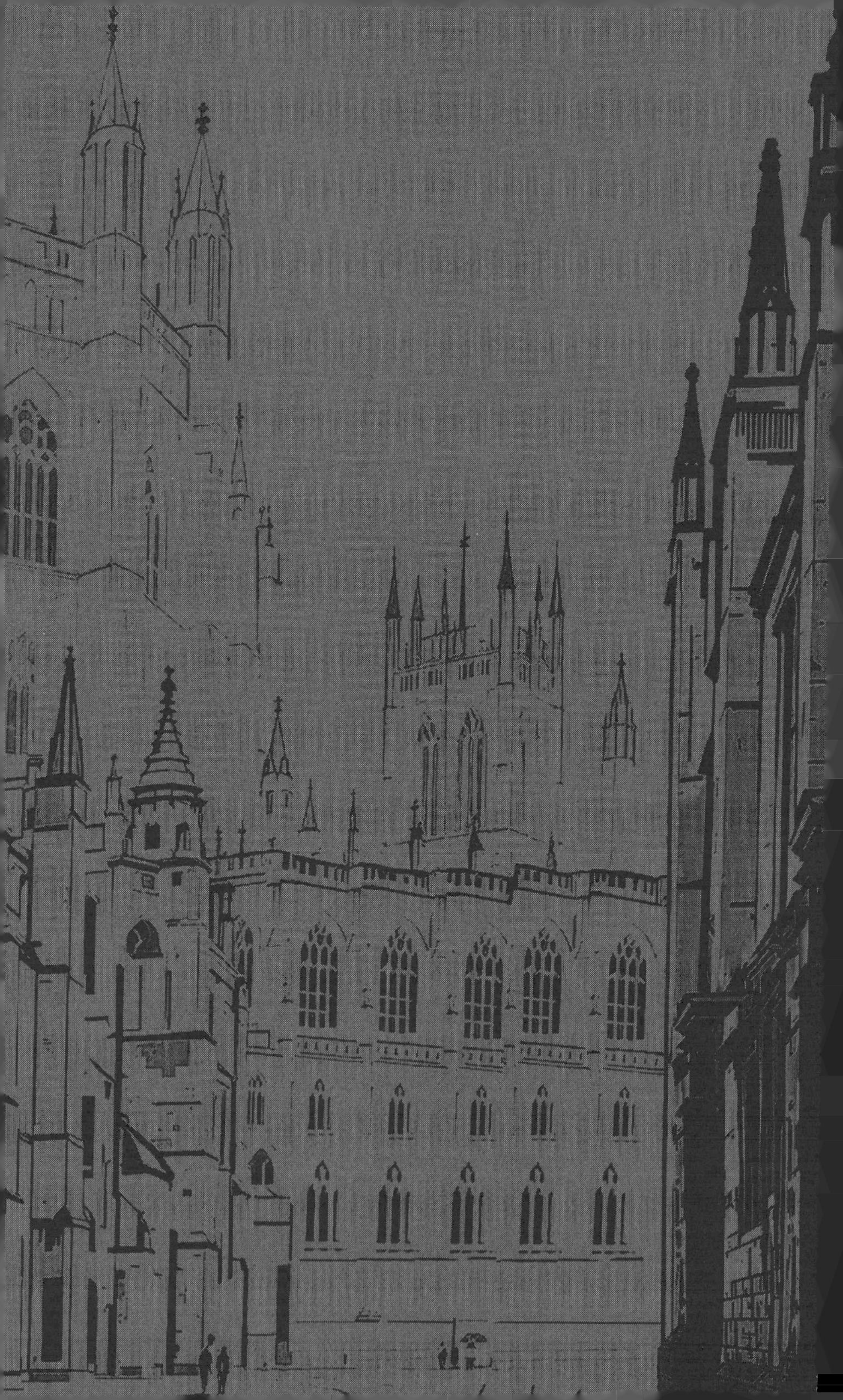

Part Four
BACK TO THE PAST

24.

CRAZED DETECTIVE MODE

07 NOVEMBER 2022, 2.05 P.M.

Phil smelled the cold in the air and felt a haze of green. As front quad slowly came into focus, all he could see clearly was the Polaroid and the scribbled *Staircase C. 07 Nov. 2022, 2.05 p.m.* on it. The doorway he was leaning against started to feel solid, and the lawn took on the formal stripes that Arbley Scrump had fastidiously etched into it with his antique, hand-me-down push-mower. Gradually, everything came into focus.

Phil looked up from the photograph and saw his other self heading to the main gate. Meanwhile, the Phil that belonged in this timeline was in Wednesbury playing with robots.

The Phil he could see was scurrying along the path at the edge of the quad. He looked on as the other Phil collided with Akito. The two of them picked up papers from the floor. They talked for a couple of minutes, and then they went out of the main gate onto Paradise Street.

As soon as they were out of sight, Phil sprinted across the grass and made a beeline to the Porters' Lodge and up to the counter. He called through to the back room, "Perkins, I need to see your CCTV from around two o'clock."

A tall, chubby, clumsy-looking man emerged through the door and slowly shuffled to the counter with a full mug of tea in one hand and a magazine in the other. He was wearing a well-worn navy-blue sweater under a navy-blue blazer, and a tatty, navy-blue peaked cap. "And a good afternoon to you too, Mr. Phil. Now then, not at all sure I can let you do that."

Phil was on tiptoes, leaning as far as he could across the counter. "Life and death, Perkins. CCTV from about ten minutes ago. I wouldn't ask, but …"

"Yes, but you would ask. You ask favours all the bloody time, as I recall," Perkins said dismissively.

"Well, one more favour couldn't hurt, could it? Life and death and all that?" pleaded Phil.

"Life and death, eh? In that case," Perkins said as he headed into the little office in the back.

Phil strained to look behind the counter to where the CCTV monitor was.

"Tell you what, I'll do you a favour if you do me one," Perkins said as he reappeared.

A damp tea towel hit Phil in the face.

"I just mopped that bloomin' floor an hour ago. You wipe your shoes on the mat like a good boy, and then wipe up the muddy footprints you just brought in here. I'll get the tape cued up."

With the floor nice and clean again, Phil was ushered behind the counter, and the two men stood in front of the console that housed the old black-and-white television that was tucked under the front desk.

CRAZED DETECTIVE MODE

Perkins pressed Rewind on the vintage VHS machine. "Nothin' much to see, though. A bunch of noisy tourists came in and I had to shoo 'em off again. Didn't want 'em in the quad getting on the grass. Mr. Scrump is on the warpath about people messing up his nice grass." Perkins glanced down at Phil's shoes and then up at Phil, and he raised an accusatory eyebrow and shook his head. "He's putting up new signs an' everythin'."

"Yes, yes. The CCTV?" urged Phil.

Phil watched as the VHS tape rewound and restarted, his eyes scanning the screen for Honey. The grainy image on the little TV set flickered, and right at 13:59:36, a group of a dozen or so came in through the open half of the main gate, all wearing coats and carrying cameras and guidebooks.

One half of the ancient, twenty-foot-high oak gateway was usually open during the day. The other half of the main gate was always closed, but the door-sized door within it was always open. This heavy, varnished, oak door, with its black metal studs and its centuries of history, was the bane of Arbley Scrump's existence. In its usual open position, the oak door completely blocked a smaller doorway that was painted green and was just inside the main gate. Behind the little green door was Arbley Scrump's storeroom.

The tourists milled around, looking like they had been expecting to find a ticket office. There was no sound, so Phil couldn't tell whether they were being loud or not. It looked as though one of them had slipped behind the door. The door in the gate was open to the street, and in its open position, it hid the green door behind it.

Then Perkins came into frame with his arms outstretched, shooing the tourists back out through the gate. Perkins then closed the big open half of the gate and stood in the gate's doorway, watching them out on the street. Then he closed the oak door within the gate, revealing a decent view of the green door. Of course, this being crappy black-and-white video, Phil had to have known the door was green. He also knew that the little sign, illegible on the tiny screen, read *Groundsman's Store*.

Then Phil watched as Perkins reopened the door in the gate and looked out. Phil watched the screen intently. Perkins went back into the lodge, but there was no sign of whoever had gone behind the big oak door. Phil looked closer at the screen. Did that person go back out with everyone else? Had he missed something?

"Then, a minute later, I goes back out an' opens the gate again when they'd all buggered off. Oh, look, and there's you, Mr. Phil, see? Coming in where I'd just opened the door again."

"Rewind a bit, please?"

The screen displayed fuzzy diagonal lines across it, and the tourists came back in walking quickly backwards.

"There. Play."

There were only two ways to get into Westgate College quads. The main gate entrance of Greyfriars Tower, off Paradise Street, and if it was open, the Backs Arch from the backs into back quad, on the other side of the grounds. If Honey had come here from the shopping centre, then she would have come to the main gate. There was definitely a dark-haired woman sliding in behind that ancient wooden door to where Scrump's green door was hidden. Was that Honey? Why would she go to that green door? When Perkins closed the big oak door, she was not there anymore. All that was revealed was Arbley Scrump's smaller, green door in the wall. If you ruled out a magic

Crazed Detective Mode

trick or some nifty video editing, the only logical conclusion was that Honey had gone into Scrump's storage room.

Phil ran out, thanking Perkins, who merely rolled his eyes, picked up his mug of tea, and pressed Record on the CCTV's video recorder.

Phil tried the green door to the groundsman's store. It was locked. He knocked. He tried the door again.

"What're you doin' rattlin' at my door?" said a familiar voice behind Phil.

Phil spun round. "Oh, Arbley. Thank God. Can you let me in?"

"That'll be Mr. Scrump to you student types, I'll thank you very much," snapped Scrump, standing with his feet planted firmly and his hands on his hips. "And why on God's green earth would I do such a thing?"

"Mr. Scrump, it's me, Phil."

"I can see that, Mr. Phil. What's in there that you want?" Scrump took off his hat, flattened it, and tucked it inside his jacket.

"A girl," said Phil.

"No girls in there, young man, Scrump replied. "Try the Slug and Lettuce. Plenty over there as I would call *girls*. Ladies, not so much. But them ones might do for ya."

"No, a specific girl. I saw her go in here," said Phil with increasing urgency.

"Did not."

"Did!"

"Can't have," snapped Scrump.

"I bloody did, I tell you!" said Phil.

"Step aside, I'll prove it to ya," Scrump said as he unlocked the door. The door creaked open, inwards, revealing a dark, dank little storage room, about fifteen feet deep by eight wide. It smelled of fresh compost and WD-40.

By the light from the forty-watt bulb hanging from the ceiling, Phil could make out a tool rack hanging on the wall at the far end, opposite the door.

"See, if it's locked and I has the only key, she can't have got in there, and unless she's magicked herself back out again, then she didn't come in here at all. See? It's empty. Except for the wheelbarrow, and tools and that, and my box of new signs."

Phil walked in and went into full-on crazed detective mode, tapping walls and looking all mysterious and baffled.

"See, I got sick of the entitled little pricks using my best lawns for picnics. There's plenty grass by the backs for picnics without using my manicured lawns for sitting on and drinking champagne. So, I got these new signs, see? They say *Please Keep Off My Fucking Grass*. Very polite, and tasteful with the gold paint an' all." Phil looked over. Scrump was holding up one of the signs. It did indeed say exactly that, picked out in gold paint on a nice dark green background.

"What are the walls made of?" asked Phil, wondering where Honey could have gone.

"Well, let's see. This wall here, with the street the other side, is solid stone, like. This one here next to the Porters' Lodge. Solid stone, also. Now, I'm not much of an expert, but I'd say there was an interior design theme for these old stone buildings, so if I was a gamblin' man, I'd plump for putting a bet on that other wall there being solid bleedin' stone."

CRAZED DETECTIVE MODE

Phil faced the tool rack, then reached up and gave the wall a good thump and, shaking his hand, said, "Yep, seems that way. Makes no sense, though. What's the other side of this wall behind the tool rack?"

Scrump thought for a moment. "I reckon that'll be the provost's staircase. That's what's the other side of the Porters' Lodge, innit. Staircase F."

Phil went back outside, followed by Scrump, who locked up behind them.

Phil paced the distance from the gate, down the length of the passageway to the other end of the Porters' Lodge. Twelve paces, give or take. The Porters' Lodge was about nine paces in length. Scrump's store was about three. Since Scrump's storeroom was as deep as the Porters' Lodge, Phil knew there must be something behind the tool rack on the wall there, but was Scrump right? Phil didn't think the provost's staircase was twelve yards long.

Phil went around the corner into the quad. Scrump shook his head at Phil and wandered off to carry on admiring the new signs in the lawn. Staircase F was the provost's hallway, and her rooms were one flight up, on the floor above the Porters' Lodge.

Phil went in through the outer door and paced the length of the hallway. Nine-and-a-bit paces. Honey had gone into Scrump's storeroom and disappeared. It seemed that there was a room beyond the storeroom, and it was not the hallway Phil was standing in. But there was no way out of the storeroom through solid stone. He couldn't make sense of it. The rooms above belonged to the provost. Phil was sure the provost hadn't kidnapped anyone. She was pious, straight-laced, and a stickler for rules—not really the type to be picking off female students. Scrump was the only one with access to the storeroom, but Phil was sure he was a jolly decent, kindly chap, and not given to bumping off students and putting them in the wood-chipper. No one was above suspicion, but Phil would put Scrump and the provost at the bottom of the list.

Phil had changed Durant's fate, and Holly had gone missing. The link had to be there somewhere. She came into Westgate and disappeared from the storeroom. He couldn't see how, but he was sure Durant was behind it. It didn't make sense, but there was definitely something behind Scrump's storeroom.

"Damn it, Durant! What have you done with Honey?" Phil said under his breath as he set off running to Staircase E.

25.
LET'S REWIND THE TAPE

07 NOVEMBER 2022, 1.46 P.M.

Honey checked her lip gloss in the mirror of the ladies toilets at the Alchemist. She was feeling confident. She had a new client. It would be nice, easy money from another lonely old professor. She packed her jeans, her favourite Burberry shirt, the matching scarf, and the cute pair of pink ballet flats into her tote bag. On her way down the corridor toward the bar, she encountered a small group of people blocking the doorway while waiting to be seated. She pushed through them, saying, "Excuse me, sorry, can I just …" and squeezed her way through to the exit.

She went down the escalators to the ground floor, then walked out of the shopping centre and crossed Norfolk Street. Her instructions from her prospective new client had been to knock on the green door, just inside the main gate. She had walked past that door a million times and never given it much thought. Maybe she was incorrect in remembering it as being a storeroom?

Honey arrived at the main gate just as a group of American tourists was bustling in through the entrance. She walked in with them through the open gate, squeezed past a few of them, and stepped to the wall on the right.

The porter came out of the lodge just as Honey had squeezed herself behind the old oak door. She stood in the tight gap behind the big wooden gate and the green door and saw a small brass sign that read *Groundsman's Store*.

This is weird, she thought.

"Sorry, folks," announced Perkins, "the college is closed to the public today. We have work going on on the grounds, and it's not safe. I would thank you kindly to come back another day."

Honey knocked on the green door, and it opened immediately. "Come in, come in. Quickly now. We don't want to be seen."

Honey felt herself being pulled in by the elbow.

Honey heard Perkins right outside, saying, "If you would, please, back the way you came, lovely, thank you." Then the massive main gate closed with a heavy, assured thud that echoed in the passageway.

The green door closed very quietly, and a key was turned slowly and quietly in the lock. Honey felt trapped and very uncomfortable. Her mind was running through her self-defence moves from the two years of Tang Soo Do she had studied as an undergrad. She knew it worked, because she had used it a couple of times before.

"I'm Professor Durant, pleased to meet you. You can call me Corvus."

"Well, this is fucking weird. What the hell are we doing locked in the gardener's storeroom?" asked Honey, looking around in the gloom and feeling significant discomfort.

LET'S REWIND THE TAPE

"I'm sorry, I needed to be discreet. One can't have young ladies seen to be coming to one's rooms. Discretion is vital with something delicate like this, don't you think?"

"I suppose. Well, yes, absolutely," she replied, totally unconvinced and trying to keep at a distance from him. If he came at her, she was ready. "But this wasn't what I had in mind for our appointment. The gardener's storeroom is not where I will be meeting clients. The other profs all see me in their rooms, so ..."

Durant laughed reassuringly. "Oh, no, my dear, you misunderstand me," he said lightly, "this is just a private entrance. I probably should have told you that in advance. I'm so sorry. I'm fortunate to have access to an ancient priest hole from my rooms. It's a fascinating bit of history. Follow me."

Durant pulled hard at the large tool rack that hung on the wall at the end of the room. Most of the wall seemed to swing open. Honey could see in the gloom that it was a hefty metal door faced with stone on the outside, and on that stone hung the large tool rack. Ahead of them was a six-foot-wide stone passageway lit by small, dim, flickering light bulbs. As they walked through, Durant stopped, turned, and closed a big metal door. The metal door clunked neatly, purposefully shut, and Durant turned the locking mechanism with the lever on the inside of the door. It was well-oiled and smooth. Not all loud and squeaky, as Honey would have thought such an ancient mechanism would be.

Honey was both creeped out and fascinated at the same time. She remembered getting the same feeling when she was a kid with her friends, and they would go exploring somewhere that was old, abandoned, dark, and sinister. This was a bizarre place to find herself.

She tried to stay calm and in control so that she didn't end up breaking the nose of an innocent prof who was just a bit of an oddball.

"So, the priest hole was constructed in the mid-sixteenth century, a hundred years after the college was built. Please, after you. Up the steps," Durant instructed, in an almost sing-song, happy voice. "It's up to the top, I hope you can manage in those delightful heels."

Even though her other clients were much less fussy about it, Honey understood that discretion was important, and the priest hole was a means to get her in and out in secret. Plus, it was very intriguing, so she told herself to get a grip. *You're being ridiculous, Holly*, she thought. *He's not Hannibal bloody Lecter, this isn't* Silence of the Lambs, *and he's not about to kill you and eat you bit by bit or wear your skin. He's just a lonely, sad old man. A harmless, pervy old professor.* She admitted to herself that it was a bit creepy, and she didn't know where the steps were heading, but she knew Durant's rooms were on the top floor, so it all kind of made sense. He was a tall man with a high centre of gravity, so he would be easy to topple. She knew that in one move she could break his nose, or his finger, and have him face down begging for his arm to be released. She fancied her chances of getting him in the groin with a stiletto too. And besides, she was determined to prove she was fine mounting the stairs in heels.

"Yep, I'm fine," said Honey, setting off up the dimly lit circular stone staircase. It was narrow and steep, but quite easily navigable, even in four-inch heels.

"The Principal of the Westgate Divinity School lived in these rooms back in those days, and he would aid and abet religious freedom by hiding Catholic priests. This priest hole was both a hiding place and a means of escape to the street when the priest hunters came. Such a fascinating bit of history."

"That's actually very cool," said Honey, catching a little of Durant's enthusiasm. She was genuinely interested and almost forgot to feel scared completely witless.

At the top of the steps, there was a wooden panel barring their way. Honey and Durant had to press their backs against the wall to allow it to swing open.

"Here we are. Please, just step in here," said Durant, jauntily. She stepped in, and he joined her in a small space that smelled of mothballs. He closed the panel behind them. "And presto," Durant said brightly as he pushed open the two light wooden doors in front of them. Stepping down onto the rug, she found herself in a bedroom, lit by a small window and a table lamp.

Durant stepped out beside her and closed the doors of his wardrobe behind them.

"Well, this is a bloody weird twist! Like some sort of backward Narnia," she said, trying to lighten her own mood.

"Indeed. Once a King in Narnia, always a King in Narnia. The priest hole is so very fascinating, though, don't you think?" Durant had a pompous air, but he seemed genuinely excited to have the opportunity to show off his priest hole. "You are one of only a handful of people in the last century to see that."

Honey glanced around at what appeared to be a pretty normal bedroom, apart from the peculiar wardrobe. There was an overstuffed bookcase, a neatly made double bed, and a bedside table bathed in a soft pool of light from the small table lamp. She was reassured by its ordinariness and relieved that the steps had indeed led to his rooms. But being in Durant's bedroom bolstered the vestige of her unease.

"Through here," Durant said, indicating the door to the living room.

The living room of a prof was a familiar space. There were walls lined with bookshelves housing an array of leather-bound tomes; tan, button-tufted leather furniture; dimly lit table lamps; burgundy velvet curtains; and the ubiquitous sideboard complete with a bottle of red wine. This seemed far more normal to Honey and made her feel a lot less creeped out. Durant had a hardcover of *The Brothers Karamazov* open on the coffee table, next to paperbacks of *Anna Karenina* and *Tess of the d'Urbervilles*. She had a glimpse of the possibility of debating faith, morality, and philosophy with him.

On the wall, in ornate, gold-painted frames, were what Honey presumed to be prints of two different London bridges. Her recollection from her fine art studies was that the originals had been painted by Monet.

She relaxed a little and told herself she was being stupid. It had been creepy in the priest hole, but this was much better. This was quite normal. He had some intriguing choices of literature and art, and she thought she would ask him about them later if they were getting along.

"Red wine, Honey?" Durant asked. When Honey nodded, he brought the bottle and two glasses over. "Do sit, my dear. You are far more beautiful than I remembered you."

"Oh, thank you, aren't you just lovely," Honey replied, trying to seem a little coy, and remembering how cheesy Limehouse was

Let's Rewind the Tape

with her. "Allow me," she said, taking the bottle and glasses from him. The bottle was unopened. She looked in the glasses. They were clean, so she set them down on the coffee table.

While Honey opened the wine, Durant said, "I'm a forgetful old fool. I meant to open the wine to let it breathe. I'm so sorry. Important to make sure it has time to breathe, though, to get the most from it. I know," he said with his big, toothy smile, "I'll get the aerator. That'll do the trick." He went back to the sideboard and returned with a small, clear, plastic device and handed it to Honey. She inserted it into the top of the bottle.

Honey poured the wine, and it swirled through the aerator into one glass. Durant picked up the empty one and held it out to be filled. "It's so very sad about old Chieveley," he said. "A jolly interesting chap, and always a hoot in the Common Room. But I'm delighted to have the opportunity to make your acquaintance. Here's to golden opportunities. Cheers!" he said. Honey picked up her wine, and Durant clinked her glass. He took a big sip and sat back.

From her student days of drinking in bars and not leaving a drink out of her sight, she felt she was pretty streetwise. Honey had opened the wine herself, seen that there was nothing in her glass, and even watched Durant drink first, so she took a sip of wine. It tasted OK. It was OK for French wine. Honey disliked French wine, as she thought it too acidic and dry. She liked red wines that were bold and deep with more than a hint of sweetness. Like her. This wine had an earthy nose. She could taste the resin and leather tannins, and the familiar mustiness of an old cellar. She was sure she could taste notes of the peasant feet that had trodden the grapes too, but perhaps she was just imagining that. She started to relax a little more.

"You like it? Châteauneuf du Pape. Jolly expensive," said Durant.

Honey knew her place. She was a potential employee, and this was a kind-of job interview; she needed to size him up, and try to figure out who he wanted her to be, so that she could be his ideal companion once a week. "Oh, yes, it's delightful. Such a complex and delicate structure."

"The luscious, textured mouthfeel. Do you taste the raspberry notes of the Grenache? Try it, try a second sip," Durant said and took another sip himself. "Hold it on your tongue, swirl it round. There, do you feel it? The firm tannins coming in. Oh, the joy of a good wine."

"Raspberry, yes, of course. I couldn't place it." But Honey wasn't altogether sure she wasn't just getting notes of her cherry-flavoured lip gloss.

"The third sip is always different again. Not a wine to hurry, normally, but we don't have long together today."

She was feeling more relaxed now, and when Durant took his third sip, she followed suit.

Durant sat forward, looking a little serious. "Now, we need to be sure of the terms, I believe," he said. "Two hundred an hour? Now, you should be tasting the finish. Do you get any chocolate and vanilla as you continue to sip?" Durant drained his own glass and sat back in his chair.

"Oh, I'm not sure I was getting any chocolate coming through. But if you've got Dairy Milk, I'd love some," she said, chuckling.

"Oh, very funny, *très drôle*," Durant said, with a completely straight face. "Occasionally, I enjoy a decent Shiraz paired with some nice, dark, seventy per cent cocoa—proper Swiss chocolate. But not Dairy Milk. Are you really a Dairy Milk kind of girl?"

"Oh, no, of course not. It was just a silly joke," she said, hoping to placate him. She took yet another sip of the brownish-red wine. A smaller sip this time, it seemed like it was quite strong wine. "And, yes, two hundred is the standard rate. Cash upfront, or we can arrange a bank thingy. A what's-it-called? Umm, yeah, I'd much rather the bank handle the money so we can just ignore that bit of it."

Then Honey put down her wine glass. She was starting to feel a bit light-headed. She had been confident he hadn't drugged her wine. She had made sure he put nothing in her glass. But this wasn't quite how getting tipsy with Wigtwizzle usually felt.

"Now, I know our introduction is only an hour, so I'm keen to impress you with a delicate, nutty Sancerre that pairs nicely with a delightful, brandy-washed Trou du Cru cheese. What do you think?"

Honey's head was swirling now. "No cheese for me. I don't feel so good." Her speech was starting to slur a little. She realized that he had managed to drug her somehow, and she knew she needed to get out.

"Are you woozy, my dear? Excellent. A few drops of mostly muscle relaxant in the aerator, along with a dash of sedative. It all gets mixed into the first glass. Who would notice the hint of bitterness in such a complex wine? Not you, eh? Oh, it's very quick acting, but we don't want you passing out, now do we? No more wine for you." Durant moved her glass away. "Let's get you to the bedroom," said Durant.

"I don't think so!" said Honey, with mounting panic. Durant took her arm and pulled her up. She stood and wobbled. She grabbed Durant's hand and tried to bend his finger back, but her grip failed. She faced him and thrust her palm upwards toward his nose, but she felt heavy and weak. Her palm smacked Durant in the face, but did not inflict the intended damage. "Help!" she screamed, before Durant managed to grab her wrist and cover her mouth. She stamped her stiletto heel on Durant's foot, but only really succeeded in losing her balance.

Durant caught her as she stumbled. Honey's legs weren't holding her up. Durant half pushed and half carried her into the bedroom and lifted her onto the bed. Honey was struggling to get away and lashing out as much as she could, and she felt the room spinning as Durant pushed her back down on the bed. She was completely fuddled, and her head was swimming, and though she couldn't focus, she did know that this was terribly wrong. There was a cocktail of drugs coursing through her, and she was trapped with a monster. She tried to scream, but realized that Durant had placed tape across her mouth, stifling her cries, and that cable ties were stopping her from fighting back.

Durant began to talk quietly and calmly to himself. "Let's take this nice and slowly. Not like last time. Not like before. That was all over far too quickly. I didn't realize how much I might have enjoyed it until it was over. You are a feisty little thing, but I do so want you conscious for this. I think perhaps you had just enough wine." Durant took a sip from a large glass of cognac. "Now, I'm going to watch the light drain from your eyes."

Oh, God, please, no, Honey thought. She tried to scream as she felt his hand on her throat. *Please, God, no, I don't want to die.*

26.

THE SECOND DEATH OF CORVUS DURANT

07 NOVEMBER 2022, 2.18 P.M.

Phil's adrenaline propelled him to the top of the stairs in spite of the fact that he was entirely out of breath. He sprinted the length of the balcony and knocked on Durant's door as though he expected Durant to just open up and invite him in. Then Phil banged on the door, his panic escalating, and finally he pounded on it, knowing more than it just being a hunch that Holly was inside and in grave danger. Assuming he wasn't already too late. He barged the door, shoulder first, like they do on TV. The door didn't even budge. There wasn't any room to make a run toward the door because the balcony was narrow, so he used all the space he had available to him as he tried again. The door barely even noticed he was there.

Phil began hammering and kicking the door again, and he was shouting. He didn't much care *what* he was shouting, but much of it would have made his mum ground him for a week. He was creating a huge disturbance. He tried charging the door again with his shoulder, but to no avail. Then he tried leaning back on the balustrade and kicking the door with both feet. *They don't make doors like this anymore,* thought Phil, fearing the balustrade would give way before the door did.

Suddenly, Durant opened the door. Phil's feet were now kicking into thin air, so he fell to the floor.

"Keep it down, or you'll have the police round here," Durant snarled.

Phil got up quickly and tried to push past Durant to get into his rooms. "Where is she?" he demanded. Durant held him back, so Phil took a step backward and charged at Durant with all his anger propelling him forward.

Phil was not a big man; he was shorter than Durant and had a much less bulky frame. Durant was a taller man with a quite muscular physique and considerably more padding from all his years of comfortable college living. Phil succeeded in making Durant stumble backward, and Phil fell forward through the door.

As Phil scrambled to his feet again at the threshold, he looked up and saw the professor turning to look behind, over his shoulder, back into the rooms behind him. Phil looked into the living room and saw Holly, in the guise of Honey, stumbling out of the bedroom with her hands and feet tied. She was trying to hop, and she was falling against furniture. She reached up and ripped the duct tape from her mouth and shouted, "Phil!"

Phil readied himself to charge Durant again, but before he could, Durant was running at him in a mad panic. As Durant's hands connected with Phil's chest, the two of them were suddenly out onto the balcony. As solid as he was, though, Phil was pretty nimble, and he instinctively stepped to the side and pushed the professor's hands away from him.

Now Durant's impetus was unhindered and heading for the balustrade. As he hit the railing, he toppled and his legs flew out behind him. He grabbed at anything he could, one hand seizing a spindle, the other clutching the lapel of Phil's jacket.

With nothing slowing his momentum, his legs followed his body over the railing, and in an instant, gravity snatched him, and Durant plunged down the stairwell. There was a sickening bang as the man hit the floor below. And then silence. *Is he dead?* Phil wondered. *Did he fall, or did I push him?*

Phil turned quickly to go to Holly. "Holly! Are you OK?"

"I will be, I think," Holly said. "The bastard was going to kill me. He was actually going to strangle me with his bare hands."

"Oh, Holly, I'm so sorry. I wish I'd gotten here sooner," Phil said, catching his breath.

"Just in the nick of time, matey. Another couple of minutes and you'd have been too late. But how did you know? How did you know I was here?" Holly asked as Phil stopped her from stumbling and propped her up.

"I just knew Durant was up to no good," Phil said, unsure of how he might explain how he'd got here. "Maybe I can explain better some other time."

Holly shook her head in disbelief. She sighed with relief and gratitude. "Help me get these ties off. Try the kitchen. Scissors, or a knife, or something."

"I'm on it," said Phil, letting go of Holly as she perched on the back of the sofa.

Phil freed Holly's hands and feet. She was still unsteady, but the adrenaline was doing a good job of focusing her mind.

They slowly walked out together and peered over the balcony. Durant lay twisted at the foot of the stairs.

"Is he dead?" asked Holly, kind of rhetorically.

"Reckon so," said Phil as he popped open his camera."

"Good. He was talking like he's done this before," she said, staring at the body.

Phil took a picture of the dead man and wrote *Staircase E, 07 Nov. 2022, 2.21 p.m.*

"Really? You're doing your Polaroid thing, right now?"

"You know, no one is going to believe I didn't murder him," said Phil. "They've got me on CCTV. They are going to know I had a motive."

"Don't you think saving my life is enough to explain what just happened?" Holly said.

"Yes, but … no, not necessarily. I'll go to prison for manslaughter, for sure." Phil was thinking that calling the police would be a big mistake. He would get stuck in this timeline, and everything would be in the news. It would be impossible to explain to the police, his mum, or to Holly. He was better off thinking about trying to undo what he had just done some other way, and he couldn't do that from a jail cell in the wrong timeline. "We can't call the police. We just need to tidy up and get out of here."

"We can't just walk out like nothing happened and leave him there for somebody to find!"

"I think we can. I think we bloody well have to. I need to get somewhere where I can work out how to fix this," Phil said, as much to himself as to Holly.

Phil grabbed the glass with Holly's lipstick on it. He grabbed the cut cable ties and the scissors. He put the cable ties in his jacket pocket.

THE SECOND DEATH OF CORVUS DURANT

Holly watched as Phil was busy tidying up and washing her glass in the kitchen. "The police will believe me that he fell, I'm sure. We need to do the right thing, don't we?"

Phil wiped the scissors and the glass with a tea towel and put them away in the kitchen.

"The right thing is that the murdering piece of shit is dead. He deserved it. The wrong thing is us getting blamed for an accident," Phil said.

It didn't seem like fleeing the scene of a crime was the right thing to do, but Phil wasn't convinced that a crime had been committed. He looked at a very uncertain Holly and held his hand out, ready to guide her through the door, down the stairs, and past the dead body.

"Come on then, Phil, if we've got to get out of here. This way," Holly said, grabbing her bag off the sofa and lurching unsteadily across the living room, doing her best to move quickly. "We can't go out via the quad."

Phil helped Holly along as she led him towards the bedroom. She opened the wardrobe. Phil was baffled, but trusted she knew something he didn't.

Holly pushed at the back of the wardrobe, but nothing moved.

"I need to sit down. Sorry, Phil," she said as she sat down on the bed. "I think it's wearing off a bit, but I'm still feeling weak." Holly took a few deep breaths. "The back opens outwards. That's how we came in."

"This is how you came in? Through the bloody wardrobe?" Phil stared at it in disbelief.

"Yep, like some fucking Narnia nightmare!" She rummaged in

her tote bag, found the little pink ballet flats, changed her shoes, and packed the heels in her tote.

Phil pushed. Nothing gave. He climbed into the wardrobe to get his shoulder on it. He felt it give a little, but it didn't open.

"We had to climb in and shut the back panel before the doors would open, if that's any help," offered Holly.

"OK, get in here with me so we can shut the doors," Phil said.

With Phil's help, Holly climbed into the wardrobe and, as Phil shut the doors behind her, he heard a faint, soft click near his feet. Then he felt around on the floor and found a raised wooden slat. He pulled at the jutting end, and it lifted up like a little lever, and there was a quiet, gentle clunk. He pushed on the back of the wardrobe, and it gracefully swung open. He took Holly's hand and carefully guided her down the stone staircase.

They reached the bottom of the stairs, walked along the passageway, and came face to face with the steel locking mechanism. Phil pulled the lever, the crossbars retracted from the metal sockets in the wall, and the door swung open. They went through the doorway, and they were in Scrump's storeroom. *Freedom!* thought Phil, and then he tried to open the outer door. It was locked.

"Bollocks! I'm not sure we can get out this way," and he turned apologetically to Holly, with his hands open in a slightly pathetic shrug.

"Will these help?" she said, dangling Durant's keys in front of Phil and dropping them into his open hand.

"Where … ?"

"Bedside table. I saw him lock that door behind us, and he dropped his keys on the bedside table as soon as we were out of the wardrobe."

"Genius. I thought for a minute I was going to have to go and raid a dead man's pockets!"

"Even half-drugged, I'm more use than you," she said, shaking her head. "Come on, get a bloody move on."

Phil turned the key in the lock and opened the door a crack. The big oak door was open in front of them, hiding them from view. Nobody was there, but the CCTV was. "No, let's wait, let's just wait a minute or two." Phil had seen how easily someone could hide from the CCTV behind a crowd. "I'm already on video from a few minutes ago, but you aren't. Not really. So let's at least keep it that way."

As always, tourists were wandering past and wandering in, but just in ones and twos. That wasn't enough cover. Then, just as Phil was thinking of making a run for it, the Westgate rugby team arrived en masse, coming down the passageway from the quad. They had a game in Abingdon, and they were heading out to board the team bus. They were singing, and they were rowdy. As they came past the green door, Phil and Holly slipped out, hidden by at least fifteen huge men as they walked through the door in the gate and out onto Paradise Street.

"This way," said Phil, "you look like you could do with a nice cup of tea."

27.
THE RELATIONSHIP COMPLICATION

07 NOVEMBER 2022, 2.40 P.M.

They got to Mrs. T.'s B & B without getting too wet. The light drizzle was cold and had woken Holly up considerably, and she had been walking unsupported, and telling Phil how grateful she was that he had arrived when he did. Phil rang the bell, and after a minute or so, the door opened and a perplexed-looking Plumbus Thistle stood peering out, squinting in the daylight.

"Sorry to disturb, Mr. Thistle. I was just bringing Holly here to recuperate. She's had a bit of a shock. This is Holly," Phil added lamely, pointing to her. "Is Mrs. T. about?"

"No, mate, she's at the shops, ain't she," said Mr. Thistle.

"Oh, perhaps we could cadge a cuppa, do you think?" asked Phil.

"Of course you can, Phil. You'd better get her in out of the wet. She looks awful."

"I know I'm not looking my best, but I'm standing right here!" Holly said.

"Sorry, luv, just woke up," Plumbus said, turning to Holly. "Afternoon nap, you know how it is. I'm not altogether with it yet."

"I do," said Holly, "I know how you feel."

"So, what's up here, then?" Plumbus asked Phil.

Holly replied, "Someone tried to, um, snatch my bag. Phil stopped them, so nothing taken. I'm just a bit shaken up."

Plumbus pushed the door open wide, and they walked in. "Best sit 'er in there, Phil," Plumbus said, indicating the front room that was hardly ever used, as it was reserved for very special occasions. "I know the missus saves it for best, but I reckon a bit of a shock would be a good enough reason to use the front room, eh?"

"Thank you, Mr. Thistle," said Holly.

"Please, call me Plumbus. Shall I phone the police?"

"No, thank you, Plumbus. Erm, nothing taken and neither of us actually saw his face or anything. So, no real point troubling officers who arguably have better things to do."

"Alright, have it your way. Cuppa tea then, luv?"

"Oh, coffee, please," said Holly.

"Cuppa coffee, mate?" asked Plumbus, looking at Phil.

"Cup of Coffee-mate? That would be weird," replied Phil absently, looking at Holly.

"Do you want coffee?" Plumbus repeated slowly.

"No, tea please, Mr. T."

Plumbus left the room muttering something about Phil being a bloody idiot.

Phil turned to Holly and saw the concern on her face. He didn't really know what to say to someone who had just nearly died. "How are you feeling?"

"Dunno. OK, I suppose, considering. I'm trying very hard not to think about it, though. But, thank you, Phil, you saved my life."

The Relationship Complication

"Oh, don't mention it. Happy to help," he replied, playing it down, trying to sound like he'd just changed a lightbulb. "Happy to throw your would-be murderers off a balcony anytime."

"Too soon for humour, Phil."

"Can I call someone? A friend, maybe?" Phil asked, feeling like he wasn't going to be able to help.

"Not right now. I'm not feeling up to explaining any of this to my friends. Not sure I am feeling much yet, but I can't stop trembling. I keep remembering Durant's hand on my throat, and then I try to think about something else. Then I can't help thinking about feeling grateful to you. And then I think it kind of changes things with us." Holly said with a sad look.

Phil took Holly's hands. She was shaking and cold. Her pupils were dilated, and she wasn't focusing. "What does? Why?" he asked.

Holly pulled her hands away. "Maybe I'm just not feeling so good right now, but as we were walking, it just felt like things are different, you know?"

"I don't know, sorry. What do you mean *different?*"

"A while ago, when I was an undergrad, I was seeing this guy. He was a bit older, had a job, a flashy car, and a nice flat. He had a lot more money than I did, and I was eking out a living, so he was always paying for things. You know, weekends away, or buying me gifts. It seemed a bit like I always had to be grateful for something. Which I was, don't get me wrong. He was very generous. But it always felt very one-sided. You know? He was different to you, though, I'm sure. He was a bit controlling. Turns out, he was a bit of a jackass. Turns out, he was married, but that's not my point. I'm just remembering that sense of always feeling a bit indebted. It just feels a bit like that, me feeling indebted to you for saving me, and I don't think I like that feeling. You see?"

Phil shook his head. "No, not really."

"You kind of want to feel like you're sort of equal," Holly said, "and not one person who owes their life to the other. Kind of feels like there's more debt on my side than anyone would really want starting a new relationship. I think it's like until I save your life, I'm always going to feel like I owe you more than I can ever pay back."

"I hadn't thought of that. I don't think I would have thought of it like that. I'm just so grateful I got there in time," Phil said, not liking where this seemed to be heading.

"Yes, well, you're the hero. It's probably pretty simple from your perspective," Holly said. "But it feels kind of complicated for me."

"You just said *thank you*. That's enough for me." Phil hoped that would be convincing, but he could hear the doubt in Holly's voice.

"It isn't really that simple, though, is it?" Holly said.

"For me, it is." Phil felt like this was unfair. He'd just saved her life, and she was being like this over it!

"Maybe I'm just being stupid. Maybe the drugs are still messing with my head. But what if it would all end in obligation and resentment, you know?" Holly said.

"But I won't resent you for saving your life," Phil attempted to reassure her.

"No, me, you dozer. I'm worried I will end up resenting you for feeling obligated to you. Like I did before, but on a bigger scale this time. Obviously, not as resentful as I would be finding out you're married, but still. I don't know Phil. It's just how I feel right now. That's what sitting here with you is making me think. And then I feel bad for thinking like this, so I try to stop myself thinking it. And then I think I'm doing that out of a sense of obligation to be grateful. And maybe having to do that all the time is going to make me resentful. Maybe I'm overthinking it, but there you go. I am very grateful to you, you saved my life," she said, her voice choking, "but I'm just feeling like that changes things. Can't you see that?"

Phil felt it like a stabbing pain, right where the knot had been when he was worried when she was missing. And now here she was, safe and sound, beautiful and alive, but telling him it might all be over. She had no idea that she really had previously, actually died, while Phil had sat talking with Akito in the Slug and Lettuce. Phil felt his blood rising. Whatever it was that Holly was feeling, Phil resented the implication that it was all his fault for rescuing her. He felt like she owed him more than to just dump him. Words just tumbled out. "Well, I'm not sure I could cope with worrying about this sort of thing happening every time you visit a bloody client. I'm pretty sure I would resent you putting yourself in that situation three times a week!"

"Oh, come on, that's not fair!" Holly said, her eyes flashing with anger. "I thought he was a respectable old Oxford professor. Limehouse Wigtwizzle referred me to him. It's not like I pick up random clients in bars or on street corners. It's not like I'm not careful. But, if that's how you feel …"

"Well, you did put yourself in danger, and you would have died if I hadn't figured it out in the nick of time. You literally would have died." Phil was exasperated.

"I know, I was there, for fuck's sake, Phil. Don't be such a condescending prick," Holly shouted. "Trying to make me resent you less by being a complete arsehole isn't really the way to go about making me feel better."

Phil watched as a tear fell down Holly's cheek. She was hurt and angry, and he suddenly felt ashamed. He swallowed hard. He really didn't want to make this harder for Holly than it already was, and he felt wretched for blaming her. His mouth opened to apologize, but at that moment, Plumbus bumbled back into the room carrying a tray, not reading the room at all.

"Alright, my lovelies. One coffee, one tea. It's instant coffee, sorry, love. Boiling the kettle and opening a jar of Nescafé is the best I can do, coffee-wise. That infernal, bloody machine that does the breakfast lattes is beyond me, I'm afraid. That's the missus's domain. You'll have to wait for Marion if you want a latte."

"This is great, thank you, Plumbus, it's hot and has caffeine in," Holly said. "You're so kind."

The three of them sat quietly while scalding hot drinks were blown on and uncomfortably slurped.

The front door banged open and Marion called out loudly, "I'm home!"

Plumbus called back, "Who's home?"

To which Marion poked her head round the door to the front room and said, "Our home, silly!" Then, looking at Holly, she put her shopping bags down and said, "And what do we have here?"

"Hello, I'm Holly."

"Had a bit of a shock, so they tell me. Would-be bag-snatcher," said Plumbus, with the *CliffsNotes* synopsis of events.

"Ooh, love, that's awful. Did he do those bruises on your neck?" said Marion, with melodramatic concern.

The Relationship Complication

"Oh! Oh, yes, I suppose so," said Holly.

Phil looked over at Holly, concerned. He hadn't noticed the bruises forming. Holly's hair must have been covering them. Holly took a look at herself in the mirror above the fireplace.

"Plumbus, go and get the biscuits! The nice ones. The Chocolate Hobnobs!" barked Marion. "And the brandy!"

"Mrs. T., is number five free for a day or two?" asked Phil quietly to Marion.

"Nothing booked for at least a week, darlin'," said Marion.

"And you can just charge it to my card, right?" Phil whispered.

"Yes, love," Marion whispered back.

"So, Holly," Phil said, "Marion says you can stay here if you want. She'll take care of you for a few days, if you'd like."

"Oh, that would be lovely, actually," Holly said to Marion. Her shoulders relaxed, and she smiled for the first time since she'd been attacked by Durant.

Phil smiled at Holly, hoping she was relieved to not have to go home alone at that moment.

"This is a bed and breakfast, but I think I can stretch to half-board for a friend of Phil's," Marion said, winking at Holly.

"Thank you, Marion," said Holly.

"Well, you make yourself at home, love, and when you feel up to it, me an' Plumbus will run you home so you can pack a bag. Steak and kidney pie and chips and peas alright for your tea, my darlin'?" Marion said.

Holly nodded enthusiastically.

"There's a phone there if you want to call your mum," Plumbus then added.

The old rotary phone was about the same vintage as the cornflower and poppy upholstery of the armchairs. Holly took a sip of her coffee, which was now slightly less hot than boiling.

"Thank you, Plumbus. I think I'll phone home, talk to my dad," she said, indicating her mobile phone. "And then have a nap."

Phil stood up, clasping his hands in front of him, searching for something to say. He was unsure if they had broken up, and he felt too awkward about it to ask. "Erm, I guess I'll leave you to rest for a bit, then. I'll come by this evening and see how you're doing, if that's alright."

"Yes, I'd like that. Thank you, Phil. You're a real hero."

Phil left the B & B and wandered around aimlessly, unable to think or feel. He got some food, but he couldn't eat. A pint of beer hadn't softened his worry over Holly. And finally, after sufficient time for a nap had probably elapsed, he walked, heavy-hearted, back to the B & B on Hollybush Row.

Mrs. T. showed Phil in and through to the front room. Holly was there, sitting quietly with a pot of tea and the fancy china, and she was reading Plumbus' copy of *The House at Pooh Corner*.

"A little *smackerel* of something?" she offered. "Cucumber sandwich? Piece of cake, perhaps? I'm not hungry, but someone should make a dent in all this," she added, indicating the side table laden with the fruits of Marion's mumsy kindness, which had not taken no for an answer.

"I'm not hungry either. How are you feeling?" Phil asked, sitting opposite Holly, across from the tea-laden table, and leaning forward anxiously.

"A bit shit, really. That brandy hasn't helped. I know I was drugged, and it all happened so fast, but I was terrified, Phil. I know what terrified *actually* means, now. I thought that was it. I think I'm mostly in denial right now, and I've got a horrible feeling more trauma will come later. I'm not looking forward to that. I just can't help reliving it, going over it. Really, over and over again. I am so grateful that you came in time. So grateful. Not all heroes wear capes. Some of them wear nerdy T-shirts."

Phil knew that now wasn't the right time for a smart-arse suggestion about getting help for the trauma. He shrugged. "I didn't do much. I just figured out where you were and banged on the door. Anyone would have done what I did."

"Not only that, but I feel guilty because I'm glad he's dead." Holly smiled weakly.

"Me too," Phil laughed. "Don't feel bad about that. If he hadn't died, I'd have bloody killed him. It's not your fault. None of this is your fault."

Holly looked at Phil, the worry showing in her furrowed brow. "What do we say if the police come? You're on CCTV. What if there's DNA or something?"

"I'll see what I can find out from my friend in the police. I cleaned up in there and wiped fingerprints off things. There's nothing to incriminate you, I'm sure," Phil said. "It's all going to be OK."

"How can it be OK? The guy's dead!" she said, shaking her head in disbelief. "Nothing about this is OK."

Phil looked down, he took a breath and said, "I'm sorry if I was a bit of a shit to you earlier."

"That's your apology, is it?" Holly scoffed.

"I'm very sorry for being a condescending prick."

"That's more like it. Thank you," Holly said quietly. "I don't honestly think I can deal with you blaming me, or judging me for being there. Telling me it's not my fault doesn't change what you said earlier. You do think it was my fault."

Phil knew that he had meant what he said earlier. He didn't like what she did. He did think she was at risk doing it. He decided not to try to argue with her. "I'm sorry anyway."

"I'm not in a fit state to be thinking about us properly," Holly continued. "Maybe we should give it time. I need a bit of time to cope with what happened first."

Phil nodded, "Yes. I get it, sorry. Take all the time you need." Phil was hoping that he would sort all of this out somehow by going back in time again and fixing it. He could change what happened in some way that would stop them being implicated in Durant's death. He could make their earlier argument never happen, and leave Holly's feelings for Phil untainted by his disastrously heroic rescue.

Holly perked up a little. "I spoke to Mum and Dad earlier. Dad's coming tomorrow to get me. I'm going to stay with them for a bit. Christmas and New Year's, at least. I'll be back in January, I think. Look for a different job. Then, I dunno, we'll have to see, I suppose."

"Oh, that's a great idea. Get some time to recuperate and have some of your mum's home cooking."

"Actually, Dad's the chef at home. He makes the spaghetti, or risotto, or the Sunday roast. My mum's a beans-on-toast sort of mum. Mind you, she makes a good cuppa. It'll be nice, though. I just think I'll feel safe there."

"Good. Glad about that. I'm not sure I could be any help if you stayed here." There was a pause as they sat with a painful silence separating them. Holly stared at the cup of tea in her hands. Phil wanted to get going on a plan to fix this, and he decided now was a good time, so he stood up. "Well, this is tough on both of us, so I'm going to get going and leave you to start feeling better." Phil kissed Holly's cheek and said, "I will hope to see you in January then. Don't get up, I'll see myself out."

Holly didn't speak. She just looked sad and tried to smile. Phil turned and walked to the door. He stopped in the doorway for a moment, but decided not to turn back.

Mrs. Thistle was out in the hallway, and she opened the front door for Phil. She gave him a big hug and said, "Oh, lovey, I'm sorry. We'll see she's alright."

Phil walked out into the cold, dreary day, feeling gloomier than the grey of the clouds. The door shut behind him with a clang of the brass door knocker. It felt like that door was closing on him and Holly.

Phil needed to fix all of this. He had to prevent Durant's death again. He had to make sure that Holly didn't need to be rescued. And that would also prevent the argument about Holly putting herself at risk. He wondered if he could simply go back and stop himself bumping into Akito, and if he could he actually let Akito kill Durant.

Then a penny dropped. It wouldn't actually prevent Durant from attacking Holly. The attack must have been happening right before Akito was there. Akito must have saved Holly the first time round. Phil needed to prevent Holly from meeting Durant that day. But he thought they might just rearrange to meet, and he needed to figure out how to stop it from happening altogether. Phil decided it was time for him to go back to his own timeline and see where he stood with Holly. They hadn't gone on the date to McDonald's in that timeline yet, but having dated in this timeline, Phil would be checking on the Holly who had been attacked to see how she felt after Christmas with her mum and dad. Also, having been responsible for Durant's death, he could check on the investigation with Havarti and confirm that he was in the clear.

Phil was relieved that at least he didn't have to actually live through the next couple of months in limbo. He could just jump forward and find out all the answers. And then he could figure out what he could do about it, and have access to his Polaroid archive. That was where he needed to be. That was a step in the right direction. He walked the short distance to the college backs, and found a secluded spot. He opened his satchel and pulled out his stack of Polaroids. He flicked through them and selected one. He held the Polaroid that read *Queen St. Flat, 18 Jan. 2023, 3.54 p.m.* in front of his eyes and the backs began to dissolve. The grass and trees merged into one blurry green screen and then faded to grey.

28.

DEEPER IN TROUBLE

18 JANUARY 2023, 3.54 P.M.

Phil sensed the familiar surroundings of his flat, and he could make out the bright-orange robot arm as it gradually came into focus. Phil was regaining his bearings and remembering where he had been. He sat still, allowing his surroundings to slowly come to life, while reality settled on the scene like dew on cold grass. He couldn't believe Holly would dump him like that. *After I saved her life and everything!* he thought. *Oh, wait, maybe that was her point.*

Phil guessed that he had taken the place of Akito in Durant's death. Losing Holly seemed to be his karmic payback for it. But Phil hadn't actually shoved him off the balcony, he reasoned, so he wondered why karma would be so pissed off.

Apart from two broken hearts and Akito being free of guilt, the world should be back the way it had been. His heart was still broken, but he was determined to fix it.

After what Durant had done to Holly, Phil was not sorry he was dead. But he wanted to go back and undo Durant's attack on Holly to prevent her needing to be saved. If that meant saving Durant, then that was what he had to do.

Phil wanted to talk to someone. He thought about going to see Mrs. Thistle to ask how Holly had been after he'd left. *Should I just call Holly? Maybe I could pop over there and see her in person?*

Just then, as his phone adjusted to its new surroundings and found a signal, it started to ping. Messages and missed calls started to show up, like they would when someone's phone goes off Airplane Mode, assuming that someone has a lot of friends. They were texts and missed calls from Havarti. Phil needed to know what the police knew about Durant's death, and she could fill him in. He wanted to know what had happened after he and Holly had made their escape, and he wanted to be sure they were in the clear.

Phil picked up his phone and dialled.

"DS Frisk."

"Hi, Havarti, it's Phil. Hey, how are you?"

"Phil, where have you been?"

"Round and ab—"

"With your phone off? You dumb twat. The Firkin Folly, right now. Seriously, this bloody minute. Run, if you can, you chunky f—"

She hung up. Phil looked at his phone. He was a bit shocked, since it wasn't unusual for Havarti to be rude, usually in an offhand, almost affectionate kind of way, but it *was* unusual for her to sound like she meant it and just hang up mid-sentence. He guessed that Havarti must really need his help, so he grabbed his stuff and rushed out to get the bus.

Phil walked into The Firkin Folly and spotted Havarti sitting at the same table where he'd had lunch with her earlier today. Of course, that had been a few days ago in Phil's timeline, but it was earlier today for Havarti.

DEEPER IN TROUBLE

It was even more confusing to realize that Havarti had not eaten lunch here with Phil on this particular incarnation of 18 January 2023. Phil surmised that because of the changes in their timelines, Phil and Havarti had not had lunch together. It was just another one of those little time-change anomalies that Phil had come to expect. Lunch had happened for Phil, and the anomaly couldn't alter that for him, but the changes he had made in the past meant their lunch hadn't happened for Havarti.

But what Phil didn't know was what Havarti had been doing during her lunchtime in this version of today.

"How's it going?" asked Phil in a cheery voice, expecting Havarti to ask a favour of some kind.

"Going? Phil, it's all going really bloody pear-shaped."

"Why? What can I do to help?" he asked.

"When you came in to the station and had fingerprints done, and we showed you the CCTV footage, I told you we couldn't eliminate you. But I'd put you on the back burner because I didn't think you'd done it."

"Remind me? What CCTV footage?" he asked. He had a sinking feeling, and he was hoping to stall for more information.

She shook her head and gave an exasperated sigh in disdain and disbelief.

"You two havin' a drink, or what?" asked Ruby from behind the bar.

"Not just now, Ruby, thanks. Sorry," said Havarti.

Havarti turned back to Phil with fire in her eyes. "On the day of Durant's death, CCTV shows you in and out of the college. You come in, you walk round. You bump into some guy, and the two of you walk out together. Then somehow, there you are again, having travelled the long way around, apparently, to show up on the quad again. I don't think Usain Bolt could have run that distance faster. Now you're in the Porters' Lodge, in the garden shed, and then running out to the quad again. Never to be seen again."

"Oh, yes, that looks odd. Right, yes. That shitty, old VHS must've been on the blink." Phil was clutching at straws, but he genuinely thought that CCTV wouldn't hold up in court.

"Well, the timestamp is continuous. And it looks more than odd. It looks bloody suspicious. Just sayin'."

Phil was shifting uneasily in his seat. He had no good explanation for Havarti. He knew the CCTV put him there at the time of Durant's death, but he also knew that the other version of him had been in Wednesbury. *Couldn't that prove his innocence?* he wondered. He decided that he shouldn't be worried by the timestamp on what he could insinuate was an old and unreliable CCTV system. He was fighting the feeling of worry that was creeping up fast. He was trying to stay calm, and yet he could see Havarti getting agitated. She was sitting forward, and she was getting angry.

"Well, let's leave aside the sodding CCTV, then," Havarti said. "What about the partial fingerprints we pulled in Durant's rooms? A cable tie we found under the sofa? The wardrobe in Durant's bedroom?"

"Oh," said Phil, with the sinking feeling growing rapidly. He realized that in his desperation to rescue Holly, he had rushed his attempt to clean up. He had been the one with the clear, undrugged head, and yet it hadn't occurred to him to wipe the wardrobe as they left.

DEEPER IN TROUBLE

"Not to mention the sodding poppy in his cold, dead hand!" Havarti continued. "Not your fingerprints, but we tracked down the poppy seller, and she described you to a tee. Literally. She even remembered your sodding Westgate College T-shirt."

Phil glanced at his lapel. The poppy was gone. He remembered Durant had grabbed his jacket. "Ah, well, yes, I did buy a poppy, but you can't prove that one is the one that—"

"No, but the poppy seller's statement puts you in Oxford that morning, Phil, not bloody Wednesbury." Havarti's voice suddenly became calm and quiet. "When we brought you in for questioning a couple of months ago, you told me you'd never been in his bedroom. Yeah, right. And yet we found your partial prints on the wardrobe. What about the cable tie, though, hmmm? A cable tie, Phil! Weird, right? You had no good explanation for the cable tie. You said you'd never even seen the cable tie. And yet, it felt like you were telling the truth."

"Well, it's all a bit weird, on the face of it, yes, but I—"

"Ruby!" called the plumber who had emerged from the gents. "I love the sign you've got over the urinals that says don't throw chewing gum in them. You know, the one where somebody added *It makes it taste disgusting.*"

"S'wot you asked for, my lovely," Ruby said, with a proud smile.

"Well, can you get another one for the bogs that says about not putting size 10 flip-flops down there?" he said.

"A pair of flip-flops?" Ruby replied, shaking her head.

"Nah, just the one," the plumber said with a shrug.

"Oh, fair enough. Alright, darlin', I'll get signs made."

Havarti rolled her eyes. "Suppose I'll have to find somewhere else to get rid of all my spare flip-flops now." Phil stared at her. His mind was racing to find a good tack to take to bring up his alibi. She calmly picked up her thread. "We can't overlook the fact that you couldn't adequately explain your fingerprints in Durant's rooms, Phil." Then Havarti seemed saddened. "You said you weren't there. You seemed totally genuine. You told me you didn't kill him. I concede that you were convincing. I think we could have polygraphed you. I'm not convinced about your alibi, what with the CCTV and the poppy seller both putting you in Oxford that day. And yet I believed you. You promised me you didn't do it, Phil. And I believed you."

Phil reasoned that she would have been interviewing the other him, who would have been in Wednesbury when Durant died. The other Phil, whose timeline he had been in that day. The *other* him who knew he hadn't been anywhere near Oxford that day. Of course, *he* would have been convincing. Of course, *he* would have passed a lie detector test.

"All of that is a bit inexplicable," Phil conceded, "but surely I have an alibi if I can prove I was in Wednesbury all day!" Phil sat back in his chair like he'd made a great chess move and waited for Havarti's reply.

Havarti sighed. "You had your appointment letter with the training centre in Wednesbury, and you had some undated pictures of some orange robots. That was enough to keep you at the bottom of the chief's naughty list. So, I pursued other lines of enquiry because I didn't think you'd killed him."

"Didn't you check with them? With the Training Centre? Am I on CCTV somewhere? Did you look?"

DEEPER IN TROUBLE

"I didn't think I needed to because I believed you. And I didn't think you wanted him dead anymore, so I believed you. Then all the other leads dried up, and I failed to pursue a suspect with due urgency." She suddenly got agitated again. "A suspect with a motive. You, Phil. I failed to pursue *you*."

"Well, I do appreciate you believing me, and not just pinning it on me. I did have motive a long time ago. And yes, that sounds bad," Phil admitted, with worry giving way to rising panic. "But you can check into my alibi now."

"Well, not so much anymore. I got called in to see the chief at lunchtime. I'm being moved to Reading."

Havarti's mock-happy tone confused Phil for a second. "Oh, really? Is it a good move? Promotion?" Phil hoped for a brief moment that this meant the conversation might be going in a better direction.

"Good move, Phil? It's Reading!" she shrieked. Havarti had gone from frustrated and angry to incandescent. Ruby stopped stacking beer glasses and looked over to see what the fuss was about. "Nobody wants to go to bloody Reading!" Havarti growled at Phil.

"Amen to that," said Ruby.

Havarti lowered her voice. "No, not a promotion. I've failed, Phil. You are the only suspect, and I've dragged my feet and failed to pursue the appropriate line of enquiry for too long. I'm off the case, Phil. I'm off the case, and I can't do anything now."

Phil was flushed with a feeling of embarrassment and shame. He felt responsible for what had happened, and it seemed as though the hope he had been holding onto was draining away.

"Oh, I'm so sorry ... "

"Oh, you will be. I'm just getting to the good bit. They've given the case to DI Hunter now. As of lunchtime, he's in charge. I can't do a damn thing anymore. Hunter thinks you did it. He's got enough to make it stick, and he'll have no intention of pursuing your alibi. He will take you down, Phil. You are buggered, matey. More than me, even, being buggered all the way to Reading. You're going to Wormwood Scrubs, and you'll probably be buggered for twenty-five to life by the nastiest of the inmates. Is the picture clear enough yet?"

"Oh shit!" exclaimed Phil. The full realization of what she was saying hit him hard in the gut. "But what about my alibi?" he asked weakly.

Havarti just shook her head. "Hunter doesn't give a shit if you say you were on stage with Beyoncé with ten thousand witnesses. You haven't got an alibi as far as he's concerned. He has the CCTV footage, and he doesn't believe you were anywhere but in Durant's rooms while throwing him off the balcony. He's going to arrest you, Phil. He's going to use what they've got to try to close the case quickly. You're going to need a bloody good lawyer, Phil, and you're going to have to pray that your so-called alibi is watertight."

"But …"

"You asked me how it's going? How? Really, really, badly is how."

Havarti paused from exasperation. Her shoulders slumped, and Phil sensed a resignation in her. She continued, but much less animatedly. "If you did it, I hope you burn in hell for making me believe you. If you didn't do it, then you'd best disappear and sort something out, because if Hunter isn't at your flat already, he will be by the time you get home."

DEEPER IN TROUBLE

Phil just sat with his mouth open. His emotions tumbled around, swirling, torn between sadness for Havarti and fear for himself. He needed to get to somewhere where he could try to undo Durant's death for a second time. This time to save himself.

Havarti stood. "I can't risk being seen here with you. Bye, Phil. Good luck," she said as she touched his shoulder and walked out.

"You too," he muttered as the door closed behind her.

It seemed Phil had underestimated Havarti's friendship. He thought she would have banged him up if she had good reason to. But she had actually believed him. And now she was being sent to Reading as punishment for it. Her career was over because of him.

And he was wanted for murder. That too. He wasn't in the clear at all. He wondered how the day could get any worse.

Phil stood up, unsure where he was heading. He walked to the door and stepped out of The Firkin Folly and into the daylight.

He was immediately confronted by three men. The one he recognized was DI Hunter. He looked supremely smug. Nothing new there. He always looked supremely smug. "Phil Beans. Thought we might find you here. You weren't home when we called at the flat with the warrant and the search team."

"Sorry, Phil. They must've followed me here," said Havarti, who was standing to the side with her arm in the grasp of a fourth officer. Phil smiled at her with a resigned shrug.

"Indeed we did, Frisk. Aiding and abetting? Never mind Reading, I'll see that you lose your fucking job for this," Hunter said with a sneer.

Hunter turned back to Phil, and as two of the men took an arm each, he recited, "Philip Lydington Beans, you are under arrest.

You do not have to say anything, but it may harm your defence if you do not mention when questioned something which you later rely on in court. Anything you do say may be given in evidence. You are entitled to a lawyer. If you don't have one, we'll find you a shitty, incompetent one, and we'll stitch you up for a few other unsolved crimes while we're at it."

They bundled Phil into the back of an unmarked car. Hunter got in the passenger seat, and another man got in the driver's side. The other two men got into a second car. Phil looked back at Havarti, who just stood and watched incredulously as they drove away.

Phil thought fast. He needed to escape, and to do that, he needed his bag with him. Being in a cell without it would prevent him from doing anything. It was now or never. His bag was on the back seat next to him, and without looking, he slipped a Polaroid out of the pocket of the satchel. He had to be sneaky, so that Hunter wouldn't notice. He looked down at the photograph. It was a picture of some roses at Lydington Manor. There was no time to sit and flick through his stack to choose a better one. This one would have to do.

He stared into the picture and asked the universe to lend him the tiniest fraction of its immense energy to help him dissipate. *Quickly*, he thought, *quickly!* Phil's haste was making it difficult. He needed to feel calmer for it to happen. St. Aldate's nick was a mere half a mile away. The ride would be barely two minutes, even with the one-way system making them go around the block on Thames Street. That was not going to be long enough! It wasn't working.

But then, at the end of Speedwell Street, with the police station literally across St. Aldate's, the car just ahead at the T-junction pulled out right in front of a cyclist, causing the cyclist to swerve and tumble off his bike. This, in turn, caused a big red Hop On Hop Off bus to brake hard and come to a halt in front of the car, narrowly missing the car and the cyclist, and completely blocking the junction.

Hunter and his driver jumped out of the police car and ran forward. Then, seeing that no one was actually injured, they tried to hurry everyone along to get the traffic moving again.

The cyclist got up, unscathed except for torn jeans and a bleeding knee. He remonstrated with the car driver with righteous indignation, and having received a lame "Didn't see you there in the cycle lane," half-apology, he pedalled off, still shouting with justified disgruntlement. The bus moved off too, trailing behind the angry cyclist.

Hunter warned the offending driver, "If I wasn't in such a hurry, you'd be getting a ticket. Now fuck off quick before I change my mind!"

And with that, the car in front made its turn onto St. Aldate's without any further attempt to reduce Oxford's cycling population, and the police officers got back in their car.

"Go! Go! Go!" shouted Hunter.

The unmarked Vauxhall Astra revved its engine and screeched its tyres. It hurtled across St. Aldate's and into the police station car park. It came to rest across two parking spaces with another gratuitous squeal of tyres, with the handbrake already on. DI Hunter leapt out and congratulated his underling for his driving, "I love it. A touch of *The Sweeney*. That driving course you took was worth every sodding penny!"

Hunter yanked open the rear door and said, "Right, Beans, out. I hope you like porridge, you arsehole." He glanced into the car and did a double take. The two detectives looked wildly around. Phil Beans was gone. "Well, don't just stand there, dickhead!" Hunter shouted. "Find the motherfucker. He can't have just vanished into thin fucking air."

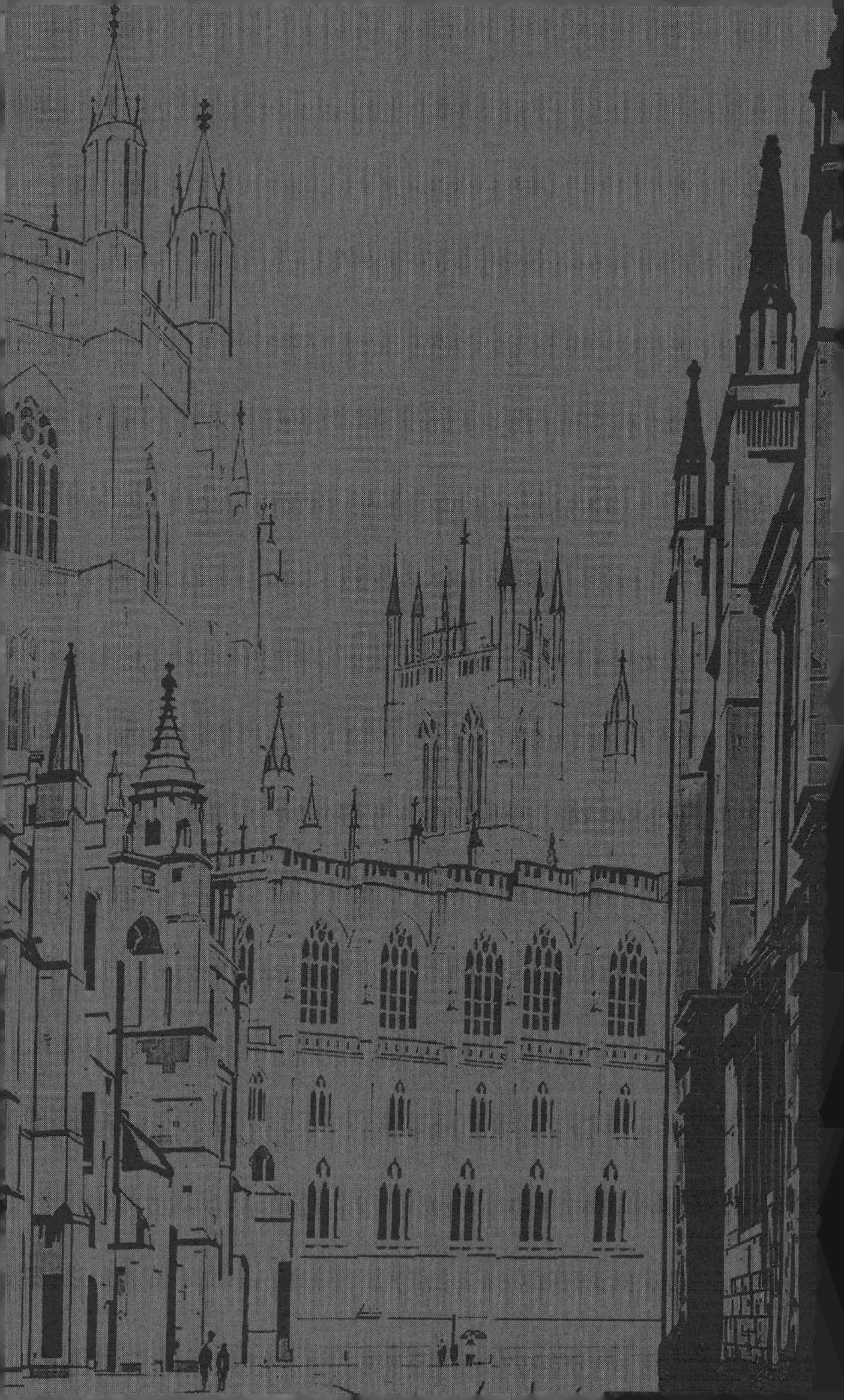

Part Five
UNCOVERING THE PAST

29.
A GRAND DAY OUT

29 MAY 2000

After his thirteenth birthday, when his mum had given him the Polaroid camera as a gift, Phil did little without the camera hanging round his neck. When he and his mum went to Brighton on the train for the following May bank holiday weekend, the camera went too. They had a wonderful, magical time at the seaside. They wandered along the promenade and the pier. They spent hours in the tiny alleyways of shops in The Lanes. They marvelled at the Royal Pavilion inside and out. They sat on deckchairs on the Palace Pier and ate ice cream while looking out over the derelict and decaying West Pier.

The Bank Holiday Monday was quite sunny and warm with a lovely breeze from the west, and they hired blue-and-white striped deckchairs to sit on the shingle beach. Phil piled up beach pebbles in little stacks to see how high he could make them, and he watched his mum sitting in her deckchair and reading her book as she began dozing off. He thought this was the happiest he had ever been. He was sure it was the happiest his mum had been in a long time too. His parents' separation had been a difficult time for his mum, but once she had got them settled in the house in Headington, she had seemed so much more joyful.

Phil loved his mum. Apart from his science teacher and a couple of friends at school, she was pretty much his whole world. He popped open his camera to memorialize this overwhelmingly special moment. Click, *whirrr,* and an instant picture was ejected out the front of the camera. Phil set the camera aside under his deckchair and left the photo to develop in the shade.

Phil had his swimming trunks on under his tracksuit bottoms, so he stripped off and ran as fast as bare feet on shingle would carry him into the sea to paddle and splash in the waves.

30.
A TURN FOR THE WORSE

SUMMER 2002

Phil and his mum lived happily in Headington. Phil got used to the long bus ride to private school and used the time to read books and listen to music. He started out reading *The Phantom Tollbooth* and *The Hobbit*, and listening to pop music. Within a couple of years, he was reading everything from Discworld novels to Shakespeare plays, anything as long as it had dark humour. And he had begun listening to dance music, though he couldn't really dance on the bus, no matter how much he wanted to. He grew in confidence and tackled puberty head-on. He became hairy and his voice dropped, he started using aftershave and hair gel, and he had turned from a boy into a young man by the time he'd turned fifteen.

The only problem was his mum. Over those couple of years, Ellie gradually became stressed and worn out. She was working full-time, enduring the stress and cost of the divorce settlement case, and even with the help she got from Phil, she was doing most of the cooking and housework in the evenings. She started to look older, and she slept a lot. And she was continually taking painkillers. She was always "too busy to see the doctor about a silly headache."

After the divorce case was settled in Lord Lydington's favour at the end of 2001, she didn't seem to get any better. She finally went to see the doctor in the April of 2002, and the news was not good. She was very ill already. After a lot of tests and scans, they determined that they couldn't operate, and chemotherapy was started straightaway. When chemo didn't seem to do any good, the doctors concluded there was nothing more they could do for her. Phil's mum went into a hospice in July, and Phil had to move back to Lydington Manor where he would be looked after by his father's housekeeper, Mrs. Mountjoy.

It was the worst time for Phil, living with his resentful father and his bitchy new stepmother, feeling unwanted, and waiting to be sent to boarding school in September. Phil visited his mum every day. His father's chauffeur ferried Phil back and forth. Bob, as his father called the chauffeur. Mr. Mountjoy, as Phil called him. Mr. Mountjoy was kind, and he was always asking after his former boss, knowing she was dying, and demonstrating his concern for young Phil. Every day, he would bring Phil to the hospice and come to collect him again in the evening. Every day, Phil sat with his mum, watching her slowly become thinner and more frail. Watching her as the pain relief stopped doing its job. Just chatting with his mum, holding her hand, and getting the nurse when she needed something. Waiting and hoping the end would come soon. Phil's heart was breaking slowly but surely, but he couldn't let it show.

Phil's mum died on an incongruously beautiful, sunny day in August.

A Turn for the Worse

At the funeral, Phil was stoic. He was determined to keep it together. He resented his father's presence, but he was not going to cry. Besides, he felt almost entirely numb.

The next few weeks and months were a blur of misery and change. Boarding school was actually worse than Lydington Manor; Phil had none of his stuff with him, and the food wasn't like Mrs. Mountjoy's cooking at all.

It was all study, sports, discipline, and sleeping in a dorm with seven other boys. Phil endured the first term with a stiff upper lip, and then he returned to his father's at the end of term. The consolation would be Mrs. Mountjoy's wonderful Christmas dinner. It was a miserable Christmas and New Year back at Lydington Manor.

31.
BIRTHDAY BLUES

06 JANUARY 2003, 10.46 A.M.

On his sixteenth birthday, Phil stayed in his room and pulled the curtains to block out the daylight and to match the gloom in his soul. He put "Adagio for Strings" on his stereo, which was the saddest piece of music he had ever heard. As was his habit, he snapped a Polaroid of the moment. He wrote *The worst birthday ever* across the bottom of the photo. Then, from his shelves of Polaroid photo albums, he pulled out the one titled *Brighton, May 2000*.

He sat on his bed and turned to the page from the beach on that Bank Holiday Monday and pulled out the photo of his mum dozing in the deckchair. Then the tears came. He looked at the picture and wanted desperately to be able to tell his mum she was already ill back then. The picture became indistinct as his tears blurred his vision. Phil wished with all his might for every atom in all the universe to just give him the tiniest bit of all their energy, just so that he would be able to see his mum and ask her to see the doctor when she got home from Brighton. He begged for help from the cosmos, and he felt like he might explode with the love and longing to see his mum again.

He sobbed and sobbed, holding the picture of his mum till he was too tired to cry any more. He wiped the tears from his eyes and looked at the picture. The picture was clear, but his bedroom was faded and indistinct. He could smell sea air, and he could hear the sound of seagulls calling. He blinked and wiped his eyes again, and gradually his vision began to clear.

32.
I LOVE YOU, MUM

29 MAY 2000, 3.47 P.M.

A few moments later, he could see the Palace Pier. He was on the beach, in Brighton, and when he lowered the photograph, he saw his mum dozing in a deckchair just as though she was real. As though she was really, actually there. Phil realized that he was not sitting on his bed anymore, but sitting on a blue-and-white striped deckchair. He looked around. It was Brighton Beach, and *he* was there as well, the thirteen-year-old Phil, running in the waves, falling backward into the water, and splashing around like a carefree kid.

Phil got up and knelt on the shingle next to his mum. "Hello, Mum. I think I might be dreaming, but I have to tell you something. I want to tell you I love you one more time, and … " Phil took her hand.

"Hmmm? I love you too, Phil. I was asleep. What d'you want? We'll get ice cream in a bit," she said without opening her eyes, and drifting off again.

"Mum," he said, "you're not well. The pain you're in is cancer, Mum. It's not stress or tiredness, it's cancer. Mum … " he continued a bit louder.

"Hmmm?" she murmured.

"Mum, will you please promise to go and see the doctor when you get home from Brighton? Will you please tell him about the pain?"

"Alright dear, I will. And we'll get ice cream in a bit." And with that, she dozed off again.

Phil expected to wake up at that moment, but he didn't. He felt like he was already awake, and this really was not a dream. He was not in his bedroom. He was actually in Brighton. He let go of his mum's hand and stood up. He wandered away, walking along the beach, and feeling confused. He didn't want to leave his mum, but this didn't seem right. It felt too real. He stooped and picked up a small pebble. This was surely just a dream, but the pebble felt solid, and somehow, he knew he was fully conscious.

He started to panic a little as he turned and saw his younger self walking back up the beach toward his mum. *Don't ask her for ice cream, you selfish little twat, can't you see she's asleep,* he thought. And just as he remembered it, he heard his younger self ask his mum for ice cream. But instead of his mum saying *in a bit* like he remembered, she woke up and said, "Alright if we really have to do that right this minute, pack up, let's go."

His mum started to pack up the picnic bag. "Get your camera. Don't forget it."

Phil watched himself pick up the camera, the towel, and the picture that had been under his deckchair. He looked down and saw that same picture in his hand. A chill ran through him that felt like frozen electricity.

In his hand, he had two pictures. The one of his mum in the deckchair and the one of "The worst birthday ever" in his room at Lydington Manor. Both pictures had been in his hands when he was

I Love You, Mum

in his bedroom, and he still had them both now. He tried to remember what he had done when he was looking at the picture of his mum, wondering if he had really made this happen by wishing it. *But that can't be,* he thought. *That isn't possible.*

Phil was more than a little bit freaked out. He looked at the Polaroid he had just taken a few minutes ago, now fully developed, that showed his stereo next to his old iMac and his chess computer crowding the top of his desk by the big oak door. Phil stared at the picture and thought how bizarre it was to wish to be back in the place he most hated to be.

He looked around. He was still on Brighton Beach, and he could see his younger self and his mum walking up onto the promenade. He began to panic as his desperation grew more intense. He looked back at the photograph and wished more intently to be back where he ought to be.

"Please, please, please!" he said aloud to himself, "This is too weird. Please let me wake up back in Oxford."

Phil was growing desperate enough to have clicked his heels three times, but when he looked up again, Brighton had blurred and faded, and if he squinted, he could see the hazy, bright-blue colour of his iMac almost in front of him. As he continued to watch, and will it to happen, his room came into focus, and the big, oak desk began to look solid, but the blue of his iMac dissolved and faded again.

33.
WHAT DID I DO?

06 JANUARY 2003, 10.52 A.M.

The iMac was there in the Polaroid, but it was not there on the actual desk in front of him. The desk was real, sturdy, and solid. Solid oak. But there was no Apple computer. No stereo. No chess game. The white, built-in bookshelves on the wall were empty. There were no books. No photo albums. Phil looked down. There was no bedding on the mattress on which he was sitting. Everything felt solid, and this was his bedroom at Lydington Manor, but there was nothing of his in the empty, echoing room. *Where has it all gone?* he wondered. *Why would it get moved?*

Then he remembered. He was due back at school in two days, and they would be packing him off to live at boarding school. This time, he would be taking all his stuff with him. No more end-of-term trips back to Lydington Manor. His father, or more likely, his stepmother, Isabella, was getting rid of him permanently. He would be gone for good. And somehow, someone must have managed to pack all his stuff while he had been dreaming. But he couldn't figure how they had taken the sheets off the bed without him being aware of it. He was disorientated and confused, so he went out of the room to see what was going on.

There was no sign of his stuff or any packing boxes out on the landing or down in the huge, echoing, white marble hallway.

Phil walked down one of the winding twin marble staircases. He stood in the grand entry hall facing the enormous double doors in the entryway that led out to the stone-pillared porch. He looked up into the grandiose gold dome, which was the first thing a visitor would notice as they drove up to the house along the mile-long driveway.

He looked around at the tall doorways leading off to the east and west wings, then turned and saw the big double doors that led to the dining room as well as the big oak door to the library.

There was no sign of any packing boxes. But in the middle of the hallway, on top of the huge circular marble table in the centre of the hall, there was a large crystal vase with a couple of dozen red roses. Phil walked up and stood looking at them. They must have just been delivered, he thought, because they weren't there earlier. And yet the roses didn't look fresh. They had a kind of darkened, dry, papery appearance, the way that red roses look the day before one decides to throw them out.

Phil unfolded the Polaroid camera that hung around his neck, and he snapped a picture of the roses. It was a thing he did. His hobby. A habit. An obsession. Ever since his mum gave him the camera, he took pictures of everything, wherever they went. He loved to sit and watch them develop. And he kept every single one. He got through a pack of film two or three times a week. He walked around the table and saw the card that had accompanied the flowers.

WHAT DID I DO?

**TO MY DARLING ISABELLA,
HAPPY FIFTH ANNIVERSARY.
WITH AFFECTION AND ADMIRATION,**

TARQUIN.

But it wasn't written in his father's scruffy, illegible handwriting, though. It was, presumably, dictated to the flower shop over the phone by his father's secretary. Phil took a second photograph of the roses, this time with the card in plain view. As it developed, he saw that the roses were in focus, but the card wasn't, so he took a third snap, as close as he could, this time with the words in sharp focus.

Then Phil heard raised voices. It sounded like men who were in a disagreement, and their voices were coming through the open door at the far end of the library. Phil walked quietly over to listen outside the nearer library door, which was closed, and though he couldn't hear clearly, with an ear right by the door jamb, he could make out some of what was said when the men were speaking loudly.

Phil heard footsteps coming, and suddenly there was a scream.

"What the hell?" shrieked Isabella. "Tarquin, Tarquin!"

Phil backed away from Isabella. The door in front of Phil opened, and the three men came rushing out of the library.

"What the hell is your little rugrat doing here?" challenged Isabella, trying to regain some composure, and failing.

Tarquin Lydington looked at Phil with an intimidating scowl. "What are you doing in my house, boy?"

Phil looked at his father, confused and frightened. He glanced around to see Mr. Pedge and Professor Durant, then he turned back to his father.

"How did you get in here? Who let you in?" said Lydington, who was red-faced and getting angry.

"Umm, I've just been up in my room," Phil said, baffled and assuming he was in trouble for snooping. "I wasn't listening. I just wanted to ask where all my stuff had gone."

"Isabella, get Bob round with the car," Lydington said.

Tarquin took hold of Phil's collar and started to drag him across the hallway.

"Why ... ? Where am I going? Do I have to leave for school? What did I do? What ... ?" Phil pleaded to know what was going on. "What's happening?"

"I say, old chap, steady on," said Mr. Pedge to Lydington, putting an arm around Phil's shoulders and edging Lydington away. "Let's get you sorted out, young man," he said to Phil. "Can't have a chap hanging about where he's not wanted, eh? What do you say, Phil, let's get you in the car safe and sound. Nice Mr. Mountjoy will see you're alright."

Phil walked with Mr. Pedge, who led him out onto the grand portico that looked across the circular gravel driveway with the ornate fountain in the middle. Phil was stunned and helpless. He had so many questions, but it seemed his life was out of his hands at that moment. Phil put his head down and his hands in his pockets. In one pocket, there were some Polaroid photographs, and in the other was a small, round pebble. Phil heard the familiar crunch of the gravel and looked up to see the large black Bentley draw up to the bottom of the steps. Mr. Mountjoy got out and respectfully held the back door open.

"Mr. Philip, please," he said politely.

What Did I Do?

"Take care, Phil," said Mr. Pedge, his face knitted with concern.

"Thank you, Mr. Pedge," Phil replied. He was grateful for his kindness, which was in sharp contrast with his father's spiteful hostility.

What did I do? thought Phil. *What have I done?* He sat in the back seat, staring at the Polaroids and the pebble. He was terrified. His heart was pounding. He wanted to ask Mr. Mountjoy what was going on, but didn't imagine that he would know. *Had my father thrown me out and sent me off to live at the boarding school?* he wondered. *Is that it? No goodbye, no good luck? Nothing?* It seemed at least that he would have the things from his bedroom at boarding school now.

"Buckle up, Mr. Philip," said Mr. Mountjoy.

So, Phil resigned himself to the long drive to boarding school, and off they drove, down the long driveway, away from Lydington Manor. Soon enough, though, they were in town, and not cruising up the M40. Then they were in Headington. Then the car pulled into the quiet little cul-de-sac.

The car stopped softly outside Phil's old house, and Mr. Mountjoy opened Phil's car door. "Here you go, Mr. Philip, home."

Phil saw the front door open. A woman with a worried expression stood on the threshold, looking out. Phil sprinted toward her.

"Mum!"

34.

TWO DOZEN RED ROSES

06 JANUARY 2003, 11.03 A.M.

Phil tried to focus on the roses in front of him while the rest of the great marble hall solidified around him. Phil was disorientated and unsure of where he was at first, but as he began to feel more steady, and the grand hallway became more apparent, Phil could feel the trepidation and angst of his childhood and knew that he was at Lydington Manor. Instinctively, he cowered down out of sight, fighting his rising feeling of dread. His heart was still pounding following his escape from police custody, exacerbated by the urgency of needing to fathom another sticky situation in which he had just landed.

Phil remembered that he had been in the car on the way to the police station just a moment before, and that he had reached into his satchel and blindly pulled out a Polaroid. His selection had been random, and this was the place and time to which he had escaped.

This was his sixteenth birthday. The worst birthday ever. It was a year or so after his parents' divorce settlement, and just a few short months after Phil's mum had died. Phil could sense the hopeless, lonely sadness that he had lived with for those months. The last time he had been here was on that birthday, when his father had thrown him out.

The day he had heard the men arguing, and the day Mr. Pedge had been so kind to him. It was not long before Mr. Pedge had taken his own life. It was the day he found out that his mum was alive, which was the best birthday present he could ever have imagined. And it was the day he first went back in time. The day he went back to Brighton.

Still in a haze and breathing as quietly as he could, he squinted at the caption on the Polaroid: *06 Jan. 2003 11.03 a.m.* Phil knew he could never use this same Polaroid to time-travel again, and the other roses pictures he had taken that day had been used as evidence in his parents' divorce. There would be no returning to this moment, so Phil knew what his next mission was. He'd thought about what he needed to do while he was here, and he slowly remembered why he had packed this picture. He needed to find out more about the meeting in the library, and to try to find out why the men were planning a diving expedition when, according to Rusty, Mr. Pedge couldn't even swim.

It dawned on Phil that he might not be alone in the hallway. He peeped over the top of the huge marble table, upon which stood the extravagant display of roses. He saw his sixteen-year-old self across the hall. The young birthday boy had one ear pressed against the library door while trying to make sense of what was going on in the meeting on the other side of the door.

Phil remembered that he had overheard some confusing talk of scuba diving, and Mr. Pedge, Rusty's dad, being talked into joining Phil's father and Professor Durant. All Phil had been able to surmise at the time was that Mr. Pedge didn't want to go on the trip. But Phil thought it odd; he had been wanting to come back to find out more.

Phil knew that his sixteen-year-old self had been interrupted before he could make much sense of what he'd heard. Then Phil realized that the interruption was about to happen any moment now. Isabella would be coming along the corridor, past the library, to discover the young, confused boy snooping at the library door.

Phil needed to get properly out of sight, which meant out of the hallway altogether. Young Phil was preoccupied, so older Phil darted quietly across the hallway, through the double doors on the right, and into the dining room. He crept along the length of the room to the door at the other end, opposite the other library door, where he could hear the discussion quite clearly. He recognized the voices at once. He started recording on his phone, hoping it would pick up the conversation. He got out his digital camera with the fancy zoom lens, and he listened as he waited for Isabella to pass by.

"If you won't do it, I can find someone who will," Phil heard his father say.

"It's one thing hiding assets from the Inland Revenue," he heard Mr. Pedge saying. "It's quite another to have done it for the divorce. I'm not doing your dirty work anymore. No more hiding assets. And I don't like what you're planning next. No more dirty accounting. I want out."

"You want out?" asked Lydington in a menacing tone of voice. "There's only one way out. That's it, right there, that bridge. You'll get your money, but only if we do it this way. In a couple of weeks' time, OK?"

"But how can you be so sure it'll go alright?" Mr. Pedge asked.

"I've told you. I'll be there with the scuba gear. You just need to keep still and breathe," said Professor Durant. "I'll swim us east, away from the bridge, and come up where Tarquin will be waiting with the boat."

Phil heard Isabella coming down the corridor, her Gucci tennis shoes squeaking on the marble tile. Phil had just heard very clearly what was being discussed, and the mystery of the fragments he had picked up so long ago now made horrifying sense. Mr. Pedge wanted out of some kind of crooked business, and Phil's father was getting rid of him. Phil knew the bridge they referred to was the bridge that Mr. Pedge had jumped from when he died. And he now knew the chilling truth that it had not been suicide.

Phil peeped around the doorway to check that Isabella was at the end of the corridor. He nipped across the passageway and peered in through the crack in the door. Three men were huddled around a desk. Phil's father and Mr. Pedge were both in their early forties. His father was handsome and greying a little, and Phil could see why the young Isabella might have been attracted to him. Apart from the money, of course. Mr. Pedge was balding and ordinary, and he was very worried. Standing on the other side of Mr. Pedge was a mid-thirties, charismatic, and athletic-looking Corvus Durant.

He pointed the camera through the door, zoomed out as much as he could, and took a photograph of the three men standing around the desk. The shutter echoed in the passageway. The men stopped talking and looked around.

"What was that?" asked Durant.

Shit, thought Phil, *that was much louder than I expected!*

Then, out in the main hall, Isabella screamed. The three men turned and went to the other door, where they discovered a confused-looking sixteen-year-old Phil and an angry Isabella.

Two Dozen Red Roses

Phil pushed open the door as his father grabbed the young Phil by the collar and began dragging him across the hallway. Phil stepped into the library. He had pity for his younger self as he remembered that the pain of being dragged away by his father was not so much the physical discomfort as it was a far more humiliating emotional hurt.

Phil watched from the library for a few seconds as kind Mr. Pedge put his arm around the young man, leading him away from Lydington, towards the main entrance. Lord Lydington and Professor Durant walked behind them. Isabella was calling Mr. Mountjoy on the phone to bring the car round.

Back in the library, Phil was outraged.

He remembered Mr. Pedge fondly, and Phil's father was plotting his death. Phil had seconds while they were out of the room to collect some evidence of what was going on. A minute or so at most. He looked at the papers spread out on the desk. Documents. *Click*. A map. *Click, click, click*. With all the palaver out in the hallway, his shutter seemed so much quieter inside the library.

The map was of the Dartford Bridge. There was an X on the bridge. There was another X close by in the water, the shape of a boat a distance away, and a dotted line connecting them. Phil needed a Polaroid for Rusty too, to pretend had been taken all these years ago. He popped open his camera with speed and dexterity, then focused and clicked.

As the motor whirred to eject the picture, Phil darted back out of the room and left the door slightly ajar just as the three men were returning to the room. He put the new Polaroid in his jacket pocket. He would tell Rusty he had discovered a picture that he had taken when he was sixteen, which was really sort of true.

As Phil crouched down at the door, he heard Durant ask, "You think he heard anything?" Phil fumbled for his phone and quickly started recording audio again.

"Doubtful, at least not much. Not with the door closed. The door's thick, solid oak, and the weatherstrip is supposed to sound-proof the room," replied Lydington.

"I don't like the plan. I don't like it," said Pedge.

"It's simple. If you want out, this is how we do it," said Lydington.

Durant added, "It's got to be here by the X. The drop into the water is the least at that point, the water will be deep enough at high tide right there." Phil couldn't see, but he knew these were instructions for Pedge. "You can't be off by much, so be sure you stop the car here. Turn in at 45 degrees, to face where you'll jump from. Your headlights will shine so you can see to climb the barrier. We don't want you falling in, now do we? Block two lanes with the car, so you attract maximum attention. We want people to witness you jumping, right?"

"Right. How far is the drop?" Pedge asked.

"It's maybe fifteen to twenty metres," said Durant. "Jump feet first. Don't dive. That's how kids do it in Hawaii off cliffs higher than this. Don't be such a baby. It'll be dark, so make sure people are there; wait till there are witnesses. Put your main beams on so your headlights illuminate the scene. Leave the note on the passenger seat, don't lock the car, and leave the engine running."

That was exactly how it was reported in the news. Mr. Pedge had stopped his car on the Dartford Bridge in the dark. Witnesses watched as he climbed up onto the parapet and jumped off into the darkness and the freezing-cold water of the Thames below.

Two Dozen Red Roses

"Suppose I jump. Suppose I do it. You're going to be there, right?" asked Pedge.

"Yes," said Durant, "I'll be in the water with scuba gear. I'll be there with a spare set for you. I will flash my torch up at you to let you know it's safe to jump. That's why place and time are important. As soon as you hit the water, I'll swim to you and give you the mouthpiece. Then you just breathe, I'll hold you like a lifeguard rescue, and you just let me swim us away, along the dotted line here, see? To the boat just here. Tarquin will help you climb on board. Change of clothes, cup of tea. He'll pilot us quietly down the river to where the car will be waiting for you, and hey presto, a brand-new life with a million pounds."

Pedge glanced up at Tarquin Lydington, who just shrugged like it was asking him to jump in a puddle.

"It's simple," added Lydington. "Then you get your pay-off, and you're free to start afresh. Abroad. Spain? Bermuda? Brazil? Wherever. I don't give a shit where. But you've got to jump. It's got to look like suicide, so that nobody ever thinks to ask you what you know. OK?"

"OK. OK. I'll do it," said Mr. Pedge. "I can't do your dirty work anymore."

The meeting seemed to be concluding, and Phil had heard more than enough. He suddenly felt exposed, so he snuck back across the corridor to the opulent dining room and crawled under the enormous table to take cover surrounded by dining chairs. This had been one of his favourite hiding places as a child.

The fragments of conversation Phil had heard when he was sixteen were suddenly making sense. Mr. Pedge didn't kill himself at all. It was the others conspiring to get rid of him. Phil knew the fall from the lowest part of Dartford Bridge, even at high tide, was probably more than fifty metres. It was definitely enough to kill someone. Even if Pedge landed feet first, holding his nose, he'd be unconscious at best with broken legs and probably worse. Then he'd drown.

Why were Phil's father and a young assistant professor mixed up together and plotting to kill an accountant? Apart from being Westgate alumni, what did these three have in common? How did his father know Durant twenty years ago? Phil thought he might never know, but he was sure they were pushing poor Mr. Pedge to jump off that bridge.

Phil began to wonder about Durant. Pedge surely wouldn't have jumped if he hadn't seen Durant's flashlight. Was Durant in the water to make sure he drowned? Had Durant held Pedge's unconscious body underwater to make sure he died? Was Pedge whohe was referring to when he'd said he'd done this before when he was busy murdering Holly? Had drowning Mr. Pedge triggered in him a fascination with killing people?

He couldn't help thinking about poor Georgia. Havarti had said there was no link between the two disappearances, but Phil knew otherwise. Durant had attacked Holly, and Phil knew Georgia had been to see Durant the day she disappeared. There had to be a link, and Durant was it. Phil wondered if Durant was the serial killer that Havarti had been so reluctant to consider. But if Durant was in his rooms all day, after Georgia had already left for Oxford Station, then it didn't seem possible.

All of this was not getting him any closer to unkilling Durant and fixing his relationship with Holly.

Phil had already worked out that he couldn't just go back and let Akito carry on and challenge Durant. There were already two other versions of Phil in front quad at that moment, and a third would surely risk more trouble. Besides, it would mean that Holly still got attacked by Durant, and saved by Akito, and it would mean that Akito would be on the hook for Durant's murder. All of that was just not good enough.

Phil needed to find a reason to stop Durant from seeing Holly that day. Intercept him somehow and make sure he never kept his appointment with Honey. Or better still, never have made an appointment with her. But if he was a serial killer, he would surely just pick a different victim. Phil had gone and changed a lot in the past lately, but that was a change that just wasn't good enough. Phil had to do better.

Phil's mind was churning like he was making butter from all his worries. He hadn't come up with anything that would work yet, and he had to be sure his plan was better than before. He had saved Durant and gotten Holly killed, then saved Holly whilst managing to simultaneously lose any hope of a future with her, and in the process, he framed himself for murder. He had messed up big time. Twice. He had to make it third time lucky without leaving anything to chance. But he had no idea how.

He decided that wallowing in his intractable woes was not getting him anywhere. Cowering under the bloody dining table was giving him a dead leg. Phil contemplated his next move. He couldn't go back to his own timeline where he was wanted for murder, so, in the meantime, he could try to figure out what happened to poor Georgia Cornwallis and find the link with Durant.

Then it clicked in Phil's head what he needed to do. He knew where he had to go next. So, Phil got out the little stack of

Polaroids from his satchel. He quickly flicked through to find the right picture. It was an arty shot of Christ Church Meadow early on a March morning, when the low, orange sun caught the few clouds and lit them with a light, golden touch of perfection.

Next, he popped open his Polaroid camera, pointed it between the rows of dining chair legs, and took a picture of his hiding place. *Just in case,* he thought. *You never know when you might need to come back this way again, right?* He labelled it and gathered up his belongings into the satchel.

Phil stared at the picture of Christ Church Meadow and willed himself to transform away. *No big rush this time. Less haste, more focus. Just relax, let it happen.*

Soon enough, the chairs and the table legs became blurry, and Phil could smell the sweet, earthy petrichor of a dewy spring meadow.

Phil felt the cool, fresh air. The brightness of a sunny March morning filled his soul with the hope of a brand-new Spring. He found himself surrounded by trees and meadow, looking out toward the River Cherwell. He turned around, and the austere edifice of the Meadow Building was coming into focus, and Phil could distinctly make out the Gothic windows. Once the Broad Walk felt firm under his feet, he set off walking toward St. Aldate's.

Phil's body hadn't just woken up, but something about the fresh, early morning air on the meadow made him want a good cup of coffee and a fry-up. Collard Green's was no good for that, so Phil wandered up to the café on Bonn Square and ordered the full English. Phil felt the need to be fuelled up and ready for a proper day of sleuthing.

Today was the last day of the conference, and he was determined to find out what had happened to Georgia Cornwallis.

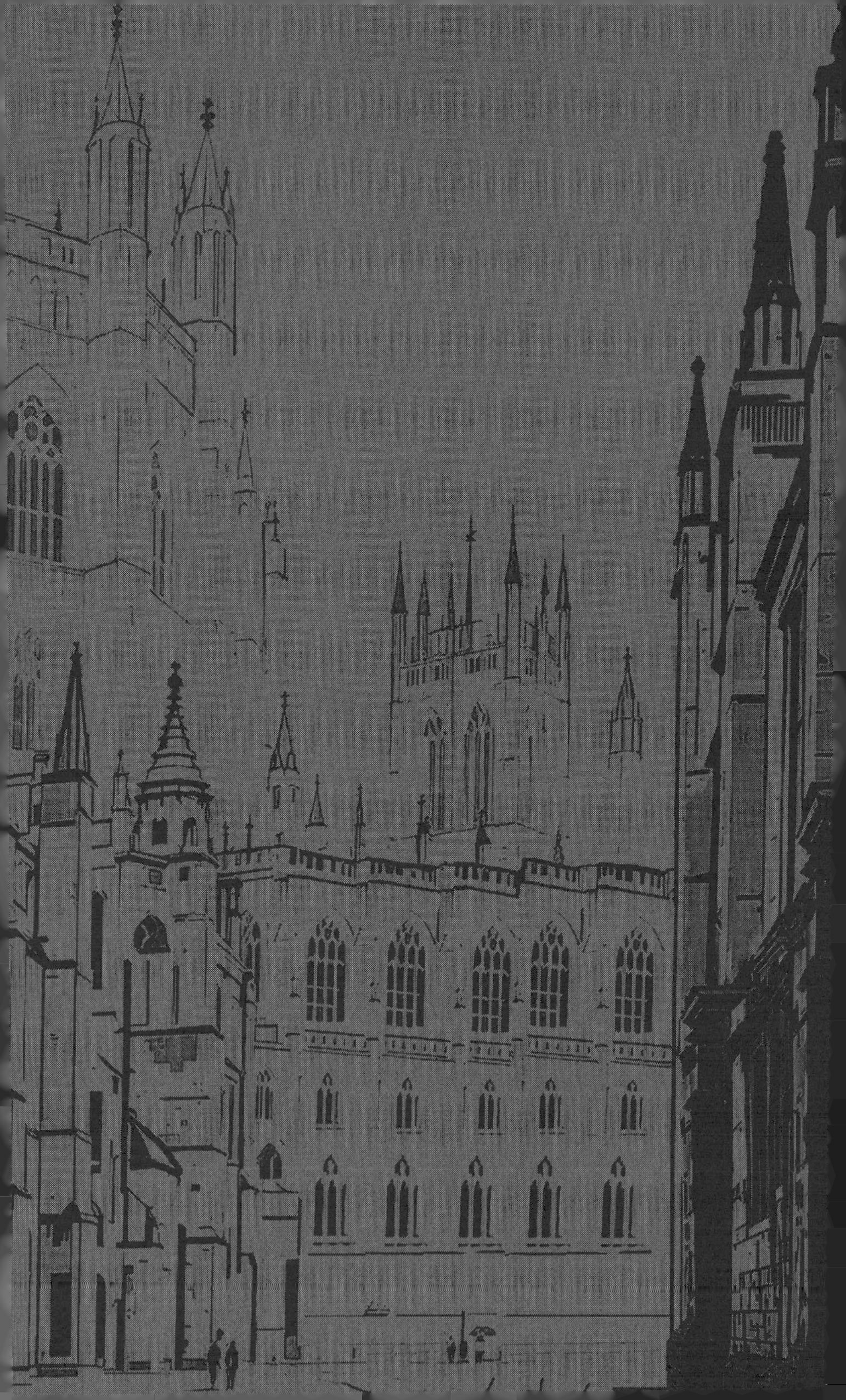

Part Six
CLOSING AND CLOSURE

35.

KEYNOTE CONTROVERSY

25 MARCH 2022, 8.30 A.M.

In anticipation of the first post-pandemic conference the world of physics had known in two years, there had been much enthusiasm about having everyone visiting Westgate College. Georgia Cornwallis was very excited. She attended every session and made copious notes in her colour-coded ring binder. There were some brilliant lectures, but naturally, the organizers had saved the best till last. The only way to keep delegates from going home early was to have the most prestigious speakers and the most interesting topics scheduled for the end of the week.

On Friday morning, there would be four talks, and proceedings would end at noon. The organizers knew that no one would stay past noon, even if Einstein himself came back to give the talk after lunch. No conference ever survived intact past lunchtime on a Friday.

Professor Corvus Durant was first up at 8.30 a.m. with his keynote address on the state of quantum gravity titled "The Grand Unified Theory of Life, the Universe, and Everything."

Durant was very good at rehashing other people's scholarly articles in review papers, and he was excellent at presenting other people's research work while making it interesting and engaging. And he was brilliant when it came to dumbing stuff down for a TV show or a podcast. Durant was a charismatic and entertaining speaker.

But today, the conference hall would be host to many of the people whose work he had reviewed, the very people he had been dumbing down. Everyone here knew just how little Durant himself had contributed for two decades. Some of the delegates would admit to being jealous of his renown and his many, many appearances on the telly. Durant was known for being controversial in his interviews, and his lecture did not disappoint.

Durant's talk was not so much a review of the progress made during the pandemic as it was an attack on the lack of progress. "Despite all the modern mathematics in our toolbox, we are hardly any closer than Einstein himself in his later years, over seventy years ago! You," Durant announced, directly referencing the assembled expertise, "have failed to make any significant inroads into physics' most urgent theoretical endeavours."

He went on as though scolding a student for coming to class late with a hangover. The irony of this condemnation coming from a man who had contributed nothing of his own in twenty years was not lost on the audience, and they were not amused.

Durant had not intended to answer questions and immediately introduced the next speaker. "So, it is my pleasure to introduce Professor Garstang Sunderland. He is Professor of Quantum Mechanics at Princeton University, and his talk is titled 'New Evidence for the Interaction between Chronons and the Higgs Field.'"

Professor Sunderland was much shorter than Durant, and as he stepped up to the podium, the microphone was on a level with the top of his head, which would have been fine if his comb-over had been giving the talk. The AV guy, wearing black jeans and a black T-shirt like he was a roadie for a rock concert, came on stage to lower the mic, and he also managed to stop it from working altogether.

"Professor Durant," came a plummy British voice from the audience, "while we have a technical interlude, perhaps you would entertain a question or two? Could the eminent Professor help us to understand whether the Marvel Universe is the one made of the antimatter he proposes in his famous paper?"

There were giggles from around that end of the conference hall, and the laughter spread as a ripple of conversation made its way across. Durant was a little annoyed. As the laughter subsided, he tried a laugh-along put-down. "Oh, yes, ha-ha, very clever, very funny," he shouted above the waning tittering. "You could say *Marvel-ously* amusing," he said with air quotes. The audience quietened considerably. "How are we doing fixing that mic? Quickly, man!"

Somewhat emboldened, another delegate—this one with a Birmingham accent—shouted out loudly, "Professor, I wonder if you could expand on your idea of quantum superposition. Could you explain where the other wreck of the Titanic could be found and why no one has yet discovered it? And could one postulate the existence of a second quantum superposition iceberg too?"

Everyone heard the question, and this time, the laughter was instantaneous throughout the whole hall. The question, couched as an academic enquiry, was an exaggeration of his throwaway line in a previous publication. Clearly, everyone thought his idea had been preposterous and warranted the ridicule. It was a neat little wisecrack at Durant's expense. And the entire audience clapped and laughed.

Almost the entire audience. Georgia Cornwallis was sitting at a table near the front of the room. The other seven occupants of the table were in hysterics. She was not. She sat open-mouthed and more than a little shocked. *My gosh,* she thought, *these Brits sure do have a twisted sense of humour. I thought these people were supposed to be polite! That's just darn rude!* She could see that Durant was humiliated, and she was horrified when he stormed past her. *Oh my,* she thought, *that's gonna make asking him about our paper real tricky.*

Georgia sat, attentively, through the next three lectures. She had been mulling over the tenet of Durant's talk, that physicists had achieved nothing significant in years. She had come to the conclusion that the professor might really want to be co-author on the paper, as it would be precisely the type of advancement he had called for in his keynote address. She had begun to get excited about the idea of speaking to him, and now she needed to find him.

The conference closed a little after noon, and in his slow, bumbling, flowery, and rather verbose manner, Wigtwizzle delivered the closing remarks in Durant's absence. It wasn't difficult for anyone to see why Durant had superseded Wigtwizzle as a spokesperson of modern physics.

Then there were goodbyes and the checking out of coats and suitcases from storage in the hallway of Staircase F. Georgia set off to the Porters' Lodge to see if she could discover Professor Durant's whereabouts.

36.

CATCHING THE TRAIN

25 MARCH 2022, 1.25 P.M.

Phil had not attended a conference in several years, and he didn't miss it. Instead, he relished the peace and quiet in the fresh air. Today was the day to find out what had happened to Georgia Cornwallis. He had wandered about the college grounds while lectures were delivered in stuffy silence. He had put a new Polaroid cartridge in his SX-70 and found some deserted and secluded spots to take a couple of pictures to keep in his jacket pocket, just in case.

Phil knew it would be grim, but it was the least he could do for poor old Chip Cornwallis. Phil was not motivated by self interest. Putting Durant behind bars would be a great outcome, and it would save him from a murder charge and give him another shot with Holly. And it might get him a million-dollar reward. Considering his recent track record of screwing up timelines, however, Phil was determined to stay out of the way and change nothing. Things hadn't gone so well before when he'd interfered. Today, he would find out what happened to Georgia and make sure Durant got his comeuppance.

Phil was thinking about Durant's history. Phil knew that Durant had killed Holly, or that at least he would have done so. Phil was also convinced that Durant had made sure Mr. Pedge had drowned in the Thames at Dartford Bridge. Phil knew, with absolute certainty, that Durant was evil.

Phil also knew that Georgia had boarded the train, so she wasn't about to be killed in Durant's rooms like Holly had been, or would have been. But he also thought that for damn sure, Durant was a murdering piece of shit.

Phil knew that Durant's alibi was that he was in his rooms for two days after he'd stormed out of the conference. He had not been seen on campus. But Phil had seen with his own eyes that Durant had a way of getting out unnoticed through the priest hole. So Phil would wait and watch. He would monitor the CCTV of the priest hole exit. This was a fact-finding mission. This was purely surveillance.

If Georgia was at the ticket machine at 13.32 p.m., she would have left at around twenty past the hour, allowing for a ten-minute walk plus a bit to account for her dragging a week's worth of dirty laundry in a pink suitcase.

Phil wandered around the backs until twenty-five past one. Then he popped into the Porters' Lodge. "Perkins, I have a big favour to ask."

"Oh, yes, Mr. Phil? Getting a parcel delivered?"

"What? No, I don't live here any … No, no, I need to take a look at your CCTV for the last twenty minutes," Phil said. "I wouldn't ask, but it's life and death."

"Oh, yes, sir? Whose?" Perkins asked dismissively, like he wasn't really listening and tidying up behind the counter.

"Ummm, one of the conference delegates, actually," said Phil, with a little indignation.

"Oh, yes?" Perkins said unfazed, stapling yesterday's visitor log and dropping it into a filing drawer. "Should I call the police, sir?"

"Not yet. Let's take a look at the CCTV and see if I'm pissing on the right lamppost, eh?"

"Oh, well, if it's your *detectiving* nonsense, I should need to see a warrant first," Perkins said, looking up at Phil.

"I'm a private detective, Perkins, we don't do warrants."

"No, sir, but the paperwork is very important." Perkins clearly could see an opportunity that was second only to charging gullible tourists an entrance fee. "There's a hefty chunk of paperwork involved, and I couldn't possibly help out without it."

"Ah, yes, come to think of it, I do have some much less formal paperwork that might suffice," said Phil, rummaging in his wallet and sliding a £50 note across the counter.

"That'll do nicely, Mr. Phil. If you come round this side of the counter, sir, and sit at this chair while I put the kettle on, I dare say you wouldn't look at the CCTV that I might happen to be in the middle of reviewing, now would you, sir."

"No, of course not. Wouldn't dream of it," Phil said, as he walked around the counter.

Perkins whistled to himself, filling the kettle and plugging it in, while Phil stared intently at the small, grainy black-and-white screen.

According to the timestamp, it was 13.12 when Arbley Scrump, dressed in a dark-grey Barbour jacket and a dark-grey hat, walked out of the small, light-grey door that Phil knew was actually green. He closed the big oak door that was in his way. He went back into the storeroom, and then he emerged again pushing a wheelbarrow that was full of potting compost and piled high with plastic planting trays of what looked like pansies.

A few stragglers who were leaving the conference and wheeling suitcases or toting army-style backpacks appeared at 13.16. Perkins emerged from the lodge to see them off. Perkins then talked to a couple of tourists who appeared to slip him an "entrance fee" and then walked through to the quad. At 13.18, Perkins opened the big oak door, concealing the smaller door again.

"There!" Phil exclaimed as he caught sight of Georgia walking into the passageway from the quad at 13.19 with her light-grey backpack and dragging her enormous light-grey suitcase. Perkins was at the lodge doorway, and they appeared to exchange pleasantries. "Have a good trip back," or some such. She left through the gate and turned left.

Phil watched intently. "Durant has to be here somewhere."

Arbley Scrump appeared again at 13.22, coming out from behind the big oak door, having presumably emerged unseen from the storeroom, just like he had seven minutes earlier. He left through the gate and turned left.

Wait just a minute, Phil thought. Scrump left with a wheelbarrow and then left *again* without coming back to the storeroom. Phil had to refer this to video adjudication. He rewound the tape, and he was able to confirm that Scrump had not returned to the storeroom.

This second Scrump wore what looked exactly like Scrump's hat and Scrump's wax jacket, but he appeared taller and less rotund. Phil had no doubt, this second Scrump was Durant in disguise.

CATCHING THE TRAIN

"Gotcha!" Phil exclaimed. "Using the priest hole. I knew it! You sneaky bastard." It was twenty-five to two. "Thanks, Perkins," Phil shouted, and then he ran out.

"I didn't do anythin', remember? Did not do you a favour at all, and no paperwork was exchanged," Perkins called after him, and then he went back to sipping his tea and reading *Private Eye*.

Phil walked briskly to the station. He knew who to look out for now. Georgia would be at the station according to police CCTV. And Phil needed to avoid being seen by an Arbley Scrump lookalike. He expertly navigated the ticket machine and got an off-peak day return ticket to Didcot. He got to the platform and hung back, prepared to jump on the train at the last minute before it left at 13.56.

He saw Georgia, who was looking exasperated. He loitered in the shadows looking for Durant. As the train pulled in, Georgia got in at the front end of the front carriage. An older lady and a tall man got in the rear carriage. Then a man wearing a wax jacket and sporting an old canvas hat jumped on at the back of the first coach. *Ha!* Phil thought. *There's Durant!* Phil ran to the rear coach just as the door beeper was beeping. The doors closed behind him. This train was already late, and it wasn't hanging around. The engines revved, and off it moved.

Phil looked around him. The carriage was almost empty, and there was one other person, along with the tall gent and the old lady who had just boarded. He was at a disadvantage being in the rear carriage. He couldn't see Georgia or Durant. He made his way to the corridor connecting the carriages. He stood near the door to the front carriage, looking in through the glass. The only people in there were Georgia Cornwallis and a thinly disguised Corvus Durant.

37.
JUMPING-OFF POINT

25 MARCH 2022, 2.02 P.M.

The train pulled in at Radley, and a woman got on at the front. Georgia looked up at her and said, "Hi, how'r you?" The woman stared at her haughtily, London style, and moved further down the carriage. Georgia watched her walk away, thinking *Jeez, these Brits take some gettin' used to. They are not friendly at all.* Then she looked at the man sitting at the other end of the carriage. She could see his hat above the seat in front of him, but not his face. He had already been sitting there with his head down, but now she could see his eyes peering over the seat back. He was looking at Georgia from under the brim of his hat, and when she looked at him, he quickly looked away.

Georgia was not unaccustomed to guys looking at her surreptitiously, checking her out, and then trying to look away all innocent-like. It happened a lot. Men usually know it was rude to stare. The nice ones generally looked away when they had been caught, or maybe just gave a smile that said *Hey*. Guys who didn't look away sometimes followed it up with a wink, or a blown kiss. Shy guys checking her out often looked down and went bright red.

Being noticed usually felt quite harmless to Georgia, but the way that the man in the hat looked away felt creepy. She found it distinctly disconcerting. Her impression was that he was an older man, but that wasn't why it was creepy. She would take it as a compliment from an older guy, but this was different. It was kind of sudden and furtive in a way that seemed really odd. She felt sure this was a weird, *stalkery* kind of look-away.

She kept glancing his way, and as the train pulled into Culham Station, he looked again. She wondered if he was watching to see if she was getting off the train or staying on.

She looked at him again. This time, it was Georgia who looked away. She recognized him. It was Corvus Durant. Her head was full of questions: *Does he need to talk to me about the paper? Why doesn't he just say hello? Is he simply going the same way I am? If he is,* she reasoned, *then why is he pretending he isn't here, and why is he looking at me so creepily?* Her mind began racing. It didn't make sense that he would be wearing that ridiculous hat unless he was in disguise, which convinced her that he *was* following her. Suddenly, she got chills. She was really very uncomfortable and wanted to jump off the train right there and then, but the beeps ended, the doors were closed, and the train moved off again.

She would have to find somewhere she felt safe with a lot of other people around when she changed trains at Didcot. Then she could see what he would do and maybe try to lose him. Georgia felt that Didcot couldn't come soon enough, and she was glad that the snooty woman was sitting in the carriage between them.

It was soon after that the train slowed again and pulled into Appleford Station. The doors opened. Nobody got on. Nobody got off. Just as the door beeps sounded, Georgia made the quick

JUMPING-OFF POINT

decision to jump off the train. She grabbed the handle of her suitcase and yanked its heavy bulk behind her. Her feet were on the platform as the doors began to close.

Durant leapt up a moment too late, heading toward the doors nearest to him. Georgia was counting on the doors closing quickly. Her suitcase didn't make the gap, and her grasp on the handle failed as the suitcase was snatched by the doors. The train's safety system caused the doors to falter and open a little, allowing the suitcase to fall back into the train as the doors began to close again. The momentary reopening of the doors had been just enough for Durant to squeeze through before the doors closed.

Georgia was about to run toward the stairs off the platform, but Durant stood between her and the exit. He had a cold, determined look in his eyes, and Georgia was afraid. She started to panic, and her instinct was to run away from him.

38.
A NICE QUIET SPOT

25 MARCH 2022, 2.09 P.M.

Durant stood looking at Georgia. She was staring back at him. He knew the exit was behind him. There was no way out for her. He saw her as just a silly girl who happened to have written a paper that could save his career. She had offered him the opportunity to be second author. *Second? Ha!* he thought. *She gave me a copy of the paper, so why should I be second? Why should I share the credit at all?* Durant wanted it for himself. He wanted to publish the groundbreaking work she had shown him. He was angry about the ridiculous questions he had faced at the conference. The impertinent laughter. He wanted that paper to prove to them all that he was to be taken seriously. He was still the best. He would be celebrated again.

She would have to get past him to get to the exit. Durant looked around at the deserted station. There was no one in sight, and no CCTV. They were alone. The diesel engines revved, and the train headed out of the station. Durant watched as Georgia turned and ran. She ran down the ramp, off the end of the platform, and then across the two railway lines. Georgia ran up the ramp on the other side and started running along the other platform towards the exit on the other side.

Durant simply jumped off the platform edge and ran directly across the rails. He was clambering up onto the platform while Georgia was sprinting back toward him, but she was hemmed in by the passenger shelter on her left. His knee was up over the platform edge, and he pushed himself up and scrambled across the platform toward her. He lunged, and just as she tried to jump from his outstretched arms, he grabbed Georgia's ankle as her trailing foot lifted from the floor.

She went down hard. She fell flat as her hands gave out in front of her. Her face bounced off the platform, and she was still for a moment. Durant knelt on her back, and Georgia didn't even struggle.

He decided this was a very exposed position, so he picked her up and threw her over the wooden railings at the back of the platform. Durant glanced around and saw that they were still alone. He climbed over the railings and jumped down beside Georgia, and he was out of sight just as an express train rushed noisily through the station. Then he was straddling her. He put his hand in his coat pocket, pulled out a long piece of blue nylon rope, and quickly wrapped it around Georgia's neck. She had fallen face down onto damp weeds and patchy moss, and she was trying to get up on her elbows, and there was blood pouring from her broken nose. Then Durant viciously pushed her head down as he pulled the rope tight. He began twisting the rope around her throat like a tourniquet. It dug in and choked poor Georgia as she lay helplessly pinned under the weight of Durant, face down in the dirt.

It was quick. She fell still and silent. Time of death, 2.13 p.m.

Durant kept the rope taut for a couple more minutes just to be sure.

A NICE QUIET SPOT

Then he lifted her tiny, limp body onto his shoulders and tossed her over the ivy-covered wooden fence behind the waiting room shelter. She thudded onto the ground in some low undergrowth.

Durant found a manhole cover at the north end of Platform 2 between the platform and the stairs. He prised it up, removed it, and left the drain open. Then he scouted a bit further off the end of the platform, and near the brick retaining wall adjoining the overbridge, he discovered a pile of heavy pieces of metal left over from past rail repairs. One by one, he pushed all the metal he could find over the fence.

Durant ducked under the stairs, near the now-open drain. He had spotted a gap where two fence panels were in disrepair, and he squeezed through, causing minimal additional damage. He pulled open Georgia's backpack and stuffed it full of rail chairs. He made sure it was strapped securely to her lifeless body. Then he used the blue rope to tie the manhole cover to her backpack straps. He dragged her a few feet across dirt and grass, and he waded out into the adjacent pond, pulling her limp body in after him. When the water was more than waist deep, he let her go, and she sank to the bottom.

He watched until the bubbles stopped floating to the surface. He left her there, weighed down by her backpack, and returned through the gap in the fence and up onto the platform. He sat in the shelter, with a puddle of pond water collecting around his feet, waiting to dry off a little.

As his adrenaline rush subsided, he realized that he felt elated, thrilled, and intoxicated. He felt powerful. It had been so easy, so simple. But he had squandered an opportunity to enjoy it more. He realized he hadn't savoured the moment. It hadn't been necessary for him to fumble and rush. He wished he had been looking at her face, not the back of her head, so that he could have watched her die, not just feel her go limp. If he'd had the guts to do it in his rooms, then he could have done it carefully, slowly. It could have been nice and civilized while he enjoyed a large glass of cognac. He was beginning to feel a little annoyed with himself.

On the upside, he thought, he had her paper, which she had handed over to him like a naïve, stupid little girl. He realized that he should be grateful for that. The paper with the SU(7) mathematics, which he could barely even comprehend, but would publish. The prissy little bitch had handed him an invitation to remove her from the equation. She had given him the motive. It was veritably Darwinian. She had just handed the paper to him, asking to be exploited, swindled, and discarded. His career was back on track, better than ever, and he was buoyed by thoughts of glory—a Nobel Prize, perhaps—and the thought of rubbing it in the face of that little *Brummie* git from the conference. Georgia had been at the conference as well, and surely she'd been laughing along with all the others. It was Georgia's own fault.

Today is a glorious day, he thought, with a smirk on his face and not even a glimmer of regard for the brilliant, beautiful young life he had just ended. He trotted briskly up the station stairs, out onto the road, across the bridge, and set off on the hour's walk to Didcot Parkway. By the time he arrived, he would be fairly dry, if a little dank-smelling.

39.

PHIL IN REWIND

25 MARCH 2022, 2.09 P.M.

Phil had seen Georgia and Durant leap from the train from inside the dark, little corridor. It happened so quickly that he had no chance to react until the doors had closed. He stumbled out of the corridor and into the carriage, then scanned the platform through the window as the train pulled away.

Durant was standing on the platform. Georgia was facing Durant. He was between her and the exit stairs that led up from the platform. Phil saw Georgia turn and run. The train picked up speed, leaving the station behind, and Phil could only look back to see Georgia run down the ramp at the end of the platform and onto the rails.

As the track gently curved to the left and the train sped on, the view was lost behind trees. Phil had a good idea what happened next, but he needed to know for sure. He needed to at least know where her body was for the sake of her poor parents, so that Chip and Marietta could bury their lil' Georgie. It would be cold comfort, but at least they would have closure.

The train rattled along, and Phil returned to the corridor between the coaches of the two-car train. He had been unable to see any more of what transpired as the train had pulled away. He was desperate to know, and not just for the sake of Chip Cornwallis. He was convinced that proving Durant killed Georgia was the only way to prevent the attack on Holly. If Phil could implicate Durant in Georgia's death, then he and Holly would be OK. Phil wouldn't need to rescue Holly, and their argument would never happen. He had to go back again to find out what happened and figure out where Georgia's body could be found, and he needed to do it quickly, before the train got to Didcot. He pulled out a Polaroid from his jacket pocket to go back earlier in the day, using the one labelled *Westgate Backs, 25 Mar. 2022, 11.10 a.m.*

He had time. He just had to relax and will it to happen. Once again, Phil's world transformed around him. The bizarre sensation of smelling fresh, cold riverside air while his body was being jostled and his ears could still hear the *clackety-clack* of the rails was a little disconcerting and disorienting. Phil supposed he would never quite get used to this aspect of time travel.

He found himself in the Westgate backs on the footpath that ran beside the river. As soon as the ground beneath his feet felt like it would support him, he set off walking out of the college and straight round to the train station. He walked at an uncomfortably quick pace even though there was no rush. He stood at the ticket machine like a man who was late for his train, all out of puff and looking anxiously at his watch. It was 11.21 a.m. The conference would be ending soon. In the next couple of hours, Georgia would go to see Durant in his rooms, leave the college, and set off walking to Oxford Station.

Phil needed to get to Appleford Station, where Georgia and Durant had jumped off the train, or rather, *would* jump off the train, without disturbing that timeline. He planned to catch the next train to Appleford and get there early, so that he might already be there waiting to see what happened. He had plenty of time. He checked his watch again. He had three hours to kill. He took a deep breath, told himself to calm down, and bought a one-way ticket to Appleford.

Phil had loved train travel ever since he was a kid. There was something special and a little bit exciting about being taken somewhere by train. Nowadays, it was nice having time to do nothing, and it was something of a guilty pleasure to buy beer and sandwiches in the buffet car. There would not even be trolley service on the local stopping train to Appleford. So, not for the first time at Oxford Station, Phil stocked up while he waited for the next train.

He got a tuna mayo sandwich on white bread from M&S. None of that healthy, seeded, brown bread that took all the joy out of having a pre-packed sarnie. And just because he thought it looked so good, he got himself a caprese salad baguette from Upper Crust, and then he got a vanilla latte from Costa Coffee. He found a copy of *Cheese!* magazine in WH Smith, and decided to get *Robotics Today* as well. Then the 11.37 was announced and Phil went to wait by the platform edge as the train approached.

Phil sat at the front of the first carriage, where Georgia had been sitting, or rather, *would* be sitting when she boarded the train that would leave in just over two hours. He started thumbing through *Cheese!* and sipped at his coffee. He opened the triangular plastic packet that contained the M&S tuna sandwich. It didn't even take him till Radley to devour it. Flicking through *Robotics Today*, he finished his coffee before the train even pulled into Culham.

A few short minutes later, the train pulled in at Appleford, and Phil alighted having stuffed his rubbish into the tiny bin by the train door. He walked along Platform 1, past the help point, the red plastic bin, and the steps up to the bridge. The big red-and-white sign, standing proudly above the notice board, announced to the world that this was, indeed, Appleford.

He walked over the bridge, plodded down the stairs that led to Platform 2, ambled to the passenger shelter and sat himself down on the rather slender and very uncomfortable metal bench seat. The time was 11.51 a.m. *Bloody bollocks!*, thought Phil as he realized he had two more hours with nothing but *Cheese!* magazine and a baguette. He pulled out his phone, googled, and confirmed that there was absolutely sod all in Appleford to pass the time of day while waiting for a murder.

Trains came and went. Mostly, they sped through the station. Express trains going to Manchester stopped at Reading and Oxford along the way. But not Appleford.

Phil thought of Holly, and his heart broke all over again. It had taken everything he had in him to kiss her cheek and leave her with Marion and Plumbus, knowing he had probably lost her. By saving her, he had lost her. The irony of that was tearing him up. Though he had to admit that acting like a bit of a prick had probably sealed it.

Phil shook himself out of it. *Come on, Phil. You have to figure out how to catch Durant hurting Georgia. A Durant behind bars can't hurt Holly!* Phil was hopeful he would soon have the answers he needed to sort out all his problems. His umpteenth time check revealed that it was 14.07.

Phil looked out of the opening of the shelter. He stared up the line towards Oxford. Georgia's train would be arriving any second. It would be the train he had been on, and it was the train another Phil was on right this minute, standing in the corridor between carriages.

PHIL IN REWIND

Then a bright dot appeared in the middle distance, coming through the arch of the bridge over the Thames. It trundled round the bend toward Appleford Station. He could see the yellow front with its big windows and its headlight shining brightly even in daylight. The engine ticking over as it coasted into the station, braking as it arrived at the opposite platform. The brakes finally squeaked as the train came to a halt.

Phil crouched down, out of sight, peeping through the shelter's plastic window pane. *Beep-beep-beep-beep.* The doors would close any second. Georgia would leap from the train, leaving her suitcase behind. Durant would make it through the doors just as they were closing. The train's engines revved, and it pulled away, revealing Durant, standing opposite Phil. As the train moved further away, there was Georgia, running away from Durant, towards the far end of the station platform. The train was out of the station now, carrying the other Phil away toward Didcot.

Georgia ran down the ramp and across the rails at the end of the platform. Seconds later, she was heading up the ramp of the platform upon which Phil was hiding.

Phil looked back to Durant. He had jumped off the opposite platform and was already running across the rails. Georgia was sprinting. She was fast. She was fit and lithe, and she was running up the platform in Phil's direction like her life depended on it.

Durant was getting older. He was overweight and not exactly nimble. He was struggling to climb up onto the platform. He had his elbows on the edge. He had one knee on the edge. He lurched forward, and then his other knee was up. Phil could see Georgia running toward Durant, and she looked like she was going to race past him. She was *fast*. But Durant lunged forward, both arms out. His grasp caught her ankle, and he held on.

Georgia's momentum carried her forward with one foot anchored by Durant's grip. She fell hard and slammed onto the platform surface. Phil was sure he actually felt her face hit the floor. She lay prostrate and stunned right next to the opening to the shelter. Suddenly, Durant was on top of her, kneeling on her back.

Phil was inches away. He could've reached out and touched Durant.

In that moment, he didn't know if he was angry, or frightened, or horrified for Georgia. He didn't know for sure because it was all so sudden, but he knew he couldn't just crouch in the shelter and watch. He stood up and stepped forward to the opening.

"Corvus," he said quietly.

Durant looked up. Phil was standing over him. Durant stood quickly with his hands out as if to defend himself.

Suddenly, Phil felt a surge of adrenaline rushing through his body. It was a result of having watched Durant attack Georgia, and his anger over killing Holly, and the remnants of hate for Durant having ended his career in physics and having contributed to the death of kind Mr. Pedge, and all of a sudden, all of it, everything, welled up inside him and he exploded in a powerful rage. With his feet firmly planted on the floor, he let out an angry roar, and then he launched himself at Durant.

His furious lunge channelled itself through Phil's hands and into Durant's chest as he shoved Durant away from Georgia. Phil managed to stay on his feet inside the shelter, stumbling back a little, with Georgia face down on the ground right in front of him. Durant staggered back, one, two, three steps, and then fell onto his backside right on the edge of the platform. He immediately pitched backward, and as he put his hands out to stop himself, he missed the edge of the platform and tumbled backward. Phil just watched him go over as his legs followed him, quickly disappearing from view over the edge and down onto the rails.

For a moment, it was silent.

Then Phil heard the rails as they began to sing and tingle.

Georgia, half crawling, half staggering, scrambled to her feet and, without glancing back, stumbled away toward the stairs, her hand clutching the fencing as she went.

There was a horn. There was a loud squeal as train brakes were fully applied. The horn sounded again and again.

Durant's face appeared above the platform edge as he tried to stand. He looked dazed, with blood coming from his head. He put his elbows on the platform edge and readied himself to try to climb up again. Then he glanced to his left as the horn blared again. Too late. Durant simply stood and looked Phil in the eyes as the train ploughed into him at fifty miles an hour.

Phil looked on in horror as Durant was flung ahead of the train and then went under its wheels as it sped by, brakes squealing. Phil heard the thuds of Durant's body hitting the underside of the carriages. If the impact hadn't killed Durant, he surely wouldn't survive that.

Most of Durant came to rest on the line, near the end of the platform. The train came to a halt some way out of the station. And all was silent again.

From the foot of the stairs leading out of the station, Georgia looked down at the mangled body of her attacker. She sat on the bottom step of the stairs, with blood dripping from her face.

Phil ducked down in the shelter and spotted the train driver up the line running back along the track.

Phil knew he had to leave here, and quickly. Looking after Georgia would surely occupy the train driver, so maybe he had a few minutes before anyone would discover him hiding in the shelter. But he didn't know where to go or which Polaroid should he use. He needed to think fast, but his mind was racing with what had just happened. He took deep breaths to calm himself.

He looked around the station. He realized that there was no CCTV, and Georgia couldn't possibly know what had just happened. He had an alibi, drinking with his friends after the last day of the conference in Oxford, so he thought he was surely in the clear. If Durant was dead, then he couldn't kill him again in November, so he wouldn't have a murder charge anymore. And Durant couldn't attack Holly, so that problem was surely solved. And Georgia was safe now. Chip and Marietta will get their daughter back.

Durant won't fall over the balcony, and he won't become a prospective client and lure Holly to his rooms. So Phil won't meet Holly until Collard Green's, next January, in his own timeline. That must mean they would be due to go on their first date at McDonald's at 2.00. Phil was excited. He may have the chance to start again with Holly. A chance to do it better this time. In spite of all the possible ripples of cause and effect that Phil could not calculate, he decided it was at least safe to go home. He grabbed his stack of Polaroids.

He picked out the photograph captioned *Queen St. Flat, 18 Jan. 2023, 3.54 p.m.*, and he tried to settle down to focus on going home. Nothing happened.

PHIL IN REWIND

Phil was getting flustered. Why wasn't it working? Was he stressed about being discovered hiding in the station's shelter? "Shit," he said aloud to himself. *Have I been in the past too long?* "Bollocks! Come on, work dammit!" he said under his breath. *Am I rushing too much? OK, calm down, take it easy. Think!* He had been in the past for a while, and he had been back to his sixteenth birthday, so maybe this trip had all added up to too long in the past, and perhaps he was stuck here now.

Then he remembered going back to his flat earlier, and he recalled it being 3.54 p.m. after leaving Holly at the B & B. Right when Havarti needed to see him at The Firkin Folly. He had used this Polaroid already, and he'd forgotten to write a big *X* on the back! He sighed with relief.

Phil quickly looked through his stash of Polaroids. He found another one from the same day at 3.29 p.m. It was a picture of a fire exit sign. He peeked through the shelter window. The driver and the guard from the train were now both tending to Georgia. There was a large red case open on the platform. It seemed to be a first aid kit. Phil could hear sirens in the distance, so he didn't have long. He stared carefully and calmly at the picture in his hand. He willed the universe to help him go home to his own timeline. But it wasn't proving to be easy. Nothing was happening. He had been away from his own timeline for a long time. He started to get anxious again. He thought of Holly. Just as he had fixed everything in the past, he couldn't possibly just get stuck here, so he tried harder. Much harder. He stared intently at the Polaroid and begged the universe to help him again. The station around him began to blur, and everything seemed to get brighter. Now he could hear the sirens close by, but felt himself fading to grey, so he focused on the picture and concentrated hard.

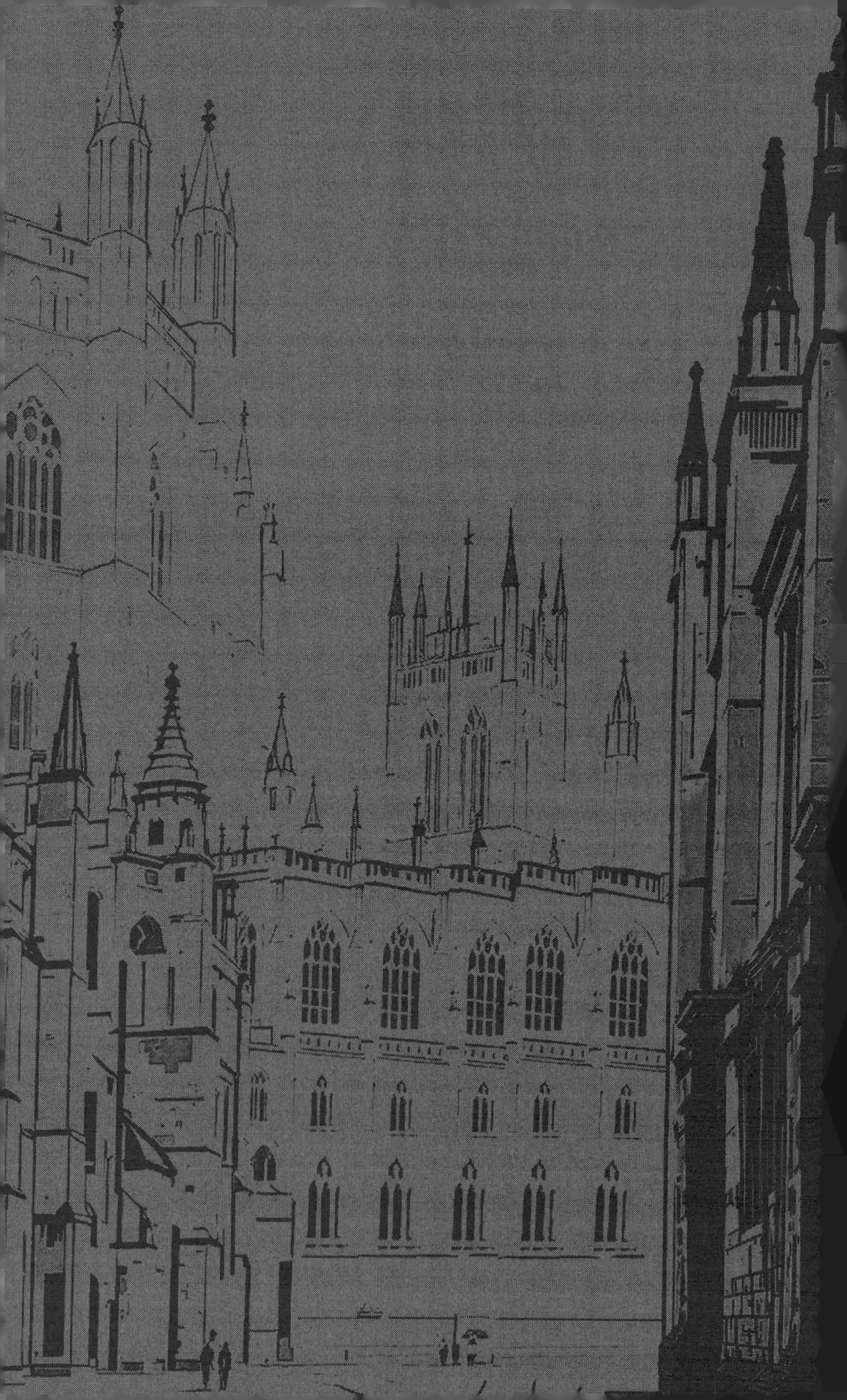

Part Seven
JIGGETY JIG

40.

MAGIC TEA

18 JANUARY 2023, 3.29 P.M.

Phil thought he might have died. Everything was white, and there was a bright light. White walls, floor, and ceiling, and stark, white fluorescent lighting. Phil was sure that heaven wouldn't have fluorescent lighting, but maybe hell would. Phil could make out some green wording. *Fire Exit.* Oh, yes, this was St. Aldate's police station, he realized. *Yep, I am in hell.*

Phil walked down the corridor to Havarti's office area. He knocked on the open door, and the whole office fell silent and watched as Phil crossed the room. You could have heard a pin drop, except it would have fallen on the hideous brown-and-black-striped nylon carpet tile. Hillman Hunter shouted out, "Look, lads, it's the boyfriend." One of the others shouted, "Didn't know you had it in you, Havarti," to which Hunter replied, "Except we all know she hasn't, right, lads?" Everyone fell about in hysterics.

"Sod off lads, you're all arseholes. If you lot are anything to go by, it's a miracle there's any straight women left." Havarti said, then swivelled her chair toward Phil. "Well, look what the cat dragged in. What can I do for you?" The question wasn't phrased that way by accident. Phil often talked to Havarti when he wanted some background on something that had been in the news.

"Nothin' really. Just checking in," Phil replied.

"You were just passing? Thought you'd drop in?" she asked, sounding a little suspicious.

"Kind of," Phil said with a shrug. "You're looking good," Phil told her, thinking about when he last saw her, and she was so stressed and looking old. "Really good."

"I'm OK, I guess. Yeah, I'm good," Havarti replied. "Work's been kind of quiet, but that's got to be better than having heinous murders on your patch, I suppose." Havarti stood up. "Let's take a little stroll, shall we? Want to get a coffee?" she asked.

They sat in a café across the street with a coffee and a Danish pastry each. Phil heard from Havarti that Durant's death had been ruled a misadventure. Phil shuddered with the memory of what he had witnessed mere minutes earlier. Georgia had said that she heard Durant roar, like he was in pain, and then he just let her go. The train driver said that all he saw was Durant just staggering backward and falling in front of the train. They thought perhaps he'd had a heart attack. The post-mortem couldn't confirm that, and the coroner concluded the cause of death was being hit by the train. The train driver said that since it seemed like Durant was going to kill the girl, he was "not actually sorry to have run the fucker over."

"Practically ethical," Phil muttered, with the responsibility for Durant's third death becoming a little lighter. "How was Georgia doing at the inquest?"

"Her face mended just fine. She had surgery on her nose, I think, but she was looking good. Really good, actually."

MAGIC TEA

Phil scowled at Havarti. "Hopefully, she got some therapy too."

"Maybe she did. The Americans excel at that. She certainly seemed to be a cheerful soul when we talked after the hearing. She was thinking of moving to Oxford. There's a professorship open at the moment, right? She was going to apply."

Phil chuckled. "I'm happy to hear that, thanks," he said. "Well, do you remember the Quinkle divorce?"

"Yes, from the news. Ages ago," Havarti replied. "You not going to eat that pastry?"

Phil pushed the plate across to Havarti. "I couldn't do half of what I do without your help. You know that, right? Well, you might not remember, but you helped me look into something for that case," he said, "and it paid out, so I think you should get your share."

Havarti took a bite of Phil's custard Danish. "I'm not sure how I helped with that, but you know, when I do you favours, I'm only really expecting lunch at The Firkin Folly. But I can't take money from you. Rules and whatnot. It's good of you to offer, though. You're a decent sort. I always said as much."

"Ha-ha, I can only imagine what you've really said, you cheeky tart."

"We need to catch up properly, though," Havarti said. "Firkin Folly at the weekend? Looks like you're buying."

"Yes, sure." Phil was delighted with the idea of meeting up with Havarti under better circumstances than last time. He was very keen for her to meet Holly, and he couldn't help himself in blurting out, "Not promising, but I might even bring a plus one."

"No way, Phil! A *girl* kind of a plus one?" Havarti took the last bite of pastry.

"Yep, a girl," Phil said, and finished his coffee.

"A real one? You do know the inflatable ones don't actually count?" Havarti said with the last bite of Danish in her mouth.

Phil laughed. "If you're going to be an arse, you can bugger off back to work."

"What about Saturday? Noon?" Havarti suggested as she got up from the table. "Ruby said they'll be showing the *Liverpool-Chelsea* match."

"Perfect," said Phil, following Havarti's lead. He wondered if Holly liked the footie. He put the tray of empty mugs and plates on the counter.

"I'd better be getting back. No rest for the wicked. Thanks for the coffee," Havarti said as she walked out.

Phil walked up St. Aldate's and back to his flat. First, he took a shower and changed into clean clothes. Then he made himself a cup of tea and settled down at his desk. He felt a whole lot better, cleaner, and refreshed. Tea was magic stuff, but the tea didn't make him feel cleaner. The shower had done that. *Tea isn't that magic, Phil thought, it refreshes parts that no crappy beer can reach.*

It was almost 4.00 p.m., and Phil was feeling optimistic. He reminded himself that he had saved Georgia and escaped unseen. He needed to look for the ripples of what his actions might have changed in this new timeline. Durant had died last March, and that meant Phil had undone all his mistakes from November. He would go back to 2.00 p.m., earlier today, to see Holly for their new first date at McDonald's, but he had some unfinished business before that.

First, he opened his bank account app. There, in his savings account, was an almost two-million-pound deposit made in August 2022. Phil started his Mac and sipped his tea. He sent a quick text to Rusty and Hasty and dialled his mum. As his Mac made its self-congratulatory fanfare sound to announce that it had booted up, Phil's mum answered.

Phil told his mum he'd done a lot of casework today, and that some of it had paid off, and that he'd be writing her a nice big cheque on Sunday. Phil's mum told him not to leave himself short on her account, while the computer screen was showing Phil his search results:

About 13,280,000 results (0.69 seconds)

Scientific American
www.scientificamerican.com/New_Theory_of_Physics
There's a New Theory of Physics and It's About Time

Phil clicked on the Scientific American link. He started to skim the article about the big breakthrough. *It was a new theory of physics, and it was about time!* Phil thought. He liked that headline. Phil's Google search was full of articles about the amazing reception that Georgia and Akito's paper had received. It had made an impact, like an asteroid colliding with the world of physics. Phil was thrilled for Georgia and Akito, and for his own part in their success. Phil felt the responsibility for Durant's death melt away a little, and weigh on him a tiny bit less.

"If today goes well," Phil said to his mum, "knock on wood, I might be bringing a date with me to meet you, if that's OK? Can't promise, it's early days yet. We only just met, in fact, but I'm sure she'll want to come over, assuming she wants to see me again after today."

"Well, that'd be lovely, dear. Jolly exciting! Good luck today then, love."

"Thanks! I really need to go and get ready," Phil said as he finished his tea.

"At least tell me her name," she said.

"Her name's Holly, Mum."

"Hollymum? Funny name," she chuckled.

"I'll see you on Sunday, you daft old dingbat."

"See you Sunday," she said, and they hung up.

Phil pulled his digital camera out of his satchel. He popped out the camera's SD card and connected it to his Mac. Moments later, his Mac pinged to let Phil know that it had imported all the new photos. He double-clicked a photo of the paperwork on his father's desk. Then he got out the Polaroid he had taken and held it up to the screen. Not a perfect match, but he could work with it. Phil adjusted the image on the screen, altering the photo with filters and blurring it a little, to match the vintage look of the Polaroid. He put some glossy photo paper in the printer and pressed *Print*. He took the picture from the printer and packed it in his satchel along with the matching Polaroid.

Phil checked the mirror. He was neat and tidy, and ready for his 2.00 p.m. date. Phil was keen to get business done so that he could focus properly on Holly. Thinking of wanting to be able to focus, he went to pee in his own nice clean toilet before leaving the flat. Phil was getting better at learning from his mistakes. He grabbed his satchel, his Polaroid SX-70, and his jacket. He was hoping Rusty and Hasty would already be waiting for him, so he rushed out of the flat and round the corner to Pedge & Co. He had some news for Rusty that Phil believed was actually good news. *Why wouldn't Rusty be happy to find out his dad was murdered?* he thought.

MAGIC TEA

Laira was on the phone when Phil arrived. "Hi, Laira, I'm Phil Beans. I'm here to see Mr. Pedge."

Laira looked surprised. "He's expecting you," she said, pointing to the door.

Rusty and Hasty were both there, sitting in the dimly lit gloom. Both of them had a mug of whisky in hand. Phil knew their timelines had changed, so Phil would not have seen either of them earlier that day. This morning's visit was now the past for Phil, but not for Rusty or Hasty. Phil was quite used to these little time paradoxes by now. He thought of them as fun little things that were quite happy to exist, and they didn't cause anyone any trouble. People just accepted a world where some things had happened, other things hadn't, and were unaware that anything had changed.

"Good afternoon, gents," said Phil as he breezed into the room. The others responded in kind. "Sorry about today, mate. Your dad's anniversary, right?"

"Yeah, hence the wee dram," Rusty said. "You remembered," he added quietly, almost to himself, seeming surprised, but touched. Phil felt a twinge of guilt as he smiled gently, grateful for the opportunity to revisit this moment and be a better mate.

Phil explained that he'd got his payout from the Quinkle case, but neither Rusty nor Hasty could remember helping him with it.

"That's bloody brilliant news," said Rusty, reaching for another mug and the bottle. "But last July? I have trouble remembering last week, mate."

"Nice work, Phil!" said Hasty. "I remember the news. Glad Mrs. Quinkle got justice. Quinkle had that coming. The old scrote was lucky he didn't go to jail. I had no idea you'd sorted that. You kept that quiet, bro. No idea what I did to help either. I don't need the money, though, just happy to help, man."

"I'm not saying no to my share," said Rusty, quickly. Phil accepted the mug he offered, and they toasted Phil's success. Rusty topped them up and sat back in his chair. Phil basked for a moment in the feeling that he was a bit of a hero for a change.

"There's more, though, Rusty. And this is big. This is, believe it or not, the real good news, so brace yourself." Rusty looked at Phil, trying to focus, as though he knew he needed to look a little bit sober for this. Phil looked deadly earnest.

"I was at Lydington Manor for a short while on my sixteenth birthday. I overheard your dad planning something with my father and Durant. They were having a meeting in the library, and I overheard them talking about scuba gear and a boat, and I thought they said something about an insurance payout. Well, I've worked out what it was all about."

"Come on, Phil, spit it out, mate," Rusty said with a frown of anxious anticipation.

"Your dad didn't kill himself. It was staged to look like he did. My father and Durant bullied your dad into staging his own suicide. Your dad thought it was so he could get his payoff and start over. But instead of rescuing him from the water, they made sure he died. They either killed him, or they made sure he was dead, having conned him into jumping off that bridge."

Rusty was wide-eyed and open-mouthed. "What?"

"Your dad didn't ... "

"I heard you. It was rhetorical. How the hell did you figure all that out?"

MAGIC TEA

Phil reached into his satchel as Rusty drained his mug and poured himself another. "I have a Polaroid I had forgotten I'd taken that day. I found it earlier, after I remembered today was your dad's anniversary," Phil said, stretching the truth a bit. He handed over the Polaroid that he had taken while he was in the library a short time earlier.

"Hard to see much in this picture, Phil. Not sure this shows anything much," said Rusty, looking a little deflated.

"But look, I scanned it and enhanced the image," Phil said, bending the truth to the breaking point. Phil handed over the printout of the digital photograph he'd made a bit blurry and pale. It looked as though it could be a sharpened, enhanced, cropped, and enlarged version of the Polaroid image. The Dartford Bridge was clearly detailed on the map. "See, I always assumed your dad felt guilty for helping hide my father's assets from my mum, and that's why he killed himself. But for them to want him dead? I reckon it was something much worse, something pretty big. I reckon they were getting into something really dodgy. From that image and what I overheard, I think your dad wanted out. He didn't want to do whatever it was, so they killed him. I can't prove it in court, but I'm convinced of it."

"This is a map of where my dad jumped," said Rusty, "and Lydington and Durant were persuading him to do it?"

"Yep. From what I heard, they were forcing him into it," said Phil, gently.

Hasty stood up and walked around the desk, next to Rusty, and looked down at the printout. "Man, those bastards," he muttered in disbelief.

Rusty looked at Phil through thankful, tear-filled eyes, then he looked back at the picture. "Dad didn't just check out. He didn't just abandon us." He looked up at Phil again. "My dad didn't kill himself. My dad loved us, after all."

"Yep. Looks that way, mate," Phil said, trying not to get choked up too. "Well, what I knew of your dad, it didn't really make sense. It always bothered me somehow."

"Thank you. This is better than money," Rusty said. "Better than therapy too! It's the best thing I've ever heard."

"You're welcome." Phil stood to leave. "Sorry it took twenty years to figure it out. I'll see you guys soon."

Phil walked out and back through reception toward the front door; Laira was still remonstrating on the phone. "No, Dad, new tyres for the car don't count as Mum's birthday present," Laira said.

Phil opened his satchel and looked in the pocket for the Polaroid that said *Collard Green's Alley, 18 Jan. 2023, 2.09 p.m.* This was the picture he had taken earlier today, when he had gone to Collard Green's only to find Em working there, and Holly completely missing. It seemed like half-a-lifetime ago since he had taken it. Phil set off in search of a quiet, secluded spot. Now it was time for Phil to check on Holly's newest timeline, see if everything had been restored, and find out if Holly was at the café expecting him to take her to McDonald's.

41.

THE WINDOW TABLE

18 JANUARY 2023, 11.22 A.M.

Holly watched Phil walk out of the café. She was excited. He was a cute guy who had been coming in every lunchtime for a week, and today he'd spoken to her. He'd said he'd been plucking up the courage. Holly thought that was sweet. Most guys would just say some cheesy line. But Phil didn't seem so cocky. She liked that. He was going to come back at 2.00 and take her to McDonald's. That was also exciting. She loved a Big Mac, and having that to look forward to would get her through today's lunchtime shift.

Holly went over to clear the plate and coffee cup that Phil had left behind. She thought about how Phil had sat at the one dirty table in the café, and she had said, "Sorry, let me clear that." She knew there was no need for an apology. He'd sat there because he wanted the seat by the window, and he had been the one who'd made it a priority for her to clear his table. A server can always leave a dirty table and clear it when they get a minute, but as soon as some arse goes and sits at it, it becomes the new next task. And for some bizarre reason, she felt the need to apologize for it.

Holly had told herself not to get snippy with him. He obviously liked the window table, and she didn't blame him. She would sit there too, if she was the customer. While sitting in McDonald's, or at a quiet café in some little village with a good bookshop, she loved a window seat where she could read for a couple of hours with just a cup of tea or a milkshake for company. She was glad she had reminded herself of that and had not been rude to him. Holly was glad that she had forced a smile back.

She laughed about how neither of them were vegan. She looked out of the window and saw Phil walking away up the street. She watched for a minute feeling really thrilled. She had a good feeling about Phil. He seemed really nice.

"Customers, Holly! Please!" shouted Collard Green.

I cannot wait for this shift to be over, she thought. Then she smiled to herself, thinking about Phil showing up at the end of her shift. *I can't wait,* she thought.

Holly put Phil's dishes on the counter and went over to the couple who had been waiting. The woman was confident-looking, in her mid-thirties, and wearing a blouse with a pencil skirt. He was fortyish, wearing a sweater and jeans, and a bemused expression. Holly enjoyed people-watching as she worked, and she guessed this was either a first date or, more likely, a *morning-after* late brunch. Holly had had a few of those in her time, so she could recognize the telltale awkwardness. It was obvious the woman was a vegan; she hadn't looked at the menu for more than a few seconds. But her date was not, of that she was sure. He stared blankly at the menu, looking lost.

"What can I get you?" asked Holly.

THE WINDOW TABLE

"I'd like the brown rice and hempseed bowl. Can I have far-out vegan chickin with that, and the honey-mustard dressing on the side, not all over it. And some mac and cheez, and a side of kale slaw. And I'd like sparkling water and an almond milk latte."

"Certainly madam," Holly said, scribbling on her order pad. "Have you chosen yet, sir?" she asked the bewildered gentleman customer.

"What would you recommend?"

"For you, sir?" Holly thought for a moment. "Big Mac, large fries, and a vanilla milkshake."

42.

SHIFT HAPPENS

18 JANUARY 2023, 2.09 P.M.

Phil saw a big black wheelie bin and boxes and bin bags around him. The dingy alleyway was now in focus, but Phil was a little disorientated. He looked closely at the photograph in front of him. 2.09 p.m. OK, so when this picture was taken, Phil had just left Collard Green's after failing to find Holly. Em had been the lunchtime waitress, and Phil had left distressed that Holly wasn't there. Things should be different this time. Phil quickly walked out of the alley and almost right into Holly coming out of the café.

"Hi, Holly, hey. Sorry I'm late. You *literally* would not believe the day I've had."

"Oh! Hi, Phil," Holly said. "And there was me thinking I was late. The new late shift girl only just turned up, and of course, the delightful Mr. Green won't let you finish till the next shift is on. Well, shift happens, so here I am. Take me for that burger, I'm bloody famished."

"OK," said Phil, smiling with relief.

Phil looked in through the window and waved to Em. She stared blankly back at him and carried on not clearing tables.

Not only was he not later than Holly was, she was also not late, as in the late Holly Farthing, which had been so widely reported in the press last year. He was also relieved that this Holly hadn't been saved from Durant. Or at least this Holly was oblivious to the notion that a different incarnation of her had been rescued by Phil, and this Holly had no idea that he could be a condescending prick.

Since they were meeting right now to go to McDonald's, Phil concluded that the dates they shared in November had never happened. That all made sense to Phil as he thought for a moment, his brain working fast to think it all through again and make sure of everything.

If Durant had died last March, Havarti would never have asked Phil to help investigate his plunge down the stairwell, and Phil wouldn't have gone back and bumped into Honey at the pub that night three months earlier.

That meant there was a lot this Holly did not know. She did not know Phil yet. She had no idea he was the son of Lord Lydington. She did not know he could dance. She did not know that his favourite thing ever was pleasuring her. With a bit of luck, she would find all that out soon enough.

"McDonald's then?" he asked, after a moment's thought.

"Yes, God, I could eat a horse," she giggled.

They walked up St. Aldate's and she linked arms with him. Somehow, they seemed really comfortable together. Phil had to remember that he did not, or at least should not, know Holly. They had first spoken only this morning. He had plucked up the courage to chat, and as far as she was concerned, he hadn't known her before this. He should have no idea she loved to dance. He should have no idea she liked Baileys or funfairs. He should not know where she lived or that she had been an escort. He would have to discover all that all over again. This was going to be quite tricky.

They stood looking at the big, overhead screens displaying a menu they both knew off by heart.

"Next customer, please."

"Big Mac, large fries, and a vanilla milkshake," said Holly.

"Same for me, please," said Phil.

"I'd say that just felt like déjà vu, but I suppose I'm always in here ordering the same thing," she said.

"Ha-ha, yes. Big Mac and fries gives me the chills every time too, don't worry," Phil replied.

They got their order and sat in a window seat.

Phil talked about Lydington Manor, and when Holly said she really wanted to see it, he promised to take her there next weekend. Holly talked about her thesis, and Phil agreed with her conclusions about the future of humanity seeming pretty bleak. Phil told her about being a detective and specializing in divorces like the Quinkle case, and she made a joke about *catching the bad guys at it*, and being a *privates* detective. Phil told her he sometimes helps the police with murders and cold cases. Holly seemed impressed. They chatted about all sorts.

When Holly's milkshake made the slurpy, empty noise, they knew it was time to go.

"Well, this McDonald's thing was meant to help me decide if you're worth investing a whole evening," Holly said. "I know we only just met, but it already feels like I've known you for ages."

"I get that. I feel like I've known you for a week already," Phil replied.

"I reckon I could risk wasting an evening with you. I'm free tonight, so, my place, later?" Holly said. "About sixish? Or is that moving too fast for you? Did you want to play it cool and wait three days before calling me?"

"Oh, yes, I'd love to," said Phil. "See you tonight, I mean, not play it cool. I've never actually tried playing it cool before. Maybe that's where I've been going wrong."

Holly laughed. "You seem pretty cool to me," she said with a flirtatious smile.

As they stood outside McDonald's, Phil softly, slowly kissed Holly on the cheek, which Phil hoped she would think was sweet. Holly smiled at him with a glint in her eyes, turned, and walked away. As she did, she called back, "Top jacket pocket," answering the question that should have been forming on his lips. Phil pulled out the piece of paper with Holly's phone number and address on it, and he chuckled to himself. He checked Holly's details in his phone to make sure nothing had changed. Then he set an alarm for 5.30 p.m. If there's one thing time travel can do, it's giving a person the chance to not make the same mistake twice. He wouldn't be late for Holly this time.

Then he headed home thinking whether to take chocolates, or flowers, or a decent bottle of wine to Holly's tonight. He decided on flowers and walked home via the florist.

When he got home, he had a sit-down with a nice cup of tea with two sugars. He put the washing on and he spent a while putting his Polaroids back in their albums, checking each one for the *X*s on the back, and filing away the new ones. Then he spent half an hour choosing which T-shirt to wear. To the untrained eye, he looked no different than he had earlier, except this light-pink tee was an old favourite. It read *There are 10 types of people*. If you looked closer, you could read the small print that read *Those who understand binary and those who don't*.

When the alarm went off at 5.30, Phil was already ready, with his shoes on, and he was pacing nervously. He immediately set off to Holly's full of eager anticipation. Phil would have to bear in mind that Holly was completely new to this relationship. He was contemplating when he might broach the subject of time travel. He would have to play that by ear.

Phil arrived at 5.55 p.m. with a full tank of petrol and the flowers, having made sure that he was a little early. He parked the car, intending to sit and wait for five minutes, but the door opened, and there was Holly. He jumped out of the car and went to kiss Holly's cheek. She grabbed his face and kissed him full on the lips. It was a real kiss. A movie kiss. The kind where you can feel the passion without really having to show it.

Phil held out the flowers.

"Freesias! Lovely," Holly said, and she held them close to breathe in the scent. "My favourite. How did you know?"

"Oh, lucky guess," said Phil.

To be continued ...

BEFORE YOU GO,
A SMALL (BUT VERY IMPORTANT) REQUEST

Well done, dear reader. You made it to the end of Phil Beans' pastry-fueled, Polaroid-powered misadventure. I hope it didn't leave you stuck in the wrong decade, covered in vanilla cream, or paying excess charges for overdue parking fines.

Now, here's the thing: **your review is worth so much more than one of Phil's chess-game mulligans.** Reviews are the lifeblood of books—they help other readers decide if they want to jump into the madness, they tell booksellers and all those fancy algorithms that this story is worth recommending, and (let's be honest) they make authors do a little victory dance that would put Phil's moves to shame.

So, if you enjoyed this book even half as much as Phil enjoys a sausage roll at The Lawns café, please take a moment to leave a review wherever you found or bought it. Amazon, Goodreads, your local bookseller's website—anywhere that lets you shout, "This was bloody brilliant!" into the void.

It doesn't have to be an essay. Just a few words, a star rating. Each review is like one of Phil's Polaroids. Small, instant, and powerful enough to bend time (or at least, in this case, to help another reader discover this book).

With gratitude (and a fresh mug of tea),
MARK J. WILSON

KEEP IN TOUCH

If you'd like to see what I'm working on next—or just want to say hello—you can find me at:

markjwilson.com

To keep up with Phil Beans and to explore some of the places mentioned in the book, visit:

geekygumshoe.com

westgatecollege.org.uk

firkinfolly.com

collardgreensvegancafe.com

Made in the USA
Middletown, DE
18 September 2025